W9-ASZ-212
PINO

ROMANTIC TIMES PRAISES MADELINE BAKER'S PREVIOUS BESTSELLERS!

THE ANGEL & THE OUTLAW

"Readers will rave about Madeline Baker's extraordinary storytelling talents."

LAKOTA RENEGADE

"*Lakota Renegade* is as rich, passionate, and delicious as all Madeline Baker's award-winning romances!"

APACHE RUNAWAY

"Madeline Baker has done it again! This romance is poignant, adventurous, and action packed."

CHEYENNE SURRENDER

"This is a funny, witty, poignant, and delightful love story! Ms. Baker's fans will be more than satisfied!"

THE SPIRIT PATH

"Poignant, sensual, and wonderful...Madeline Baker fans will be enchanted!"

MIDNIGHT FIRE

"Once again, Madeline Baker proves that she has the Midas touch...A definite treasure!"

COMANCHE FLAME

"Another Baker triumph! Powerful, passionate, and action packed, it will keep readers on the edge of their seats!"

GONE WITH THE WIND

He was staring at her as if he'd never seen a woman before, and she was staring back. The air seemed to vibrate between them. Earth, trees, and sky all seemed to fade away, and he was aware of nothing but the young woman standing before him. He could see the pulse throbbing in the hollow of her throat, hear the uneven rasp of her breathing. Was she real, or merely a vision sent to tempt him?

For a moment, he thought of taking her in his arms, putting her on his horse, and carrying her far away from this place. He had the strangest feeling that she would go with him without question or complaint.

"It's you," she murmured inanely, and again felt that warm surge of energy, of awareness, that had speared her when she met his eyes in front of the general store in town. Never before had she felt such a rush of recognition, as if she had been waiting for this one man for all her life.

Other *Leisure* and *Love Spell* Books
by Madeline Baker:
THE ANGEL & THE OUTLAW
LAKOTA RENEGADE
APACHE RUNAWAY
BENEATH A MIDNIGHT MOON
CHEYENNE SURRENDER
WARRIOR'S LADY
THE SPIRIT PATH
MIDNIGHT FIRE
COMANCHE FLAME
PRAIRIE HEAT
A WHISPER IN THE WIND
FORBIDDEN FIRES
LACEY'S WAY
FIRST LOVE, WILD LOVE
RENEGADE HEART
RECKLESS DESIRE
LOVE FOREVERMORE
RECKLESS LOVE
LOVE IN THE WIND
RECKLESS HEART

Writing As Amanda Ashley:
DEEPER THAN THE NIGHT
EMBRACE THE NIGHT

Chase the Wind

MADELINE BAKER

LEISURE BOOKS  NEW YORK CITY

For all my readers who asked for a sequel to
Apache Runaway. This one's for you.
And for my cyberfriends Erik and Stefanie who share
my love of music and theater.
Much love to you all.

A LEISURE BOOK®

September 1996

Published by

Dorchester Publishing Co., Inc.
276 Fifth Avenue
New York, NY 10001

Printed in the United States of America.

Chase The Wind

Prologue

Apache Reservation
Fort Sill, Oklahoma
May, 1895

Chase the Wind had always known he was a half-breed. As a young boy, he hadn't understood what that really meant. Half-breed. Part Apache. Part white. What he had understood was that his mother had left him, that she had chosen to go off with a white man rather than stay at the rancheria with him and his father.

As he grew older and prouder, he told himself his white blood didn't matter. His heart and soul were Apache; he was Apache—a proven warrior, with a warrior's name. He had fought alongside Mangus and Geronimo, fighting against the armies of Crook and Gatewood during the Apaches' last desperate bid for freedom.

A long sigh escaped Chase's lips. There was no

point in dwelling on the past. The Apaches would never fight again, and he was a man alone. And yet, on nights like this, when the earth was quiet and the sky was clear and sprinkled with stars, he was haunted by the ghosts of his past, tormented by thoughts of the mother who had deserted him when he was no more than an infant.

When he'd been a child, he had often asked his father about the white woman who had given him birth, but Kayitah, like Alope, had refused to speak of the past. And now they were both gone. His father had been dead these past eight years; Alope, the only mother he had ever known, had died three days ago.

He had resigned himself to the fact that he would never know anything about the woman who had given him life other than the fact that his father had called her Golden Dove. But then, shortly before her death, Alope had told him that, among the whites, his mother had been known as Jenny. She'd had pale hair and bright green eyes, Alope had said, her voice tinged with bitterness. And his father had last seen her with the white man she had run off with near a small settlement called Twin Rivers.

Was his mother still alive? Did she ever regret giving him away? Had she married the man she had run off with? Had other children?

Questions without answers. A hurt that refused to be ignored no matter how often, or how deep, he tried to bury the pain beneath layers of indifference and insolence.

Why had she left him? he wondered bleakly. Had she been so ashamed of having an Indian baby that she had refused to accept him, refused to claim him as her own?

Shivering from the cold, he stared up at the heavens, wondering if he would ever see the land of his birth again, if he would ever find the answers to the questions that had plagued him all his life.

Chapter One

Fallon Ranch
Twin Rivers
June, 1895

Dusty swung out of the saddle and stretched the kinks out of his arms and legs. Breaking and training horses was never easy: it was backbreaking, bone-jarring hard work. But it was always satisfying.

He took a few minutes to stroke the zebra dun's neck. She was a fine mare, bridle-wise, with a soft mouth and a smooth gait. Jim Patterson had selected the pretty little mare for his youngest daughter, and Dusty was sure Patterson would be pleased. The dun had plenty of bottom and a willing heart.

Removing his hat, Dusty ran a hand through his hair, then glanced up at the sun. Almost four. The little zebra dun was his last horse of the day, the last horse he'd be breaking for his father. Tomorrow, he'd start his new job.

Dusty grinned as he replaced his hat, then brushed the dust from his jeans. Sheriff Fallon. His mother hadn't been happy with his decision to run for sheriff, but she had supported him all the way, understanding his need to make his own way in the world. He had a good job here, and his father paid him well, but he felt the need to get out on his own, to leave his own mark on the world.

Dusty gave the mare a final pat on the shoulder before removing the saddle and bridle and turning her loose in the corral.

Leaving the pen, Dusty walked across the yard toward one of the horse troughs. Removing his hat, he dunked his head in the water, reveling in its coolness. Shaking the excess drops from his hair, he waved at his mother, who was hanging a load of wash.

A sound from one of the other breaking pens drew his attention, and he went over to see what the fuss was about.

"Hey, Pat, Clancy, what's goin' on?" Dusty called as he neared the corral.

Clancy flashed a grin as he jerked a thumb toward the pen. "We're trying to decide who's more stubborn, the bronc or your father."

"My old man," Dusty said as he took a seat on the top rail, "without a doubt."

The horse, a big, bald-faced black stallion, was as wild as a Saturday night in town. Determined to rid itself of the burden on its back, the stud bucked and crow-hopped from one end of the corral to the other. Hoots and hollers filled the air as the ranch hands cheered his father on.

Dusty shook his head. His father was the best rider he'd ever seen—but even the best could be thrown now and then.

Dusty grinned as his father hit the dirt, hard. "Hey, old man! Want me to take over?"

Ryder Fallon glared at his son as he stood up and brushed the dirt from the seat of his pants. "That'll be the day."

Face set in determined lines, Ryder took up the reins and swung into the saddle again.

"He's gonna break his neck one of these days," Jenny remarked as she took a place at the rail beside her son.

"Naw. He's the best."

"Yes," Jenny murmured. "He is that."

She felt a thrill of excitement as she watched her husband cling like a cocklebur to the stallion's back. It was a sight she never tired of. Thick yellow dust rose in the air as the horse bucked its way from one end of the corral to the other. Sweat plastered Ryder's shirt to his back. Dusty and the cowhands whooped and hollered and Jenny raised her own voice in encouragement.

Twenty minutes later, the battle was over. The stallion stood in the center of the corral, ears twitching, nostrils flared.

Dismounting, Ryder patted the animal's neck, then handed the reins to one of the men. "Dry him out, Pat, then give him a good rubdown and a quart of oats."

"Right, boss."

Ryder smiled at Jenny as she entered the corral. "Been a long time since you've ridden a wild one like that," she said, slipping her arm around his waist.

"Yeah. What's up?"

"Nothing. I just wanted to come down and watch my favorite cowboy at work." She winked at him. "Why don't you take a break? I made some fresh lemonade."

"Sounds good. You coming, Dusty?"

"Sure."

Dusty walked behind his parents, grinning inwardly. Sometimes they reminded him of newlyweds, the way they were always gazing into each other's eyes, or sneaking kisses when they thought no one was looking. It used to embarrass him, the way they were always carrying on. As he grew older, he realized what a rare and precious love his parents shared. Now he hoped that one day soon, Elizabeth Johnson would look at him the way his mother looked at his father.

When they reached the house, Dusty accepted a glass of lemonade from his mother, then sat on the porch rail, listening idly to his parents talk about ranch business.

There had been numerous changes in the ranch in the last fifteen years. His parents had built a new house about ten years ago and converted the old place into a bunkhouse. They had built a barn and corrals, planted fruit trees.

There had been other changes, too. Twin Rivers had become a good-sized town. Twenty-five years ago, there had been only thirteen cabins in the valley; now more than sixty houses lined the riverbanks and hillsides. The town had its own newspaper now, a telegraph office, two banks, a blacksmith, a cooper, a barber shop, a post office, a doctor and a dentist, a couple of saloons, and three churches. Mace Carson, one of the valley's first settlers, had built a new general store. Melinda and Ivy, two of Abel and Laura Patterson's daughters, taught at the new schoolhouse; Daisy Patterson owned a millinery store; their youngest daughter, Opal, worked in the general store. Solid wood boardwalks fronted most of the buildings, saving wear and tear on skirts and footwear in rainy weather.

The Indian problem had been settled. The Apache wars had ended in the middle of the 1880s. In 1886, 498 Chiricahua Indians from Arizona had been sent to Florida as prisoners of war. Of course, there'd never been an Indian problem in Twin Rivers. The Howard brothers had been the original settlers in the valley. Both men had been married to Comanche women and had come to the valley looking for a place where they could raise their children. As more people had drifted into the valley, the Howards had made it clear that anyone willing to live in peace was welcome.

Dusty remembered his mother saying that years ago, the valley had been a refuge, a sanctuary for men and women who were running from an unpleasant past. After the Howards' arrival, a handful of others had found their way into the valley—an outlaw on the dodge; a woman running away from an unhappy love affair, a drifter who stopped by and fell in love with her; a retired sheriff and his wife; a priest; a Negro family. The Howards had made them all welcome. Mace Carson had married an Apache woman and raised a brood of black-haired daughters. Carson had traded with the Indians who came to the valley, giving them a fair price for their furs. In the old days, the Apaches had come often to the valley, bringing their wives and children with them.

Dusty slid a glance at his parents, who had been through some hard times. Life hadn't been easy for his father. In his prime, Ryder Fallon had been known as a fast gun. Dusty remembered hearing one of the men in town remark that Ryder Fallon could "draw quickern' you can spit and holler howdy." Not only that, but his father was a half-breed. Fewer than thirty years ago, that had been a dirty word. In some places, it still was. But it had never been a problem in Twin Rivers, at least not until recently. Half the population seemed to carry Indian blood of one sort or another. Hell, Dusty was proud to be one-quarter Cheyenne. But lately, with more and more people arriving from the east, there'd been some name calling that had led to more than one barroom brawl. A month ago, one of the Howard boys had been lynched by three outsiders who claimed he'd stolen one of their horses.

It was that incident that had led the town fathers to decide they needed a full-time lawman. At first, they had been reluctant to hire Dusty. They'd told him it was because he was so young, but he suspected it had more to do with the fact that he was part Indian. In the end, he'd got the job because no one else wanted it.

Rising, he gave his mother a quick kiss on the cheek. "Thanks for the lemonade, Mom."

"Going to see Elizabeth at the dance tonight?" Jenny asked, smiling up at him.

"Right the first time. I'd better get cleaned up, or I'll be late. Don't wait up."

Whistling softly, Dusty went into the house, a thrill of anticipation running through him as he contemplated seeing Elizabeth again. If he was lucky, she might let him steal a kiss.

Later than night, Jenny stood on the porch, gazing into the vast empty darkness that surrounded the ranch. It was late, almost midnight, and the whole earth seemed to be sleeping.

She felt an uncharacteristic wave of melancholy as her gaze moved over the ranch. There had been many changes since she had first come here with Ryder twenty-five years ago: changes in their lives, changes in the valley, in the world.

The ranch had prospered. The little cabin in which they'd spent the first years of their marriage had been replaced by a rambling three-bedroom house with oak floors and leaded-glass windows. She had insisted on painting the new house yellow with white trim to remind her of the old place. The corrals out back were filled with blooded stock; people came from near and far to purchase a horse that had been raised and gentled by Ryder Fallon. They'd built a new barn last year. Where had the time gone?

It seemed like only yesterday that Dorinda and Dusty had trailed at her heels, tugging on her skirts, asking questions quicker than she could answer them. Only yesterday, her children had been babes, eager to grow up, to take that first step that would allow them to take another and another, until they no longer needed a helping hand, no longer needed her. . . .

Leaning back against the porch upright, Jenny closed her eyes. Maybe it was the fact that Dorinda had recently left home for the first time that had her feeling so blue. One of Dorinda's friends had moved to New York and had invited Dorinda to come for a visit. Dorinda had jumped at the chance, eager to visit the East, to take in the theater, visit the museums. It was just a visit, Jenny mused ruefully, yet it was one more step away from home. . . .

How old had her firstborn son been when he took his first step, spoke his first word?

Cosito . . . the son she had traded for her husband's life.

Cosito . . . he would be twenty-five now, a man grown. She had not seen him since he was a baby. She remembered how Ryder had risked his life by riding into the Apache rancheria to kidnap her son. He had known how she missed Cosito, how she grieved for her son, and so, without telling her what he planned, he had ridden out to bring him back.

When she discovered what Ryder intended to do, she and Will Howard had gone after him. She would never forget the soul-shattering joy she had experienced when she saw her husband riding toward her with Cosito in his arms. Nor would she forget the heart-wrenching fear that had engulfed her when Cosito's father, Kayitah, overtook them. She had pleaded with Kayitah for Ryder's life and, in the end, she had surrendered her son to his father in order to save her husband's life.

She had never regretted her decision, but sometimes the pain of not knowing what had become of her firstborn son was more than she could bear.

"Jenny?"

She turned at the sound of Ryder's voice. "I'm out here."

Familiar footsteps crossed the porch, and then Ryder was gathering her into his arms, holding her close. Lamplight filtered onto the porch from the parlor, and she smiled up at him, thinking he was the most handsome man she had ever known. His hair was still long, black as pitch save for a few gray strands; his eyes were the same compelling shade of blue. It was hard to remember that he had once been a drifter, a gunfighter without equal. To her, he would always be a knight in shining armor, the man who had rescued her from the Apaches, given her a home, children. . . .

She sighed as she thought of Cosito again.

"Something troubling you, Jenny girl?" Ryder asked.

"No, not really."

"You're thinking of him, aren't you?" Ryder remarked.

She didn't deny it, and Ryder felt a twinge of guilt. Jenny was the sweetest, kindest, most soft-hearted woman he had ever known—and the most courageous. She had endured two years of captivity with the Apache, and she had saved his life at the risk of her own when he had been captured by the Indians. Then she had saved his life a second time, giving up her firstborn son in exchange. In all the years of their marriage, she had never once hinted that she felt she'd made a bad bargain, never said or done anything to make him think she regretted that decision.

"Jenny." He gazed deep into her eyes, eyes as green as spring grass, thinking that she was even more beautiful now than she had been twenty-five years ago. Jenny.

He brushed his lips against her hair, remembering the first time he had seen her. He had been Kayitah's prisoner at the time, badly wounded, when she had come to him under cover of darkness, her bright golden hair hidden beneath a blanket. That night, she had saved his life.

Ryder couldn't help grinning as he recalled how she had brought him water when he would have sold his soul to the devil for just one drop, and then, turning that same need for water against him, had extracted his promise to help her escape from the rancheria.

He stroked her hair as she buried her face in the hollow of his shoulder. "I still miss him, Ryder."

"I know, honey."

"I wish . . ."

"What, Jenny girl? What do you wish?"

"I just wish I knew he was all right."

With a sigh, Ryder drew her closer. The Apache, like the Sioux and the Cheyenne and the Crow, had been sent to live on the reservation years ago. "Do you want me to see if I can find him?"

"Do you think it's possible?"

"I don't know. Maybe. There must be records of some kind on the reservation."

"It's been so long, so much has happened since then. How would you even know where to start?"

"I can ask around."

"I'd love to know how he is, but . . ." Jenny shook her head.

"But what, honey?"

"I feel like I gave up all my rights to him years ago. He probably doesn't even know I exist." She took a deep breath. "The house seems so quiet with Dorinda gone. Do you think she's having a good time in the big city? I wish she'd taken someone with her."

"Me, too, but you know Dorinda. Stubborn and independent. Kind of like her mother." Ryder grunted softly as Jenny cuffed him on the shoulder. "She was determined to go alone. I'm sure she's fine." Ryder rested his chin on the top of Jenny's head. He understood why she had changed the subject—thinking of Cosito was too painful to endure for long. "Besides," he said, hoping to cheer her, "it's not forever. She'll be back soon."

"I know. It was fun at the dance tonight, wasn't it? Dusty looked so handsome."

Ryder grunted. "Yeah. He's a good-lookin' kid, and he knows it, too. Did you see the way those fool girls swarmed around him? Especially Johnson's daughter." He looked up at the sky and frowned. It was after midnight and his son wasn't home yet.

Jenny laughed softly. She couldn't blame the girls for following Dusty. Except for his eyes, which were green instead of blue, Dusty looked just like his father, with the same thick black hair, the same wide shoulders and long, long legs. The same heart-stopping smile.

Ryder drew back a little. "What's so funny?"

"Nothing, except Dusty looks just like you."

And once again her thoughts turned to her other son, her little lost lamb. Had Cosito grown up to look like *his* father?

"Jenny?"

"I'm all right." She leaned against him, grateful for his love and understanding, for the unfailing strength of the strong arms around her.

Dusty slid his arm around Elizabeth Johnson's waist and drew her to him. "Warmer now?"

Beth snuggled against him. "Much. I heard something funny today."

"Oh?"

She nodded. "I overheard my dad talking to Mr. Carson. Mr. Carson said your father used to be a gunfighter. Is that true?"

"Yeah. According to my mother, he was the best there was."

Beth laughed softly as she ran a finger over the badge pinned to Dusty's vest. "I guess you're not exactly following in his footsteps."

Dusty shrugged. "Not exactly."

"Does your father ever talk about those days?"

He grinned. "No. My mother does, though. Sometimes, when my dad's out working in the fields, she gets to talking about the old days before they came here."

"Did they have a lot of adventures?"

"More than their share, I'd say."

"I'd like to hear about them. Life is so dull here."

"It won't be dull for long if I don't let you go in soon."

Beth laughed softly. "Kiss me good night?"

"What do you think?" Bending, Dusty kissed her gently. "See you at church tomorrow?"

"I'll save you a seat."

"See you tomorrow, then."

"'Night, Dusty."

"Good night."

Whistling softly, Dusty walked down the path toward the street. He turned and waved, then swung into the saddle and headed home.

He'd been courting Elizabeth for almost four months, and it was getting harder and harder to say good night. His dreams were filled with images of Beth, her long honey-colored hair falling loose over her bare shoulders, her brown eyes warm with desire. Just thinking about her made him ache.

Urging his horse into a lope, he tried to think of something else, but the scent of Beth's perfume lingered in his nostrils, making it difficult to concentrate. He hadn't proposed yet, but they'd talked about marriage, and Dusty was certain that when he finally popped the questions, she would say yes.

He was still thinking of Beth when he reached home. He unsaddled his horse, tossed it some hay, then left the barn.

"'Bout time you got home."

"Hi, Dad. Mom."

Ryder grinned at his son. "How's Elizabeth?"

"Pretty as a spring flower."

"Did she ask you over to Sunday dinner?"

"No, but she will."

Jenny shook her head. "You seem mighty sure of yourself."

Dusty shrugged. "She's invited me every week for the last four months."

"Could be we'll be having a wedding soon, Jenny girl," Ryder remarked.

"Do you love her, Dusty?" Jenny asked.

"Yeah."

"And does she love you?"

"I don't know. I think so."

"Well, she's a lovely girl," Jenny said. "I'd be proud to have her in the family."

"Thanks, Mom." Dusty gave his mother a hug. "See you in the morning. 'Night, Dad."

"Night, son."

Jenny leaned against Ryder, her head pillowed on his shoulder. "The house will seem empty when they're both gone."

Ryder nodded. "You can't keep them home forever."

"I know."

"Cheer up, Jenny girl. You'll always have me."

She smiled up at him as he swung her into his arms and carried her inside. Whatever else happened in her life, she would always have Ryder. And someday soon, God willing, she would have grandchildren.

Wrapping her arms around his neck, she let out a sigh of contentment as Ryder carried her down the hallway to the bedroom and shut the door, closing out the rest of the world.

Chapter Two

Mounted on a stolen horse, Chase the Wind left the reservation without a backward glance, everything he owned stowed in his saddlebags.

He had said a final prayer at his stepmother's grave, said his good-byes to a few close friends, and ridden into the darkness. With luck, he would never see the reservation again.

He felt a rush of excitement as he urged the horse into a lope. He was going on a pilgrimage of sorts, back to the land of his birth. And perhaps, if *Usen* smiled on him, he would find someone who knew his mother.

Chapter Three

Dusty sat back in his chair, his feet propped on his desk, idly admiring his new Justin boots. They were Texas-made and about the best footwear he'd ever owned. The most expensive, too.

Glancing out the window, he saw Beth Johnson enter the millinery shop across the street. Lordy, but that girl was the prettiest thing he'd ever seen.

Grabbing his hat, he stepped out onto the boardwalk, his back propped against the jailhouse wall, his gaze fixed on the door of Patterson's Millinery Shoppe.

He pushed away from the wall and crossed the street as Beth emerged from the store.

"Hey, Miss, can I carry your packages and walk you home?"

"Why, that's mighty kind of you, Sheriff," she replied, handing him a parcel wrapped in brown paper and tied with string. "Do you extend this courtesy to all the girls?"

"Just the pretty ones with hair the color of summer honey and eyes as brown as beaver fur."

Beth felt a wave of color sweep into her cheeks. "Thank you, kind sir."

"What'd you buy?"

"A new hat," she said, her eyes sparkling. "It's peacock blue with black feathers and white lace. Wait until you see it! It's beautiful."

"So are you."

"You mustn't say such things," Beth said primly. "It isn't proper."

"Says who?"

"Mama. She says you're just trying to sweet-talk me out of my innocence."

Dusty scowled. Theda Johnson had made it perfectly clear that she was dead set against a match between her only daughter and Ryder Fallon's son. Oh, she was polite enough when Beth invited him to dinner, but he knew Theda thought her daughter too good for the likes of him. If Theda Johnson had her way, Beth would marry someone like Ernest Tucker, the banker's son.

"Are you, Dusty?"

He glanced at Beth, realizing she'd asked him something. "What?"

"Are you trying to sweet-talk me?"

"No. I wouldn't tell you lies, Beth. *My* mama taught me better than that."

Beth sighed. Dusty Fallon was the most handsome man she'd ever met. He was tall and dark and well-mannered. If only her mother wasn't so set on her marrying Ernest Tucker. Not that Ernest wasn't a nice young man. It was just that he was so . . . so boring. All he ever thought about was money—how to make it, how to save it, how to make more. He never wanted to do anything fun, like run barefoot in the rain, or go swimming in the river. He didn't like to read, and thought it scandalous that she'd read *The Strange Case of Dr. Jekyll and Mr. Hyde* and *Ships That Pass in the Night.* Ernest thought it improper for a lady to read novels, and had told her, more than once, that if she had to indulge her passion for reading, she should stick to *Vogue, The Ladies Home Journal,* and the Bible.

Beth placed her hand on Dusty's arm and smiled up at him. "Will you come to Sunday supper?"

Dusty hesitated a moment, dreading the thought of spending another afternoon under Theda Johnson's baleful eye, and then he nodded. He'd endure a dozen like Theda Johnson to be with Beth.

"We're having turkey and all the fixin's."

"Sounds good."

"And apple pie. I'm making it myself."

"I'll look forward to it."

"Well, here we are," Beth said.

"Yeah." Dusty glanced up at the big white house. Beth's father was the richest man in the valley. He'd been a banker back east and had come west for his health. Their home, built on a large lot at the end of Main Street, was reminiscent of Southern-style mansions, with six white columns and a wide veranda that spanned the front of the house. A shiny black carriage was parked at the carriage block; a dozen blooded horses grazed alongside the house. He half expected Theda Johnson to come running out of the front door to rescue her daughter from his evil clutches.

"See you tomorrow," Beth said, taking her package from his hand.

"Tomorrow." He let his fingers slide over hers, wishing he dared steal a kiss.

Beth stood at the gate, watching Dusty walk away. Her mother might think she was going to marry Ernest Tucker, but Beth knew it was never going to happen. Beth craved excitement, not security. And when a woman wanted excitement, she didn't pick a plow horse; she chose a stallion.

And Dusty was the finest stallion in the valley.

The following afternoon Ryder drew his horse to a halt, his head cocked to one side as he heard the sound of gunshots coming from behind the house. Instinctively, his hand went to the gun on his hip, and then he grinned self-consciously. Old habits died hard, he mused as he urged his mount toward the back of the house.

Rounding the corner, Ryder reined his horse to a halt. For a moment, he stared at the thin curl of blue-gray smoke rising from the barrel of the Colt in his son's hand. There'd been a time, years ago, when he had worn his own gun as if it were as much a part of him as his hands and feet. It wasn't a life he wanted for Dusty.

Dusty turned around, reaching for the box of ammunition sitting on an upended crate behind him. "Hi," he said. "I didn't hear you come up."

"Doin' some practicing, I see," Ryder remarked, gesturing at the cans lined up on the corral fence.

Dusty grinned sheepishly, like a kid caught smoking behind the schoolhouse. "I thought, well, even though we don't get much action in town, I thought I should . . . you know."

"Yeah," Ryder said. Dismounting, he dropped the reins to the ground and took a place beside his son. "How're you doing?"

Dusty jerked a thumb in the direction of the cans. "See for yourself."

Ryder grunted softly. "Not bad."

"Not good, either."

"Let me see you draw."

Feeling a trifle self-conscious, Dusty holstered his Colt, then drew and fired. One of the cans toppled off the fence.

"You're jerking the trigger," Ryder remarked. "Cock the hammer as you draw so the gun comes out of the holster ready to fire. Just be sure you don't shoot yourself in the foot."

"That's real funny."

"You won't think so when it happens. Drawing your weapon and cocking it should all be one smooth motion. Don't draw, cock, aim, and shoot. It slows you down. You need to pick your target and know where your first shot's going before you even draw your weapon."

"How about a demonstration?"

"Dammit, I haven't fast-drawn my gun in twenty years."

"They say you never forget."

Ryder shook his head. "I don't know," he muttered, and then, in one swift motion, he drew his Colt and rapid-fired five rounds.

Dusty whistled softly as five cans flew off the fence. "That's shootin'."

Ryder grinned, inordinately pleased with himself. By damn, he still had it. "Well, that's what I was talking about."

Dusty holstered his Colt. "You never told me how you got to be a gunfighter."

"I was never really a gunfighter. I was a gambler who just happened to be fast with a gun." Ryder shook his head. "I found an old Colt's Dragoon when I was just a kid. I remember I practiced drawing that old gun for hours on end, until I could draw and fire that old Colt with the same speed and accuracy as I had once had with a bow and arrows. I admit I killed my share of men—maybe more than my share. But I never thought of myself as a gunfighter."

"Do you think I could learn to shoot as good as you do?"

"That's up to you. Just remember, once you take a man's life, he becomes a part of you whether you like it or not."

"I don't understand."

"Like I said, I've killed men. And sometimes, late at night when I can't sleep, I see their faces."

Dusty nodded, his expression suddenly sober.

"One other piece of advice. If you draw that gun on a man, you'd best be prepared to kill him. Don't try anything fancy, like winging him or shooting the gun out of his hand. Most times, you'll only get one shot, so you'd best make it count."

"I'll remember."

"Good." Ryder slapped his son on the shoulder. "You going over to the Johnsons' again tonight?"

"Yep. Six sharp for Sunday dinner."

"Old Theda still givin' you a bad time?"

"Same as always."

"If you marry Beth, you'll be marrying her mother, too, you know."

"I know," Dusty replied mournfully.

"Well, I guess your mother and I can stand it if you can."

Dusty watched his father swing into the saddle, then glanced at his watch. Four o'clock. He'd best get cleaned up if he hoped to be at the Johnsons' on time.

Dusty held Beth's chair for her, then took a seat beside her, uncomfortable, as always, in her mother's presence. He had the feeling that Theda Johnson watched his every move, waiting for him to commit some horrible breach of etiquette that would prove him to be the savage she thought him to be.

He stifled a grin as he stared at the silverware laid out beside his plate, and silently blessed his mother for teaching him which fork to use with which dish.

Dusty bowed his head as Walter Johnson said grace, asking the Lord's benediction on the food, the hands that had prepared it, his family, and especially his daughter. He felt a wave of heat climb up the back of his neck as Mr. Johnson pleaded with the Almighty to bless his daughter with wisdom at "this important time of decision making in her life."

Beth slid a glance at Dusty, her eyes begging his forgiveness for her father's rudeness.

"So, young man," Walter Johnson said, "how are things going at the sheriff's office?"

"Fine, sir."

"Do you plan to spend the rest of your life as a small-town sheriff?"

"Daddy!"

"Hold your tongue, Elizabeth," Johnson said, his gaze on Dusty.

"I'm not sure what I plan to do with the rest of my life, sir. I've only been the sheriff a week."

"True, true, but a young man has to decide on a career early in life," Johnson remarked, glancing at his daughter. "A man needs security if he intends to settle down and raise a family."

"Yes, sir."

"Banking is a respectable occupation."

"Yes, sir." Dusty slid a furtive glance at Theda Johnson. She was watching him over the rim of a crystal water goblet, no doubt waiting for him to say or do the wrong thing.

"I might be able to get you a position at the bank."

"Thank you, sir, but I think I'll stay where I am for the present."

"As you wish," Johnson said curtly. "Mother, pass me some of those potatoes, please."

The rest of the meal passed in near silence. When it was over, Johnson insisted Beth play the piano.

Dusty sat in a spindly-legged chair covered in rose damask, his back straight, his face carefully impassive. He applauded politely when Beth finished playing.

"That was lovely, Elizabeth," he said formally. He bowed in Theda Johnson's direction. "Thank you for dinner, ma'am."

"You're welcome, Mr. Fallon," Theda replied stiffly.

"Thank you for having me, sir. Good evening."

"Good-bye."

"I'll walk you out," Beth said. As soon as they were outside, she grabbed him by the hand. "I'm sorry, Dusty. They were horrible."

"I'd like to disagree," he replied with a smile, "but I can't."

"I'll be shopping in town tomorrow," Beth said, smiling up at him. "Will you be in your office?"

Dusty nodded.

"I'll see you tomorrow then."

"I'll looked forward to it." Placing his hands on her shoulders, he kissed her good night. "Till tomorrow."

Beth watched him walk down the porch steps. She waved when he paused at the gate and glanced back at her.

She stayed on the veranda for a few minutes, wishing her parents weren't so snobbish. All her life, she'd been told to be aware of her position in the community, that it was important for her to behave like a lady, that she had a duty to be a good example. As much as she cared for Dusty, she doubted her parents would ever allow her to marry him. And if she refused to marry Ernest, she knew her mother would follow through on her threat to send her back east in hopes Beth would make a "good match" by marrying into one of the respectable Boston families.

But that was next year, she mused as she climbed the stairs to her bedroom. A lot could happen in a year.

Chapter Four

The desert surrounded him, endless shimmering waves of sand that seemed to go on forever. Reining his big buckskin mare to a halt, Chase lifted his face to the sky. The sun seemed brighter here, the sky more blue.

Moving on, he passed the Rock Springs waterhole, and Foxtail Creek, and every mile took him closer to the land of his birth until, at last, he saw the high purple cliffs that enclosed the valley that had once sheltered Kayitah's band.

He urged the mare into a lope. She was a fine animal, with a deep chest and nostrils that drank the wind. The fact that he had stolen her from a bluecoat made her all the more valuable.

His heart pounded with anticipation as he reached the narrow passage that led into Rainbow Canyon. Reining the mare to a halt, he took a deep breath, his nostrils filling with the remembered scent of earth and sage and pine.

He closed his eyes, and memories of the past filled his heart and soul. . . .

It was here that he had taken his first steps; here that Kayitah had taught him to ride, to hunt, and to track. To be a warrior.

It was here that he had met Geronimo; here that he had made his first kill.

Loosing a deep sigh, he rode into the heart of the canyon. Nothing remained of the rancheria save a few stones blackened by fire and smoke. Everything of value had been destroyed or carried away by the bluecoats; what was left had been obliterated by time.

Dismounting in the place where Kayitah's lodge had once stood, Chase unsaddled the buckskin, then turned the mare loose to forage on the rich green grass that spread like a blanket over the canyon floor.

Spreading his saddle blanket on the ground, he sat with his back against a cottonwood tree, his gaze fixed on the darkening sky, as he listened to the night, to the serenade of the crickets and the soft sighing of the wind as it whispered good night to the trees.

And there, crying in the wind, he heard the voices of those long dead. *Welcome home, ciye,* they sang. Welcome home, my son.

He closed his eyes and memories assailed him once more: the pungent scent of meat roasting over an open cookfire, the sound of children playing, Alope's smile as she welcomed him home, the look of pride on his father's face when he put away his childhood name and became a man, the love in

Clarai's eyes when he asked for her hand in marriage . . .

He felt the sharp sting of tears as the good memories were swallowed up by the horrors that had come after—the battles that had been fought as the bluecoats pursued them, relentless as winter-starved wolves. He had fought for his life beneath the scorching summer sun and in the bitter cold of winter. He had been wounded numerous times, had taken numerous lives. He had seen his friends and his loved ones killed—shot, knifed, hanged. He had seen children trampled to death beneath the iron-shod hooves of the soldiers' horses. He had held Clarai in his arms while her life's blood poured from a bayonet wound in her breast. And he had vowed he would never surrender, never forgive, never love again.

And then Gatewood had taken the field, accompanied by Tom Horn and his Apache scouts.

Chase fisted the tears from his eyes, sorrow replaced by hatred as he thought of Chatto and the other Apaches who had scouted for the Army.

In the summer of 1886, Kayitah had surrendered. By November of that year, 498 Apaches had arrived in Florida as prisoners of war. Fewer than a hundred were warriors. It was there, far from the land of his birth, that Kayitah had died, his heart broken, his spirit crushed.

From Florida, the Apache had been sent to Mount Vernon Barracks. To the dismay of their parents, 112 Apache children had been sent to the Indian School at Carlisle. Thirty died there; twelve had been returned to the reservation because of sickness. In October of 1894, the Apaches, now numbering fewer than three hundred, of which only fifty were able-bodied men, had been sent to Fort Sill.

With effort, Chase wiped the bitter memories from his mind. The wind, cold now, stirred the leaves in the trees, and in their quiet rustling, he heard his father's voice echoing the words, *Welcome home, ciye. Welcome home.*

He spent a week in the valley, and each day his spirit grew stronger. It was good to be there, to contemplate the lessons he had been taught in childhood, to remember the people he had loved and lost, to recall the ancient stories of the Apache. He walked along the riverbank and swam in its chill water. Occasionally, he found an arrowhead buried in the sand.

And always, in the back of his mind, he wondered about the mother he had never known. Had she been lively or quiet, pretty or plain? Why had she left him? He tried to remember what his father had said about the woman he called Golden Dove, but Kayitah had been close-mouthed about the white woman he had taken to wife, saying only that she had harbored no love for the Apache and that, when given the choice, she had gone back to her own people.

Chase gazed into the depths of the slow-moving river. He was a grown man, yet it rankled deep inside that his own mother had abandoned him. Of all the ghosts that haunted him, his mother's betrayal was hardest to bear.

Tomorrow, he would ride out of the valley in hopes of finding answers to the questions that plagued him.

* * *

Chase urged the mare into a lope, a sense of exultation riding with him. According to the last man he had talked to, Twin Rivers was just over the next hill.

During the previous week, he had stopped at every farm and ranch he'd come across, asking after his mother. He hadn't told anyone who he was, just asked if they knew if a woman named Jenny still lived in Twin Rivers. He'd had the feeling that they all knew of her, but, except for the old man, they had all refused to tell him anything. Most of the people he questioned had denied knowing her. One man, more outspoken than the rest, had declared he'd be damned before he'd tell a "dirty redskin a damned thing about a decent white woman."

Even now, a week later, Chase could feel the anger that had surged through him at the man's words. Dirty redskin. How often had he heard those words, always spoken with derision, always accompanied by a look of disdain. When he'd been a child, those words had hurt. As he grew older, he'd learned to conceal the hurt behind a mask of insolence. Later, insolence had given way to a cold and bitter rage. He had learned to hate the bluecoats who had hunted them, the black robes who had tried to steal away their religion, the white women who had come to the reservation, their pasty faces filled with pity. He had despised them all, but the young white women had been the worst. They had looked at his people, at him, as one might look at a wild animal whose spirit had been broken but who might attack them at any moment.

Would his mother look at him like that?

He put the thought out of his mind as he topped a rise and caught his first sight of Twin Rivers. The town, located between the gently sloping hills of a verdant valley, was situated on both sides of the two rivers that had given the town its name. He saw many of the small square houses favored by the white man. Some were located within the town, others had been built on the hillsides.

His mouth felt suddenly dry as he realized his mother might be living in one of those houses.

Reining his horse to a halt, Chase brushed the dust from his clothes and ran his fingers through his hair. Then, shoulders squared, he urged the buckskin forward.

It was mid-afternoon, and the streets were crowded. He was aware of being watched as he neared the center of town. Most of the looks were merely curious; a few were contemptuous.

Unconsciously, Chase stroked the handle of the knife sheathed on his belt and wished he had a rifle.

He hesitated as he approached the sheriff's office. No doubt the lawman would know if his mother was in town, but he didn't want anything to do with the white man's law. Clucking to the buckskin, he rode on down the street until he came to the general store. The man who ran the trading post on the reservation knew everyone. Perhaps the man who ran the general store possessed similar knowledge of the people who lived in town.

Dismounting, Chase tethered his horse to the rail that ran the length of the building, then climbed the steps to the boardwalk.

He was reaching for the latch when the door opened and he saw a young woman standing in the doorway. She wore a pale blue dress with puffy sleeves and a full skirt. The square neck, which was edged with rows of fine white lace, revealed a modest amount of smooth, sun-tanned skin. Long, honey-blond curls peeked from beneath a white bonnet. Her cheeks were rosy, her lips full and pink.

In that moment, Chase knew he had never seen anyone more beautiful.

"Excuse me," she murmured, and her voice moved over him, as soft and light as a summer breeze.

With a nod, Chase took a step backward.

And then her gaze met his. Her eyes were a luminous shade of brown, intelligent and curious, and as he stared at her, he had the strangest feeling that he knew her, that he had always known her.

Awareness flowed between them like the ripples in a stream, and for one moment out of time, no one else existed in all the world but the two of them.

Chase cleared his throat, trying to summon the courage to speak to her, to tell her how he felt, but before he could form the words, an older woman, clad in a severe black dress, stepped between them. The crone looked down her nose at him, her nose wrinkling as if she had just smelled something vile, and then she took hold of the young woman's arm and they walked down the boardwalk together.

The young woman glanced over her shoulder, her gaze meeting his once more, and again Chase felt the attraction that hummed between them, singing like the white man's telegraph lines. She sent him a shy smile, her lips curving ever so slightly, her eyes crinkling at the corners, and then she was lost to his sight.

He had a sudden urge to run after her, to learn her name, hear the sound of her voice. To feel the touch of her hand on his face.

Shaking the fanciful notion aside, Chase opened the door and entered the building. It was a large, high-ceilinged room. Shelves lined the walls; counters and tables were piled high with goods.

For a moment, he stood inside the door, staring at the bounty before him. Never in all his life had he seen such an abundance of merchandise. Unlike the trading post on the reservation, the shelves here were filled with bolts of cloth in every color imaginable. There were stacks of blankets, cowboy hats in a variety of styles and colors. Enough canned goods to feed the Apache for a year. He saw barrels of crackers and pickles and cheese, smelled the rich aroma of freshly ground coffee. There were sacks of flour and sugar and cornmeal. There were rows of ready-made dresses, shirts, pants, and vests.

He glanced at his own cotton shirt and canvas pants, both of which were badly worn. Only his moccasins were new, made by Alope shortly before she died.

"Can I help you?"

Chase turned to see a stoop-shouldered elderly man walking toward him. "I am looking for someone."

The man nodded. "I might be able to help you. Name's Mace Carson." Mace took in the younger man's appearance in a quick glance. "Looks like you've come a fer piece."

"Yes."

"So, who might you be lookin' fer?"

"A woman."

Mace laughed. " 'Fraid you've come to the wrong place. I got lots of things fer sale here, but no women."

Chase shook his head. "I am looking for a particular woman. Her name is Jenny."

Mace frowned. "Jenny Fallon?"

"I do not know her last name."

"You a friend of hers?"

"No."

Mace stroked his chin thoughtfully. "You're Apache, ain't ya?"

Chase stiffened, and then he nodded. "Does she live here?"

"That she does. Why don't you go on down to the Red Horse Saloon and have a drink? I'll ride out and tell her yer here."

"How long will it take?"

"Not long. Half-hour, hour, maybe."

"I will wait."

"Maybe I oughta tell Jenny yer name."

"She will not know it."

Mace grunted softly. "I reckon she'll wonder who you are."

"I reckon," Chase said, parroting the white man's words.

"Have it yer own way," Mace said.

"Will she meet me in the saloon?"

Mace grinned. "No. Why don't you come back here in an hour?"

Feeling awkward, Chase held out his hand. "Thank you."

"You're welcome," Mace replied, shaking the younger man's hand. "Tell Clem I sent you."

"Clem?"

"The bartender at the Red Horse. Tell him to take care of you."

With a nod, Chase left the store. Taking up the reins to his horse, he walked down the street until he saw a sign with a red horse painted on it. Looping the buckskin's reins over the hitch rail, he entered the saloon.

The interior was dark and smoky. Chase coughed as he made his way to the bar. He had never been in a saloon before. The walls were covered in dark red paper. Oil lamps hung from the ceiling. Round tables covered with green cloth took up a good portion of the floor. Several women wandered around the room. Even knowing it was rude, he couldn't help staring at them. Never before had he seen women dressed in such a manner. Their brightly colored dresses were cut scandalously low in front, revealing an indecent amount of flesh.

"What'll it be, fella?"

With an effort, Chase drew his gaze from a raven-haired woman clad in a bright red dress and looked at the bartender.

The man sighed. "You buyin' or just lookin'?"

"Mace Carson sent me."

"That right?"

Chase nodded.

"You want a beer?"

Chase nodded again, wondering if the white man's beer was anything like *tiswin.* Moments later, the bartender placed a glass of amber liquid in front of him.

Taking the glass, Chase walked toward the back of the room and sat down at an empty table. What would his mother think when told that there was an Indian waiting in town to see her? Would she think it was a mistake? Or would she know that her past had finally found her? Would she acknowledge him as her son, or call him a liar and turn him away? He wondered again why she had left him, if she had ever given any thought to Kayitah and the infant she had deserted.

He blew out a deep breath, then downed the beer. Soon, he would have the answers to the questions that had plagued him as long as he could remember.

Jenny stared at Mace Carson, her mind reeling. A young man, an Indian, looking for her. "He didn't tell you his name?"

Carson shook his head. "He said you wouldn't know it. It ain't my place to say, but he looked like trouble to me."

"How old would you say he is?"

"Oh, I don't know, early twenties, maybe. Hard to tell with Indians sometimes."

Feeling light-headed, Jenny reached across the table for Ryder's hand. "You don't think . . . ?"

Ryder shrugged. "There's only one way to find out."

"You're right, of course." Rising, she removed her apron and ran a hand over her hair, smoothing it back from her face. "Do I look all right?"

"Beautiful, as always."

"I'm serious."

Ryder grinned. "So am I. Come on, let's get this over with. Thanks for coming, Mace."

"No problem. I'll meet you at the store."

"Right."

Jenny smoothed her skirts and put on her hat. "I'm so nervous. What if it *is* him?"

"One step at a time, Jenny girl," Ryder said, opening the door. "One step at a time."

Pat was waiting outside, whittling idly.

"Thanks for bringing the rig up," Ryder said.

Pat nodded. "Want me to drive?"

"No." Ryder helped Jenny onto the seat, then swung up beside her and took up the reins. He clucked to the horses, and they moved out at a brisk walk.

"Ryder, I'm so scared."

"Try to relax, honey."

"I wish I could. Oh, Ryder, what if it *is* him? What will Dusty think? And Dorinda?"

"Let's worry about one thing at a time, okay?"

"We should have told them."

"There didn't seem to be any point at the time."

"I know, but maybe we should have said something. What will they think now?"

Ryder slipped his arm around Jenny's shoulders. "I don't know, Jenny girl. Maybe we should have told them they had a brother, but hell, when they were young, they wouldn't have been able to understand what happened, and then . . ."

Ryder shrugged. There hadn't seemed any point in telling the kids they had a half-brother they'd never see.

There was a lot of their parents' past that Dusty and Dorinda didn't know. Like the fact that Jenny had once been married to another man, or that she'd been captured by Indians on her way to join her first husband. Jenny hadn't been keen on the idea of talking about the time she'd spent with the

Apache, or discussing the fact that she had borne Kayitah a son. As for Ryder, he had a skeleton or two in his own closet that he'd just as soon forget.

He felt Jenny's hand tighten on his arm as they reached the outskirts of town. "We don't have to do this," he said as he drew rein in front of Mace Carson's store.

"No, I want to. I have to."

Alighting from the carriage, Ryder tossed the reins over the hitch rack, then helped Jenny to the ground. "Smile."

"Easy for you to say," she remarked. He'd told her that once before, she recalled, when he'd taken her to Widow Ridge to meet Hank. *Smile, honey,* he'd said. *I'm sure the Christians weren't half so pale when they went to meet the lions.* And she'd retorted, *I'll bet they weren't as scared, either.*

She took a deep breath, then lifted her skirts as they climbed the stairs to the boardwalk. "Nothing to be afraid of," she murmured, but couldn't still the pounding of her heart as they entered the general store.

Carson was standing just inside the door. "He's in back," Mace said, jerking a thumb toward the room he used for his office.

"Thanks, Mace." Ryder gave Jenny's hand a squeeze. "You want me to go with you?"

Jenny nodded. "Please."

"All right, let's get it done."

The door was closed. Jenny paused a moment, then opened the door and stepped inside.

Chapter Five

He was sitting in a rickety straight-backed chair, his hands resting on his knees. He looked up as she entered the room, and Jenny found herself staring into a pair of deep black eyes. Kayitah's eyes.

"Cosito." The name whispered past her lips, stirring memories of a daring escape on a stormy night.

He stood up, tall and straight, like his father. "I am called Chase the Wind."

Jenny nodded, unable to speak past the lump in her throat as she stared at her son. He was not quite as tall as Dusty, though he was wider through the shoulders. His skin was dark, his waist-length hair shone blue-black in the light filtering through the window. But it was his eyes that held her attention. They were the eyes of a man who had seen much, endured much. Lost much.

"You are Jenny?" he asked.

"Yes."

"The same Jenny who was once known as Golden Dove?"

She nodded, grateful that Ryder was standing behind her. "How is your father?"

"He is dead."

"I'm sorry."

"Are you?"

She recoiled from the animosity in his eyes, the bitterness in his voice. "Yes, I am. He was a good man."

"Then why did you leave him?" Chase demanded, the cumulated anger and bitterness of more than twenty years evident in every word. "Why did you leave me? What kind of woman abandons her child?"

"Listen here, boy," Ryder said. "I won't have you talking to your mother in that tone of voice."

"Who are you?"

"I'm Jenny's husband, and if you don't start treating her with some respect, I'm gonna beat the crap out of you with my bare hands. That's who I am."

For the first time, Chase took a good look at the man standing behind his mother. The realization that this man, who obviously had Indian blood, was his mother's husband, hit him with the force of a blow. It didn't make sense, Chase thought, bewildered. He had assumed she hated Indians. Why then, had she married one?

"I think you owe your mother an apology."

Chase felt the hot blood of shame climb up the back of his neck. The man was right. This woman was his mother and should be treated with respect.

Hands clenched at his sides, Chase met her gaze. "I am sorry for my angry words. Forgive me."

"I should be asking you to forgive me."

"I cannot."

Jenny's tears came then, hot, stinging tears that burned her eyes and made her throat ache. She felt Ryder's hands on her shoulders and she took a deep breath, drinking in his nearness, his support. "What do you want of me?"

"I want only to know why you left me. Were you so ashamed of having an Indian for a son that you ran away?"

"No! No, I loved you."

"Is that how a white woman shows her love, by running away?"

"This isn't the place to be havin' this discussion," Ryder said. "Why don't you come out to the ranch where we can talk in private?"

It was in Chase's mind to refuse, but something, some nagging sense of curiosity, urged him to accept. "I will come."

"Good. We've got a buggy outside."

Chase shook his head. "I will follow you."

"All right." Ryder put his arm around Jenny and led her out of the store, aware of the inquisitive gazes that followed them. He lifted Jenny onto the seat, took up the reins, then vaulted up beside her. Backing the team away from the hitch rack, he headed out of town, acutely aware of the angry young man riding behind them.

Jenny pressed close to Ryder, needing his comfort, his strength, as she relived the night that Cosito—no, Chase the Wind—had been born.

She remembered gazing down at her newborn son and wondering if, for his sake, she should have stayed with Kayitah. She had known the Apaches would love her son, known than no one would belittle him because his mother was a white woman. With the Apache, he would have been accepted without question. But she had wanted to go home, back to Hank, back to the life she knew. And Ryder Fallon had agreed to take her because she had saved his life.

But the escape, which had sounded so easy when they talked about it, didn't go as planned. It had stormed that night, her horse had taken a bad fall, and she had gone into labor.

She remembered the joy that had filled her heart when Ryder placed her son in her arms, remembered asking him if it was hard, being a half-breed. He had been reluctant to answer her.

It's bad, isn't it? she'd asked, needing to know, and still he'd hesitated, and then, when she insisted on an answer, he had said, simply, *It's bad.*

And then Kayitah had come, flanked by twenty warriors, and demanded his son. He had threatened to kill both her and Ryder if she refused to surrender the child, and because they'd had no choice, Ryder had given her son to its father. She had begged Kayitah to take her back, but he had been a proud man, and he had refused.

You have chosen the path you will follow, he had said, his voice harsh and cold. *I give you the freedom you have begged for so often.*

"Just tell him the truth, Jenny girl," Ryder said. "That's all you can do."

It sounded so easy. Just tell him the truth. She only hoped she could make Cosito understand.

And forgive.

* * *

When they reached home, Ryder lifted Jenny from the rig. "I think you two should be alone," he remarked, giving her a hug. "I'll be in the barn if you need me."

Jenny nodded, her smile tremulous, as she waited for her son to dismount.

Chase the Wind swung out of the saddle, feeling as edgy as a rabbit about to enter a snake hole as he took a quick look around, noting the size of the house, the numerous corrals filled with blooded stock, the barn. A half-dozen dogs burst from under the porch, hackles raised, and barked at him.

"Quiet," Jenny scolded as the dogs surrounded them, nosing her hand, sniffing at Chase the Wind's moccasins.

Patting the nearest hound on the head, she smiled at Chase apologetically. "Come in, won't you?"

He followed her up the porch steps, across the wide veranda, and into the house. The parlor was a large, square room painted a pale shade of sky blue. Standing there, he perused the furnishings: a sofa made of brown leather, an overstuffed chair of the same material, a large oak rocking chair. A large hearth took up most of the wall across from the door. In addition to a vase of wildflowers and a clock, there were several gilt-edged picture frames on the mantle. One held a photograph of his mother and Ryder; the other two were of a young girl and boy.

A pair of tables made of dark oak stood on either side of the sofa. A buffalo robe was spread on the floor in front of the hearth; a Navajo rug hung on one wall, a painting of a desert at sunset hung on the opposite one.

Jenny watched her son's face as he took in his surroundings. How many times had she imagined him here, in this room? A hundred times, a thousand? She wondered where he had lived for the past twenty-five years, what he had done.

"Please," she said, "sit down and make yourself at . . ." Her voice trailed off and she felt a wave of color sweep into her cheeks. "Home."

She saw a muscle jump in his clenched jaw as he sat down on the sofa, his back rigid.

"Would you care for something to drink? A cup of coffee, or perhaps a glass of lemonade?"

"No." He ran his hand over the back of the sofa, noting the soft, supple feel of the leather beneath his hand.

Hiding her hands in her skirt pockets so he couldn't see them trembling, Jenny sat down on the opposite end of the sofa. "How have you been?"

"I am well."

Jenny fidgeted under his intense scrutiny. "I'm sorry about your father, truly I am. He was always kind to me."

"And you repaid his kindness by running away."

"Cosito, you must try to understand . . ."

"I am called Chase the Wind," he reminded her, his voice cool.

Jenny nodded. "Of course. I'm sorry."

She bit down on her lower lip as she searched for the words that would erase the scorn from his eyes, that would make him understand how it had been.

"I was very young when your father captured me. I already had a husband. Surely you can understand why I wanted to return to my own people?"

"He loved you." Chase stared at his mother. Though she was no longer young, she wore her age well. There were only a few faint lines at her mouth and eyes, and while her figure was no longer youthfully slim, it was softly rounded.

"I know, but I didn't love him. And even though he was kind to me, I was still his prisoner."

Something that might have been compassion flickered briefly in Chase the Wind's eyes, and then was gone.

"You can understand why I wanted my freedom, can't you?"

"Yes," Chase said quietly, remembering all too clearly what it had been like to be imprisoned on the reservation, his freedom and his way of life forever lost to him. "I understand."

"It wasn't easy for me when I returned to my husband," Jenny said. "He couldn't forget that I had been with another man, even though it was against my will. We quarreled, and he . . ." She lifted a hand to her cheek, remembering. "He hit me."

"Why have you not left him then?"

"Not Ryder," Jenny said quickly. "Ryder helped me escape from the rancheria and took me back to Hank, my first husband. It's all so complicated. I was in love with Ryder by then, but I was married to Hank. I tried to make Hank happy, but too much had happened while we were apart."

She shook her head, remembering the silent accusation in Hank's eyes whenever he looked at her, the endless arguments. He'd started drinking, and then one night he'd hit her.

"When I realized I couldn't live with Hank, I ran

away and went back to your father. I intended to stay with him, to be with you, but Hank and his brother, Charlie, came after me. I didn't want to go with them, I told Hank I wouldn't leave without you. But he wouldn't listen. They forced me to go with them. We almost made it out of the valley, but then Kayitah rode up with some of his men. Hank's brother was killed. Hank was shot. At the time, I thought he was dead, too. And then, somehow, Ryder was there, and I knew there was no way I could ever go back, no way I could ever convince Kayitah that I hadn't come back to steal you away. Ryder brought me here, to this valley. Once, he went back to try and get you, but it wasn't to be."

As she related the story to her son, she saw it all again: Ryder coming toward her with Cosito cradled in his arms; how much her son had grown; her sadness when she realized he hardly remembered her. And then, like the echo of distant thunder, they had heard the sound of horses approaching.

She had heard Ryder mutter Kayitah's name, and then he had told Will Howard to take Jenny and get the hell out of there while he tried to hold them off.

She hadn't wanted to leave Ryder, but Will had grabbed the reins to her horse and ran for cover. Heart pounding with trepidation, she had watched Ryder draw his rifle, and then, with the Cheyenne war cry on his lips, he had lit out in a dead run, leading the Apaches away from her.

He had made a valiant effort, might even have gotten away if Kayitah hadn't shot his horse out from under him. And then Ryder, too, had been shot. Kayitah's face had been dark with anger when he demanded to know the whereabouts of his son.

When Ryder refused to tell him, Kayitah staked Ryder out and began to skin him alive, one inch at a time.

It had been more than she could bear. Tears streaming down her face, she had ridden forward and begged for Ryder's life, promising to give up her son forever if Kayitah would spare Ryder.

"I knew it was the right thing to do," Jenny said, blinking back her tears. "You cried for your father when you saw him, and I knew then that you belonged with Kayitah. But there's never been a day that I didn't think of you. You must believe that."

Chase nodded. She was speaking the truth. He had heard it in every anguished word, seen it in the clear green depths of her eyes.

"One more thing," Jenny said. "You have a brother and a sister."

Chase stared at her. Moments before, he had been alone in the world, and now he had a brother and a sister. And a mother, if he could bring himself to accept her as such. It was more than he could handle.

Rising quickly, he headed for the door. He needed time; time to consider what she had said, time to absorb the fact that he was no longer alone.

Jenny hurried after him. "Chase, where are you going?"

He paused, his hand on the door. "I need time to think."

"Won't you stay for dinner?"

"No."

"I'll see you again, won't I? You won't leave town without saying good-bye?"

He turned to face her, noting for the first time,

that she barely came to his shoulder, that there were a few fine gray hairs sprinkled among the gold. She was a remarkably pretty woman, and it occurred to him that she must have been quite beautiful when she was young. No wonder so many men had desired her.

"Chase?"

"I will see you again before I leave," he promised.

"Chase, would you mind if I . . . could I give you a hug?"

It was in his mind to refuse. He owed this woman nothing. No matter what her reasons, she had abandoned him. And yet, looking into her eyes, eyes as green as new grass, he knew he could not deliberately cause her pain.

Jaw clenched, he opened his heart and put his arms around her. She felt light in his arms, fragile. He could feel her heart pounding like that of a wild bird caught in a trap. Or was it his own heart beating so frantically? He drew in a sharp breath as he felt her arms go around his waist. She gave him a squeeze and then quickly let him go, as if she were afraid of offending him.

Jenny smiled self-consciously as she backed away. "We still have a lot to talk about. Will you come back tomorrow evening and stay for supper? Dusty's coming. I know he'd like to meet you."

With a nod, Chase opened the door and stepped out onto the porch. He didn't look back, but he knew he would never forget the love he had seen shining in his mother's eyes as they embraced.

Swallowing the lump in his throat, he swung into the saddle and rode out of the yard.

* * *

Muttering under her breath, Beth found a shady place alongside the stream and sat down, arranging her skirts around her.

After a moment, she removed her shoes; then, with a defiant toss of her head, she took off her stockings and let her feet dangle in the water. And then, feeling wonderfully wicked, she removed the pins from her hair and shook her head. Someday, she thought, someday she'd be able do to what she wanted, go where she wanted. Someday.

Leaning forward, she propped her elbows on her knees and stared into the water. She looked like a wanton, she mused, barefooted, with her hair tumbling down around her shoulders. If her mother could see her now, she'd likely swoon.

With a sigh, Beth dragged her hand through the water, blurring the image. She was so tired of living at home, tired of her mother's nagging, her father's matchmaking. Tired of having to act like a lady when she wanted to ride astride like a man, when she wanted to learn to hunt and fish, to spend the night under the stars.

Sometimes she hated having to wear corsets and bloomers and layers of petticoats. Sometimes she wanted to shed all the trappings of civilization and swim naked in the river. She wanted to go barefooted in the summer, to climb trees and dance in the rain, to say what she really meant instead of what was expected.

Not that she wasn't happy being a woman. She loved parties and pretty clothes and dressing up, it was just that women—were always expected to act like *ladies*.

"Oh, bother," she muttered. What was the use of

wishing for things that could never be? Why think of flouting convention when she didn't have the nerve? Letting Dusty court her took all the courage she possessed, even though she knew her parents would never let them marry.

She frowned at her reflection, then stuck out her tongue. "Coward," she muttered. "You know you'll marry Ernest Tucker, just like your father wants, and spend the rest of your life regretting it."

Beth closed her eyes, wishing she could swear. She was searching her mind for a mild epithet that might relieve her frustration when she heard a noise behind her.

Her eyes flew open. She saw him then, or rather his reflection, in the water beside her. A tall man with long black hair and dark copper skin. His face was all sharp planes and angles, totally masculine. Totally beautiful. Dark brows arched above black eyes that were slightly slanted at the corners. His shoulders were broad beneath a faded blue cotton shirt. His legs were long, his feet encased in a pair of moccasins.

An Indian. Her heart seemed to stop, then began to pound heavily in her breast. There was nothing to fear, she told herself. There weren't any wild Indians roaming the countryside anymore.

Taking a deep, calming breath, she glanced over her shoulder and found herself staring into a pair of the most beautiful black eyes she had ever seen. Familiar eyes.

"Oh, my," she murmured, recognizing the man she had seen briefly in town. "Oh, my."

Chase frowned, confused by her odd greeting.

Hardly aware that she was moving, Beth stood up. And smiled. "Hello."

Chase nodded, his gaze moving over the girl. It was she, the girl he had seen in town. But how different she looked now! Before, he had noticed nothing but her eyes. Her hair, the color of wild honey, had been hidden beneath a floppy-brimmed hat. Now it tumbled over her shoulders and down her back in wild disarray. She wore a yellow dress that clung to her breasts, then flared out at the waist. An incredibly tiny waist, he noted. Her skin was a pale golden brown; a handful of freckles were scattered across her cheeks. Bare feet peeked out from the hem of her skirt.

Feeling as though someone had just punched him in the stomach, Chase took a deep breath, and his nostrils filled with the scent of flowers and earth and an intoxicating fragrance that he realized came from the woman herself.

He was staring at her as if he'd never seen a woman before, and she was staring back. The air seemed to vibrate between them. Earth, trees, and sky all seemed to fade away, and he was aware of nothing but the young woman standing before him. He could see the pulse throbbing in the hollow of her throat, hear the uneven rasp of her breathing. Was she real, or merely a vision sent to tempt him?

For a moment, he thought of taking her in his arms, putting her on his horse, and carrying her far away from this place. He had the strangest feeling that she would go with him without question or complaint.

"It's you," she murmured inanely, and again felt that warm surge of energy, of awareness, that had speared her when she met his eyes in front of the general store in town. Never before had she felt such a rush of recognition, as if she had been waiting for this one man all her life.

Incapable of speech, Chase nodded.

"My name is Elizabeth," she said, hardly recognizing her own voice. "Elizabeth Johnson, but folks generally call me Beth."

"I am called Chase the Wind."

Chase the Wind. It conjured up romantic images of a dusky-skinned man riding across the plains, of Indians chasing a herd of buffalo, of campfires and moonlit nights. "Are you staying in town?"

"Yes."

"Will you be staying long?"

Chase nodded, though until this moment, he had intended to stay only long enough to meet his mother and find out why she had abandoned him.

"What are you doing out here?" he asked.

"Nothing, really. I just like to be alone sometimes."

Chase nodded. He, too, had often found comfort in solitude.

Beth lifted one foot and wiggled her toes. "My mother doesn't approve of ladies going barefooted"—she ran a hand through her hair—"or of letting their hair down, so I come out here where she can't see me."

"Or speaking to Indians," Chase mused, remembering how the woman in town had hurried her daughter down the street before they could speak.

"My mother has a lot of old-fashioned ideas," Beth said with a shrug. But she wasn't thinking about her mother, could think of nothing but the man standing before her.

She took a step forward. She wanted to reach out and touch him, to slide her fingers down his arm, to feel the warmth of his skin beneath her hand, to brush her fingertips over his broad chest, to measure the width of his shoulders with her hands. To keep from touching him, she clasped her hands together. Licking lips gone suddenly dry, she wished she could run her tongue over *his* lips, feel his mouth on hers.

The thought shocked her even as a wave of desire swept through her. Disconcerted, she took a step backward.

"I . . . I should go," she said, and turning on her heel, she ran toward town, her shoes and stockings forgotten in her haste to get away.

Chase stared after her, confused by her sudden departure.

"Beth." He picked up one of her stockings and wound it around his hand, marveling at its softness, imagining it next to her skin.

"Beth." He whispered her name again, liking the sound of it, the taste of it, wondering if he would ever see her again.

Chapter Six

Feeling somewhat dazed by his encounter with the young white woman, Chase caught up his horse and headed back to town. He looked for her on the way, but there was no sign of her, and he decided she must have taken a path through the woods to her home, wherever that might be.

He had seen her, spoken to her, for only a few minutes, yet her voice and her image would linger forever in his mind. He had vowed to hate the whites for as long as he lived, but one look into Beth's eyes—into her beautiful brown eyes—had shattered that vow.

He was aware of people staring at him as he rode into Twin Rivers. He reined his horse to a halt in front of the Red Horse Saloon. Dismounting, he tethered the buckskin to the hitch rack and entered the saloon.

The bartender grunted softly as he offered Chase a beer. "Didn't expect to see you in here again."

"I did not expect to be back," Chase replied. He took a sip of his drink, then made his way to the same table he had occupied before.

He sat there, gazing out the window, while day faded into night. His thoughts turned inward. So much to think about. His mother hadn't left him because she'd wanted to. He had a brother. And a sister. Amazing as these things were, it was Beth who overshadowed every other thought. Beth . . . She had captured his heart and soul with one look.

Chase sat there far into the night, oblivious to the noise and the laughter around him. Once, a woman wearing a bright red dress and black lace stockings sauntered up to him and sat on his lap, her arms winding around his neck.

"Buy me a drink, cowboy?" she purred.

"I am not a cowboy," Chase replied.

She leaned back a little and took a good look at his face. "Well, I'll be," she muttered. "You're an Injun! Well, no matter. Cowboy or Injun, the price is the same."

"Price of what?"

"For what, honey?" she asked, laughing. "Why, for me."

"You are for sale?"

"More like for rent."

He understood then. She was a *bija-n-ata,* a whore. Shaking his head, Chase lifted the girl from his lap. "I have no money."

"Oh, well, perhaps another time," the girl said and walked away, her hips swaying.

It was near midnight when Chase left the saloon. Taking up the reins of his horse, he walked down the dark street toward the edge of town, heading for the stream where he had last seen Beth.

He would sleep there, under the stars, and perhaps, if he was lucky, he would dream of her.

Chase came awake with a start. Jerking to a sitting position, he heard the sound of dogs barking, followed by the sound of gunshots and running feet.

Rising, he drew his knife, then stood in the shadows, waiting, listening. He whirled around as two men came crashing through the underbrush.

The man in front was leading a big chestnut stallion. He came to an abrupt halt when he saw Chase. "What the hell!" he exclaimed.

Chase took a step backward, his hand tightening on the hilt of the knife as the second man leveled a rifle at him.

"He's an Injun," the man leading the stallion remarked.

"No shit."

The horse handler looked over his shoulder. "They're comin'! I hear 'em. Dammit, Rance, I hear 'em! I knew this was a dumb idea."

The man called Rance smiled. "Stop worrying, Joby," he said, grinning. "I've got an idea."

"Yeah? Well, I hope it's a damn sight better than the last one."

"Trust me," Rance said. And in the blink of an eye, he lifted his rifle to his shoulder and sighted down the barrel.

With a cry, Chase hurled his knife at the man called Rance. He felt a brief moment of satisfaction as the blade sank into the man's chest.

There was a roar of gunfire, a flash of gunpowder. Chase saw the stallion rear up, jerking the lead rope from the white man's hand, and then everything went black.

Dusty opened the jailhouse door, frowning when he saw Joby Berland standing on the boardwalk. He'd never trusted Berland. There was something about the man that set Dusty's teeth on edge, and the fact that Joby never looked him in the eye was only part of it.

He saw that Kurt Harvey and his brother, Sean, dressed alike in overalls and plaid shirts, stood behind Joby.

"What brings you all out here at this time of night?" Dusty asked.

"We caught him, Sheriff," Joby said jubilantly. "Me and Rance, we caught the Injun what stole the Harveys' stud." He jerked a thumb at the horse hitched to the rail. "Bastard shot Ned. He's bad hurt. He shot Rance, too, but we caught him."

"Where's Rance?"

"He's home. Martha's lookin' after him."

"And Ned?"

"We dropped him off at Doc's on our way here."

Dusty glanced at the body draped over the back of a big buckskin mare. "Is the Indian dead?"

"No, just bleedin' bad."

"Kurt, Sean, carry him on in here, then you can tell me what happened. Joby, you go tell Doc I need him here as soon as he can make it. Then take the Indian's horse down to the livery."

Dusty went back inside. Climbing the stairs to the second floor where the cells were located, he spared a glance at the prisoner in the first cell. Greg Paxton, arrested for being drunk in public, was snoring loudly.

Moving down the narrow aisle, Dusty opened the door to the last cell and drew back the blankets on the cot. He'd been the sheriff for a couple of weeks, and up until now, except for arresting an occasional drunk on Saturday nights, things had been quiet.

Kurt and Sean dumped the unconscious man on the cot.

"So, what happened?" Dusty asked.

"We heard the dogs barkin' about midnight," Sean Harvey said. "When we went out to check, we saw a man running across the pasture with our stud horse."

"Running?" Dusty asked. "Why didn't he ride?"

"Horse ain't broke."

"Just one man?"

Kurt Harvey nodded. "When he heard us coming, he turned and took a shot at us. He hit our foreman. Doc doesn't think Ned's gonna make it."

Sean nodded, as if to back up his brother's story. "Ned Greenway's a decent man. He's got a wife and three kids that depend on him. We chased the Injun into the holler near the stream. Joby was there with Rance. Rance was bleedin' pretty bad. Joby said the Injun shot Rance, and Rance shot the Injun. The Injun was out cold."

Dusty grunted softly. "What were Rance and Joby doing in Piney Hollow?"

"Said they'd been out huntin' coons and were on their way home when this Injun attacked 'em. Joby said Rance shot the Injun in self-defense."

"Okay. I'll need the two of you to come back in the morning and make a statement."

"Right, Sheriff," Kurt said. "Can we go now?"

"Yeah. I'm sorry about Ned. Tell Emma to let me know if there's anything I can do."

Sean nodded soberly. "I'll do that, Sheriff. Good night.

"Good night." Dusty shook hands with both men, then turned to study the Indian. His shirt front was soaked with blood. His moccasins were cut in the Apache style.

Curious, Dusty mused. Besides Carson's wife and daughters, he hadn't seen an Apache in these parts in years.

The sound of footsteps drew his attention. A short time later, Doc Forbes entered the cell, followed by Joby Berland.

"Is the redskin gonna live, Doc?" Joby asked.

"I don't care for that word," Dusty said.

Joby looked down at the floor. "Sorry, Sheriff," he mumbled.

"How about it, Doc?" Dusty asked. "Will he live?"

"Can't say till I have a look at him," Forbes replied. Opening the Indian's shirt, he examined the wound. "I'll need some water, Sheriff."

"I'll get it. Joby, I won't be needing you anymore tonight," Dusty said, heading for the stairs, "but I'll need you to come by in the morning and make a statement. Bring Rance with you if he's fit to travel."

"Yes, sir, Sheriff," Berland said, following Dusty down the stairs into the office.

"One more thing," Dusty said, frowning. "Where's the Indian's rifle?"

Joby looked blank for a moment, then grinned. "Still in the holler, I guess. See you tomorrow."

"It's already tomorrow," Dusty muttered.

After taking a bucket of hot water up to the doctor, Dusty went back downstairs and dropped into the chair behind his desk.

Smothering a yawn, Dusty wondered if he could persuade the town fathers to let him hire a deputy so they could trade off staying the night when there was a prisoner in the jail.

He was on the verge of sleep when he heard the doc's footsteps coming down the stairs.

Sitting up in his chair, Dusty leaned forward and braced his elbows on the desk. Doc Forbes was a man who commanded respect despite his short stature. He had graying red hair and dark brown eyes that met the world head on. "Is he gonna make it?"

Forbes nodded. "Shouldn't be any problem. The bullet went in low on his left side. Didn't hit anything vital, but he's lost a lot of blood. Still, he's young and healthy, so I'm not anticipating any trouble unless that wound gets infected. You might want to see that he gets plenty of red meat the next few days."

"Did he regain consciousness yet?"

"Briefly. You might want to check on him a couple times, make sure he drinks plenty of water when he wakes up. I'll stop by and look in on him tomorrow."

"Right. What about Ned Greenway?"

Forbes shook his head. "He's hurt real bad. I told Emma there was a chance he'd make it, and there might be. But I wouldn't stake my reputation on it."

"Thanks for coming by, Doc."

Forbes nodded. "Should have been a dentist," he muttered as he left the office. "Never hear of dentists having emergencies in the middle of the night."

Grinning, Dusty closed and locked the door. It was going to be a long, sleepless night. And sometime tomorrow he'd have to find time to ride out to Piney Hollow and see if he could find the missing rifle.

"A horse thief," Beth exclaimed, her eyes growing wide. "Why, we haven't had a horse thief in Twin Rivers since I was a little girl."

"Well, they caught this one dead to rights."

"What'll happen to him?"

Dusty shrugged. "I don't know. That's up to a judge and jury."

"Is it anyone I know?"

"Not unless you've been seeing an Indian on the sly."

Beth's heart caught in her throat. "An Indian?"

Dusty nodded. "Apache, by the cut of his moccasins. I don't know what he's doing here. Last I heard, all the Apaches had been rounded up and sent to Florida."

"What's his name?"

"I don't know. He's hasn't been conscious long enough to tell me."

It was suddenly hard to speak. "He . . . he's hurt?"

"He got shot, but . . . Beth? Beth, are you all right? You look right pale."

"I'm fine." Beth stared out the window. Her parents were sitting on the porch swing. Her father was reading the newspaper, her mother was shelling peas for dinner. She could hear a bird singing in the tree that grew alongside the porch, smell the pot roast cooking in the kitchen. But none of it seemed real.

"Beth? Beth, are you all right?"

She shook her head. "I don't feel very well, Dusty," she said. "I think I'll go upstairs and lie down for a little while."

"Yeah, you do that." He stood up, frowning. "I'll call on you tomorrow and see how you're feeling."

"All right."

"Well, okay, I guess I'll go on over to the hotel and get some dinner."

Bending, he kissed her cheek, but she hardly seemed aware of it. Puzzled by Beth's strange behavior, Dusty grabbed his hat off the rack and left the house.

Beth stared out the window, worrying her lower lip with her teeth as she watched Dusty take up the reins to his horse. Was Chase the Wind the Indian in the jail? How could she find out? She had gone back to the river to look for her shoes yesterday. At least that was the excuse she had given herself. In truth, she had hoped to see Chase the Wind again. She had found her shoes and one stocking on top of a flat-topped rock, but there had been no sign of Chase the Wind. And no sign of her other stocking.

Rising, she paced the floor. Dusty would be over at the hotel having dinner for at least half an hour. Did he leave the jail unlocked when he was away?

Grabbing her bonnet, she quickly put it on, then went out the back door. Picking up her skirts, she began to run through the woods toward town, praying that no one would see her.

When she reached the end of town, she stopped to catch her breath; then, head high, she made her way to the rear of the jail. Murmuring a silent prayer, she put her hand on the latch, felt a wave of relief as the door swung open.

She stood there a moment, listening, before she closed the door and hurried toward the steps.

Too late, she wondered what she'd do if the Indian wasn't the only prisoner. At the top of the stairs, she peered around the corner, relieved that all the cells were empty save one.

Heart slamming against her ribs, she tiptoed toward the last cell, murmured, "Oh, no" when she saw Chase the Wind lying on the cot, his eyes closed, his breathing labored. A thick bandage was wrapped around his torso. The cloth was very white against the dark bronze of his skin, but it was the ugly reddish-brown stain on the cloth that held her gaze.

Chase stirred, his nostrils filling with a familiar fragrance. Beth? Turning his head toward the cell door, he blinked, and blinked again. Dressed in a gown of lavender plaid trimmed with yards of white lace, she looked like a porcelain doll he had once seen in a store window. He shook his head, certain he must be dreaming.

"Chase?" Beth wrapped her hands around the bars. "Chase, are you all right?"

"Beth," he said, gasping with the effort it took to speak. "What are you doing here?"

"What happened to you?"

With an effort, he sat up, his arm wrapped protectively over the wound in his side. For a moment, the room spun wildly out of control. When the dizziness passed, he stood up. His legs felt like wet reeds as he crossed the few feet separating them.

"Beth." Hesitantly, he placed his hand over hers. "You should not be here."

"What happened?"

"I have been accused of stealing a horse and shooting a white man."

"No!"

He nodded, and then, succinctly, he told her all that had happened the night before.

"Joby Berland!" Beth exclaimed in disgust. "Everybody in town knows he's no good. And Rance Crenshaw is just as bad. Surely Dusty doesn't believe their story."

"I am afraid he does, and so will everyone else."

"No!"

Chase smiled down at her, the hard shell he had erected around his heart melting a little beneath the warmth of her touch, the trust in her eyes. "How do you know I did not do it?"

Beth stared up at him. The thought that he might be guilty had never occurred to her. "You didn't, did you?"

"No."

"I'd better go," Beth said. "Can I bring you anything?"

Chase shook his head.

"I'll come see you again if I can," she said, and rising on tiptoe, she pressed her lips to his, then turned and hurried toward the stairs.

Chase stared after her, the pain in his side forgotten in the wonder of seeing her again. Reaching into the pocket of his trousers, he rubbed his hand over the silk stocking he had taken that day by the river. It was smooth and soft, like her skin.

Withdrawing the stocking from his pocket, he pressed it to his face and took a deep breath. The fragrance that was Beth filled his nostrils.

Wadding the stocking up, he put it back in his pocket, then slowly sank down on the cot, afraid that what he felt for Beth Johnson was far more dangerous than being accused of being a horse thief.

Chapter Seven

Jenny frowned as she glanced at the grandfather clock ticking quietly in the corner.

"He isn't coming," she said despondently. "We might as well eat."

"Maybe something came up," Ryder suggested, hoping to comfort her. She'd been moping around the house for over an hour. Time and again, she'd gone to the window, only to sigh and turn away. "Or maybe he's just on Apache time," Ryder said with a wry grin. The Indians didn't have clocks, didn't do things by set times. They ate when they were hungry, slept when they were tired, hunted when they needed meat. It had been a good way to live.

Jenny shook her head. "He hates me."

"I doubt it."

She whirled around to face him, her hands fisted on her hips. "Then where is he?"

"I don't know, honey."

Jenny blew out a long breath. First they'd gotten a message from Dusty saying he had a prisoner and couldn't leave the jail, and now Chase the Wind had apparently changed his mind about coming to supper. She'd hoped that somehow she could make amends, that if Chase the Wind wouldn't accept her as his mother, they might at least become friends.

Going into the kitchen, she opened the oven and pulled out a pan of biscuits, her frustration making itself known in the way she slammed the oven door.

Ryder grinned as he stood in the doorway watching her. "Hey? Is it safe for me to come in there?"

"Somebody has to eat all this food before it burns," she muttered, stirring the gravy that was simmering in the pan on the stove. "It might as well be you."

"Thanks."

Jenny looked up at his wry tone. "I didn't mean it like that."

"I know." Taking the wooden spoon from her hand, Ryder drew Jenny into his arms and gave her a hug. "Chicken smells good," he said, nuzzling her ear. "Come on, let's eat."

Jenny rested her cheek against Ryder's chest. "It's not just that Chase the Wind didn't show up. I thought it would be a good time for Dusty and Chase to meet and get acquainted. I was hoping they might get to be friends. I was hoping . . ." She sniffed back a tear. "Chase seemed so lonely, I was hoping that he'd, that we could . . ."

Jenny buried her face in the hollow of his shoulder. Old hurts couldn't be mended in a day. Maybe, like a plate once broken, trust could never be whole again.

"I wanted so much for him to like me. To forgive me."

"I know, honey, I know." Placing a finger beneath her chin, Ryder tipped her face up and kissed her. "But let's not judge him too harshly until we hear his side, okay? I'll ride into town tomorrow morning and see what I can find out."

Ryder left the ranch early the following morning, determined to find Chase the Wind, sit him down, and find out what the hell was going on. No matter how Chase felt about his mother, he had no cause to upset her. Jenny had done what she felt was right for all concerned, and she paid for it every day of her life. If Chase couldn't understand that, then Ryder, by damn, intended to make him understand.

It wasn't until he reached town that he realized he had no idea where to find Chase. Thinking perhaps Dusty would know, he reined up outside the jail, nodding at May Ellen Coombs, who was sweeping the boardwalk in front of her father's store.

Dismounting, he settled his hat on his head and opened the jailhouse door.

Dusty was sitting behind the desk, thumbing through a stack of wanted posters.

"So," Ryder said, stepping into the sheriff's office, "how's it going?"

"Fine," Dusty replied. He gestured at the seat in front of his desk. "What brings you into town so early in the morning?"

Ryder leaned back in his chair, collecting his thoughts. "It can wait. I've got a couple of things to tell you, and I want you to hear me out before you say anything."

"Is something wrong at home?"

"No," Ryder said, and taking a deep breath, he told Dusty about Chase the Wind.

"Why didn't anybody ever tell me this before?" Dusty asked. Rising, he began to pace the floor. "All these years, I've had a brother and didn't know it. Dammit, Mother should have told me." He came to an abrupt halt, his eyes narrowed as he faced his father. "Why now?" he asked. "Why tell me now?"

"He's here, in Twin Rivers," Ryder said. "He was supposed to come to dinner last night, but he never showed up. I told your mother I'd come in and ask around, see if I could find out if he's still here."

"You didn't tell me his name."

"He calls himself Chase the Wind."

Dusty sat down hard. "Chase the Wind? Are you sure?"

"I'm sure."

"He's here," Dusty said, feeling as though someone had just pole-axed him. "Upstairs."

Ryder swore under his breath. "He's in jail?"

Dusty nodded. "The Harvey brothers have accused him of stealing that big chestnut stud of theirs and shooting Ned Greenway."

"Did he do it?"

"He's got no alibi."

"Are there any witnesses?"

"Just Berland and Crenshaw."

"Berland and Crenshaw!" Ryder swore again. "I wouldn't take their word that it was raining if I was standing knee deep in mud and soaking wet."

"Well, they claim to have caught him dead to rights. And the Harveys claim he's the one who shot Greenway."

Ryder dragged a hand across his jaw, wondering how the hell he could go home with a story like this. "When's the trial?"

"It's set for a week from Friday. Judge Brooks should be back from Santa Fe by then."

"You know I can't let him hang."

"I know."

"If he's convicted . . ." Ryder didn't finish the thought. There was no need.

"Does he know about me?"

"Your mother told him."

"Damn! What do I do now?" Dusty ran a hand through his hair. "I like being the sheriff. I like knowing I'm doing something worthwhile in this town, something that makes a difference."

Ryder sat back in his chair, his chin resting on his folded hands. This was a decision Dusty would have to make for himself. Like most important decisions, it wouldn't come easy.

Dusty slammed his fist on the desk. "Dammit, I don't even know the man, but I'm with you. I can't let him hang."

Ryder grunted softly. "For now, let's just sit tight and see how the hand plays out. If he's tried and found guilty . . . well, we'll worry about that when it happens. Okay if I go up and see him?"

Dusty nodded.

"You want me to tell him who you are?"

"Yeah. It might make it easier on both of us."

Rising, Ryder clapped his son on the shoulder, then headed for the stairs. He'd been a law-abiding citizen for the last twenty-five years. He hoped that wasn't about to change.

* * *

Chase came awake at the sound of footsteps on the stairs. Thinking it was the doctor, come to check his wound, he kept his eyes closed. It hurt to move, to breathe.

"Chase?"

At the sound of Fallon's voice, he opened his eyes, then slowly sat up, his back resting against the wall.

Ryder glanced around the small iron-barred cell. He'd always hated small places, hated feeling closed in. Leaning one shoulder against the bars, he met Chase the Wind's shuttered gaze. "How are you, son?"

"I am not your son."

"True enough, but I'd still like to know how you are."

"Why do you care?"

"Because I love your mother," Ryder said quietly. "And she cares."

"Then why isn't she here?"

Ryder blew out an exasperated breath. "Listen, Chase, save the insolence for somebody else. I don't need it."

Chase met his gaze, his face impassive.

"I didn't know until a few minutes ago that you were here." Ryder's gaze swept the cell again. It wasn't much bigger than an outhouse, and it smelled little better. All the cleaning in the world couldn't wash away the jailhouse stench. "Damn," he muttered, "I hate jails."

Chase raised a skeptical brow.

"I've been where you are now," Ryder said quietly. "I know what you're thinking, and I know how you're feeling. I'm only gonna ask you this once. Did you steal the Harveys' stud horse?"

"No."

"Did you shoot Greenway?"

"No."

"I believe you."

"The jury will not."

Ryder grinned ruefully. "Probably not, but you're gonna have to trust me when I tell you that you won't hang. No matter what verdict they decide on, you won't hang. I promise you that."

Chase stared at the man who had married his mother. "What do you want from me?"

"I don't want anything except your trust." Ryder shook his head, frustrated by the younger man's stoic expression. And yet he understood it all too well. How many times had he covered fear with bravado, anger with arrogance?

"Listen, Chase, I love your mother. I'd do anything for her. Anything. Including breaking her son out of jail if it becomes necessary. Now, you can believe me or not, that's up to you. But one thing you have to know, Jenny loves you. It broke her heart to leave you behind. I know. I was there. You've been in her thoughts every day since then."

"I believe you," Chase replied quietly. "But the hurt remains."

"I reckon so. I've got one other thing to tell you before I go." Ryder took a deep breath. "Your mother told you that you had a brother."

Chase nodded.

"Well, he's the sheriff."

Chase stared at Fallon. "The man who locked me up is my brother?"

"He didn't know who you were until today." Ryder pushed away from the bars and resettled his hat on his head. "He'll be up to see you in a few minutes. Do you need anything?"

"Only my freedom."

"I'll work on it. In the meantime, I'll see that you get a change of clothes. And I reckon your mother will be coming by to see you first thing tomorrow."

Chase nodded, uncomfortable with the tide of emotions swirling through him.

"Well, so long," Ryder said. Turning away from the cell, he started toward the stairs.

"Fallon."

Ryder paused and glanced over his shoulder.

"I . . . thank you."

"You're welcome."

Feeling shaky, Chase closed his eyes. He heard the faint murmur of voices from below, the sound of a door opening and closing, and then the sound of footsteps on the stairs.

He took a deep breath, surprised at how nervous he was at the idea of meeting his brother face-to-face. And then Dusty was there, staring at him through the bars, and Chase's nervousness was swallowed up by a wave of humiliation.

Dusty shifted from one foot to the other, wondering why it was so hard to think of something to say. Chase the Wind was his brother, for crying out loud. They had years to catch up on.

"So, I guess Dad told you we're related."

"He is not my father."

"Sorry. Listen, I just thought the two of us ought to meet." Dusty gestured at the bars between them. "I wish it could be under different circumstances."

A faint smile tugged at Chase's lips. "It would have been my wish, too."

"How are you feeling?"

"I am all right."

"This is really awkward," Dusty remarked. "You know, if it was up to me, I'd turn you loose."

"Would you?"

"I'm a pretty good judge of character, Chase. You said you were innocent, and I believe you."

"Your father has also said he believes me."

"Nothing gets by my old man," Dusty said proudly. "He's the best. I'd like to ask you one question, though. What happened to your rifle?"

"What rifle?"

"The witnesses all claim you had a rifle. Berland says you shot Rance with it. The Harveys say you shot their foreman."

"I had no rifle. Only a knife. I threw it at the man who shot me."

Dusty crossed his arms over his chest. Someone was lying, and he didn't think it was Chase.

It would bear some thinking about later, but now he wanted to get to know his brother. "If you feel like talking about it, I'd like to know a little about your past . . . you know, what it was like growing up with the Apache."

Right hand pressed over the wound in his side, Chase moved to the end of the cot so there was not quite so much distance between them. "And then I would like to know about you."

"Fair enough," Dusty said. Pulling a battered wooden chair close to the cell, he sat down and made himself comfortable.

Beth fidgeted all through dinner, wishing her father would just shut up. All he could talk about was the Indian who had been arrested for stealing a horse. There would be a trial on Friday, her father said, and then he would be hanged for his crimes.

Beth stared at her father. He never mentioned the possibility that Chase might be innocent. To hear him tell it, the trial was merely for show, the guilty verdict a foregone conclusion.

"Enough talk about horse thieves," Theda Johnson said. She looked at Beth and smiled. "We're leaving for New York next month."

"Next month! Why?"

"Your father and I have decided that Ernest Tucker isn't the man for you."

Thank goodness, Beth thought, careful to keep her face impassive. Now that she'd met Chase the Wind, her determination not to marry Ernest was stronger than ever.

Theda Johnson folded her napkin and placed it on the table beside her plate. "I had a letter from an old acquaintance of mine. Lydia Cummings. Her brother was widowed a year ago, and now he's looking for a wife to help raise his three daughters."

Beth stared at her mother, a horrible feeling growing within her.

"Lester Harbaugh is a lawyer, and quite well-to-do. Your father and I think he would be a good match for you."

Beth bit back a groan of despair. She could just picture Lester Harbaugh—short and rotund, with oily hair and fat fingers. He'd call her "my dear" and kiss her on the cheek. He'd expect her to be obedient and ladylike, and to give him more children, preferably sons to carry on the family name.

"You might show a little enthusiasm," her father remarked.

"He sounds very . . . very nice," Beth replied. "How old are his children?"

"I believe the oldest is twelve, and the youngest is six."

Twelve! Beth stared at her parents. Did they seriously expect her to marry a man who had a child who was only five years younger than herself? "How old is Mr. Harbaugh?"

"In his early thirties, I believe."

Thirties! He was almost old enough to be her father!

"We'll begin shopping for our trip next week," her mother said, beaming. "Imagine, Elizabeth, a lawyer!"

"Yes," Beth said, swallowing the lump of disgust in her throat. "Imagine."

As soon as she could, she excused herself from the table and went to her room. Standing at the window, she stared into the darkness. How could her parents marry her off like this? She wasn't ready to have children of her own, let alone look after someone else's. She wasn't ready to settle down and be a matron.

Putting such depressing thoughts behind her, she gazed toward the far end of town, wondering if Chase the Wind was all right, if he was thinking of her.

She hardly knew him, yet he had been constantly in her thoughts from the moment she had first seen him outside the general store. And then she had seen him at the river, heard his voice, deep and rich. Ever since that day, she had dreamed of him, thought of him, fantasized about what it would be like to be held in his arms, to be kissed. Innocent that she was, her daydreams ended with love's first kiss and happily ever after.

They were going to hang him. Pressing her forehead against the windowpane, she closed her eyes. The memory of a hanging she had glimpsed when she'd been a little girl came unbidden. She remembered watching the man climb the thirteen steps to the gallows, remembered how pale he'd looked as the hangman placed the noose around his neck. She clearly remembered the audible gasp of the crowd as the hangman reached for the lever that would spring the trap, the awful, animallike cry of terror that had been torn from the man's throat just before the trap was sprung. She hadn't watched the hanging itself, nor had she ever been able to understand why anyone else would want to witness such a gruesome sight.

A low moan rose in her throat as she imagined Chase the Wind standing on just such a gallows, a thick rope pulled tight around his neck, his hands bound behind his back, his long black hair fluttering in the breeze . . .

"No." Opening her eyes, she shook her head. "No!"

Her hands were shaking as she undressed, pulled on her nightgown, and crawled into bed. He couldn't hang, not now, not when she'd just found him.

Chapter Eight

For Chase, the next three days passed in a haze of pain and confusion. His mother came to visit him every day. She brought him a change of clothes—a dark blue wool shirt and a pair of black trousers. She brought him underwear, which he frowned at and cast aside. And she brought him a pair of Apache-style moccasins. He had looked at her, a question in his eyes, and she had said, with a hesitant smile, "I made them for you. I hope they fit."

They did. Perfectly. The knowledge that she had taken the time and effort to make them for him caused something painful to dislodge in his heart.

Every day, she brought him a basket filled with food: fresh-baked bread, thick slices of cheese and beef, apples and carrots, a piece of cake or a dozen cookies. Never, in all his life, had he eaten so well, he mused ruefully.

Ryder Fallon also came each day. Sometimes he didn't say much, but Chase found a certain comfort in the older man's presence, though he couldn't say why.

And always, Dusty was there. Dusty. His brother. Remarkably, since the day of their talk, a bond had formed between them. Chase was at a loss to explain why. Perhaps it was his brother's unquestioning belief in his innocence; perhaps it was Dusty's generosity of spirit that manifested itself in numerous small ways. Perhaps it was merely a bond of blood founded on nothing more than their shared ancestry. Whatever it was, it made Chase's captivity easier to bear.

Thursday night, Jenny and Ryder came to see him, assuring him that everything would work out.

It was near ten when Ryder stood up. "Come on, Jenny girl," he said. "We'd better start for home."

Jenny stood up, her eyes bright with unshed tears. "Don't worry," she said, squeezing Chase's hand. "We'll get through this."

Chase nodded. "Sure."

And then Ryder reached through the bars and clasped his hand. "You won't hang, Chase. I promise."

And in that moment, Chase the Wind knew that Ryder Fallon was a warrior, a man to be reckoned with, and for the first time, he felt a slender ray of hope.

The trial was held at nine o'clock Friday morning in the courthouse. To Chase, it seemed as though every man and woman in the town was packed into the building, craning their necks to get a look at him.

He sat near the front of the room, his hands

cuffed behind his back, listening to the low murmurs that ran through the crowd. They had already tried and convicted him, he thought bleakly. As far as they were concerned, he was guilty, and a hanging was sure to follow. He heard their excitement, sensed their anticipation, as they looked forward to the hanging. Stores would close. People would come to town, watch the hanging, and have a picnic lunch afterward.

Sickened, he glanced once at his mother and Ryder, and then his gaze rested on Beth Johnson. She was seated between the grim-faced older woman he had seen her with in town and a man with dark gray hair. Her parents, he guessed. Dressed in a frothy pale pink dress, Beth looked like a flower in a field of weeds.

Her tremulous smile went right to his heart, lodging there like a tiny ray of golden sunshine. His gaze still on Beth's face, Chase paid little attention as four white men took the stand to accuse him of stealing a valuable horse and shooting Sean and Kurt Harvey's foreman. Chase watched Beth's expression change from mild worry to concern as the lawyers argued the case.

The biggest hole in the prosecution's case was the fact that the rifle Chase had allegedly used to shoot Rance had never been found, but, in the end, it didn't matter. The jury reached its decision in less than ten minutes—guilty as charged.

The judge declared the hanging would take place Monday morning at ten, the jury was dismissed, and the trial was over.

Numb, Chase stood up. He forced a half-smile for Beth, then turned and preceded Dusty from the courtroom. Angry whispers followed him from the building.

"Dirty redskin . . ."

"Who does he think he is? Shot Ned Greenway . . ."

"Doc doesn't think he'll recover . . ."

Hardly remembering how he got there, Chase found himself locked in his cell again. Minutes later, his mother and Ryder were there, along with Dusty.

Chase faced them through the bars. A short time ago, he'd been a man alone. Now he had a family who cared for him. There were tears in his mother's eyes, compassion in Dusty's, determination in Ryder's.

"Don't worry, Chase," Ryder said, "we'll get you out of this."

Jenny glanced at Dusty, and then at Ryder. "You're going to break him out of jail?"

"You got any better suggestions, Jenny girl?" Ryder asked, grinning.

"No, but . . ." She put her hand on Dusty's arm. "If anyone finds out . . ."

"We'll have to hightail it out of town," Dusty said.

"No." Chase shook his head. "I cannot let you do this."

"I don't see how you can stop us," Ryder said.

"Anyway, maybe no one will find out," Dusty remarked. "We can make it look like you escaped, and then, when we clear your name, you can come back home."

Home. It was a word that conjured up thoughts of love and security and permanence, something he hadn't had since Kayitah had surrendered to the white man.

"Sounds simple enough," Ryder said. He looked at Dusty and grinned. "You can bring Chase his dinner Sunday night and arrange for him to get hold of your gun, accidental-like. He'll take your gun, lock you up, take your horse, and leave town. He can hide out in Rainbow Canyon until we find out who really stole the Harveys' stud and shot Greenway, and then Chase can come forward and clear his name."

"It might work," Dusty said.

"It has to work," Jenny declared fervently. "It has to."

"If the people in town find out that Dusty is my brother, they will not believe that I escaped without help."

"They can think what they like, but they won't be able to prove a thing," Dusty said. "Hell, you can hit me over the head with my gun on the way out. A good-sized lump on the back of my head ought to be convincing enough."

"I cannot let you do it," Chase said again. "The risks are too great." He wrapped his hands around the bars. "Make them listen, my mother. You have much to lose."

"Are you suggesting that I stand by and let them hang you just to save a house and a few acres of land?" Jenny exclaimed.

"You do not even know me."

"You're my son, Chase. I knew you before you were born, and if I have to spend the rest of my life hiding out in the hills to keep you from hanging, then I'll do it gladly."

Chase sent a pleading look at Ryder. He didn't want to be beholden to these people, to this woman. He had hated her all his life. "You cannot let her do this."

Ryder reached through the bars and clapped Chase on the shoulder. "Son, I've never been able to tell your mother what to do, and I don't imagine she'll let me start now."

Chase paced the floor of his cell, the ache in his side forgotten as he tried to absorb the fact that his brother, who was supposed to uphold the white man's law, was planning to let him out of jail, with the full knowledge and approval of his parents. Even more incomprehensible was the knowledge that they were all willing to risk everything they had to help him escape.

All the bitterness and anger he had harbored melted away in the face of their love. He had done nothing to deserve their affection, yet they had welcomed him with open arms, accepting him as one of them simply because Jenny was his mother . . . his mother.

Chase felt his heart grow warm at the thought of her. Someday, when all this trouble was behind him, he wanted to hear about her life, starting from the day she had met his father, and every day since.

His musings came to an abrupt halt when he heard Beth's voice downstairs. What was she doing here? She had been much on his mind since the trial yesterday. Whether he hanged or Dusty helped him escape, he knew he would never see her again. The sound of her laughter filled him with a longing for something that could never be. Though he knew little of the ways of the white man, he was certain it was not customary for young women to visit men in jail. And then, hearing her soft laughter float up the stairs, he realized she had probably come to see Dusty.

Chase knew a sudden, fierce rush of jealousy as he pictured Beth talking to his brother, smiling at him.

Hands clenched around the bars, Chase tried to hear what they were saying, but try as he might, he couldn't make out their words.

"Hello, Sheriff."

Dusty came to his feet, smiling. But then, she always had that effect on him. His gaze swept over her, admiring the way her lavender shirtwaist and gathered skirt emphasized the fullness of her breasts, her narrow waist. She wore a perky little bonnet that tied under her chin.

"Hi, Beth. What are you doing here?"

"I just wanted to see you. My mother got one of her headaches and went home. Father thinks I'm over at the millinery shop."

"Here," he said, holding a chair for her. "Sit down."

"Thank you." Beth folded her hands in her lap. "The trial was interesting. I've never been to one before."

"Short," Dusty remarked, "but interesting."

"You don't think he's guilty, do you?"

"I'm sure he isn't."

"You're not going to let them hang an innocent man, are you?"

"He was tried and found guilty," Dusty replied.

"I'll have to carry out the sentence of the court."

"But . . ." Beth bit down on her lower lip. It wouldn't do to protest too much. She couldn't afford to make Dusty suspicious. "Are you coming to dinner Sunday night?"

"'Fraid not. I'll have to stay here and keep an eye on the prisoner."

"Oh." Beth stared at her folded hands. "Maybe I could bring you something to eat."

"That would be real nice," Dusty said, "although I doubt if your mother will allow it."

"I'll manage somehow." Beth stood up and offered Dusty her hand. "Till Sunday, then."

Taking her hand, Dusty drew Beth into his arms and kissed her lightly, gently. "Did I tell you how pretty you look today?"

"No."

"Well, you do. Pretty as a spring flower."

Beth closed her eyes as Dusty kissed her again. His mouth was warm and soft and she felt her heart beat a little faster as he deepened the kiss. Yet even as Dusty was kissing her, she was wondering what it would be like to be in Chase's arms, to feel his mouth on hers. *Chase.* It came to her in a blinding flash of insight. She loved him. Impossible as it seemed, it was true nonetheless. She loved him. She admitted it, and realized that he was not only the man she had been waiting for her whole life, but he was the answer to her problems, the fulfillment of all her dreams.

Heady with excitement, she placed her hands on Dusty's chest and eased out of his embrace.

"I'd better go," she said, the daring idea that had occurred to her making her feel fluttery inside. "My father will be looking for me."

Dusty nodded. "I'll be looking forward to Sunday."

"Me, too. 'Bye, Dusty."

"So long, Beth."

Whistling softly, Dusty sat down and propped his feet on the desk. Life was good, he mused. And Beth was the best part.

Sunday morning dawned gloomy, with dark gray clouds that shrouded the sun. Standing at the barred window looking out, Chase prayed that it would rain before the night was out, knowing that a good heavy storm would eliminate his tracks.

His mother and Ryder came to visit him in the afternoon. Ryder informed him that there would be a cache of supplies, including a rifle, a couple of canteens, a change of clothes, and a bedroll waiting for him in the hollow where Rance had shot him. Jenny smiled, saying she'd packed plenty of dried beef and venison, a dozen fresh-baked biscuits, some fruit, and as much canned goods and coffee as the pack would hold.

Chase had stared at the two of them, his throat clogged with emotion. He had never seen two people who were so much in love, so united in their thinking. Kayitah had been a good man, and Alope had been a dutiful wife, but they had not shared the kind of devotion that was so readily apparent between Jenny and Ryder as they stood outside his cell, holding hands. It was difficult to say good-bye, knowing he might never see them again.

"Don't worry," Ryder said in parting. "Everything will work out."

His mother hugged him fiercely, her eyes bright with tears. "You'll be in my heart and my prayers every day until you come back to us."

He hugged her once, hard, unable to speak past the rising lump in his throat.

That had been hours ago. Now, he paced the narrow cell, his nervousness mounting with each passing minute. How soon would Dusty come to turn him loose? In spite of all Ryder's assurances that there wouldn't be many people around on a Sunday night, Chase couldn't help wondering if he'd make it out of town.

Hours passed. He judged the time to be about eight o'clock when he heard Beth's voice downstairs, the lilting sound of her laughter. He felt his heart ache at the thought of never seeing her again. Ryder and Dusty made it sound so simple—they would find out who had stolen the stallion and shot the white man, clear his name, and he could return to Twin Rivers. In spite of their confidence, Chase doubted it would be that easy. There was a good chance that they would never find out who had stolen the Harveys' stallion, in which case he would never see Beth Johnson again.

Perhaps it was just as well. He was a half-breed. He had no way to care for a woman, nothing to offer. He owned nothing. His horse had been stolen; the clothes he wore were a gift from his mother.

He stared into the night. Though he couldn't see it in the darkness, he knew the gallows was out there. Yesterday, he had stood at the window, watching in morbid anticipation as the trapdoor was tested, imagining himself standing on the wooden platform, a noose around his neck. Hanging. It was a bad way to die, the rope choking the life from his body, trapping his soul within a prison of flesh.

With a shudder, he turned away from the window. It was getting late. How much longer would he have to wait?

Moving to the door of his cell, he cocked his head to one side, listening. Where was Dusty?

Thirty minutes passed. And then he heard the soft sound of footsteps on the stairs.

Chase frowned. No light showed from below.

He felt a rush of apprehension as a dark form materialized at the head of the stairs. And then he caught the faint fragrance of flowers. "Beth?"

"Shhh." She was at the cell door now, and he heard the faint jingle of keys. "I've come to get you out of here."

"What?"

She muttered something under her breath as she struggled to fit the key into the lock.

"Beth . . ."

"Got it!" she exclaimed. "Hurry." Opening the door, she grabbed his hand. "Let's go."

Feeling somewhat stunned, Chase followed Beth down the stairs. She paused at the door, opened it, and peered out. It was then that Chase saw Dusty. The lawman was slumped over his desk, his head pillowed on his arms.

"All clear," Beth said. "Come on." When he didn't move, she glanced over her shoulder. "Don't worry about Dusty," she said, placing the keys back on their hook. "I put some of my mother's sleeping powder in his coffee. He'll be fine when he wakes up."

Chase nodded. He didn't understand why Beth was helping him, but, in one respect, it made things easier. His family wouldn't be involved now. They wouldn't have to lie to protect him; he wouldn't have to worry about his mother being forced to leave her home.

He followed Beth out the back door of the sheriff's office. Two horses waited in the alley behind the building.

Taking the reins to a long-legged sorrel mare, Beth glanced at him over her shoulder. "Hurry!" she called softly, and tossed him the reins to the other horse.

Chase's gaze ran over Dusty's horse. It was a red-roan Appaloosa, with wide-set intelligent eyes. Grabbing a handful of the gelding's mane, he swung into the saddle, grimacing as pain lanced through his left side.

"Thank you," he said, glancing down at Beth. "I . . . I guess this is goodbye."

"I'm going with you."

Chase stared at her as if she'd suddenly grown two heads and a tail. And then he shook his head. "No."

"Oh, yes."

"No," Chase repeated, and reining his horse around, he urged it into a gallop. He would ride for the hollow, find the supplies Ryder had promised to leave him, and return to Rainbow Canyon. He would hide out there, as planned, until Ryder sent word that his name had been cleared.

Chase leaned low over the roan's neck, the ache in his side forgotten, swallowed up in the knowledge that he was free! He grinned, reveling in the bite of the wind against his face. He was free! The week he'd spent behind bars had seemed like a year. Never again, he vowed, never again would he let anyone lock him up.

For a short time, he considered heading for Mexico. He would be safe there. But he would have no way to get in touch with his mother, no way to find out if his name had been cleared.

His hands tightened on the reins. He didn't want to spend the rest of his life on the run, always looking over his shoulder, afraid to settle down in one place. He wanted to get to know his mother, to have a home of his own—perhaps here, in Twin Rivers.

He felt a peculiar tug in his heart. He wanted a woman of his own, a woman of courage and honor like his mother. A woman like Beth Johnson.

The hollow loomed ahead, and Chase slowed his horse to a walk. It was then that he heard the sound of hoofbeats coming up fast behind him.

Fearful that his freedom was only an illusion, that a posse was already in pursuit, he glanced over his shoulder to see Beth riding toward him. Her long blond hair had come loose from its knot and blew in the wind like a banner made of gold silk.

She smiled brightly as she drew rein beside him. "That was wonderful!" she exclaimed.

"Wonderful?" Chase shook his head.

"Yes! I've never ridden at night before. Never ridden so fast."

She was beautiful. The most beautiful creature he had ever seen. Her honey-colored skin glowed in the light of the full moon, her brown eyes sparkled with excitement.

"Go home, Beth."

She shook her head. "No. I want to go with you."

"It is not possible."

"Oh, but it is." She patted the saddlebags tied behind the cantle of her saddle. "I'm all packed and ready to go."

"Foolish woman! I am not making this journey for pleasure."

"I know." The smile faded from her lips, though her gaze remained warm and vibrant as it met his. "But we can make it a wondrous adventure, Chase. It's all in your attitude."

"Attitude?" Chase snorted softly. "I have been accused of shooting a white man and stealing a horse, and you think I should try and make a game of it? Go home, woman. Go back where you belong."

Beth lifted her chin defiantly. "If you want me to go back, then you'll have to take me."

"You know I cannot do that."

She tried to hide her triumphant smile, and failed miserably. "I know, so we should get going."

What was he to do with her? Dismounting, he led the roan into the hollow. The packhorse and supplies were waiting, just as Ryder had promised. Beth must have been surprised to see them, but she said nothing.

He checked the rigging, using the time to try and sort out his chaotic thoughts. He couldn't send her back to town alone, in the middle of the night, nor did he dare take her back. What to do?

He was aware of her standing behind him even before she spoke. "We should be going."

He whirled around and grabbed her by the arms, holding her in a grip like iron. "Why are you here?" he demanded.

"Because I want to go with you."

"Why? You do not know me. I do not know you." But even as he uttered the words, he remembered the first moment he had seen her, remembered thinking that he knew her, that in some part of his soul he had always known her. But such a thing was impossible.

Confused, he stared down at her, felt himself drowning in the depths of her eyes.

"Beth." His voice was thick, ragged with an emotion he didn't understand.

"Take me with you, Chase. Please."

He shook his head. He was in enough trouble. No one would ever believe she had gone with him willingly. No matter how tempting it might be to have her along, in the end, she would only slow him down, cause him trouble.

Her gaze was fixed on his, her big brown eyes silently begging him to take her with him.

"I can't," he said hoarsely, but even as the words passed his lips, he was lifting her onto the back of her horse.

His hands lingered at her waist, and he felt the heat flowing from her body to his, felt an unmistakable stab of desire as she smiled down at him. It was that smile that was his undoing.

Turning away, he swung into the saddle and took up the reins of the packhorse. He sat there for a moment, beset by doubts, and then he clucked to the horse.

Taking her with him was wrong, and he knew it. But in all his life, he'd never had anything he wanted. And he wanted this white woman, wanted Beth, as he'd wanted nothing else.

He glanced over his shoulder once to make sure she followed, and then he rode out of the hollow.

Chapter Nine

Dusty groaned softly as he opened his eyes. His mouth felt thick, his head fuzzy, as though he'd spent the night drinking.

Sitting back, he cradled his head in his hands. What the hell had happened?

A glance at the clock put the time at just after five A.M. He swore under his breath as he stood up. Damn! Chase should have been long gone by now.

Taking up the keys to the cells, he climbed the stairs.

For a moment, he stood there, staring at the open door, the empty cell. Chase was gone all right. But how the hell had he gotten away?

His brow furrowed in thought, he went downstairs to check the alley. His roan was gone. Hunkering down on his heels, he examined the ground. Two sets of tracks. The prints of the lead horse belonged to his roan.

With a sigh, Dusty stood up. He recognized the

second set of tracks, too. They belonged to Beth's sorrel mare.

He stared at the hoofprints, his thoughts turned inward. Where had she met Chase, and why had she gone with him?

Muttering an oath, he walked down the street to Ruddman's Livery. Old Man Ruddman wasn't happy about turning out one of his horses at six A.M.

"Gonna cost you extra," he grumbled as he saddled a raw-boned gray gelding.

"Bill the town for it," Dusty retorted irritably. Taking up the reins, he rode out of town.

"But, how?" Jenny asked, frowning. "How did he get away if you didn't turn him loose?"

Dusty sat back in his chair and shook his head. "I don't know."

Ryder sat forward, his elbows braced on the kitchen table. "You say the keys were in your desk?"

"Yeah."

"And no came to see you besides Elizabeth?"

"That's right." Dusty looked at his father. "What are you suggesting?"

"I'm not suggesting anything."

"You think Beth let him go? Why would she do that? They didn't even . . ."

"Didn't even what?" Jenny asked.

"Nothing." Dusty stared into the depths of his cup, remembering Beth's interest when he'd mentioned there was an Indian in jail.

"Son?"

"Nothing," Dusty said. "I'm gonna ride out and see if the packhorse is gone. Can I take one of your horses? I had to rent one from Ruddman. I think he gave me the worst of the lot. Horse's got a mouth like iron."

"Sure. Take the chestnut."

"Thanks." Pushing away from the table, he grabbed his hat and left the house.

"What do you make of all that talk about Beth?" Jenny asked.

"I don't know," Ryder replied. "But I've got a bad feeling about this."

Instead of riding for the hollow, Dusty rode back to town to return the gray to Ruddman and see if Beth had returned.

He was riding away from Ruddman's when he heard a voice calling his name. Glancing over his shoulder, he saw Ralph Johnson riding toward him.

"Sheriff! Sheriff! She's gone! Beth's gone." Ralph reined his horse to a dirt-scattering halt in front of the boardwalk. "Is she here? Is Beth here?"

"I haven't seen her, Mr. Johnson. I'm sorry."

Ralph Johnson slumped forward in the saddle, his face pale. "Where could she be?"

"I don't know. Did she leave a note, anything?"

"No." Ralph Johnson's head jerked up. "She said she was bringing you something to eat last night."

Dusty nodded. "She came by about eight, but she didn't stay long."

Johnson frowned. "She didn't come back later?"

"No."

"She went up to bed about nine-thirty. That was the last time I saw her."

Dusty rubbed the back of his neck. "Do you or Mrs. Johnson keep any kind of sleeping powders in the house?"

"Mrs. Johnson takes them sometimes. She gets headaches. Doc gave her something to help her sleep."

"Go on home, Mr. Johnson. If I hear anything, I'll let you know."

"Thank you, Sheriff." With a sigh, Johnson reined his horse toward home.

Dusty stared after him. He didn't like what he was thinking, but it was the only thing that made sense. Beth had drugged him, then turned Chase loose. But why? And where was she now? He didn't like the answer that came readily to mind.

Swearing softly, he urged the chestnut into a lope and headed out of town.

The hollow was empty. Dismounting, he checked the ground. The signs were plentiful and easy to read. Moccasin prints. Smaller prints that he knew belonged to Beth. The hoofprints of his roan and Beth's sorrel. A third set of tracks that belonged to the packhorse.

His brother was gone, and Beth had gone with him.

There was a crowd gathered in the street in front of the jail when he returned to town. A check of his pocket watch showed the hour to be a few minutes shy of ten.

Dusty swore softly. Looked like the whole town had turned out for the hanging.

Settling his hat on his head, he swung out of the saddle. The crowd parted before him like the Red Sea.

"What's going on, Sheriff?"

"Where's the prisoner?"

"Cell's empty. What happened?"

Dusty tuned out the questions as he climbed the stairs. He turned to face the crowd, lifting one hand to silence the noisy throng. "The prisoner escaped last night," he said, speaking loudly. "That's all I know."

"Escaped? How?"

"I don't know," Dusty said. "I fell asleep at my desk, and when I woke up, he was gone."

He held his ground, face impassive, as a flood of angry questions and accusations was hurled at him.

"I don't know," Dusty repeated, his voice taut with the strain. "When I find the answers, I'll let you know. For now, I want you all to go home."

Most of the crowd complied, but a half-dozen men remained, muttering under their breath about getting up a posse and seeing that justice was done.

"If I need help tracking him down, I'll ask for it," Dusty said.

"Could be we need a new sheriff," one of the men remarked. "One who can stay awake nights."

Dusty stood firm, his hand resting on his gun butt, as the men began making thinly veiled threats.

"You heard what he said. Now, all of you, go home where you belong."

Dusty glanced over the heads of the men in the crowd. His father, mounted on a big black stallion, rode toward him, a rifle negligently cradled in the crook of his left arm. Ryder Fallon knew his way around a rifle, and every man in town was aware of it.

"Go on," Fallon said, reining his horse to a halt at the rear of the dissenters. "Git!"

The men glanced at Dusty, glanced at Ryder, and then, apparently deciding they were outmaneuvered, they shuffled down the street toward the saloon.

"So," Ryder said, dismounting, "any idea what happened?"

"She drugged me." Dusty felt the back of his neck grow hot. "She drugged me and turned him loose."

"She?"

"Beth."

Ryder frowned. "Beth? Are you sure?"

Dusty nodded. "She's missing, too. Her old man came by earlier this morning, looking for her. She must have taken some of her mother's sleeping powder and put it in my coffee, then came back later, after I'd passed out, and turned him loose."

"That doesn't make sense. Why would she do a thing like that?"

"How the hell do I know? Dammit, I thought she loved me."

"Hey, take it easy."

"How can I? Dammit, she betrayed me."

"Let's go inside," Ryder suggested, conscious of passersby.

"Yeah." Unlocking the door, Dusty entered the office. Removing his hat, he tossed it on the desk, ran a hand through his hair. "I feel like a damn fool."

Ryder closed the door, then leaned against it, his ankles crossed, his arms folded over his chest. "I don't understand. When could they have met?"

"I don't know." Dusty dropped into the chair behind his desk.

"So, what are you gonna do now?"

"I don't know." He bit off each word.

"You can always go after them."

"Not me. I courted her for five months. I thought

I knew her. I thought she loved me. I guess I was wrong on both counts. Well," he said, slapping his hands on the desktop, "I've got work to do."

Ryder nodded. "Guess I'd better go. I've got some work to do myself." He pushed away from the door. "Your mother's expecting you for dinner tonight. Don't forget."

"I'll be there." Dusty looked up. "Thanks for your help out there."

"You didn't need it," Ryder replied, "but when your mother asks, I want to be able to say I would have been there if you got in a tight. See you tonight, son."

Dusty nodded. He stared out the window for a long time, but it was Beth he saw. Beth smiling at his brother.

It was after four when Dusty left the office. Lost in thought, he walked down the boardwalk, hardly aware of the people he passed, the thought of Beth and Chase burning like acid in his gut.

He didn't see Rebecca Winterburn until he'd practically knocked her off her feet.

"I'm sorry," he said, grabbing her arm to keep her from tumbling off the boardwalk. "Are you all right?"

"Fine." Rebecca straightened her hat, then smiled up at the man standing in front of her. "How have you been, Dusty? I haven't seen you for a while."

"Fine, fine," he replied absently. "And you?"

"Fine. I heard about your trouble at the jail. I'm sorry."

He shrugged. "It's not the first time a prisoner has escaped from jail. I don't reckon it will be the last."

"I guess that's true. I got a letter from Dorinda today."

"Yeah? What'd she have to say?"

"She said she's having a wonderful time, shopping and touring all the museums. I wish I could have gone with her. She said she's met a lot of nice people, but she misses everyone here."

"Yeah, well, I know my mother sure misses her." Dusty smiled at Rebecca. She was a pretty woman in a soft, understated sort of way. Her hair was dark brown, kind of curly; her eyes were the soft gray of a dove's wing.

"How are things going at school?" he asked. She'd been teaching for a little over a year.

"Same as always. Brad Simms spends every recess clapping erasers. That boy will never learn!" She laughed softly. "How are your folks?"

Dusty shrugged. "Same as always."

Rebecca clasped her hands, her gaze sliding away from his. She'd been in love with Dusty Fallon ever since he'd asked her to dance at the Christmas party last year. She had hoped he'd come courting, but he hadn't. Oh, he smiled at her at church, and he had occasionally accepted her invitation to lunch, but then he'd started courting Elizabeth Johnson.

"Well," Dusty said, "I guess I'd better go. My folks are expecting me for dinner."

"Say hello to your mother for me."

"I will. See ya."

"See ya." Rebecca stared after him as he walked away, wishing she was prettier, wishing she had the gumption to make her feelings known.

Perhaps someday, she mused, when he was over Beth.

* * *

Chase and Beth had ridden all that night and the next day, stopping only at noon to eat and rest the horses.

Beth, accustomed to riding no more than an hour or two at a time, thought they'd never stop for the night. Time and again she was tempted to complain, to tell him she couldn't go any farther, but each time she bit back the words. He hadn't asked her to come along, she reminded herself. If her back was sore and her body dead from the waist down, it was no one's fault but her own. Besides, if he could ride for miles and miles with a bullet wound in his side and not complain, she could surely endure a little discomfort.

She fastened her gaze on Chase's back, distracting herself by watching the way the breeze ruffled his long black hair, admiring the way he sat in the saddle, the spread of his shoulders. When he glanced back to check on her, she felt the touch of his eyes clear to her soul. What was there about him that touched her so, that made her feel as though she had known him all her life? It made no sense, no sense at all.

Until a few days ago, she hadn't even known Chase the Wind existed. Until a few days ago, she had thought herself in love with Dusty.

But then she had seen Chase's reflection in the river, and she had known, known in the very depths of her heart and soul, that he was the reason for her existence.

A faint smile tugged at her lips. She had never realized what a romantic she was until now, she thought, bemused. Never believed in love at first sight. But she believed now.

Her gaze ran over Chase again. Did he feel the same, or had he merely let her tag along because she hadn't given him any other choice?

As the sun began to sink below the horizon, she was beset by doubts. The landscape, which had seemed beautiful in the sunlight, suddenly seemed ominous. Her parents would be worried sick by now. No doubt Dusty had come to the conclusion that she had drugged his coffee.

Running away with Chase, which she had viewed as an adventure at first, no longer seemed as romantic as it once had.

It was near dark when Chase drew rein in a shallow draw that would protect them from the wind as well as conceal their presence.

Dismounting, he glanced up at Beth, felt the instant attraction that hummed between them whenever their eyes met. And yet, mixed with the stirrings of desire came the realization that he should not be with her. She was a white woman, and he was an Indian. On the reservation, he had been told, time and again, that her kind was forbidden to him, that he was not good enough for a white woman.

He shook the thought from his mind. A sharp pain knifed through his left side as he reached up to lift her from the saddle, but the pain was forgotten the minute his hands closed around her waist. Her hands were warm on his shoulders, and her body brushed against his as he lifted her from the saddle. Even when Beth's feet were on the ground, he continued to hold her. The top of her head just reached his shoulder. He stared down at her, unable to look away, unwilling to let her go.

"Beth, I . . . Beth." He seemed unable to say anything but her name.

She smiled up at him, her eyes luminous. "I know." She shook her head. "It's like magic, isn't it?"

Maybe that was it, he thought. The Apache were strong believers in magic. Medicine men, especially, were thought to possess powerful magic. It was believed that special virtue resided in the hair of the medicine man, and he took special care that no one touched it. *Hoddentin* was a bit of magic that each warrior possessed. Made of powdered tule, it was used for anointing the sick. A pinch was thrown toward the sun at planting time, and whenever a war party rode out. It was believed to restore the sick.

Chase lifted his hand to the small buckskin bag he wore beneath his shirt. It held a small amount of *hoddentin,* and a turquoise stone that was smooth and perfectly round.

He had never seen or felt anything more magical than the woman in his arms. Slowly, he bent his head and kissed her.

All her earlier doubts and fears vanished like morning mist at the first touch of his lips on hers. Her eyelids fluttered down, and she pressed herself against him, reveling in the solid strength of his arms around her.

After a moment—or was it a lifetime—he drew back, shaken to the core of his being.

"Beth, I . . ." *I have never felt like this before.*

The words, unspoken, hovered in the air between them.

"I know," she whispered.

Reluctantly, he released her and took a step backward. "I must look after the horses."

"I'll help."

Side by side, they unsaddled the horses, tethering them to a clump of brush growing out of the side of the draw. After spreading their bedrolls, Beth rummaged through the packs, looking for something to eat. Along with a variety of dried and tinned food, she found a small pot of salve and some clean cloth for bandages.

Since there was no wood available, they ate beef jerky and cold biscuits for dinner and washed it down with water from one of the canteens.

Later, they sat side by side, their backs propped against the hard-packed earth, Chase's arm wrapped loosely around Beth's shoulders.

"Do you feel all right?" she asked. "Does your wound pain you very much?"

"Not much." Not at all, when you're beside me, he thought to himself.

"Maybe I should change the bandage?"

Chase nodded, pleased by the thought of her taking care of him. He removed his shirt, and she unwound the cloth from his middle, then checked the wound. "I don't know much about such things, but it seems to be healing."

Chase studied the wound a moment, then nodded. The hole had closed and the surrounding area didn't appear infected.

With a hand that trembled only for fear of causing him pain, Beth spread a thin layer of salve over the wound, then placed a clean square of gauze over it and wrapped a strip of cloth around his side to hold it in place.

"There," she said, sitting back. "How does it feel?"

"Better." He put his arm around her shoulders. "Thank you."

"You're welcome." She glanced into the darkness. "I've never slept outside before. It's kind of scary."

"Scary?"

"It's so dark. So quiet." She shivered as a wolf howled in the distance. "Maybe not quiet enough."

Chase drew her closer, glad for any excuse to hold her against him. "He will not hurt you."

"Are you sure? He sounds hungry. Like the Big Bad Wolf in Little Red Riding Hood."

Chase shook his head. "Who is Little Red Riding Hood?"

"It's a fairy tale."

"I have no knowledge of such things."

"Fairy tales are stories mothers tell their children, like Cinderella, and Sleeping Beauty."

"What is the purpose of such stories?"

"Some of them have a message."

"Like Apache hero stories?"

"Maybe."

"Tell me one of your stories," he urged.

"All right." She frowned a moment, then took a deep breath. "Once upon a time . . ."

Idly, Chase stroked her hair as he listened to the story of Cinderella and her ugly stepsisters.

". . . and they lived happily ever after," Beth finished.

"Happily ever after," Chase mused aloud. "Is there such a thing?"

"I think so. I hope so!" Beth turned her head to

the side so she could see his face. "Were your parents happily married?"

"No."

"I'm sorry." Beth shrugged. "I don't know if my parents are happy together, but Dusty's are. . . . Dusty!" she exclaimed. "Oh, my."

"What about Dusty?"

"Nothing. It's just that I . . . that we . . . Never mind."

"Tell me."

"He asked me to marry him."

Chase stared at Beth as if seeing her for the first time. "My brother has spoken for you?"

"Your brother! Dusty's your brother?"

Chase nodded.

Beth blinked at him. "Oh, my," she murmured. "Oh, my! Does Dusty know you're his brother?"

"Yes."

"Where've you been all this time? How come Dusty never mentioned you?"

"He didn't know about me until I came here."

"Why did you come here?"

"To find my mother."

"Your mother . . . You don't mean Mrs. Fallon?"

"Yes."

"But you're . . ." Beth's eyes widened.

"Apache," Chase said, his voice carefully controlled.

"Oh, my." Beth shook her head. "Dusty said his parents had some adventures in their youth, but I never thought . . ." She frowned at him. "Where's your father?"

"He is dead."

"Oh, I'm sorry, Chase. Where have you been all this time?"

"On the reservation at Fort Sill."

Beth bit down on her lower lip. She didn't have to ask if he had liked it there. The tone of his voice, the look in his eye, told her that it had been terrible. "You're not thinking of going back there, are you?"

"No."

"Will they come looking for you?"

"I do not know. I only know that I will never go back to that place. But you should go back to Twin Rivers. I will take you home tomorrow."

"No! I don't want to go home."

"You belong to my brother."

"I don't *belong* to anyone!"

With a shake of his head, Chase stood up and walked away from her. Why hadn't she told him she belonged to another man? Another man! She belonged to his brother. Dusty would never forgive him for this, he thought bleakly. He had to take Beth back to town, he had to try and explain.

He snorted softly. He didn't dare show his face in Twin Rivers. And what could he say to Dusty? How could he explain the way he felt when he looked at Beth? She was the first good thing to come into his life in more years than he cared to remember.

"Chase, listen to me."

"How could you do this?" He whirled around to face her. "Why did you not tell me?"

"Because I didn't think it was important."

"Not important?"

"It's not like we're betrothed or anything. I mean, he asked me to marry him, but I never said yes." She shook her head, wondering how to make him understand. "My parents would never let me marry Dusty anyway."

"They do not approve of him?"

"Are you kidding? He's part Cheyenne . . ." Horrified by what she'd said, Beth bit down on her lower lip, wishing she could call back the words.

She stared at Chase, and even though she couldn't see his expression in the darkness, she knew she'd hurt him, hurt his pride. Suddenly there was more distance between them than a few feet of arid ground.

"Then why are you here with me?" he asked, his voice as cold as winter frost. "If they will not let you marry a man who is only a quarter Cheyenne, they will surely object to one who is half Apache."

Even in the darkness, she could feel his gaze probing hers as he weighed her reasons. Weighed them and found them wanting.

"Perhaps you hope that, by running away with me, it will make my brother seem more desirable?"

"No. No, no, no!" She blinked rapidly, refusing to cry. "Why are you doing this? I love you. I loved you the first moment I saw you outside of Carson's."

He stared at her as if she were speaking a language he didn't understand.

"Say something," she begged. "Tell me you understand."

Slowly, Chase shook his head. "I have no words," he replied quietly. "I look at you, and my mouth goes dry. My heart beats fast, like the wings of a hummingbird. I hear your voice, and it makes my soul glad."

"Oh, my," Beth murmured tremulously. Never had anyone said such beautiful things to her before.

She took a step toward him, but he held out his hand, warding her off.

"I am afraid to love you."

"Afraid?" she asked. "Why?"

"I have lost everyone, and everything, I ever loved. My mother left me. The woman I had hoped to marry was killed by the bluecoats. My father died a prisoner in a distant land. My stepmother also." Chase took a deep breath. "It is enough."

"Oh, Chase, I'm so sorry. I wish I could make things better for you, that I could wipe away the past." She slipped under the hand he held out to keep her at bay and wrapped her arms around his waist. "Let me love you, Chase. You don't have to love me back."

"Beth." He groaned softly as his arms folded around her. It was impossible that she should love him, inconceivable that she would leave her home and family to be with him, and yet she was there, her arms locked tightly around him, her face pressed against his chest, and he knew he would never let her go, that he would kill anyone who tried to take her from him.

Chapter Ten

Chase glanced at the woman riding beside him. They had been on the move since early morning, stopping only occasionally to rest the horses. He had expected Beth to complain of the long hours in the saddle, the heat, the dust. He had expected her to slow him down, but she did none of those things. She marveled at the beauty of the desert, looked at him, her eyes shining with wonder, when they saw a hawk circling overhead. She drank sparingly from her canteen, recognizing the need to conserve water.

She had changed her clothes that morning and now wore a long-sleeved blouse of pink gingham and a brown skirt spilt in the middle so she could ride astride. A wide-brimmed straw hat shaded her face, kidskin gloves protected her hands.

Feeling his gaze on her, Beth looked over at Chase and smiled. "Where are we going? You never did tell me."

"Rainbow Canyon."

"Is it far?"

"Another few days."

"Have you been there before?"

Chase nodded. "I grew up there."

Beth smiled, pleased by the prospect of seeing where Chase had grown to manhood. She drew in a deep breath, thinking she had never felt so free. There was no one to tell her what to do, no silly conventions to adhere to. All her life, she'd dreamed of having a great adventure, and now the dream had become reality.

"It's beautiful out here," she remarked. "You must have hated to leave."

"Yes." He drew rein in the scant shade offered by a small stand of trees. "We will rest the horses."

Beth reined her horse to a halt alongside his. "It's beautiful, but so desolate. How did your people survive? I mean, there are hardly any trees, and I haven't seen any game. What did you eat?"

"Many things. There is food everywhere, if you know where to look. The central stem of the narrow-leaved yucca is edible. The new shoots of the tule rush, the agave. There are wild onions and potatoes, sumac berries and choke cherries. Mesquite beans can be ground into flour. There are acorns and piñon nuts. And honey."

Chase grinned. Apache boys often made a war game of stealing the honeycomb from a hive, showing off their bravery by stoically withstanding the stings of the furious insects.

"Rainbow Canyon has good grass and water," he remarked. "We hunted deer and antelope, turkeys and rabbits. And when game was scarce, we went raiding into Mexico for food and blankets." Pride filled his voice. "Our warriors knew every spring and waterhole, every crevice and canyon, for hundreds of miles. Our men required little to survive. A little food and water would last for days. If necessary, they could travel great distances on foot. I was taught early to read the signs of the sky and the earth."

He had been a warrior. It was a thought that hadn't occurred to her before. "Did you ever go to war?" She asked the question certain she would not like the answer.

"I fought with Geronimo."

Geronimo! Beth shuddered. She didn't know much about the Apache, but everyone knew the name of Geronimo. He had cut a wide and bloody swath throughout Mexico and the Southwest, and had been among the last Apaches to surrender.

"How old were you?"

"Sixteen."

"Sixteen!" Only a year younger than she was now. "How old are you now?"

"I have seen twenty-four winters."

"Did you . . . did you kill many men?"

"I did not count them."

"Oh." Staring out into the desert, Beth felt the blood drain from her face. She could almost hear the hellacious cries of the Indians, the sound of gunfire. She took a deep breath, and imagined that she could smell gunsmoke, and death. "It must have been awful."

"I did not think of it in that way. I was a warrior fighting to protect my home, my people. We fought even when we knew we could not win, fought until even Geronimo said he had had enough."

Chase paused, his thoughts turned inward. Though he had never been a chief, Geronimo had been feared and respected as a medicine man. The Apaches believed that no bullet could kill him. As a young warrior, Geronimo had been resourceful, daring, and impudent; he had, on occasion, also been cruel. Though he was now an old man and a prisoner of war along with the rest of the Apaches, the People still viewed him with a sense of awe. As enterprising as he was shrewd, the old warrior had recently taken to selling photographs of himself to the whites for a dollar apiece.

It had shamed Chase to see their people brought down, their pride crushed, everything they had loved and fought for lost to them forever.

"We surrendered," he went on, his voice heavy with defeat, "and they sent us away. To Florida, and then to Alabama, and finally to Fort Sill. Geronimo is still there. He is an old man now, and he will die there, in the land of his enemies."

He gazed into the distance. "I will never go back there. I will die first."

Beth stared at him. His profile was strong and cleanly chiseled, like a statue carved from bronze. His hair fell to his waist like a river of ebony. She had never seen such beautiful hair.

"It must have been a hard life," she mused.

"In many ways. And yet we were free as no white man is ever free."

He turned to face her then, and she saw the sadness in his eyes.

"And now my people are free no more. The government sends our children away to school. Your people dress them in the clothes of the white man. They cut their hair, and forbid them to speak their native language. They refuse to let us worship our gods. Our old ones grieve for the past. Our young men have no hope. The hearts of our women have turned to ashes."

"I'm sorry," Beth murmured, stricken by the kind of life his words painted in her mind. "I wish there was something I could do for you, for your people, but . . ."

He looked at her, his expression bleak. "There is nothing anyone can do now. Whether our people live or die is in *Usen's* hand."

"U-sen?"

"The Great Spirit."

"Oh." It had not occurred to her that the Apache were a religious people, or that they worshipped a god different from the one she believed in.

She pondered that as she urged her horse after Chase. She had been taught there was only one God. If that was true, then *Usen* must be the same God she believed in. Wasn't it Shakespeare who had wondered, What's in a name?

She studied Chase's profile as they rode across the barren land. As always, just looking at him filled her with a tingling feeling of warmth, as if a thousand fireflies were dancing in her heart.

It was most peculiar. Even since she'd been a little girl, she had loved to read, especially fairy tales. Time and again, she had read stories of the handsome prince rescuing the fair princess, of love at first sight, of brave and noble knights saving maidens in distress. Though she had dreamed of such things, she had never really expected them to happen to her. And yet, Chase the Wind was the embodiment of every fantasy she had ever had. He was tall and strong and brave. She knew he was an honorable man, and that he would never hurt her. Just how she knew these things was a mystery, and yet she knew they were true, knew that she had nothing to fear from this man she had just met.

That night they made camp a short distance from a winding stream. Sitting on one of the saddle blankets, Beth watched Chase water the horses, then hobble them in a patch of sun-bleached grass.

She watched him stroke Dusty's roan, shivering as she imagined his hands stroking her neck, her shoulders, her back. She knew it was wicked to entertain such thoughts, and even more wicked to welcome them.

Mesmerized, she watched him walk toward her, admiring the way he moved, silent and supple, like a jungle cat. The moonlight silvered his hair.

She felt the fireflies take flight in her stomach as he drew nearer. She looked up at him, felt her breath catch in her throat. How handsome he was, like a bronze statue come to life.

"I . . . I'd better fix something to eat," she stammered.

"That would be good."

She nodded, unable to draw her gaze from his. His eyes were deep and black, filled with hurts she yearned to heal. He lifted a hand as if to touch her, and she went suddenly still, waiting, wanting.

He took a deep breath and turned away, releasing her from his gaze.

"Oh, my," Beth murmured. "Oh, my!"

Later, after they had eaten, they sat on opposite

sides of the campfire. Chase stared into the flames, but Beth had eyes only for the man across from her. What was he thinking? Was he remembering times long past? Or regretting the fact that she was there?

A coyote howled in the distance, and she wrapped her arms around her waist, feeling suddenly vulnerable and alone.

"Do not worry," Chase said quietly. "He is far away."

"Are you sure?"

"Yes."

"What were you thinking about?"

Lifting his gaze from the fire, he looked at her. "I was thinking of you."

Pleasure rippled through her, as intoxicating as the brandy she'd sipped one Christmas eve. "What about me?"

"I was thinking how beautiful you are, and how brave."

"Brave? Me?"

Chase nodded. "It was a brave thing you did, getting me out of jail. Leaving your family. Coming with me."

"I couldn't let them hang you."

"You could have." He considered telling her that Dusty and Ryder had promised to set him free, then thought better of it. Thinking of Dusty made him wonder if it was wise to go to Rainbow Canyon. It would not take Dusty or Ryder long to realize that Beth had set him free and then run off with him. If Dusty wanted revenge, he would know where to look for it.

Picking up a stick, he turned it round and round in his hands. Would Dusty regret his decision to help his brother? Would Dusty feel honor bound to come after him to save face? Take him back to jail? See him hanged, not for killing the white man, but for taking Beth? Would he blame Dusty if he did?

Chase looked across the fire at Beth, felt the warmth in her eyes, the powerful attraction that hummed between them. Her hair fell down her back and over her shoulders like a river of wild honey. Her eyes were as brown and warm as sun-kissed earth.

Hardly aware that he was moving, he stood up and circled the fire. He reached for her, drawing her to her feet, his gaze never leaving her face as he lowered his head and kissed her.

Her lips were as pink as the wild roses that grew along the banks of the Little Big Horn, as sweet as wild strawberries. She moaned softly, a purely feminine sound of pleasure, as her eyelids fluttered down and she pressed herself against him.

His body came instantly alive, tingling with awareness as he wrapped his arms around her and held her tight. Her breasts were soft against his chest. He could feel her thighs against his, her fingers caressing his nape, her hand moving restlessly up and down his back.

"Chase." Her voice was low and husky, her breath warm against his cheek.

He drew back so he could see her face. Her eyes were luminous, her lips slightly parted, her cheeks rosy. So beautiful, he thought, dazed. Like a goddess come to earth.

But he was only a man. A half-breed, and not worthy of her.

"What's wrong?" Beth asked.

"Everything."

"I don't understand."

"You should not be here with me."

"Are you going to start that again?"

"It is true, and you know it. Only trouble will come of this."

"I don't care."

Fool that he was, he knew he would not send her away. Not as long as she wanted to stay. And he knew, just as surely, that once she was truly his, he would never let her go.

"It is late," he remarked. "We should sleep now."

Beth nodded. She wasn't sure how, but they had crossed an invisible line that night. No words had been said, but she knew a bond had been forged between them.

It was a beautiful day! Beth felt herself smiling as they rode across the prairie. She'd never felt so happy, so carefree, in her whole life.

She glanced at Chase and felt a flutter in her stomach as she remembered the kiss they had shared the night before. She had no words to describe the feelings that his kiss had brought bubbling to life. One little kiss, and her blood had turned to flame and her knees had gone weak. One little kiss, and it had changed her forever, had made her dreams of love and happy-ever-after seem within her grasp for the first time.

They stopped near a narrow, winding stream shortly after noon. A few scraggly trees grew nearby, offering a bit of shade. Beth sat on a patch of yellow grass, chewing on a piece of jerky, while Chase watered the horses.

Her heart did a somersault as she watched him strip off his shirt. The bandage swathed around his middle seemed very white against the dark bronze of his skin. He knelt beside the stream and doused his head and shoulders. She felt herself smile with admiration and feminine pleasure as she watched the play of muscles in his back and arms as he sat on his heels and ran his hands through his hair. Such wondrous hair, long and thick and blacker than sin. Sunlight glinted off his copper-hued skin and danced in the wet sleekness of his hair.

Heat flooded through her as she stared at him. She'd never known a man could be beautiful, but he was, more beautiful than anything or anyone she had ever seen. She yearned to go to him, to run her hands over his chest, to touch the drops of water sliding down his skin.

She pressed a hand to her thundering heart. Never before had she entertained such thoughts about a man, but then, she had never met a man like this one. Tall and dark and dangerous. It was so easy to imagine him riding into battle, an eagle feather braided into his hair, bold slashes of war paint drawn across his cheeks. Had he killed many men? Taken scalps?

She licked lips gone suddenly dry, glad that her parents had lived back east during the Indian wars. She had overheard Dusty's parents talking about such things once when they didn't know she could hear them. They had been talking about an Indian attack on a stagecoach bound for Widow Ridge, and the unfortunate fate of all the passengers save one . . .

Beth frowned, suddenly certain that the survivor

of that coach had been Dusty's mother. She gasped as bits and pieces of conversations she had overheard through the years fell into place. Jenny Fallon had been abducted by the Apache, and Chase was the result.

"Beth?"

Startled, she glanced up to see Chase staring down at her.

"Are you ill?"

"Ill? Me?" She shook her head. "No, why?"

"The color has left your face."

"I'm fine."

She held out her hand, and he took it, drawing her to her feet, and then into his arms.

With a sigh, she rested her head against his chest. She could hear the beat of his heart beneath her ear, strong and steady, heard it beat stronger and faster as his lips moved in her hair, as his hands stroked her back.

She tilted her head back, giving him access to her mouth, closing her eyes as his lips claimed hers, gently at first, as if he feared to hurt her.

She kissed him back, her tongue sliding over his lips, wanting to taste him. She heard his gasp of surprise, and then, tentatively, his tongue caressed her lower lip. Lightning, she thought, I've been kissed by lightning. How else to explain the fire lancing through her?

Time ceased to exist as they stood there, locked in each other's arms, discovering how potent something as simple as a kiss could be.

She savored the taste and the touch of him, the raw wildness, the controlled strength. Her hands explored his broad back and shoulders, her fingers slid up his neck into the heavy black fall of his hair. She pressed herself against him, noting on some distant level that she fit him perfectly. Sparks seemed to radiate from each point where their bodies touched.

His voice was low and deep, like the rumble of thunder, as he whispered her name. She felt his hands brush against her breasts, felt the proof of his desire. A spiral of exhilaration rushed through her, a feeling of feminine power. He wanted her. And she wanted him. Here. Now.

She made a soft sound of protest when he took his mouth from hers.

Chase took a deep breath and then, with great force of will, he let her go. She looked up at him through eyes dazed with passion. He could see the pulse pounding in the base of her throat, hear the uneven tenor of her breathing. If only she were his woman, he thought desperately, if only he had the right to plant his seed within her. But he was afraid to trust in her love, afraid to admit he loved her, for fear he would lose her as he had lost everyone else he had ever loved. And always, in the back of his mind, loomed the thought that she belonged to Dusty.

He ran a hand through his hair, took a deep, calming breath. "We should go."

She gazed up at him through long dark lashes. "Go? Now?"

He nodded. "We can travel for a few more hours before we find a place to spend the night."

Beth blinked at him. "We could spend the night here."

He shook his head. He needed to put some space

between them, needed some time to get his desire for her under control. No matter how tempting it might be, he would not take her here, in the dirt, like some wild beast. He would not defile her as if she was one of the women at the Red Horse Saloon. She deserved better than that.

Turning away, he picked up his shirt and slipped it on, then went to the horses, tightening the cinch on the roan, and then on the sorrel. Taking up the reins, he led the horses to Beth.

His gaze held hers for a long moment, and then he lifted her into the saddle and handed her the sorrel's reins. She took them without a word, but the promise he read in her eyes was more meaningful than anything she could have said.

Chapter Eleven

Jenny drew rein beside Ryder. Removing her hat, she ran a hand through her hair, then smiled at her husband. "It's been a long time since we rode up this way."

"Too long," Ryder replied. Dismounting, he lifted Jenny from the saddle. "What'd you bring for lunch?"

"Oh, the usual. Fried chicken and potato salad. A couple of apples for the horses. Chocolate cake for you."

"Sounds good." He spread a blanket on the grass while she removed the picnic basket from the back of her saddle. Then he unsaddled the horses while she unpacked their lunch.

"Looks good," Ryder remarked. Sitting cross-legged on the blanket across from her, he reached for a chicken leg. "Smells good, too."

"Well, of course it's good," Jenny exclaimed. "I made it, didn't I?"

Ryder grinned at her. "And a fine cook you are, too, Jenny girl."

"I should think so, after all these years."

Ryder took a bite of chicken, his expression thoughtful. "They've been good years, haven't they?"

"The best. Remember the first time we came here? You threatened to put a fish down the front of my dress."

Ryder laughed. "I remember."

"You should. You made me tell you what a mighty fisherman you were."

"And a mighty hunter?"

"The mightiest," Jenny said, mimicking the words she had said so many years ago.

Ryder smiled roguishly. "You also told me I was a mighty lover."

"So I did," Jenny murmured with a grin. "And it's still true."

"Is it?" He wiped the grease from his hands and put the basket aside.

"What are you doing?"

With a shake of his head, he took the chicken leg from her hand and tossed it over his shoulder. And then, with a wicked grin, he reached for her. "I want to prove I'm still a mighty lover."

"Here?"

"Why not?"

"But what if someone comes?"

"You didn't worry about that back then."

"But . . ."

He silenced her protests the best way he knew how: He kissed her, long and hard, until she melted against him, soft and supple and pliant. She smelled of fresh-baked bread and fried chicken, of lilac water and powder and scented soap. And woman. His woman. It was the most intoxicating scent he'd ever known.

He deepened the kiss as he bent over her, until she was lying on the blanket. He covered her body with his, his hands cupping her face as his tongue plundered her mouth. She tasted of chicken and lemonade and warm, willing woman. His woman.

Slowly, as though he had all the time in the world, he kissed her, his lips caressing her eyelids, the tip of her nose, the curve of her cheek, the pulse that throbbed in her throat. He smiled as a low moan of pleasure whispered past her lips. He knew, after all these years, what she liked.

His hands slid down her arms, stroking softly, moving to the curve of her waist, the flare of her hips, along her thighs. She moved restlessly beneath him, her hands delving under his shirt, her nails skimming over his bare back, cupping his hips, drawing him closer.

With the ease of long practice, he undressed her and then himself.

"You're still a mighty lover," she purred, her eyes slumberous with desire. "But then, you always were."

"And you always tempted me beyond the power to resist."

She laughed softly as his body molded itself to hers, steel sheathed in satin. And she was a young woman again, willing to risk any danger to be with the man she loved beyond all else.

She held him tight, her body moving in unison with his, wishing, for one fleeting moment, that she could be that young woman again, that her hair was not streaked with gray, that her skin was still youthful, unlined by time. And then she looked in his eyes and knew that, to Ryder, she would always be that young woman, just as he would always be the tall, dark, dangerous man she had fallen in love with.

And then there was no more time for thought, only the feeling of belonging, of rapture, as ecstasy and pleasure blossomed within her.

With a sigh, Jenny snuggled against Ryder, her head pillowed on his shoulder, her arm draped across his chest, the blanket pulled over both of them.

"Have you talked to Dusty lately?" she asked.

"Last night. He came home pretty late."

"I wish I knew what to say to him. He seems so withdrawn."

"He's bad hurt, Jenny girl, but he'll get over it."

"Will he?"

"I think so. I think his pride's hurt more than anything else."

"How can you say that? He loves her."

"Maybe, but . . ."

"But what?"

He shrugged. "I don't know. Don't get me wrong, I like Beth well enough, but I never thought she was quite right for Dusty."

Jenny propped herself up on one elbow and stared down at her husband. "You never said anything to me."

"I never said anything to him, either."

"I thought they were perfect for each other."

"Who knows, maybe they are."

"But?"

Ryder ran a hand through his hair. "Dusty's always been down to earth, hard working. You know what I mean. He wants a home and a family. He wants to make something of himself. He wants to make a difference in the valley. I don't know how to explain it, but I've always sensed a wild streak in Beth."

"A wild streak!" Jenny exclaimed, sitting up. "Are we talking about the same girl? Why, she's always been a perfect lady."

"Maybe, but I think there's more simmering under the surface than she's let on."

Jenny shook her head. "Goodness, Ryder, I've never even heard the girl raise her voice."

"Yeah, well, it's always the quiet ones you've got to look out for. I remember a girl who was afraid to talk back until she took some good advice, and then . . ."

"And then I set Kayitah and Alope on their ears," Jenny said.

Grinning, Ryder sat up and gave her a playful punch on the arm. "Right the first time."

" 'Give 'em hell, honey,' that's the advice you gave me." She laughed with the memory. "When I got back to the lodge, Alope told me to get the wood, and I told her to get it herself." And that night, when Kayitah had reached for her, she had pushed him away.

"I was right, wasn't I?"

"Every time. Whenever I've been in trouble or lonely and in need of comfort, you've been there. I was hoping Dusty would find what we have with Beth."

"I know, but I don't think Beth is the kind of girl who would have been happy being married to a lawman, and I don't think Dusty will be happy doing anything else, except maybe running for governor."

"Governor! Ryder Fallon, where are you getting these crazy ideas?"

"You saying our son isn't good enough to be governor?"

"Of course not, but he's never said anything about wanting to run for public office."

"He's a sheriff."

"That's hardly the same thing. Twin Rivers is just a small town. But governor!" Jenny smiled. "He'd be good at it, wouldn't he?"

"He'll be good at whatever he sets his mind to," Ryder replied.

"Where do you suppose Beth met Chase?"

"Beats the hell out of me."

"They can't know each other very well. She's lived here most of her life, and Chase has never been here before. It just doesn't make sense."

"Maybe it was love at first sight, sort of like you and me."

Jenny made a face at him. "Be serious."

"I am being serious. I loved you the minute I saw you, Jenny girl." He slipped his arm around her waist and pulled her up against him. Her skin was smooth and warm beneath his hands, her lips still swollen from his kisses.

"Dusty's a big boy," he murmured, running his tongue along the curve of her neck. "He can take care of himself."

His tongue laved her ear. "Chase is all grown up, too."

His hand cupped her breast. "And Beth's not our concern."

"I know, but . . ." Her voice trailed off as his lips rained kisses along her shoulder, and then he was lying back on the blanket, drawing her down on top of him, crushing her close, and all rational thought fled her mind as his hands and lips worked their familiar magic.

Dusty sighed and tossed his napkin on the table.

"Something wrong, son?" Ryder asked.

"Ned Greenway died this morning. There's some talk of getting a posse together and going after Chase."

Jenny sent a worried glance at her son. "You mean a lynch mob, don't you?"

"Berland and Crenshaw are behind it."

"I can't imagine those two having the gumption to start anything," Jenny exclaimed.

"Me, either," Dusty said, "but they were at the saloon most of the day, stirring up trouble."

"Why didn't you arrest them?"

"For what? There's no law against talkin' in a saloon."

"What about inciting a riot?"

"They weren't inciting a riot, Mother," Dusty said, grinning in spite of himself.

"Seems mighty suspicious to me," Ryder mused. "In fact, it seemed mighty suspicious to me that they were out in Piney Hollow that night."

"There's no law against coon huntin', either," Dusty pointed out.

"I know." Ryder swore softly. "Maybe the two of us ought to ride out after him."

"And then what?"

Ryder shook his head. "I don't know. If he does as planned, he'll hole up in Rainbow Canyon until he hears from one of us."

A muscle twitched in Dusty's cheek as he imagined Beth and Chase living together in the canyon, just the two of them. Jealousy rose up within him as he imagined Beth in his brother's arms, imagined his brother holding her, kissing her . . . With an oath, he stood up, his hands clenched at his sides.

"Dusty, what's wrong?" Jenny asked, alarmed at the fierce expression on her son's face.

"Nothing, Mother. Thanks for supper." Turning away from the table, he plucked his hat from the hook by the back door. "I'm gonna spend the night in town."

"Dusty . . ." She stood up, intending to follow him out the door.

"Let him go, Jenny."

"But . . ."

"Let him go."

With a sigh, Jenny sat back down. "He's hurting, Ryder. It pains me to see him like this."

"There's nothing you can do, Jenny girl. He's got to work this out for himself."

Chapter Twelve

Beth felt a thrill of excitement as she followed Chase through the narrow passageway that led into Rainbow Canyon. Once, hundreds of untamed Apaches had lived in this place. Was it merely her imagination, or could she really feel their disapproval as she rode into their ancient stronghold?

She stared in wonder at the craggy cliffs that surrounded the verdant valley. In the distance, she saw a winding river. A stand of tall timber provided shade and firewood.

She slid a glance at Chase the Wind. He seemed to belong here, in this wild place.

He reined his horse to a halt near the river. After dismounting, he turned and lifted her from the saddle.

"We will camp here," he said.

They spent the next few minutes unsaddling their horses. Then, while she arranged their bedrolls, he removed their supplies from the packhorse. When that was done, he turned the horses loose.

"I will build a shelter for us," Chase said.

"And I'll fix something to eat."

He looked at her a long moment, his expression shuttered, and then, taking an ax from the supplies stacked on the ground, he turned away. She watched him walk toward the trees, admiring the way he walked, his long legs eating up the distance. Sunlight glinted in his hair. Such beautiful hair for a man, she thought. Long and straight, it reached his waist, flowing down his back like a waterfall of dark silk. She touched her own hair. How often had she wished for hair like his, hair as black as night?

She watched him until he was out of sight, and then she turned back to the pile of foodstuffs. Humming softly, she began to sort through the sacks and tins.

Hidden behind a tree, Chase watched Beth. What was he going to do with her? She seemed to look on his exile as some kind of great adventure. He should never have brought her here, and yet he was glad for her presence. He watched her walk along the riverbank, admiring the unconsciously graceful way she moved, the sway of her hips, the curve of her breasts.

A thin thread of desire spiraled through him as she removed her shoes and stockings, lifted her skirts to her knees, and waded into the water. She stood there a moment, her head tilted back, her face lifted to the sun.

After a time, she returned to the shore and began gathering rocks.

And he continued to watch her, noting the way the sun danced in her hair, making it sparkle like molten gold, the way her skirts swished about her ankles as she made her way downriver. She smiled with obvious delight when she spied a squirrel peeking from beneath a fallen log near the river. Kneeling, she spent a few moments trying to coax it from under the deadfall.

Failing that, she went back to the task at hand until she had an armful of rocks, and then she turned and headed back the way she'd come. Every move she made enticed him. He looked at her and saw perfection. And seeing it, he wanted to touch her, to taste her, to draw her deep into himself. He knew, somehow, that she had the power to erase the ghosts from his past.

With a sigh, he drew his gaze from the girl and walked deeper into the timber, searching for a tree that would suit his purpose. A short time later, he found what he was looking for. Stripping off his shirt, he took up the ax. Some hard physical labor was just what he needed.

Beth looked toward the timber as the sound of an ax striking wood rang out in the silence. For some reason, the thought of Chase cutting wood made her smile. Perhaps because it seemed like such a domestic task, and he was far from being domestic.

Putting the last rock in place, she took a step back. The rocks were all of a size, placed in a perfect circle around a shallow pit.

"Not bad for the first time," she thought, pleased with her efforts.

With a nod of satisfaction, she picked up one of the canteens and headed for the woods, drawn by the sound of the ax and by the prospect of seeing Chase. Never before had she been drawn to a man in such a compelling way. He was a stranger and yet she felt as though she had been waiting for him all her life. One look at his face, and she had known he was her destiny. It made no sense; she could not explain it.

Beth threaded her way through the trees, the sound of the ax growing louder, until she came to an abrupt halt, her gaze fixed on Chase. He swung the heavy ax with agile strength. He had braided his hair to keep it out of the way, and he had removed his shirt, exposing his broad back. For a moment, she could only stare at the powerful muscles that rippled beneath the smooth copper-hued skin. Beads of sweat trickled down his spine. Her gaze drifted slowly down his back, over the bandage wrapped around his middle, to his lean hips and muscular thighs.

"Oh, my." The words whispered past the lump in her throat as he turned toward her. "Oh, my."

He drove the blade of the ax into a log. Sweat glistened on his brow and dampened his chest. She felt her mouth go dry, curled her hands into tight fists to keep from reaching out to touch him. He was by far the most beautiful creature she had ever seen.

"Did you want something?" His voice was low and husky and slightly breathless.

"No. Yes. I mean . . ." She shrugged. "I just wanted to see you."

I want to touch you, she thought, feeling a little breathless herself.

I want to hold you, he thought, his body feeling suddenly heavy with desire.

Tension stretched between them, humming like a telegraph wire.

"Are you thirsty?" She held out the canteen, grateful for an excuse to break the silence.

He reached for it, his fingers brushing hers. For a moment, he gazed deeply into her eyes, and then, uncapping the canteen, he took a long drink, wishing the cool water could chill his desire as it eased his thirst.

"Thank you." He returned the canteen, his fingers brushing hers again, but this time he caught her hand in his. Fire raced up his arm and settled in his heart. "Beth."

She stared at him, her dark eyes wide and uncertain. "Do you feel it?" she asked, her voice sounding foreign to her ears.

He nodded.

"I've never felt like this before," she confessed. "It frightens me."

"I will not hurt you."

"I know. It's not you I'm afraid of. It's . . . it's me. I . . ."

"You have changed your mind about being here with me?"

"No! No, I . . ." Lifting her free hand, she placed it on his chest, over his heart. "I want to be with you. I love you."

How could he help himself? Unable to resist, he took the canteen from her hand and tossed it aside and then, with a low groan of surrender, he drew her into his arms.

"Beth, what are we to do?"

"I don't know." She looked into his eyes, her heart racing. She'd never felt this way before. It was as if she were standing on the brink of a high cliff, knowing one wrong move would send her plummeting over the edge. In spite of the danger, she wanted to reach out and grab for what she wanted even as a part of her warned that, once committed, there would be no going back.

As if reading her doubts, Chase drew in a deep breath and then took a step back. "Perhaps we need to get to know each other before we make any decisions about the future," he suggested, certain that, in time, she would realize she didn't belong here, with him, that she belonged with her own people.

Beth nodded. Maybe he was right. Maybe they should get to know each other better. "I'll go fix dinner," she said.

Chase nodded, his expression thoughtful as he watched her walk away. He never should have brought her here.

By nightfall, he had erected a crude peeled-pole shelter. A small but cozy fire blazed just outside the lean-to; a good-sized pile of firewood was stacked nearby.

Sitting cross-legged on his bedroll, Chase rubbed his shoulder. He had chopped firewood until it got too dark to see what he was doing, taking a break only to eat the meal Beth had prepared.

"Here, let me."

He looked up to find her watching him. A half-smile touched her lips as she gestured at his shoulders. "I could massage your back for you."

He shook his head. The last thing he needed was her hands on him.

"You deserve it," she insisted. "I've never seen anyone work so hard."

He started to protest, but before he could form the words, she was kneeling behind him, her hands kneading his shoulders. Soft hands. Warm hands. Moving from his shoulders to his back, massaging his biceps, the back of his neck. Sending shivers of pleasure spiraling through him.

His head fell forward and he groaned softly as he imagined her hands touching his chest, his thighs.

"Is something wrong?" Beth asked, her hands resting on his shoulders.

"No." He forced the word through clenched teeth.

"I thought maybe I'd hurt you."

It hurt, he thought, in ways she couldn't begin to imagine.

He clamped his lips together as she moved closer, her breasts grazing his back as her fingers began to massage his scalp.

With a wordless cry, he jumped to his feet, careful to keep his back to her lest she see how her touch affected him.

"Chase?"

"Go to bed," he said gruffly. "I'm going out to check on the horses."

Grabbing his shirt, he left the shelter, his heart pounding like a war drum.

Outside, he drew in several deep breaths. How could he be with her and not touch her? How could he feel this way for a white woman? His whole body burned for her. He thought of the story of the bird and the fish who fell in love but could not live together, and he knew his love for Beth could never be. Like the bird and the fish, they came from different worlds, and no matter how much he might want to share her life, he would never fit in. And even if she could adapt to his world, he had nowhere to take her, and nothing to offer.

He could not send her home alone, and he could not take her back to Twin Rivers himself. He would just have to wait and hope that Dusty found the horse thief soon, that Ryder would come to Rainbow Canyon and tell him it was safe for them to leave.

Until then, he would have to be careful not to get close to her, or let her get close to him.

His decision made, he checked the hobbles on the horses, then took a long walk along the river, giving her plenty of time to get to sleep.

He woke to the scent of bacon frying. Rolling out of his bedroll, he went to the door and peered outside.

Beth was sitting on a rock, turning bacon in a big black skillet. Sunlight poured over her; he could hear her humming softly.

She turned at the sound of his footsteps. "Good morning," she said brightly. "Isn't it a beautiful day?"

Chase nodded as he sat down across from her.

"I don't know who packed for you, but they were thorough." In addition to the frying pan, there was a coffee pot and a dutch oven, as well as enough food to feed an army for a month.

He nodded again, noticing how her hair gleamed in the sunlight.

"Of course, there's only one plate, one knife and fork and spoon, and one cup, so we'll have to share."

His mouth went dry as he imagined eating from a spoon she had used, putting his mouth where hers had been.

"I will use my knife and eat from the pan," he said.

"Don't be silly."

He didn't argue, could only stare at her, thinking again how beautiful she was, wondering why she had left her comfortable home to run away with him.

"Did you like living here?" she asked.

"Yes."

She looked up, glancing at the high purple cliffs that surrounded the valley. "It's pretty, but kind of . . . I don't know. Intimidating."

Chase frowned. "Intimidating? I do not know that word."

"It means scary. I'd hate to be here alone. I know it's silly, but last night, it seemed like I could hear voices."

"The spirits of the dead do not rest in peace."

"Spirits!"

Chase nodded. "Many of my people were killed here. Sometimes you can hear their spirits crying for vengeance."

His words sent a shiver racing down Beth's spine. She'd never given much thought to ghosts before, but Chase sounded as if he believed there really were such things.

Chase insisted she eat first, then took the plate from her hand, all too aware that she had eaten from the same plate, used the same spoon.

He ate quickly, then stood up. "I am going hunting," he said. "Stay close to the shelter until I come back."

"You're going to leave me here, alone?"

"You will be all right." He went into the lean-to and returned carrying a pistol he had found in one of the saddlebags. "Do you know how to use a gun?"

She looked at the weapon as if it might bite her. "No."

The hunt would have to wait. Unloading the gun, he handed it to her.

"It's heavy," Beth said.

"Yes."

Moving behind her, he stretched out his arm, then folded his hand around hers. The moment he touched her, every nerve ending in his body came alive.

In clipped tones, he instructed her how to aim and fire the weapon, but on a deeper level, he was only aware of the girl standing so close. She smelled of smoke and bacon, of sunshine and woman. Her hand was small and soft, and when he felt her trembling, he wondered if his nearness was affecting her, as well.

When he felt she was comfortable holding the pistol, he showed her how to load and fire. The first five rounds missed the target—a good-sized tree branch—but she hit it on the sixth try.

"That will do for now," Chase said. "We can practice more tomorrow."

She followed him to the lean-to, stood in the doorway while he picked up the rifle and a handful of ammunition. "How long will you be gone?"

"As long as it takes."

"What are you after?"

Chase shrugged. "A deer. A rabbit. Anything. We need fresh meat to make our supplies last longer."

"I'll make some soup stock," Beth said, "and we can add the meat when you get back."

With a nod, he turned away, unable to ignore the domestic quality of the moment. He would hunt, and she would prepare his kill, and later, they would share it.

He risked a glance over his shoulder as he saddled the roan, praying that Ryder would come for him quickly. Praying that he would never come.

Chapter Thirteen

A growing sound of unrest drew Dusty from the office. Picking up his hat, he went outside, a sense of dread moving through him as he saw the men gathered outside.

"What's going on?" he asked, though he knew, deep inside, what the answer would be.

"We're goin' after the Injun," Sean Harvey said.

"I said I'd take care of that," Dusty replied, his gaze sweeping the crowd. He counted a dozen men, all heavily armed. He saw Rebecca standing across the street and hoped she had the good sense to go inside before things got ugly.

"Don't look like you're doin' much," Joby Berland retorted. He glanced around, as if to make sure he had the backing of the crowd. "The redskin escaped days ago, and you ain't done nothin' yet."

"Joby's right," Alan Kelton called.

A rising murmur of agreement rippled through the crowd.

"Maybe you're draggin' yer heels 'cause that murderer's an Injun," suggested a man from the back of the crowd.

"That you, Rance?" Dusty said. "Why don't you come up here and say it to my face?"

The crowd parted as Crenshaw shoved his way to the front. "We've known you a long time," Rance said. "We know your folks. I ain't sayin' nothin' aginst you, but if you ain't got the stomach to go after that redskin, then step aside."

"I don't like the word 'redskin,' " Dusty said, his voice deadly quiet. "You people elected me sheriff. Now go on home and let me do my job."

"Don't look like yer doing it," Kurt Harvey said, his voice apologetic but determined.

Dusty took a deep breath. "I'm just going to say this once. I followed the prisoner's tracks out of town as far as the hollow. I'm only a town marshal, and my jurisdiction ends there. If I see him in this area again, I'll arrest him. Until then, I've done all I can do within the limits of the law. Now, go on home."

"'Fraid not," Sean Harvey said. "Joby here can track near as good as you can. It ain't rained since that last little drizzle. Any tracks out there will be easy to find."

Dusty swore under his breath. Beth's sorrel left a distinctive print.

Kurt shifted the coil of rope resting on his shoulder. "When we find him, we're gonna string him up."

"Damn it, Harvey, that's murder!"

Kurt Harvey shook his head. "He's been tried and found guilty. Only thing ain't been carried out is his sentence. We aim to take care of it."

Dusty rested his hand on the butt of his gun. "I can't let you do that."

"You can't stop us. He shot Ned Greenway, and he ain't gettin' away with it!"

"As sheriff of this town, I'm ordering you all to go home."

There was a taut moment of silence, and then the crowd surged together, seeming to meld into one being. From the corner of his eye, Dusty saw a man on the edge of the crowd reach for his gun. His reaction was instinctive.

Dusty drew his gun, knew a moment of relief as his weapon cleared leather.

The other man was still tugging his pistol free of the holster when there was a gunshot.

Dusty stumbled backward, feeling as though someone had punched him in the stomach. Fire exploded in his gut.

From somewhere in the distance, he heard a woman scream, and then everything went black.

"Dammit, this is all my fault!" Muttering under his breath, Ryder paced the floor, pausing every few minutes to glance down the hallway. Now and then, Jenny hurried into the kitchen for more hot water, more towels. Her face was drawn, her eyes shadowed with fears that neither of them had dared put into words.

He glanced at Rebecca Winterburn, who sat in the parlor, her heart-shaped face as white as the sheet she was tearing into strips. She was a pretty girl, with curly brown hair and serene gray eyes. To the best of his recollection, she had started teaching school earlier in the year.

Resuming his pacing, Ryder wondered briefly what she was doing here, but it was Dusty who held his thoughts. He was bad hurt, and Ryder couldn't help feeling it was all his fault. He should never have left Dusty in town to face things alone once Greenway died. He should have known this would happen, should have known that Berland and Crenshaw would stir things up. Indian haters, both of them.

Damn!

He whirled around at the sound of footsteps. "How is he, Doc?"

"Not good," Forbes said. He took the bandages from Rebecca's hand. "I think this will be enough," he said. He glanced at Ryder, then hurried back to Dusty's room.

Ryder began pacing again, his hands clenching and unclenching at his sides. It galled him that there was nothing he could do but wait. He'd never been good at waiting. He'd never been good at anything except fast-drawing a Colt.

"Would you like a cup of coffee, Mr. Fallon?"

"No." Ryder swore softly. "I'm sorry, Rebecca, I didn't mean to bite your head off."

"It's all right, Mr. Fallon. I understand. I'm sure he'll be all right."

Ryder was spared having to answer by the appearance of the doctor. Hardly daring to breathe, Ryder met the other man's gaze. "Spit it out, Doc."

"That slug tore him up pretty bad inside. I'm afraid I've done all I can, Ryder. You'd best prepare yourself for the worst."

"Does Jenny know?"

"I'm afraid so."

Jonas Forbes placed his hand on Ryder's shoulder. "I'm sorry," he said, his eyes filled with compassion. "I'll be back tomorrow."

"Thanks, Doc."

"I wish I could have done more. I left some laudanum for the pain."

Ryder nodded. He walked Forbes to the door, then stood there, staring blankly into the distance, seeing Dusty as a little boy, learning to walk, to talk, eager to ride, copying everything his father did, wanting to learn to fast-draw a gun, practicing with one made out of wood.

Resting his forehead against the edge of the door, he closed his eyes, remembering the morning Dusty had been born. Through a bizarre twist of circumstances, Jenny's first husband, Hank Braedon, had been staying with them then. Ryder felt a twinge of self-disgust as he remembered how jealous he'd been of the time Jenny had spent taking care of the man. They'd all known there was no chance Braedon would recover. Hank had died the same day Dusty had been born.

Even now, Ryder could recall that morning, the exultation he had felt as he'd held his son for the first time. The cabin had been too small to hold his joy and he'd gone outside into the light of a new day, a day filled with golden sunshine.

My heart soars and my spirit sings. He remembered murmuring those words, the same words his own father had said the day Ryder became a warrior. Filled with a deep sense of well-being and the wonder of life renewing itself, he had lifted his face to the sun and loosed the ululating victory cry of the Cheyenne.

Later, he had gone inside to see how Hank was doing. The bedroom had been cool and quiet, pungent with the faint, musty scent of death. He had looked down at Jenny's husband, reminding himself that the Indians believed that life was a circle, that nothing was ever lost. A man had died, and a new life had begun.

A new life . . . Ryder hammered his fist against the door frame. Dusty couldn't die, not now, not when he still had his whole life ahead of him. And Jenny . . . He'd rather cut off his arm than put her through this.

Pushing away from the door, he walked down the hallway to Dusty's bedroom. He needed to hold Jenny, to offer her what comfort he could, needed to draw on the deep inner strength that had always been hers.

Jenny looked up as Ryder entered the room.

"How is he?"

She shook her head, her beautiful green eyes dark with pain. "I'm so afraid."

"I know." Crossing the floor, he drew her into his arms.

"I don't think I could bear it if he died."

"He won't," Ryder said. "Don't even think it."

"Should we send a wire to Dorinda?"

Ryder hesitated, then shook his head. "Let's not worry her. There's nothing she can do. . . ."

He glanced over Jenny's shoulder, blinking back tears of his own as he looked at Dusty. He looked so young lying there. His face was pale, his jaw shadowed by a day's growth of beard.

"Sit down, Jenny girl," he said, leading her to the chair beside the bed. "I'll get you something to eat."

"No, I'm not hungry."

Standing behind the chair, Ryder placed his hands on her shoulders. "You need to keep your strength up, honey."

"I can't eat," she said, clasping Dusty's hand in hers. "Not now. Did you . . . did you find out who shot him?"

Ryder shook his head. "No. Whoever made up that mob is keeping quiet. But I'd bet my last dollar that Berland had a hand in it somewhere."

Ryder brushed his hand over Jenny's cheek, then bent and kissed the top of her head. "Rebecca Winterburn is still out there. Should I send her home?"

Jenny nodded.

Ryder stood there a moment more, then went into the parlor.

"How's Dusty?" Rebecca asked, her expression anxious.

"Still unconscious."

"Is there anything I can do?"

"I don't think so. You might as well go on home."

Rebecca lowered her gaze to the strip of cloth in her hands. "I . . . would you mind terribly if I stayed a while longer?"

"I guess not." Ryder looked at the girl's bowed head, at the nervous way her fingers toyed with the length of sheet. "Rebecca, if I'm out of line, I'm sorry, but why are you here?"

Her head jerked up, two bright spots of color in her cheeks. "What do you mean?"

Ryder lifted a hand and let it fall. "I was just wondering . . . I mean . . . You know what I mean."

"I was there when he got shot," Rebecca replied. "I just wanted to . . . to . . ." She looked up at him, begging him to understand what she couldn't say.

"You're in love with him, aren't you?"

Mute, she stared up at him, her cheeks scarlet.

"Does he know?"

She shook her head. "No. He loves Elizabeth. He's never even looked at me."

Ryder grunted softly. Comparing Rebecca to Elizabeth was like comparing a dove to a canary. Both were beautiful in their own way, but unfortunately, no one would notice the dove if the canary was in the same room.

"Did you see who shot him?"

"No. There were so many men, and it happened so fast."

"Do you want to go in and see him?"

"Are you sure it's all right?"

"Yeah. I think Mrs. Fallon could use a break."

Rebecca rose quickly to her feet. "Thank you, Mr. Fallon."

It took Ryder five minutes to pry Jenny away from Dusty's bedside.

"I'll be right back," Jenny assured Rebecca.

"Yes, ma'am."

"Call me if he wakes up."

"Yes, ma'am."

"Come on, Jenny," Ryder said, tugging on her arm. "A cup of good strong coffee will do you good."

Rebecca waited until Dusty's parents left the room, and then she took a seat in the chair beside the bed. For a time, she just sat there, watching him sleep. Then, unable to keep from touching him, she brushed a lock of hair from his brow, smoothed the sheet over his chest, her hand lingering a few moments longer than necessary.

When he didn't stir, she took his hand in hers, alarmed by how hot his skin felt.

"Get well, Dusty," she whispered. "Please get well."

Jenny sat at Dusty's bedside, sponging his face and body in an effort to bring down the fever that raged through him. She glanced out the window, wishing morning would come. Fears seemed worse at night. Fevers seemed to burn hotter. The soul seemed closer to heaven than to earth.

She shook the thought from her mind, but she couldn't help thinking that Dusty's getting shot was all her fault. If she hadn't asked Chase to stay so she could get to know him better, none of this would have happened. He wouldn't have been arrested, Beth wouldn't have run off with him, and Dusty wouldn't have been shot by a bunch of stupid, angry men with manure for brains.

And yet she couldn't be sorry that she'd had a chance to see Chase. After years of worrying and wondering, it had been a relief, a joy, to know that he was still alive, that he had survived the Indian wars and grown into a handsome young man that any woman would be proud of. She didn't believe for a minute that he had stolen the Harveys' stud or shot Greenway. Chase had said he was innocent, and she knew he was telling the truth.

Dusty stirred restlessly, and she smoothed the hair from his brow. His skin felt cool and damp beneath her hand. The fever had broken at last.

"Praise the Lord," she murmured as she wiped the perspiration from his body and covered him with a warm blanket. "Oh, thank God." He was going to be all right.

Chapter Fourteen

Chase stood out in the darkness, his face lifted toward the sky. Three weeks had passed since they had left Twin Rivers. Only twenty-one days. How could he feel this way about a woman, a white woman, in such a short time? She filled his waking thoughts and haunted his dreams . . . His dreams, he thought ruefully. Never before had he had such dreams—dreams from which he awakened drenched in sweat, his body hard and aching for her touch.

He tried to keep his distance from Beth. He spent long hours hunting, or just exploring the valley, visiting favorite childhood haunts. He had the uncomfortable feeling that she knew what he was doing, and why. He could not help but think her the braver, the more honest, of the two of them. She had said she loved him, and it showed in everything she did, everything she said.

And she wanted him. Though she never spoke the

words aloud, she told him so in ways subtle and not so subtle. When she looked at him, he could see the yearning in her eyes. She touched him whenever he passed close to her. Nothing sexual or overly bold—sometimes it was no more than the brush of her hand against his—and yet her touch burned him like fire, kindling the desire that smoldered within him, under control but never quenched.

Now it was evening, and she had gone to the river to bathe.

He glanced at the sky, impatient for her return. Dark clouds were moving in, driven by an east wind that was growing ever stronger, ever colder. He could smell rain in the air, hear the distant rumble of thunder growing closer. A great bolt of lightning arched across the sky.

A nagging worry began to scratch at the back of his mind. Surely she knew it wasn't safe to stay in the river with a storm coming.

Suddenly restless, he began to pace back and forth, and then he was running toward the river, driven by an unreasoning fear.

Before he reached the shore, the heavens opened.

"Beth!" He shouted her name, knowing as he did so that she wouldn't be able to hear him over the rising wind and the pounding rain.

When he reached her usual place, he glanced up and down the river, but she was nowhere in sight.

"Beth!"

Which way would she have gone? He wasted precious moments trying to decide, and then turned downriver.

"Beth!"

"Here!"

Chase came to an abrupt halt, his head cocked to one side. Had he heard her voice?

"Chase! Over here!"

He peered into the growing darkness, and then, through the pouring rain, he saw a faint movement.

"I'm coming!" he shouted, and sprinted toward her.

Beth fell back against the rock, relieved beyond words.

"Beth, are you all right?"

"My foot's caught," she said.

"What happened?" he asked.

"I slipped, and when I tried to stop myself, my foot got wedged between the rocks."

She grimaced with pain as he touched her foot, cried out as he tried to draw it from between the two huge rocks.

"I am sorry," he said. "Lift your other foot while I try to move one of the rocks."

She did as she was told, wincing as the movement sent a shaft of pain up her leg. She focused on Chase, staring at the give-and-take of the muscles in his back, bulging with effort as he took hold of the rock and pushed.

"Now," he said, and with a mighty heave, he managed to shift the boulder a few inches to the right, holding it just long enough for her to withdraw her foot.

She groaned as pain shot through her ankle.

Chase darted a glance at the river, which was rising rapidly. "We must get out of here," he said.

Hearing the urgency in his voice, she looked at the river, feeling a shiver of alarm at what she saw.

Usually slow-moving and placid, it was now a surging mass of dark water.

As gently as he could, Chase picked her up and started running toward their shelter, which was located a safe distance from the river.

Beth was shivering with cold and pain by the time they reached the lean-to. Gently, he put her down on the stump she used for a chair.

"Can you get undressed?" he asked.

"Y—yes."

With a nod, he struck a match and lit the fire. "I will wait outside."

"But it's raining."

"I am already wet," he said, grinning. "Call me if you need help."

The thought of him helping her caused another kind of shiver to tiptoe down her spine.

Some minutes later, she knew she needed help. The laces on her shoes were wet and refused to give way to her shaking hands. Not only that, but her left foot was so swollen, she didn't think she'd ever get the shoe off anyway.

"Chase? I need you."

Those four simple words caused an odd stirring in his heart. She needed him.

Ducking into the shelter, he saw she was sitting as before. She had unfastened her dress, and she held the bodice together with one hand.

"I can't get my shoes off," she said.

With a nod, he knelt before her and lifted her uninjured foot. After a few minutes, he managed to untie the knot. Slipping the shoe from her foot, he tossed it aside, then placed her injured foot in his lap. The shoe looked oddly misshapen, and he knew her foot was badly swollen.

"I will have to cut the shoe from your foot," he said, drawing his knife.

She nodded. "Okay."

Knowing it would cause her pain, he worked as quickly and carefully as he could, cutting away the sturdy leather, then peeling off the long cotton stocking. He grinned as he wondered what she would say if she knew he carried one of her stockings in his pocket.

Her brow was damp with perspiration by the time he finished. Her foot was badly bruised and swollen. She flinched when he examined it, and he flinched as well, her pain becoming his.

"I do not think it is broken," he said.

"It hurts."

"I know. We need to wrap it."

"You can tear one of the ruffles from my spare petticoat."

"No need to ruin your clothes," he said, and withdrew the stocking from his pocket.

"Where did you get that?" she asked, her eyes widening in surprise. "From the river that day," she said, answering her own question. "You took it."

Chase nodded as he wrapped the stocking around her ankle. The cotton was cool and damp. It would help to keep the swelling down.

"I went back to look for you the next day," Beth said

"You did?"

Beth nodded. "Uh-huh. I pretended I was looking for my stocking, but I was really looking for you." She ran her hand through his hair. "I'm glad I found you again."

"I, too, am glad." He tied off the stocking, nodded with satisfaction. "I will help you get into bed, and then I will bring you something for the pain."

"Where are you going to find a doctor out here?"

"My people lived here for many years," he reminded her. "Our doctors looked to the land for their medicine."

It made sense, she thought. She tried to keep thinking about that as he helped her out of her clothes. *All* of her clothes. She stood on one foot, her hands braced on his shoulders, her cheeks burning with embarrassment, as he helped her into her nightgown, then carried her to bed, tucking her in as if she were a child.

"I will not be gone long," he said, placing the pistol within reach.

"Hurry."

The shelter seemed larger without him, the night darker, the storm more fierce. She placed her hand on the pistol, thinking it would give her courage, but it only made her more afraid.

Closing her eyes, she listened to the wind and rain beat upon the thatched roof.

She was almost asleep when she heard a horse whinny. Startled, she reached for the gun, but it was only Chase.

She watched him through heavy-lidded eyes as he fussed around the fire. A short time later, he sat beside her and helped her to sit up.

"Here," he said, handing her a cup. "Drink this."

"What is it?"

"Willowbark tea."

She drank it all, willing to try anything if it would ease the throbbing pain in her ankle.

When she was finished, Chase put the cup aside and tucked her into bed. "Sleep now."

She nodded, suddenly drowsy. "You should get out of those wet clothes before you catch a chill."

"Do not worry about me."

He started to rise when she caught his hand. "Aren't you going to kiss me good night?"

He hesitated for the space of a heartbeat, and then he kissed her gently.

"Good night, Beth," he murmured, but she was already asleep.

Beth sat outside, her injured foot propped up on one of the saddles as she watched Chase butcher a deer. Ordinarily, such a sight would have made her stomach queasy, but in this case, it was the man who held her attention. She had never realized a woman could be so mesmerized by the sight of a man's bare back, yet she thought she would be content to sit there for hours, just watching the play of muscles in his back and shoulders, the way his hair caught the sun's light. Tall and lean, he moved with an easy grace that was beautiful to see.

She resented the bandage wrapped around his middle because it hid part of his flesh from her sight. She glanced at the jagged scar on his right shoulder and wondered what kind of wound had left it. He would have another scar when the wound in his side healed. Such a shame, she thought, to mar such a beautiful body.

Her gaze slid down his arms, remembering how they had held her. He turned, and she stared at his profile, the finely shaped nose and strong jaw, the high cheekbones. She wished she had the ability to paint so she could capture his image on canvas, and even as the thought crossed her mind, she doubted anyone would be able to do him justice, to capture the wild spirit that dwelled within him, the vibrant masculinity.

Chase stood up, stretching his arms and legs. His side ached, yet there was no help for it. He had to hunt if they were to eat. An Indian woman would have been able to butcher the carcass, but Beth knew nothing of surviving in the wilderness. Perhaps one day he would teach her. Until then, they would have enough fresh meat to last a while, as well as plenty of dried venison.

He looked over at the deerskin pegged on the ground. Such work was best left to the women, he mused, and then shrugged. He didn't mind the work. Skinning a deer and tanning the hide were arduous tasks, ones that might ruin the softness of her hands.

He slid a glance in her direction, her beauty striking him anew. He would not have her any different, he thought. He was glad her hands were not rough and calloused from hard work, that her skin was smooth and clear.

His gaze lifted to hers, met, and held. Before he was aware of what he was doing, he was walking toward her, his heart pounding faster with each step.

Beth looked up, shading her eyes against the sun. With the sun shining behind him, he looked like a statue carved in bronze.

"Here," she said, reaching for the canteen at her side. "You must be thirsty."

With a nod, he took the canteen from her hand

and took a long drink. "Thank you."

"We should have enough meat to last a long time," Beth said, wondering at the sudden nervousness she felt.

Chase nodded. "How is your foot?"

"Still sore, but not as bad as it was yesterday."

He nodded again. "What are you reading?"

"*Wuthering Heights.* Would you like to read it when I'm done?"

A shadow passed over his face, and then he lifted his chin. "I cannot read."

"You can't?"

"Nor write."

"Did no one ever try to teach you?"

"At the reservation, but I refused to learn."

"Why?"

"I wanted nothing to do with the white man."

"You should learn to read and to write, Chase. I could teach you, if you like."

He considered it a moment, then nodded. "I would like that."

"Good." She smiled up at him, her pleasure warming him. "What was it like, on the reservation? Why didn't you like it there?"

"How would you like it if you were taken far from your home and made to live in a way that was not your own?"

Beth glanced around the valley, at the raw, untamed beauty, and then at the man standing in front of her. "I like it fine."

"But you were not brought here by force," Chase replied bitterly. "No one forced you to leave your home, or tried to make you learn a new language and a new way of life. Your children have not been taken from you and sent away to school."

"I know. I'm sorry for making light of it. Forgive me."

"There is nothing to forgive."

"It must have been awful for you," Beth said, wanting to understand and knowing she never would.

"Yes," he said. "Awful. Awful to watch our old ones give up hope, to watch our young men grow old before their time, to hear our women weep when their young ones were taken away. At the Indian school, the children were forbidden to practice their religion, or to speak their own language. The teachers cut off their hair and made them wear the clothing of the whites. Our children sickened and died."

Beth looked away, ashamed of what her people had done to his. No wonder he was bitter.

"My people yearn for home." He made a broad gesture that encompassed the valley and the high purple cliffs. "They are part of the land. Their blood has nourished the earth. Their bones are buried here, in the land of their ancestors."

"Maybe some day they'll be allowed to come back."

"Do you think so?"

"No. I'm sorry, Chase, I wish . . ." What did she wish? That he was still living wild and free with the Apache? If that were true, she might never have met him, and even though she'd known him only a short time, she couldn't imagine her life without him.

"What do you wish, Beth?"

"I was going to say I wished that the Indians had

never been sent to the reservation, but it would be a lie because then I might never have met you. I know how selfish that sounds, but I just can't help it," she finished in a rush, then stared up at him, daring him to chastise her for thinking more of her own happiness than the good of his people.

The hard expression faded from his face as he knelt beside her. "I am glad I met you, too," he said, smiling.

"You don't think I'm terrible?"

"I think you are beautiful."

"So are you."

"Foolish woman. Men cannot be beautiful," he scoffed, but she could tell he was pleased, and flattered, by her words.

"You are," she insisted.

He knelt there for stretched seconds, trapped in the warmth of her gaze, and then, unable to deny the longings of his own heart, he bent forward and brushed his lips across hers.

He had no idea how long they kissed. It might have been an hour or a moment, but when they drew apart, he knew something had forever changed between them.

Chase woke with a sense of foreboding. Rising, he pulled on his moccasins and padded noiselessly from the shelter.

Outside, the horses were stirring restlessly. He watched them a moment, noticing that they were looking east, toward the entrance of the rancheria.

Hurrying back into the lean-to, he grabbed his shirt and rifle.

"What's wrong?"

"Nothing, perhaps. Go back to sleep."

"Something is wrong. Tell me."

"I do not know. Something has spooked the horses."

Beth sat up, his alarm evident to her. Moving carefully, she stood up, the pistol clutched in one hand. "I'm going with you."

"No."

"Chase . . ."

"You will wait here. Please, Beth."

"All right."

She followed him to the door, watched him throw a saddle on the roan. And then she heard it, the distant sound of hoofbeats.

In the clear morning air, she could see riders coming toward them. The intruders had not yet spotted the lean-to, which was built near a stand of timber and hard to distinguish from the forest itself.

"White men," Chase muttered.

Beth stared hard at the men riding toward them. Unless she was mistaken, Joby Berland was riding at the front.

"Chase, get out of here!"

"I will not leave you."

"They won't hurt me!" Beth cried. "Please, go!"

Dismounting, he ran toward her. "I will not go."

"You must! Please, go. Hurry. I don't see Dusty with them."

"I will find you," he promised.

"Go!" The men were close now. They'd seen the horses. Soon they'd see the lean-to as well.

Chase grabbed her and kissed her hard, then swung aboard the roan.

"There he goes!"

She heard Berland's cry and Chase disappeared into the forest.

Praying that Chase would escape, she limped away from the lean-to and hobbled into the path of the oncoming horses.

Several of the men swore as they reined their horses to a dirt-scattering halt. Three of the men, Berland among them, detoured around her and kept going.

"Miss Johnson," Sean Harvey said, "what the hell . . . heck . . . are you doing here?"

A dozen answers crossed Beth's mind. Then, with a sob, she collapsed on the ground. "Help me," she begged, and burying her face in her hands, she began to cry.

She was immediately surrounded by men, all offering her their kerchiefs as they demanded to know if "that dirty redskin had laid a hand on her."

"No," she said vehemently, "no, he didn't hurt me."

She was sitting up, a blanket wrapped around her shoulders, when one of the men who had gone after Chase came back.

"We lost him," Fred Walker said, dismounting.

"Lost him!" Sean Harvey hollered.

Walker nodded morosely. "He jumped off his horse and lit out on foot. But don't worry, we'll get him. Joby's got him trapped in a box canyon. He wants the rest of you to come up and help flush the redskin into the open."

Harvey looked thoughtful for a moment, then nodded. "All right. I'll stay here with Miss Johnson. The rest of you go on."

Walker grinned as he swung into the saddle. "Pick out a tree with a sturdy branch," he said. "We won't be gone long."

Beth felt suddenly sick as she realized the men meant to hang Chase as soon as they caught him. She stood up, clutching the blanket in hands that trembled. "Mr. Harvey, where's Dusty?"

"He . . . uh, that is . . ."

"What?" Beth asked, grabbing Harvey by the arm. "What happened to him? Why isn't he here?"

"There was a little misunderstanding at the jail, and he was . . . uh, that is, he got shot."

"Shot! Is he dead?"

"I can't say. He was alive last I saw him."

"You're nothing but a lynch mob!" Beth exclaimed. "You have no authority, no right, to hang anyone."

"That damn redskin killed my foreman," Sean Harvey replied, his voice tinged with anger. "Ned Greenway was a decent man, and that Injun gunned him down. We don't need no more right than that."

"You'll be no better than a murderer yourself if you take the law into your own hands."

"Redskin's already been sentenced to hang," Sean retorted. "We're just carrying out the court's order."

There was no point in arguing with the man, she thought bleakly. If they caught Chase, they would hang him.

Minutes seemed to pass like hours as they waited for the others to return. Beth felt her nerves grow taut as an hour slipped by, and then another. She told herself that as long as the men were still out there, it meant that they hadn't found Chase.

It was near dusk when the posse returned.

"What happened?" Harvey asked.

"He got away," Joby said sullenly.

"What?" Harvey bellowed. "How?"

"Near as I can figure, he found a way over the cliffs."

"That's impossible!"

Joby shrugged. "That's what I thought. But we combed every inch of that canyon, and he ain't there."

"Where's Murphy?"

"His horse went lame. He's riding double with your brother. They'll be along."

"Why didn't he ride the Injun's horse?"

"Alton's still trying to catch it. Horse is faster than a jackrabbit."

Sean Harvey grunted. "We'll bed down here for the night," he decided, "and head out at first light. Murphy can ride the packhorse. If the Injun's on foot, he won't get far."

"Like hell," Walker chimed in. "Apaches have been known to cover over fifty miles in a day. You can be sure this one won't stop until he's out of the territory."

"Fifty miles on foot," Joby said skeptically. "You're joshin'."

"I'm dead serious. My pa rode with Crook. He said the 'Paches could cover more ground in a single day than mounted cavalry."

There was some grumbling as the men took care of their horses, then bedded down for the night.

Later, lying in her bedroll inside the shelter, Beth uttered a silent prayer of thanks that Chase had gotten away. It wouldn't be easy, going back home, having to face her parents, but none of that seemed important now. Chase had gotten away, and that was all that mattered.

Chapter Fifteen

Chase huddled, shivering, near the entrance to Rainbow Canyon. His hands and chest were scraped raw from his descent down the backside of the box canyon. It had taken two hours to make his way down the steep rocky slope, and another hour to reach the entrance to the rancheria.

The cold air stung the numerous cuts on his hands and chest; muscles he had not realized he had ached from the arduous climb and descent.

Chin tucked against his chest, he closed his eyes. There was an hour until dawn.

Beth felt a wave of regret as she rode out of the canyon. She had been happy there with Chase. Like Adam and Eve, they had been the only two people in the world, living off the land. She had needed no one else, only Chase.

And now he was gone, and she knew she'd never see him again.

She uttered a silent prayer that he had escaped unharmed.

The posse rode in sullen silence. Joby Berland had wanted to ride into the desert that stretched away behind Rainbow Canyon to search for Chase, claiming the Indian would be easy to track down now that he was on foot, but the rest of the men had disagreed. Sean Harvey had declared that, without food and water and on foot, "the dirty redskin" would die out there. Besides, his brother had added, they'd been away from their ranch too long already. Posters had been issued for the Indian's arrest, so even if he somehow managed to survive the desert, he'd be caught sooner or later. And that seemed to be the general consensus of the men. Whatever anger had driven them to ride out after Chase had apparently been played out, and now all they wanted to do was go back home.

Home. Beth looked in her heart and knew the big white house in Twin Rivers would never be home again. Chase had become her home, her family.

She blinked back her tears, not wanting the men to see her weeping. They all thought she had been kidnapped, and she let them believe so. Had Chase been there, she would have been proud to acknowledge him as the man she loved, but practicality had reared its head. It would be easier to face the town and her parents if everyone thought she'd been forced to go with Chase.

At dusk, the men made camp alongside a shallow stream. Feeling the need for privacy among so many men, Beth spread her bedroll a good distance from the others.

Huddled beside the fire, she listened to the men

talk about crops and cows, about the possibility of a train coming to town, about the upcoming church social. After a time, her thoughts turned inward, and she wondered if Dusty had survived his wounds. And then, no longer able to keep him at bay, she let herself think of Chase, of the kisses they had shared, the sound of his voice, the yearning she had seen in his eyes. She wished now that he hadn't been so honorable, that he had made love to her when they had the chance. She wished she'd been brave enough, bold enough, to seduce him, even though such a terrible sin would have dammed her soul for eternity. . . .

Gradually, she realized that the men were bedding down for the night.

With a murmured "good night," she sought her own blankets. Only then did she let the tears fall.

She woke with a start, wondering what had jolted her from a sound sleep. And then she felt it again, a soft tap as something hit her shoulder.

Sitting up, she gazed into the darkness.

"Beth."

Was she hearing things? Eyes narrowed, she peered into the trees to her left.

"Beth."

Chase! Heart pounding with excitement, she stood up, stifling a groan as she put her weight on her injured ankle. Glancing around, she saw that all the men were sleeping. Grabbing a blanket, she wrapped it around her shoulders and limped toward the trees. Should anyone wake up and see her leaving camp, they would think she was answering a call of nature.

It was all she could do to keep from running to him. And then she was there, in his arms, and he was holding her close, his hands running up and down her back.

"Are you all right?" he whispered.

"Fine. And you?"

He hesitated only a moment. "I am all right. I have two horses waiting. Do you wish to go with me?"

"Do you have to ask?"

He blew out a deep breath that seemed tinged with regret. "I was going to take my horse and go, but I could not leave without seeing you again. I have no right to ask you to go with me . . ."

She'd heard it all before, and she was having none of it. With a huff of irritation, she kissed him soundly on the mouth. "Does that answer your question, you silly man?"

She couldn't see his face in the darkness, but she had a feeling he was staring at her, his mouth open in astonishment.

"Where are the horses?"

"Back here." Taking her hand, he led her deeper into the trees.

A short time later, they reached the horses. He had taken Dusty's roan and her own mare and had saddled both horses. Canteens hung from the pommels; their saddlebags, which one of the men had stuffed with their supplies from the lean-to, were tied behind the cantles.

Beth slanted a grin in his direction. "Pretty sure I'd come with you, weren't you?"

"I hoped you would," he admitted, "even though I think it is a mistake."

He lifted her into the saddle, his hands lingering at her waist before he turned away and mounted his own horse.

Beth felt a shiver of excitement rise within her as she urged her horse after his. She might never know another moment's peace, she thought, but she'd found more excitement with this man than she had ever dreamed of.

They rode until well after sunup, then took shelter in the lee of a rocky overhang. Exhausted, Beth sank down on the ground and was instantly asleep.

When she woke, it was almost dusk. For a moment, she stared up at the gray rock over her head and wondered where she was, and then it all came back to her; Chase's appearance at the posse's camp, the long ride through the night.

Turning her head, she saw Chase lying beside her, his eyes closed. The blanket had fallen away and for the first time, she saw the numerous bloody scrapes and abrasions on his arms and chest. There was a jagged gash on his right cheek, another on his left arm, and still another across his chest.

She was sitting there, still staring down at him, when his eyelids fluttered open and he smiled at her. And in the warmth of that smile, she forgot everything else.

It wasn't until he reached for her, groaning softly as he did so, that she came back to herself.

"You're hurt," she said accusingly.

Sitting up, Chase considered the bloody cuts that adorned his chest and arms. None was serious, but the cut across his chest was deep and painful.

"The canyon has sharp rocks," he remarked.

"Let me see your hands."

With a sigh, he held out his hands, palms up.

"Oh, Chase," she murmured. "They must hurt terribly."

He didn't deny it, only shrugged. He would have sacrificed another layer of skin to gain his freedom.

He glanced at her ankle, still tightly bound. "Your foot," he said, "how is it?"

"A lot better than your hands."

He didn't object as she soaked a strip of her petticoat in water and began to wash the blood from his chest. The cold water stung the cuts, but he thought it a small price to pay to have her near, to see the concern in her eyes, to hear the worry in her voice as she fretted over the possibility of infection.

There was a multitude of cuts on his legs, as well. Even though none of his injuries was life-threatening, she knew he'd lost a bit of blood, knew he'd followed her thirty miles on foot.

The thought made her heart ache with tenderness.

When she had the blood washed away, she wrapped his hands in layers of cloth, then sat back, watching him as he regarded his bandaged hands.

"I cannot do much with my hands like this."

"What do you want to do?"

"We need wood, food, fresh meat."

"Didn't you look inside the saddlebags when you saddled the horses? There should be enough food in there to last until your hands are better," she said. "I don't mind eating jerky for a couple of days."

But he wasn't thinking of food. With his hands bandaged, he couldn't hold the rifle.

Leaning back against the rock, Chase watched

Beth rummage through the saddlebags. It had been a mistake to go after her, but the thought of leaving her behind, of never seeing her again, had overcome his good sense.

"There's plenty of dried meat and canned goods," Beth called. "Oh, and a side of bacon and the makings for biscuits. That should hold us for a couple of days." She smiled at him over her shoulder. "You sit back and rest, and I'll fix something to eat."

Chase grunted softly. They'd have to be on their way soon, but for now, he was content to sit back and watch her.

Beth brushed a lock of hair from her forehead, glad that dusk was approaching. Her back and legs ached, and she had a dreadful notion that, when it came time to dismount, she'd find her backside had become part of the saddle. They'd been riding all day and most of the night before.

She wished fleetingly that they could go back to Rainbow Canyon. It had been so pretty there, so peaceful, but Chase had feared that Rainbow Canyon was the first place the posse would look.

That night, they made camp in a cut-bank arroyo. She insisted Chase sit down and rest while she prepared dinner.

"I am not helpless," he muttered irritably.

Beth grinned. Her father was that way, too, always refusing to admit he might need help. "Why don't you see if you can find some wood, then?"

"Woman's work," he complained.

"Well, that's all that needs doing at the moment, unless you want to cook."

He scowled at her, then turned around, limping

slightly as he walked away from her.

We're a fine pair, Beth mused, watching him. *Only two good legs between us.*

She had their bedrolls spread out and a hole dug for the fire by the time Chase got back. Dumping an armful of wood on the ground, he squatted on his heels and busied himself with building a fire.

"I never cared much for jerky before," Beth remarked, handing him a chunk of dried venison, "but it's not bad. Of course, I'd rather have a steak."

Chase grinned wryly, thinking of the many times when he had eaten raw meat and been glad to have it, times when there had been nothing at all to eat, when the children cried because their stomachs hurt, when the old ones had given what little food they had to the young men so they would have the strength to fight. And what had it gotten them? The very young and the very old had died and the rest of the people had been sent from their homeland.

"Chase?"

He looked up, his expression bleak.

"I found some salve in my saddlebags. Would you like me to . . . I mean, it might soothe your cuts."

He looked at her as if seeing her for the first time. What was this rich young white woman doing out here, with him?

"Chase? Is something wrong?"

He shook his head, knowing there was no way to explain what he was feeling, no way to make her understand that, as sincere as she seemed to be, he was afraid it wouldn't last, that when the novelty of living out-of-doors with him wore off, she'd go back to her comfortable home where she belonged. The worst of it was, he would not blame her for going.

She sat beside him and carefully unwrapped his hands. His palms still looked raw and red. Gently, she rubbed the ointment over the lacerations. It gave her a sense of satisfaction to know she was helping him, soothing him. She wished she had the ability to ease the pain in his eyes, as well.

Dipping her fingers in the pot of salve again, she began to massage it into the cuts on his arms. His skin was smooth and warm beneath her fingertips.

He gasped as she spread the ointment over his chest.

"Am I hurting you?"

"Not in the way you think."

"I don't understand."

He captured her hand in his and pressed it against his chest. "Do you know what your touch does to me?"

She shook her head. She could feel the rapid beat of his heart beneath her hand, could see the spark of desire in his eyes.

"Beth . . ." Releasing her hand, he took a deep breath. "I think you should go to bed now."

She started to protest and then, seeing the desire in his eyes, she murmured, "Good night, Chase," and crawled under the covers.

They traveled for three days until they arrived at a meadow set between two mountains. At her curious glance, Chase explained that it had once been a hideout for the Apaches.

There was graze for the horses, a shallow stream, a stand of timber.

"How long will we stay here?" Beth asked, looking around.

"A few days."

"And then what?"

"I do not know."

"Is there a town around here?"

Chase nodded. "Why?"

"I think we should send a letter to Mr. Fallon and find out if they've found the man who killed Greenway."

"No."

"But if they've found him, you won't have to hide anymore."

"And if they have not, they will know where to find me."

"I'm sure he won't tell anyone where we are."

"I am not willing to take that chance."

"All right." She would drop it for now, she thought. But somehow, she'd make him see that she was right. They couldn't spend their whole life together hiding from the world.

Later that afternoon, they sat side by side under a tree. The weather was cool and clear, the meadow silent save for the song of a bird.

Beth stared into the distance, acutely aware of the man sitting beside her. She had never known a man like him—virile, tender, self-confident. She knew he would take care of her no matter what, that he would protect and defend her with his very life. He made her feel safe, cherished, feminine.

She was aware of his gaze resting on her face, felt the attraction between them grow until it vibrated like a living thing. She felt herself yearning toward him, needing his touch, wanting to touch him in return.

She turned to meet his gaze. "Chase?"

"I know. I feel it, too."

"I love you."

He wanted to believe her, needed to believe her. Crushing her close, he slanted his mouth over hers, drinking in the sweetness of her lips. She was honey and fire in his arms, her mouth opening to his, her tongue teaching him an intimacy he had never known.

His hands slid up and down her spine, molding her body to his, her softness fitting snugly against him, filling years of emptiness with her nearness.

He murmured her name, his breath mingling with hers as they kissed and kissed again. She pressed closer, and he could feel her trembling, feel the need growing within her, matching the need growing within himself.

Time and place lost all meaning, until there was nothing in all the world but the two of them. He lost himself in the scent of her, the touch of her, the taste of her. She was like the very air he breathed, necessary to his survival. Years and years of feeling lost and alone melted away and she became all things—father, mother, sister, friend. He did not understand it, but he accepted it.

"Tell me," he whispered. "Tell me again."

She didn't have to ask what he meant. "I love you," she said, pouring her whole heart and soul into each word. "I love you."

Feeling suddenly weak, he drew her down beside him, one arm curled around her waist while his hand caressed her face. "How can you?" he asked, lost in the wonder of her eyes. "How?"

"I don't know. I never believed in love at first

sight, but I believe it now."

"Is that what this is?" Chase asked. He thought of Clarai. He had thought he loved her, but what he had felt for her paled to nothingness beside the depth of emotion he felt for Beth. The thought that he cared more for this white woman than he had ever cared for Clarai filled him with guilt, yet he couldn't deny what he felt any more than he could explain it.

Gently, he cupped her face in his hands. "What do you want of me, Beth?"

"Everything!"

"Tell me."

"I want you to love me the way I love you. I want to be able to tell you my deepest fears, my innermost thoughts. I want you to share my laughter and my tears. I want you to be the father of my children and grow old beside me."

"You speak of marriage."

Beth nodded. "Yes."

"Have you thought this through? Your parents will never accept me."

"I don't care."

"I do not want you to be hurt."

"Do you love me?"

"Yes."

She smiled, and it was like the sun bursting forth from a cloud, bright, beautiful.

"Will love be enough for you when your parents turn their backs on you? When people shun you because of me? I do not want your love to turn to hate, Beth. I do not want to look at you a year from now and see regret in your eyes."

"You won't," she whispered. Leaning toward him,

she brushed his lips with hers.

"Then I will be your husband from this day on."

"I wish you could, but there's no one to marry us."

"Marriage takes place here," Chase said, placing one finger over her heart. "We need no one to speak for us."

"No witnesses?"

"The Great Spirit will be our witness. I ask you again, are you certain this is what you want?"

She took his hand in hers and pressed it to her heart. "Yes."

"Then I pledge you my love this day," Chase said solemnly. "I will protect you and provide for you and love no one but you until the day I die."

Beth blinked up at him, her heart swelling with tenderness and love for the sincerity of his words, for the devotion shining in the depths of his eyes.

"And I pledge you my love in return," she said, her voice soft yet strong. "I will cherish you and comfort you and stand beside you in sickness and in health, and I will love you, and only you, all the days of my life."

"From this day, you will be my woman," Chase said.

"And you will be my husband."

"I will want no other."

"Nor I."

"It is done then," he said, his voice exultant.

Beth gazed into his eyes, her heart pounding with joy. The silence around them seemed like a benediction. Her eyelids fluttered down as Chase kissed her, deeply, reverently.

Beth wrapped her arms around him. *My husband,* she thought, and knew she would not have felt any more married if she had spoken her vows in church.

She felt her cheeks grow warm as Chase drew back and looked at her. Married. The full implication hit her as his gaze met hers. Married. She suddenly remembered her mother telling her what a husband expected of a wife: *Sharing the marriage bed is something no real lady enjoys, but you must endure if for the sake of children. In time, you will learn to close your eyes and think of other things.*

She licked her lips nervously. Would he expect to claim his husbandly rights now, in the full light of day?

"Have you changed your mind already?" Chase asked.

"No. No, it's just . . . I mean, I've never . . ."

"I will not touch you if you do not wish it," Chase said. "I may be Apache, but I am not a savage." Rising, he offered her his hand.

She was doing this all wrong, Beth thought desperately. She took his hand, let him pull her to her feet. "Chase . . ."

"I will come to you when you are ready." Gently, he brushed his knuckles over her cheek. "Do not make me wait too long."

"I don't want to wait," Beth said tremulously. "I love you. It's just that . . ." She looked away, embarrassed.

"You said you wanted to tell me your deepest fears," Chase reminded her. "I am listening."

"My mother told me it was painful, the joining between a man and a woman. She said it was something I would have to endure."

"She did not like lying with her husband?"

"I don't think so. They don't even sleep in the same room anymore."

"We will never sleep apart, Beth. And I promise I will never hurt you."

There was such love in his eyes, she knew she had no cause to doubt him. "Do you want to . . . to . . ." Mercy, but it was hard to say some things out loud.

"I want you," he said, and taking her hand, he pressed it to his chest. "Feel how my heart beats with love for you." He drew her up against him, pressing her length to his. "Do you doubt how much I want you?"

Beth shook her head and gasped with delight as he swung her into his arms. "Where are we going?"

"I know a place," he said.

"I can walk, you know."

"Not today."

With a sigh, she wrapped her arms around his neck. She had wanted an adventure, she mused happily, and she had found one.

He carried her up a shallow draw, across a narrow stream, his long legs eating up the distance. Content, she watched the scenery pass by until he came to a small blue pool surrounded by wildflowers. It was like a bridal bower, she thought, lush and green.

With his arms still wrapped around her, he lowered her feet to the ground, and then he kissed her. It was a kiss like no other he had given her, possessive, gently demanding, filled with promises unspoken and a hunger that could wait no longer.

His hands were trembling as he undressed first her and then himself.

"You are so beautiful, Beth. More beautiful than

any flower." Sitting down, he took her hand and drew her down beside him. "Do not be afraid, Beth. I will not hurt you."

She gazed into the dark depths of his eyes. "Have you done this before?"

"No."

"Me, either."

He cupped her face in his hands, his thumbs lightly stroking her cheeks. "We will find our way together."

His hands slid over her shoulders, down her arms, and everywhere he touched, her skin tingled with excitement.

"Touch me, Beth."

Eagerly, she brushed her hands over his chest, delighting in the sun-warmed bronze of his skin, in the taut muscles that bunched and relaxed beneath her hand. Leaning forward, she kissed the half-healed cuts on his arms and chest, reveling in his gasp of pleasure.

He pulled her close, drawing her down on the grass beside him, his body pressed to hers, as they continued to explore each other. She discovered he was ticklish; he discovered the soft sensitive place behind her knee. His tongue was warm as it laved her breasts, awakening sensations she had never known, until she yearned toward him, silently asking for that which she didn't fully understand.

And then he was rising over her, blocking everything from her view but his face, the fire that smoldered in his eyes. She cried his name as his body meshed with hers. She had not known what to expect, had never dreamed that the act her mother had said must be endured for the sake of bearing children could entail such ecstacy, and she knew, in that moment, that she would never be the same again, knew that, even as she had given him her maidenhead, she had also given him her heart and soul.

Chase released a long shuddering sigh as his body convulsed one last time. Being sheathed within her warmth was more wonderful than he had ever imagined. For a moment, he rested his head on her shoulder, shaken to the very depths of his being by their joining. All his life, he had heard men brag of their conquests, but none had ever mentioned the sheer wonder of possessing a woman, of becoming a part of her, so that it wasn't merely a joining of flesh, pleasurable as that had been. No, it had been more than that, as if, in their coming together, he had become her, and she had become him, a part of everything that he was.

Had his mother felt this same overwhelming sense of love for Ryder? If so, he could not fault her for risking everything to stay with him. He knew he would make any sacrifice to be with Beth, to fall asleep in her arms and awaken there in the morning.

When his breathing returned to normal, Chase raised himself up on his arms, almost afraid to meet her eyes. Had he hurt her? Was she disappointed in him? He could not bear to think he had failed her, this woman who had vanquished the hatred from his heart.

One look at her face, and all his doubts fled. Bathed in sunlight, she smiled up at him, her face radiant, and he knew he had not imagined the almost mystical bond that had flowed between them. She had felt it, too.

"I love you," she whispered, caressing his cheek.

"And I love you."

Knowing he must be heavy, he started to withdraw, but she wrapped her arms around him, holding him in place. "Don't go."

Content to be cradled in her arms, he brushed her lips with his, felt his body stir to life again as her tongue met his. That quickly, he wanted her again.

It was a day never to be forgotten. They made love again, then swam in the pool, and made love yet again in the water's cool embrace.

Later, lying in Beth's arms, with the stars shining down on them like a benediction, Chase the Wind knew he had come home at last.

Chapter Sixteen

Jenny opened the door to her son's room and peeked in. "Are you awake?"

At Dusty's nod, she stepped inside and closed the door after her. "Rebecca's here again. Shall I send her in?"

"What's she brought this time?"

"Apple pie."

"I'll soon be as fat as Old Man Cheevers," Dusty grumbled.

"Hardly, but you could stand to put on a few pounds." Jenny regarded her son for a moment. "Dr. Forbes said you could get up tomorrow."

"About time," Dusty muttered, setting aside the book he had been holding, but not reading.

"I'll send Rebecca in. Try to look glad to see her, won't you?"

"I don't know why she keeps coming here."

"Don't you?"

Feeling a flush climb into his cheeks, Dusty lowered his head. Rebecca had come out to the ranch every day since he'd been shot. His mother had told him Rebecca had sat with him while he was unconscious. He didn't know how he felt about that. Sometimes it pleased him to think she cared so much, and sometimes it annoyed him. Mostly though, it flattered his male ego to know there was at least one girl who cared about him, even if it was the wrong girl.

"I could tell her you're asleep," Jenny suggested, "if you'd rather be alone."

"I've had a bellyful of alone." He hadn't meant to speak the words aloud, but they slipped out, awash with bitterness.

"Maybe you shouldn't judge Beth too harshly until you hear her side of the story."

"What's there to hear? She drugged me and turned him loose." He slammed his fist on the table beside the bed. "I just wish I knew when they met."

Dusty looked up at his mother, his eyes dark with torment. "Do you think he kidnapped her?" he asked, then shook his head. "I know, stupid question. He was locked up."

"Dusty, don't think about it. You'll just drive yourself crazy."

"I know."

"Well," Jenny said, "what shall I do about Rebecca?"

"Might as well send her in, seeing as how she's here." He tried to make it sound as if her being there didn't matter one way or the other, but just the thought of Rebecca made him smile.

She entered the room a few moments later, looking exceptionally pretty in a gown of gold and green striped taffeta.

"Hello, Dusty," she said, returning his smile. "How are you feeling today?"

"Much better, thank you."

"You're looking better. Your mother told me you can get up tomorrow."

Dusty nodded.

Moving with an innate grace, Rebecca rounded the footboard and sat down in the chair beside the bed. "What are you reading?" she asked, gesturing at the book he'd tossed aside.

"*Twenty Thousand Leagues Under the Sea* by Jules Verne. Do you know it?"

"I've read it. Twice."

"Really?" He found it fascinating that she had read the book. Few of the women he knew read anything other than *Vogue* or *Good Housekeeping.* "Have you also read Mr. Verne's *Journey to the Center of the Earth?*"

"Oh, yes," Rebecca said, her eyes sparkling. "I thought it most exciting, though I'm sure I would never have had the courage to go exploring as his characters did."

"No? Think of it, a chance to go where no one has ever gone before, to see things no one else has ever seen."

Rebecca shook her head. "I'm afraid I lack the courage. I wouldn't have made a very good pioneer, either. I'm afraid if it had been up to me, the Indians would still own all the land west of the Missouri."

"I admire your honesty," he said, laughing. "But

it's been my experience that women have far more courage than men."

"Really?"

Dusty nodded, thinking of his mother. She had endured much in her life, had defied Kayitah to save his father's life. She had married a man who was a half-breed and a gunfighter.

"Would you like me to read to you a while?" Rebecca asked.

"Sure, if you want to."

He handed her the book, then sat back against the pillows while she read to him. Engrossed in the story, she made the characters come alive, her voice changing tone and inflection for each character.

Dusty applauded when she stopped at the end of the chapter. "You should have been on the stage, Miss Winterburn."

"Me? On the stage?" A bright pink blush colored her cheeks. "No."

"Why not?"

She shook her head. "I couldn't. Crowds make me nervous."

"I guess the stage's loss is my gain."

Her gaze flew to his. Only then did he realize how possessive those words sounded.

Suddenly flustered, she stood up, one hand worrying the wide velvet sash on her gown. "I should be going."

"Do you have to?" he asked, surprised to find that he wanted her to stay a little longer.

"Well . . ."

"Please? Stay for dinner."

"Oh, I wouldn't think of imposing on your mother."

"Believe me, she won't mind."

"Well, if you're sure . . ."

"Good. We can probably get in another chapter or two before dinner."

"Well," Jenny said, wiping her hands on a dish towel, "what do you make of that?"

"Of what?"

"Dusty inviting Rebecca to stay for dinner."

"I'd say the boy's got good taste," Ryder retorted with a grin.

"Good taste, indeed," Jenny exclaimed, flicking him with a corner of the towel.

"It's obvious she's crazy about him, and just as obvious that he's beginning to see her as more than an irritant."

"An irritant! Ryder, what a thing to say."

"Well, you have to admit he wasn't too crazy about her being here at first."

"True." Jenny wiped anther plate and put it in the cupboard. She had to agree with Ryder—Rebecca suited Dusty far better than Elizabeth ever would. Thinking of Elizabeth brought Chase to mind. It had been almost a month since the jail break. The posse had come back to town, subdued and silent. When questioned, they had said only that they'd found Chase but he'd gotten away and yes, Beth Johnson had been with him, though she, too, had disappeared.

"Jenny?"

"I wonder where they are."

Ryder shook his head. "They could be anywhere by now. If it was me, I'd head for Mexico."

"Mexico! How will we ever get in touch with him?"

"I reckon we'll have to wait for him to get in touch with us."

"I just feel so helpless."

Ryder nodded. It wasn't a good feeling. "Berland's the key," he mused. Rising, he started toward the door.

"Where are you going?"

"To talk to Dusty."

His brow furrowed in thought, Ryder made his way to his son's room and rapped on the door. "Dusty? You still awake?"

"Yeah, come on in."

Ryder picked up the chair beside the bed and turned it around, then straddled the seat, his arms resting over the back. "So, you and Rebecca seem to be hitting it off pretty good."

Dusty shrugged. "She's a nice girl."

Ryder raised one brow in wry amusement. "Nice?"

"All right, I like her, but . . ."

"But she's not Beth."

"I don't want to talk about it."

"That's not why I wanted to see you. Do you remember anything Berland might have said the night they brought Chase in?"

"What do you mean?"

"Anything that made you suspicious?"

"You mean aside from the fact that it was Joby?"

Ryder grinned in acknowledgment.

Dusty thought for a moment, then shook his head. "No. His story seemed pretty straightforward, except that he insisted Chase had a rifle."

"But you never found one?"

"No. And Chase said all he had was a knife, and that he threw it at Crenshaw."

A slow smile spread across Ryder's face. "That might be just the answer we're looking for."

"What do you mean?"

"I'll let you know after I talk to Forbes. In the meantime you should get some sleep. But first, I want you to swear me in as your deputy."

"What?"

"You heard me. You're gonna be laid up for another four or five weeks. The town needs a lawman until you're on your feet again."

Dusty grinned. "Hold up your right hand and repeat after me. . . ."

Ryder left the ranch early the next morning. His first stop was at the sheriff's office, where he picked up a badge. His next stop was Doc Forbes.

Forbes looked up from the book on his desk. "Anything wrong?" he asked, his brow furrowed with concern. "Dusty hasn't had a relapse, has he?"

"No, Dusty's doing fine. I just wanted to ask you a couple of questions."

"Well, come on in and sit down then. Want some coffee?"

"No, thanks, this'll only take a minute."

Forbes stood up and stretched. "I was about to pour myself a cup. Come on in the kitchen."

Ryder followed the doctor through the house, then stood in the kitchen doorway, his shoulder braced against the frame, while Forbes poured himself a cup of coffee.

"You said you had some questions," Forbes said,

adding a spoonful of sugar to his cup. "Fire away."

"Did you ever examine Crenshaw's wound?"

"No." Forbes sat down at the table and indicated Ryder should join him.

Ryder took a seat opposite the doctor. "Funny Martha didn't send for you," he remarked.

"I thought so, but then, lots of people don't cotton to doctors." Forbes shrugged. "Sure you don't want a cup of coffee?"

Ryder shook his head.

"I stopped by Crenshaw's the day after he got shot and offered to take a look at his wound, but he said no. Insisted he was fine. He said Martha had taken care of him." He shrugged again. "Martha's a competent nurse, so I didn't think anything of it. I take her with me on calls now and again. What's this all about?"

"Berland claims Crenshaw was shot, but the Indian denied having a rifle. Said all he had was a knife."

Forbes nodded slowly. "And you were hoping I'd seen Crenshaw's wound."

"Yeah, well, there's more than one way to skin a cat," Ryder said, and then grinned. "See ya later, Doc."

Joby Berland was slopping the hogs when Ryder rode into the yard. Ryder shook his head in disgust as he took in the man's appearance. Berland looked like a bandy rooster with his bright red hair and skinny legs. His hair was limp and greasy, his eyes were a washed-out blue. Sneaky eyes, Ryder thought. Never in all his life had he seen Berland in clean clothes. Today was no exception.

Berland tipped his hat back on his head as Ryder drew rein near the pen. "What brings you out here?" Joby asked, his expression sour.

"Just stopped by to make a friendly call."

"Yeah?" Berland asked skeptically. "How come? You ain't never bothered afore."

"Just in a talkin' mood, I reckon," Ryder replied. Dismounting, he dropped the reins of the black. "You gonna invite me in?"

"Just say yer piece," Berland growled. "I got work to do."

"I want to know about the night Ned Greenway was shot."

"I already told the sheriff everything I know."

Ryder nodded. "So you did, but I'd like to hear it for myself."

"Go to hell, Fallon. You ain't the law."

"I am now," Ryder replied softly. He pulled his vest back so Joby could see the tin star pinned to his shirt, and then he drew his gun.

Berland's expression quickly changed from insolence to fear. Raising his hands, he took a step backward. "Here now, wait a minute!"

"I'm tired of waiting."

"I don't know nothing, I tell ya!"

"We'll see. Let's go inside."

Joby started to protest, but one look into Fallon's eyes quickly changed his mind.

Ryder swore under his breath as he followed Berland into the house. The first thing he noticed was the musty smell, the second was the fact that the pigsty was cleaner.

"Now what?" Berland asked.

Ryder gestured at a spindly legged chair. "Sit down."

"Why?"

"Sit!"

Joby dropped into the chair.

"Put your hands behind your back."

A movement of the gun in Ryder's hands stilled Berland's protests, and he put his arms behind his back.

Grabbing a length of rope that was lying over the back of a ratty-looking sofa, Ryder bound Berland's hands, then holstered his gun.

Rounding the chair, he stood in front of Joby, one hand resting negligently on his gun butt. "What happened that night?"

"We was huntin' coons, me and Rance, when the Injun showed up with the Harveys' stud. He threw down on us and shot Rance, and Rance shot him." Joby shrugged. "That's all there was to it."

"I don't believe you."

"It's the truth."

"The Indian told me he didn't have a rifle."

"Who you gonna believe—me, or some dirty redskin?"

"You seem to forget," Ryder said, every syllable fraught with deadly menace, "that I'm a redskin."

"I . . . uh . . . I didn't mean you."

"Didn't you?" Ryder picked up the butcher knife lying on the kitchen table and ran his thumb over the blade. "Sharp," he mused. He pressed the edge of the blade against Berland's cheek. A fine line of red rose in the wake of the blade.

Joby yelped and jerked his head back. "You cut me!"

"I'll bet I could skin you alive with this."

Berland's face went deathly pale.

"I haven't skinned anybody in years," Ryder remarked. He held the knife up, turning it this way and that. Sunlight glinted on the blade. "I could skin you alive and toss your body to the hogs. Nobody would ever know who'd done it."

"It was Rance!" Joby said, his voice high pitched and shaky.

"Go on."

"Rance wanted that damned stud, not me. It was all his idea. I just went along to keep him company. He shot Greenway and the redsk . . . and the Injun."

"Did the Indian have a rifle?"

"No, just a knife. He threw it at Rance, and Rance shot him."

"And you lied about the rifle because Ned had been shot, right?"

Joby nodded vigorously. "Rance shot him, just like I said. It was his idea to frame the Injun," he said, meeting Ryder's eyes for the first time since they'd known each other. "I swear it."

Ryder nodded. "I'm taking you into town with me. When we get there, I want you to go see Judge Brooks and tell him everything you just told me."

Berland's eyes grew wide. "I can't. . . . Rance will . . ."

"Everything you just told me. Understand?"

Berland nodded sullenly.

"And we'll keep my little visit here today a secret, right?"

"Right."

"After you see the judge, I want you to come to the jail and turn yourself in."

Berland's eyes grew wide as he realized he wasn't going to get away without facing the consequences of what he'd done.

"I can see you're thinking about leaving town," Ryder said, his voice harsh. "If you do, I'll hunt you down and hang you with your own innards. Do we understand each other?"

"I understand," Joby muttered, his gaze resting on the knife in Ryder's hand.

"Good." Walking behind Berland's chair, Ryder cut the man's hands free, then tossed the knife onto the table. "Remember what I said. Not a word about this to anybody."

"I won't forget."

"Good. Let's go."

"I wish I'd been there," Dusty said, wiping tears of laughter from his eyes. "Damn, I'll bet he was ready to puke."

"Close," Ryder said, grinning with the memory. "Right close."

"I never believed his story," Dusty said. "Not for a minute."

"Then Chase can come home," Jenny said exuberantly. Throwing her arms around Ryder, she kissed him soundly. "We've got to get in touch with him right away." Her words trailed off. "But we can't, can we?"

"I don't know how. Damn Berland! If they hadn't gone off on their own, Chase would still be in Rainbow Canyon."

"There's got to be a way," Jenny said. "Think of something."

Ryder put his arm around her shoulders and gave

her a squeeze. "Don't worry, Jenny girl, the worst is over."

"Over? How can you say that? What if they've run off to Texas or Mexico? We might never see him again."

"We could put a flyer out on him," Ryder suggested.

"A wanted poster!" Jenny exclaimed, horrified by the very idea of seeing her son's face on such a thing.

"Not a wanted poster, exactly," Ryder explained. "We could say he's wanted for questioning in a murder case."

Jenny shook her head. "I don't like the sound of that."

Ryder nodded. "Maybe you're right. It might be safer for both of them if we offered a reward for information about Beth."

Dusty looked at his father. "Beth?"

"Yeah. We could say she's a runaway and offer a reward for information on her whereabouts. Might cause less trouble for Chase that way."

Jenny nodded. "That might work. What do you think, Dusty?"

"She's . . . It's no longer my concern," Dusty retorted, his voice tinged with bitterness. No matter how he tried, he couldn't forget that she had betrayed him.

The following morning, Ryder rode out to Rance Crenshaw's place.

Martha Crenshaw looked surprised when she opened the door. "Why, Mr. Fallon, what brings you out this way?"

"I've come to see Rance. Is he here?"

"Yes. Come in."

She stepped back so he could enter the house. Unlike Berland's place, the Crenshaw house was clean and neat.

Rance was sitting on the sofa, sipping a cup of coffee. His right arm was in a sling.

"What'd you want to see me for?" Rance asked, his expression wary.

"I've got a warrant for your arrest," Ryder replied.

"Arrest," Martha Crenshaw exclaimed, her face pale. "What has he done?"

"He killed Ned Greenway."

"No!"

"I'm afraid so."

Martha shook her head. "No. He said an Indian did it."

She looked at her husband, her eyes begging him to tell her it was a lie. "Tell him, Rance. Tell him you're innocent."

Crenshaw looked at his wife for a long moment, then shook his head. "I ain't sayin' anything until I get a lawyer, Martha."

"Let's go," Ryder said.

He regarded Crenshaw's injured arm a moment, then pulled a pair of handcuffs from his back pocket. He locked one cuff around Crenshaw's left wrist, then drew Crenshaw's left hand behind his back and locked the other handcuff around one of the sturdy belt loops in Crenshaw's Levi's.

"Rance!" Martha threw her arms around her husband's waist, clinging to him as if she was afraid she would never see him again. "What will I tell the boys?"

"Just tell them it's a mistake," Crenshaw replied flatly.

"I will," Martha said, nodding emphatically. "I will."

Outside, Ryder saddled Crenshaw's horse, then helped the man into the saddle. Taking up the reins to Crenshaw's mount, he headed for town.

"How'd you get that warrant?" Crenshaw asked.

"On some solid evidence."

"What evidence?"

"You'll find out soon enough. Why'd you steal the Harveys' stud, anyway? You must have known you couldn't keep it, and you sure as hell couldn't sell it to anyone in town."

Crenshaw scowled at him. "You tell me how you got that warrant, and I'll answer your questions."

"Can't do that. You know, it might go easier on you if you confessed."

"Go to hell."

Ryder shrugged. "It's a possibility, I guess. For you, I'd say it was a sure thing."

"My boys," Crenshaw said. "What about my boys?"

"What about them?"

"They need me."

"You should have thought of that before you killed Greenway."

With a muttered oath, Crenshaw fell silent.

They reached town forty minutes later.

Reining his horse to a halt in front of the jail, Ryder dismounted. He started to help Crenshaw dismount, but the man jerked his arm away.

Lifting his right leg over the saddle, Rance Crenshaw slid to the ground. He glanced up and down the street, as though considering his chances of making a run for it; then, with a sigh of resignation, he climbed the steps to the boardwalk.

Opening the jailhouse door, Ryder motioned him inside. "Upstairs, Crenshaw."

Sullen-faced, Crenshaw crossed the floor to the stairway. "You gonna take these cuffs off?"

"Soon as you're locked up."

"What the . . ." Rance came to an abrupt halt as he saw the other prisoner. "Berland!"

Ryder opened the door to the cell at the far end of the hall. "Inside, Rance."

Muttering under his breath, Crenshaw entered the cell, glaring at Berland while Ryder locked the door, then reached through the bars and removed the handcuffs.

"Berland, you dirty sonofa . . ."

"That's enough, Crenshaw," Ryder warned. "I want it quiet up here, understand?"

"Yeah, I understand," Rance replied.

"Ryder, don't let 'im get me," Berland said, his expression one of near terror. "He'll kill me sure."

"He's not gonna get you, Joby. I reckon you'll do some time in jail, but he's sure to hang."

Whistling softly, Ryder went downstairs. Jenny would be pleased as punch when she learned of this day's events.

Shortly after dusk, Pete Hampton entered the jail. Pete was a middle-aged widower who lived above the saloon. Ryder had hired him on to take the night watch at the jail.

" 'Evenin', Ryder," Pete said. Removing his hat, he tossed it on the desktop. "Anything new?"

"We've got another prisoner. Rance Crenshaw."

"Crenshaw! No kiddin'? What's he in for?"

"As of today, he's the number-one suspect in the Greenway killing."

"Rance! Naw, I don't believe it."

"Berland's willing to testify against him."

"Joby." Hampton shook his head. "I just can't believe it. Joby's scared to death of Rance. Everybody knows that."

Ryder nodded. "I reckon so, but he's gonna testify just the same."

"Well, I'll be damned."

"Take care," Ryder said, plucking his hat from the rack near the door. "I'll see you first thing in the morning."

"I'll be here."

Chapter Seventeen

It was like being in heaven, Beth thought. Or Eden. Like carefree children, they ate when they were hungry, slept when they were tired, made love beneath the bold blue sky or the silvery light of the moon.

She had never realized how restricted her life had been until she came here, to this place, with this man. Nothing she had learned before seemed important. She had no need to speak softly, to wear a corset or shoes. She left her hair unbound because Chase liked it that way. She ran barefoot in the dew-damp grass, swam naked in the pool, slept in the arms of the man she loved.

She could not get enough of him, never tired of looking at him, of hearing his voice. She taught him to read. He taught her to speak his language. But at night, cradled in each other's arms, they spoke a language of their own.

She glanced up at the sound of his footsteps, a

smile of welcome curving her lips. Just looking at him made her heart leap with joy.

"No luck, I see," she remarked as he sat down beside her.

Chase shook his head. "Game is scarce here. I think we will have to leave." He laid his bow and arrows aside, grinning a little as he recalled how surprised Beth had been to learn he knew how to make weapons. He had reminded her, somewhat ruefully, that he had once been a warrior, had kissed her when she replied that, to her, he would always be a warrior.

"Where will we go?" she asked.

"South."

"To Mexico?"

"Yes."

"But . . ."

His gaze probed her. "But what?"

"Nothing."

"Tell me, Beth."

"I think we should try to get in touch with my parents, or with Dusty. Maybe we're running for nothing. Maybe they've found out who really took the Harveys' horse."

Guilt rose up inside Chase at the thought of his brother. No matter what Beth said to the contrary, he felt as if he had taken her when he had no right.

"It's worth a try," Beth insisted. "No one knows us around here. I can send a wire to Dusty, or to your mother."

"Very well," he said heavily. "But if nothing has changed, we will go to Mexico. Agreed?"

"All right."

"We will leave tomorrow. There's a small town not far from here."

Beth glanced around. She would hate to leave this place. Sidling closer to Chase, she placed her hand on his knee, and then, oh so slowly, ran her hand up his thigh.

"Beth?" She loved the husky sound of his voice, the sudden flare of desire in the depths of his eyes.

"Hmmm?" She ran her other hand over his bare chest, felt his muscles tighten beneath her fingertips.

"Beth . . ."

She smiled up at him through heavy-lidded eyes. Twining her arms around his neck, she lowered herself to the ground, drawing him down on top of her.

With a low groan, Chase claimed her lips with his. It still seemed like a miracle that she was his, that she wanted him. His response to her touch was immediate and unmistakable. Heat infused him, then settled in his groin, as her hands played over his back and chest. His mouth plundered hers. Her lips were sweeter than wild honey, the small purrs of pleasure that rose in her throat stoked the fires of his own desire. She was his, he thought exultantly. His woman. His wife.

They undressed each other, tossing their clothes aside with careless abandon in their haste to be together. Her skin was smooth and soft, warmed by the sun. Her soft curves fit against him, molding to his body as though she had been fashioned solely for him, even as her love filled the cold empty places in his life, making him feel as if he belonged.

She whispered that she loved him, and he knew

he would ask nothing more of life than to spend the rest of his days in her arms.

They left the meadow the next morning. For a time, they rode at a walk and then, with a whoop, Beth urged her mare into a lope.

Glancing over her shoulder, she yelled, "Can't catch me!"

Chase quickly took up the challenge. He drummed his heels against the roan's sides, and the gelding shot forward.

A thrill of exhilaration spiraled through Beth as the sorrel lined out in a dead run. The wind whipped her hair back and stung her eyes as she urged the mare on, her ears were filled with the roar of the wind and the quick tattoo of the mare's hooves as she flew over the ground.

And then a new sound was born to her on the wings of the wind, a shrill ululating cry that sent shivers down her spine.

Darting a glance over her shoulder, she saw Chase riding up behind her. He was leaning low over the roan's neck, riding with the ease of a man who had learned to ride before he could walk. He threw back his head, and the war cry rose on the wind again. It was a horrible, blood-curdling sound, and it carried with it a quick image of Chase clad in nothing but a loincloth, a feather in his hair, black paint streaked across his face. The image imprinted itself on her mind, and she felt a sudden sense of unease. For the first time, the fact that he was an Indian registered in her mind. He had fought against the Army, had killed white men. Women and children, too, for all she knew.

Spurred on by a sudden unreasoning panic, she kicked the mare again, then slapped the end of the reins across the sorrel's neck. "Faster!" she begged.

She screamed as an arm snaked around her waist, lifting her from the saddle.

"Beth. Beth!" Chase reined his horse to a halt, grunting with pain as Beth pounded her fists against his chest. "Beth!"

Breathing hard, she blinked at him. "Chase? Oh, Chase, for a moment I was so scared."

She felt him stiffen. "Of me?"

"Yes . . . no . . . that is . . ." She looked away, feeling suddenly foolish for letting her imagination run wild.

Very carefully, he lowered her to the ground, then swung out of the saddle. "Tell me." It was not a request.

Beth stared at the two horses, who were standing together, heads hanging, tails swishing.

"Tell me what frightened you."

"Nothing. It's silly."

"I would have no secrets between us."

"It was that war cry," Beth said, not meeting his gaze. "It scared me and . . ." She swallowed the lump rising in her throat. "I looked at you, and I imagined you riding to war against the Army," she said, her words coming in a rush. "I imagined your face streaked with paint and your hands red with blood, and . . ."

"And you saw an Indian."

She nodded, feeling more miserable than she'd ever felt in her life.

"I will take you home."

"What?" She stared up at him, certain she had misunderstood him.

"I will take you home," he repeated, his voice void of emotion. It no longer mattered that he was wanted for stealing a white man's horse. He no longer cared if they hanged him.

"But I don't want to go home."

He looked at her, his expression unreadable.

"Chase, please. I'm sorry. I just let my imagination get the best of me, that's all."

He didn't say anything, only continued to stare at her as if she were a stranger.

"Chase! Please, talk to me. Tell me what I can do to make things right."

"You will never look at me the same again," he replied, his voice so quiet, his eyes filled with such pain, that it broke her heart.

"That's not true. I love you." She started to touch him, then jerked her hand away at the warning look in his eyes. "Chase, please don't turn me away. I didn't mean to hurt you. You've got to believe me."

He turned his back to her, not wanting her to see how badly her words had wounded him. What had started as a harmless game had opened a chasm between them, one he wasn't sure he could cross again.

And then he felt her arms curl around his waist, felt her cheek press against his back. The warmth of her tears penetrated his shirt, and he knew he would risk his heart, his very life, to stay with her.

"Say you forgive me." Her voice was soft and low and thick with anguish.

"Beth." Turning, he placed his hands at her waist and gazed down into her eyes, beautiful earth-brown eyes glistening with tears. "It's true, I fought against the whites. I killed many men. There was hatred in my heart; my hands were stained with the blood of my enemies. But I never killed women or children. I would never hurt you."

"I know." Her hand trembled as she reached up and caressed his cheek. "I know."

"I love you, Beth. If you do not wish to stay with me, you have only to say so, and I will take you home."

"I *am* home," she said, smiling. "Here, with you."

He drew her up against him, his arms wrapping around her in a hug that threatened to crack her ribs. It felt wonderful.

They reached the town of Sandy Flats three days later. Chase reined his horse to a halt just outside of the town, his expression ambivalent.

"I can go in alone, if you want," Beth said.

"No."

He clucked to the roan, urging the horse forward, but Beth could see he was uncomfortable.

"I'm sure no one's looking for you," she said, hoping to reassure him. "Anyway, we won't stay long. Look, there's the telegraph office."

They drew up in front of the small wood-frame building. Dismounting, Beth pulled a coin purse from the bottom of her saddlebags. She didn't have much money, only a couple of dollars she had stolen from her mother's pin money the night she helped Chase escape from jail.

"Who shall we send the wire to?" she asked. "My mother or yours?"

Chase considered that for a moment. He didn't

want to be in debt to his mother, but to ask Beth's mother for help was out of the question. "My mother."

"Okay. Are you coming?"

"I will wait here."

"All right." Dusting off her skirts as best she could, Beth stepped up on the boardwalk and entered the building. It took only a few minutes to send the message.

"Are you going to wait for a reply, miss?" the telegrapher asked.

"I'll be back later."

"Are you staying at the hotel?"

"I'm not sure."

"Well, I'll just hold it here for you then."

"Thank you."

She was on her way out the door when she saw the poster.

$500 REWARD FOR
INFORMATION AS TO THE
WHEREABOUTS OF
ELIZABETH JOHNSON
17 years old, 5' 5" tall
Blond hair, brown eyes
Please contact Sheriff Fallon
at Twin Rivers

A small pen-and-ink sketch of her face adorned the bottom half of the poster.

Frowning, she hurried outside. Chase was the one wanted by the law, she thought, confused. Why was there a poster for her, but not for him? Did that mean his name had been cleared?

"Was there trouble?" Chase asked.

"Trouble? No, why?"

"You look worried."

"I saw a wanted poster with my name on it."

"*Your* name? But why? What have you done?"

"My parents have put up a reward for information as to my whereabouts. They must be worried to death by now." She felt a rush of guilt as she realized how little thought she had given to her parents, or what her running away would mean to them. They had always taken good care of her, provided for her, but she'd never thought they really loved her, that she was important to them. Had she been wrong?

"Perhaps we should not stay here," Chase said. He glanced around, expecting to see people staring at them, but there were only a few people on the street, and they seemed caught up in their own business.

"I think we should wait for a reply to the wire," Beth said. "Let's go to the hotel and get something to eat. I don't know about you, but I'd like a meal that wasn't cooked over a campfire."

At his nod, Beth took up the reins to her horse and walked across the street toward the hotel, wondering if they had money enough for a room for the night. A hot bath and a bed with a mattress sounded like paradise.

After tethering their horses to the rail, they went into the hotel dining room. Clad in her travel-stained dress, Beth felt highly conspicuous as she took a place at a table in the back. Chase sat across from her.

A few minutes later, a waitress handed them each a menu.

"What are you going to have?" Beth asked.

Chase glanced at the menu. Most of the words were foreign to him.

Looking up, Beth saw him scowling at the menu. "I'm going to have fried chicken and mashed potatoes," she remarked. "If that doesn't sound good, you can have steak, pork chops, or lamb."

"Steak," Chase said. He put the menu aside.

Beth smiled at him as she dropped her menu on top of his. "Rare?" she guessed.

"Yes."

"With all the trimmings?"

"What are trimmings?"

"Potatoes, vegetable, bread and butter, and coffee."

Chase nodded.

Beth gave the waitress their order, then sat back in her chair and looked around. The dining room was painted pale green. White cloths covered the tables. Paintings of meadows and sunsets hung on the walls.

"Do you want to spend the night here?" Beth asked.

Chase looked around. He'd never been in a hotel before. "Do you think it's safe?"

"I think so. Wouldn't you like to take a hot bath, sleep in a bed?"

"I don't care about the bed," Chase said with a shrug, "but a hot bath sounds good."

Beth attacked her dinner with gusto when it arrived. The chicken was moist and tender, the mashed potatoes smooth and creamy. Ordinarily, she didn't care for green beans, but she was so hungry, she ate them, too.

There was little conversation as Chase was also concentrating on his dinner. Once, meeting Beth's eyes, he smiled, amused by the image of the two of them as ordinary people enjoying an ordinary meal.

With a sigh of contentment, Beth sat back. "That was wonderful. How about some dessert?"

Chase finished his steak and pushed the plate aside. He'd never had a meal like that in his life. "What kind of dessert?"

Beth repeated the question to the waitress when she came to clear away their dishes.

"We have chocolate cake, apple pie, blueberry pie, and custard."

"Chocolate cake," Beth said.

"And you, sir?"

Sir! It was all Chase could do to keep from laughing out loud. In all his life, no one had ever called him sir! "Apple pie."

The waitress smiled at Chase. She was a pretty woman, with curly black hair and green eyes. "Coming right up," she said, batting her eyelashes at him.

Beth made a very unladylike sound as the waitress walked away from the table, hips swaying provocatively. "I think she likes you."

Chase grinned at Beth. "Jealous?"

"Should I be?"

The amusement faded from his eyes as he reached across the table and took her hand in his. "No. Never."

Beth felt her insides melt. "Maybe we shouldn't have ordered dessert."

"What?"

"Suddenly I'm hungry for something else," she explained, and then blushed furiously.

Chase looked at her askance, and then he grinned. "I am sure we will have time for both."

The hotel room was not large, nor was it particularly sumptuous, but Beth didn't care. As soon as Chase closed the door, she was in his embrace, running her hands over his shoulders and down his arms, reveling in the hard muscular strength of him, in the smoldering heat in his eyes.

She had planned to take a bath first, but Chase's kisses quickly changed her mind. His mouth was hot and hungry on hers, igniting a fire deep within her that would not be ignored.

Sweeping her into his arms, he carried her to the bed, undressed her between hot hungry kisses. He groaned as he felt her hands skim over his flesh as she removed his shirt, then reached for his trousers. In less than a minute, their clothes lay in an untidy heap on the floor.

"Beth," he groaned softly, "I can't wait."

"No need," she whispered breathlessly, and then he was hovering over her, his black hair falling forward, enclosing them in a dark cocoon as his flesh merged with hers in a joyous explosion.

Slowly, slowly, reality returned.

Chase gazed at Beth. Her eyes were slumberous, her smile that of a woman who had been well and truly satisfied.

Much later, after they had both bathed and dressed, they walked back to the telegraph office.

"It's here," the telegrapher said when Beth entered the building.

Beth quickly scanned the paper he handed her. *Beth, come home,* the message said. *Parents worried. Crenshaw confessed.*

"Everything's all right!" Beth exclaimed. "It says Crenshaw confessed to shooting Greenway." She looked up at Chase, her eyes shining. "We can go home!"

Chase nodded. It was good news, yet he could not help feeling that, once they returned to Twin Rivers, everything would change.

Chapter Eighteen

Dusty smiled as Rebecca handed him a glass of lemonade. In the last six weeks, he had grown fond of the girl. There was a sweetness about her, a genuine warmth, that helped soothe his bruised ego. Beth's betrayal had cut deeper than he let on. He had been so certain she loved him. So certain.

"Ready for another game?" Rebecca asked.

"What?" He looked up, frowning.

"Another game," Rebecca repeated. She gestured at the checkerboard spread on the table between them.

"Oh, sure."

"Is something wrong, Dusty?"

"No. No, I was just . . ."

He was saved from explaining by the timely arrival of his father, who entered the house waving a sheet of paper. "Dusty, where's your mother?"

"In the kitchen. Is anything wrong?"

"No." Ryder nodded at Rebecca. "Tell ya later. Jenny! Hey, Jenny!"

"I wonder what that's all about?" Rebecca said.

"I don't know." But he could guess. Beth had sent a wire.

Distracted by thoughts of Beth and Chase, he lost the game.

"Well," Rebecca said, "I should be going."

"You're welcome to stay for dinner."

"No, I don't think so."

Dusty stood up when she did and walked her out to the front porch.

"Pretty sunset," Rebecca remarked.

"Yeah. Listen, Rebecca, I'm sorry about before, for being distracted, I mean."

"That's all right, Dusty. I know you're in love with Beth."

Dusty stared at her, taken aback by her candor. In all the time she'd been coming to see him, she'd never mentioned Beth's name, not once.

Rebecca smiled sadly. "I don't think I'll be coming around anymore, Dusty. Good night."

"Rebecca, wait . . ."

"There's nothing more to say. Good night, Dusty."

Feeling as though he'd just been punched in the gut, Dusty watched Rebecca ride out of the yard, surprised by the overwhelming sense of loss he felt at the thought of not seeing her again.

He blew out a deep breath. Hell, maybe it was for the best.

Returning to the parlor, he found his folks waiting for him.

"Did Rebecca leave?" Jenny asked.

Dusty nodded.

"Didn't you ask her to stay for supper?"

"I asked her, but she said no."

"I like that girl," Ryder said.

"So do I," Jenny remarked. She smiled at Ryder, then held up the telegram she'd been clutching in her hands. "They're coming home. Chase and Beth are coming home."

Later, lying in bed, Dusty pondered the implications of their return. Chase was a free man. Rance Crenshaw had been tried and convicted of killing Ned Greenway. Berland had been implicated in the killing as well. Both had received long prison sentences.

Justice, he mused bitterly. It was never the same for whites and Indians. Chase had been sentenced to hang for the same crimes that had earned Berland and Crenshaw time behind bars.

Beth and Chase were coming home. Beth . . . When he'd thought she was gone for good, he'd told himself he was glad, that he didn't love her, that maybe he never had. Now, knowing she was coming back, he admitted that he still loved her. Maybe he always would.

Closing his eyes, he thought about Rebecca. She was everything he had ever wanted in a woman—pretty, generous, kindhearted, good-natured. He liked her well enough, enjoyed her company. He'd even thought he was falling in love with her. Sitting with her in the evening, listening to her talk about her day, telling her about his, had made him think about settling down, having a couple of kids. The kisses they'd shared had been sweet and passionate and made him yearn for more.

But now Beth was coming home.

Beth's nervousness increased with each mile that carried them closer to home. How was she going to face her parents? What was she going to say? And what about Ryder and Jenny Fallon? What would they think of her? Everyone in town knew Dusty had been courting her. For the first time, she felt a twinge of guilt for what she'd done. She could just imagine the old cats gossiping over the back fence, their heads together. *Imagine,* they would say, *courting one brother and running away with the other one.* No doubt Dusty and his parents hated her now. Why had she ever agreed to go back home?

"Chase?" She reined her horse to a halt.

He drew up beside her, a question in his eyes. "You are tired?"

"No. No, I . . . I was just thinking . . ."

"Thinking what?"

"Maybe we shouldn't go home."

"Not go? Why?"

"My parents . . . I'm afraid . . . I mean . . ."

"Of what are you afraid, Beth?" His voice was quiet, but she heard the hard edge beneath, saw the knowledge in his eyes.

"I'm just afraid my parents won't let us be together."

"They cannot keep us apart."

"But they can!" She leaned toward him and placed her hand on his forearm. "Let's go somewhere else. I don't care where."

"That is the only reason you wish to run away, because you are afraid of your parents?"

"Of course." She looked away. "What other reason could there be?"

"Perhaps you are ashamed to be seen with me."

The tone of his voice had not changed. It was still low and quiet, but the arm beneath her fingertips was suddenly taut.

"That's not true," she exclaimed.

He didn't say anything, only continued to stare at her, his dark eyes void of expression.

"It's just that . . ." She let out a deep sigh, wishing she'd never said anything at all. "I never thought what people would think about me running away with you. Everyone assumed that Dusty and I . . . that we'd . . . It might be embarrassing for him if we go back home."

"Everyone expected you to marry?"

Beth nodded.

"Do you wish to leave me and marry my brother?"

"No, of course not."

"I ran away from a crime I did not commit. I will not run away now. You are my woman. I will not hide as though we have done something to be ashamed of." Brave words, he thought, and yet, deep inside, he knew he would rather face an army of bluecoats than see hatred in the eyes of his brother.

"You're right," Beth said. "I'm sorry for being such a coward. Forgive me."

"There is nothing to forgive."

"How much longer till we get there?"

"An hour, perhaps less."

Beth nodded. An hour. She straightened her shoulders and took a deep breath. She'd be glad when it was over, she thought, and yet she couldn't help wishing she could put it off for one more day.

They had decided to go see Chase's mother first, but fate took the decision out of their hands. They were about to turn down the road that led to the Fallon ranch when they saw Beth's parents coming toward them.

Ralph Johnson reined his matched bays to a halt, his face going white when he saw his daughter. "Beth!"

Alighting from the carriage, he took hold of her horse's reins. "Where have you been, young lady?"

"You will not speak so to my wife," Chase said, edging his horse nearer to Beth's.

"Wife!" Ralph Johnson glared at Chase. "What the hell are you talking about?"

"Father, please, if you'll just let me explain."

"Damn right you'll explain. Get in the carriage, young lady. I'm taking you home."

He was grabbing her arm as he spoke, yanking her out of the saddle.

Dismounting, Chase took hold of Ralph Johnson's arm. "You will not treat her that way."

"She's my daughter, and I'll treat her any way I like. Now, unhand me!"

"Chase, please," Beth looked up at him, begging him not to interfere.

"Did he kidnap you?" Ralph Johnson asked. His grip tightened on her arm. "Did he take you against your will?"

"No." Beth shook her head. "It wasn't like that."

"You ran off with this . . . this redskin, of your

own free will!" Ralph Johnson exclaimed. "I don't believe it."

"Can't we discuss this at home?" Beth asked.

"There's nothing to discuss. Get in the carriage."

Beth glanced past her father to where her mother sat in their shiny black carriage, a lace-edged handkerchief pressed to her mouth, and knew she would get no help from that direction.

"She is my wife. She stays with me," Chase said.

"Like hell." Reaching into his jacket, Ralph Johnson withdrew a snub-nosed pistol. "You get the hell out of here, right now. If I ever see your face again, I'll put a bullet in you, no questions asked."

Chase took a step backward. Hands clenched at his sides, he glared at Beth's father, then looked at Beth.

"Chase, just go, please," she said. "I don't want any trouble."

"No. You are my woman. I will not leave you."

"She's my daughter, and she's underage. I don't know who married you, but I intend to have it annulled."

"What does that mean?" Chase asked. "Annulled?"

"It means like it never happened." Ralph looked at his daughter. "Who performed the ceremony?"

"We . . . I . . ."

"Well?"

"No one. We said the words ourselves."

Ralph Johnson grunted. "Well, that makes it easy. Go on," he said, giving her a push. "Get in the carriage with your mother."

Chase took a step forward, and Johnson eared back the pistol's hammer.

"Come on," Johnson said, beckoning Chase with his free hand. "Make a move. I'd love an excuse to put one in you."

"Chase, please," Beth pleaded, "just go."

"It is your wish that I leave you?"

Beth glanced at the pistol in her father's hand, at the rage in his eyes. The finger wrapped around the trigger was white and trembling. "Yes, please, go." Better he should leave her than be killed in front of her very eyes.

She saw a muscle twitch in Chase's jaw; then, head high, he took up the reins of his horse and swung into the saddle. He looked at her for one long moment, then clucked softly to the horse.

He looked back at her only once, and then he urged the roan into a gallop.

She watched until he was lost in a haze of dust, and then she climbed into the carriage beside her mother.

Dusty was sitting on the front porch reading the newspaper when he heard the hoofbeats pounding down the road. Glancing over the top of the paper, at first all he saw was a cloud of dust. He recognized the horse immediately, and then, catching a glimpse of the rider's face, he stood up.

They were back.

Chase reined his horse to a walk as he neared the house. He could see Dusty standing on the porch, and he had a sudden desire to turn tail and run. What could he say to his brother, to this man he hardly knew? How could he explain the love he felt for Beth? How could he expect Dusty to understand, or forgive?

Reining his horse to a halt, he met his brother's gaze. And waited.

Tension strung out between them and might have gone on forever if Jenny hadn't stepped onto the porch.

"Chase!" she exclaimed. She ran down the stairs. "I'm so glad you're home."

Not knowing what to say, Chase dismounted and tossed the reins over the hitch rack.

"You're all right?" Jenny asked. Her gaze, filled with a mother's concern, ran over him. "Your wound healed all right?"

"I am fine."

"Come in and sit down." She reached for his arm, then withdrew her hand, afraid he might not welcome her touch. "We've got so much to talk about."

Chase met Dusty's gaze. "Yes," he said. "We have a lot to talk about."

He followed his mother inside, aware of Dusty entering the house behind him.

"I'll make some coffee," Jenny said.

Chase and Dusty followed her into the kitchen. Dusty sat down at the big oak table and after a moment, Chase sat down across from him.

"Where's Beth?" They were the first words Dusty had spoken, and they emerged from his throat as though torn.

"With her parents."

Dusty looked surprised.

Jenny placed three cups of coffee on the table, then sat down between her two sons. She could feel the tension radiating from Dusty, feel Chase's unease. She wanted to know everything that had happened since Chase left town, but she wasn't sure where to start.

Dusty went right to the heart of what was bothering him. "Where did you meet Beth?"

"Near the river."

"When? How long have you known her?"

"We met at the river the day before I was arrested."

"And she ran away with you?"

Chase nodded.

"Why?"

Chase stared into his coffee cup, as if he hoped to find the answers somewhere inside. "I cannot explain it to you. I looked at her, and . . . I did not know she was yours."

"So, you admit she's my girl and you ran off with her!" Dusty ran a hand through his hair. "Dammit, how could you do such a thing?"

Chase looked up and met his brother's gaze. "I did not know then. She did not tell me until later."

Dusty stood up and began to pace the room. "I don't understand."

"I do," Jenny said. "Sometimes it just takes one look, Dusty. That's all. Just one look."

"Dammit, I loved her. I asked her to marry me, and she ran off without so much as a good-bye! Ran off! Hah! She drugged me and broke him out of jail."

"Dusty, calm down."

Dusty came to a halt in mid-stride. Slowly, he turned to face his father, who had just come in the back door. "I will not calm down. I have every right to be angry. If he wasn't my brother, I'd call him out."

Ryder closed the door behind him. "I asked you to calm down. Now I'm telling you."

Dusty took a deep breath, and for a moment, Chase thought he'd argue, but then, with a muttered oath, Dusty sat down, his arms crossed over his chest, his expression mutinous.

"I heard everything," Ryder remarked. He sat down across from Jenny and reached for her hand. "Sounds to me like it's your pride that's hurt, not your heart."

Dusty snorted softly.

"For a man with a broken heart, you turned to another mighty fast."

"Rebecca's just a friend."

Ryder nodded. "Maybe, but she'd like to be more. And from the way I saw you kissing one night when she was here keeping you company, it looked like you might feel the same."

Dusty blushed from the roots of his hair to his toes. "One kiss doesn't mean anything. I was lonely. She was willing . . ." He shrugged.

"So it didn't mean anything?"

"All right, I like her. She's a nice girl. But I don't want to talk about Rebecca, I want to talk about Beth."

"I think Beth's made her choice." Ryder looked at Chase. "Where is she?"

"Her father took her home."

"What do you mean?"

"We were coming here when we met him on the road. He took Beth home."

"And you let him?" Dusty asked, a sneer in his voice.

"He pulled a gun on me."

"A gun!" Jenny exclaimed.

Chase nodded. "He said she was not old enough to marry without his permission, and that he would have our wedding a . . ." He searched for the word. "Annulled."

"You got married!" Dusty stared at Chase, his green eyes dark with anger and disbelief.

"In the Apache way."

Ryder grunted softly. "Last time I looked, that still wasn't considered legal in these parts."

"She is my woman," Chase said. "I will not let her go."

"Hold on now," Ryder admonished. "No sense going off half-cocked. Dusty, when's Beth's birthday?"

"Sometime in December. The fifteenth, I think."

"That's a little less than five months away. Until then, maybe we'd better just sit tight and let things cool off."

"She is my wife," Chase said, biting off each word. "I do not wish to wait a few months."

Ryder looked at Jenny and grinned. Ah, the impatience of youth! "So, what do you want to do? Kidnap her and carry her off again? Have her father hate you, hunt you down, charge you with kidnapping a minor?"

"She is mine," Chase said stubbornly.

"Chase, please try to be reasonable," Jenny urged. She placed her free hand over his. "Ralph Johnson is a very powerful man. He has a lot of money, and a lot of influence. And he's Beth's father. Wouldn't you rather have all this settled peacefully?"

"Your mother's right. Why not give it a few days? Give Beth a chance to explain things to her father.

Maybe he'll cool off when he's had a chance to think."

"Time will not change what I am. No matter what Beth says, no matter how hard she argues, he will never accept me as his son."

And that, Ryder mused, just about summed it up.

Chapter Nineteen

Beth paced her room, growing more agitated by the moment. Knowing the door was locked, she turned the handle anyway, then shook it in frustration.

When they had reached home, she had tried to talk to her mother, tried to reason with her father, but to no avail. Her father had dragged her to her room and locked her inside.

A short time later, her mother had unlocked the door and informed Beth that she was to bathe and dress for dinner.

And now she paced, waiting, wondering. Where was Chase? Had he gone to see his mother? Would he come after her? Would her father really shoot him if he did?

They never should have come back here. Her father would never let her marry Chase, not in a million years.

The sound of a key turning in the lock stilled her thoughts.

"Dinner is ready, Miss Elizabeth."

"Thank you, Dottie."

With a slight bow, the maid turned away.

It was in Beth's mind to sulk, to refuse to eat, but she knew it wouldn't do her any good. It never had.

A quick look in the mirror assured her that her hair was neatly combed. Smoothing the front of her dress, she left the room and went downstairs. *Into the lion's den,* she thought ruefully.

Her parents were already seated. Wordlessly, she took her usual place, spread her napkin in her lap, bowed her head while her father said grace.

"Lord, we thank you for this food, and for the return of our daughter. We pray that she will forget her foolishness and the shame she has brought upon us. Amen."

"There's to be a party at the Carter's on Friday," Theda remarked. "We've all been invited."

"I don't wish to go."

"You will go," Ralph said, his voice firm yet mild. "Tomorrow you will go shopping with your mother and buy a new dress. Something white."

"White, father?" Beth regarded her father with wry amusement. Did he think that if he clothed her in a white gown, people would be foolish enough to think she was still innocent, that she had run away with a man and nothing had happened between them?

"White. Lester Harbaugh has asked for your hand in marriage, and I have accepted for you."

"Accepted! But I've never even met the man."

"That will be remedied. As it happens, Lester is coming out here the first of October. If your mother and I approve of him, and he approves of you, the wedding will take place after Thanksgiving."

"And what about me? What if I don't approve of him?"

"You have no say in the matter."

"It's my life!"

"And I am your father. And you will do as I say."

"What about Ernest Tucker?" Beth asked, playing devil's advocate.

"After the shameful way you've behaved, he is no longer interested in marrying you."

Theda shrugged. "It's just as well. Lester is a much better match."

"But he's so much older than I. And he's got three children."

"He'll make you a good husband. You're far too headstrong for your own good. You need an older man to look after you."

"I won't do it!"

"You will," Ralph said, his voice smug. "If you oppose me in this, I shall send you to school at the convent in New Mexico."

"Convent! We're not even Catholic."

"A minor point, if one can pay the price."

"I don't believe this. You don't care anything about me, about my happiness."

"Of course we do, dear," her mother said. "You'll thank us for it later."

Beth groaned softly. How often had she heard those words in the past? A hundred times? A thousand? Had she ever felt like thanking them for interfering in her life? Never! Well, maybe once or twice, but not in this. She loved Chase; she would never be happy with anyone else.

Her appetite ruined, Beth pushed her plate away.

"Finished, dear? Perhaps you should go to bed, then. You need your rest."

"Yes, bed," Beth said. Folding her napkin, she placed it on the table and stood up. "Good night, Mother. Father."

"Good night, Elizabeth."

"Good night, dear." Theda Johnson watched her daughter leave the room, unable to ignore the tiny voice in the back of her mind that questioned if they were doing the right thing.

Chase stood at the window, staring out into the darkness. His mother had insisted he stay at the ranch, though he had been reluctant to do so. He knew Dusty didn't want him here. He had seen the surprise in his brother's eyes, the surprise and the disapproval. The animosity between them was almost tangible. Try as he might, he couldn't help feeling guilty about Beth. And yet he wouldn't give her up. Not for Dusty. Not for anyone. She was his, for now and for always.

A movement in the darkness caught his eye. It was Ryder, standing near one of the corrals. Chase watched him a moment, then left the house.

Ryder whirled around at the sound of footsteps coming up behind him. He grinned ruefully when he recognized Chase. It had been over twenty years since he'd hung up his guns, he mused, and he still reacted to people coming up behind him.

"You're up late," Ryder remarked. Leaning back against the corral, he crossed his arms over his chest.

"So are you."

Ryder nodded. "Pretty night."

Chase grunted softly, remembering the warm summer nights he had spent with the People, the buffalo hunts, the feasts, the dances. So many good memories, so many people he would never see again.

"Something on your mind?" Ryder asked.

"I think I should not stay here. This is Dusty's home, and he does not want me here."

"Be that as it may, it's your mother's home, too, and she wants you here. And so do I."

Chase swallowed against the sudden tightness in his throat. He didn't really want to leave. He wanted a chance to get to know his mother. And he wanted to get to know Ryder Fallon.

"You've got as much right to be here as Dusty," Ryder remarked. "Maybe more."

"I cannot blame him for hating me."

"Yeah, well, that might be true. On the other hand, it was Beth's decision. I never thought they were right for each other." Ryder studied Chase for a moment. "But I think the two of you will make it."

"Not if her father has anything to say about it," Chase replied bitterly.

"Can't argue with that."

"Beth did not want to come home. She wanted us to go away, but I said no. I told her I was tired of running. I think now I should have listened to her."

"It probably would have been the easiest thing to do," Ryder agreed, "but that don't make it the right thing."

"Her father will not let me see her."

"I might be able to get a message to her."

"You would do that?"

"Hate to stand in the way of true love."

"You are a good man, Ryder Fallon. I think my mother was wise to marry you."

Grinning, Ryder clapped Chase on the shoulder. "I think so, too."

Chase laughed, surprised at how good it felt, at how good *he* felt. For the first time since returning to Twin Rivers, he thought things might work out for the best after all.

Sunday morning, Beth sat between her parents in church. As always, they had arrived early and sat in the right front pew that her father considered his.

Hands folded in her lap, Beth stared at the church's single stained-glass window. It was situated above the pulpit and depicted several biblical scenes interwoven in bright rainbow hues. Her favorite scene was Adam and Eve in the Garden surrounded by flowers and trees. She remembered the days she had spent with Chase in the canyon, and how she had felt like Eve then, alone in a beautiful place with the man she loved.

Gradually, the church filled up and the service began. Standing to sing the opening hymn, she glanced across the aisle, felt her heartbeat increase when she saw Chase looking at her. She smiled for the first time in days as she felt the warmth of his gaze wash over her.

The music faded into the background, and she was aware of nothing but Chase, of the love in his eyes. He smiled at her, that wonderful smile that made her believe everything would be all right.

She glanced up at her father when he tugged on

her arm. Only then did she realize that the hymn was over and everyone was sitting down.

She sat quickly and folded her hands in her lap again. She had no idea what the minister said that day. She was aware of nothing but Chase sitting across the aisle. Occasionally, she leaned forward a little, just enough so she could see him. He was still here, she thought, still in town. One night he'd come for her, and she'd be ready.

When the service was over, she followed her parents outside, stood beside them while they conversed with other members of the congregation.

Ryder and Jenny Fallon stood nearby, talking to Mace Carson. Chase stood behind his mother, saying nothing. Beth noticed that most of Reverend Cleghorne's flock avoided speaking to Chase, though he received numerous speculative glances.

Surprised, Beth watched Ryder approach her father. "Good morning, Ralph," Ryder said. "Mrs. Johnson. Beth."

"Good morning, Ryder," her father replied. "Something I can do for you?"

"No, I just came by to make sure Beth is all right."

"She's fine."

"I'm glad to hear that. I want to apologize for any worry that my family has caused you."

"No harm done," Ralph Johnson said stiffly.

"I'm glad. Good day to you then," Ryder said. He nodded at Ralph and Theda Johnson, then took Beth's hand in both of his. "I'm glad you're back," he said, squeezing her hand.

"Thank you," Beth replied. Slowly, she drew her hand from his, then slid her hand into the pocket of her skirt. "Good day to you."

"And you."

"He has a lot of nerve," Theda Johnson said indignantly.

"Well, what can you expect of his kind," Ralph replied. "Come, Beth, let's go home."

"Yes, Father," she replied.

At home, she pleaded a headache and went upstairs to lie down. In her room, she withdrew the small piece of paper from her pocket.

Beth,
I will be waiting for you tonight, at the river where we met. Come if you can. If not, I will wait for you every night until you can get away. I love you.

Chase

She stared at the words, written in a bold hand. Chase had learned the rudiments of reading and writing, but not enough to compose this note. Tears stung her eyes as she realized that Ryder Fallon must have written the note for Chase. The fact that he was an accomplice indicated approval. It lifted her spirits to think that Chase's family, at least, was on their side.

She thought the day would never end. She was too nervous to eat much. She spent the evening in the parlor with her parents, pretending to read a book, though none of the words made sense. All she could think of was seeing Chase again, hearing his voice, feeling the touch of his hands in her hair, on her skin. Her pulse raced as she imagined kissing him again, making love to him again . . .

"Elizabeth, are you all right?"

"What? Yes, of course. Why do you ask?"

"You look flushed, dear. You're not coming down with something, are you?"

"I might be. I do feel rather warm." It wasn't a lie, she thought. Thinking of Chase always made her temperature rise.

Theda stood up and crossed the room. She frowned as she placed her hand on Beth's brow. "You do feel a trifle warm, dear. Perhaps you should go up to bed."

"Yes, I think I will. Good night, Father. Mother."

"Good night, Elizabeth," her father said. "Sleep well."

"Thank you, Father."

"Call me if you need anything," Theda said.

"I'm sure I'll be fine after a good night's sleep."

"Of course," her mother said, smiling. "I'll have Dottie bring you a cup of tea to help you relax."

"Thank you, Mother. Good night."

Trying to look properly fatigued, Beth left the room and slowly climbed the stairs. Undressing, she slipped into bed, wishing she could make the hours pass faster. She drank the tea that Dottie brought her, extinguished the light, and slid under the covers.

At ten, she heard her parents climb the stairs. Her mother opened her bedroom door and peeked inside. Satisfied that all was well, she closed the door.

Five minutes later, Beth sat up, drumming her fingertips on the counterpane. How long would it take for her parents to go to sleep? How long before it would be safe to sneak out of the house? How long would Chase wait for her?

When she couldn't wait any longer, she stepped

out of her nightgown and into a navy blue dress. She didn't bother with underwear or shoes. Barefooted, she tiptoed down the stairs and out of the house. Then, picking up her skirts, she ran toward the river.

Chase paced along the shore, wondering if Beth would come. It had been all he could do to keep from grabbing her that morning in church. Only Ryder's whispered reminder that such a thing would only lead to more trouble had kept him from sweeping her up in his arms and running away.

Ryder and Jenny had both urged him to be patient in hopes that Beth's parents would come around. Chase knew they would never approve of him, knew that Ryder advised patience because Jenny was hoping everything could be resolved in such a way that Beth and Chase could stay in the valley. He could not blame his mother for that. In the last few days, he had come to realize that his mother was a warm and caring woman, that the decisions she had made in the past had been made because she loved him, and because she loved Ryder Fallon.

Life on the ranch would have been pleasant but for Dusty. Chase couldn't blame his brother for being distant, for being resentful of the fact that Chase was living in the house, that Jenny seemed to go out of her way to make Chase feel at home. She cooked his favorite meals, made sure there were always sugar cookies in the cookie jar because Chase liked them . . .

The soft sound of footsteps interrupted his reverie, and he whirled around, all his senses alert.

"Chase, where are you?"

"Over here." He walked toward the sound of her voice. A moment later, Beth was in his arms.

"I missed you," she said, running her hands over his face, down his arms.

"And I missed you." He held her close, his hands moving restlessly over her back, absorbing her warmth, her nearness. She was here, in his arms, at last.

"Kiss me," she whispered. "Kiss me, kiss me."

Only too willing to oblige, he slanted his mouth over hers, his tongue sliding over her lower lip, exploring the soft inner recesses of her mouth. She tasted warm and sweet and familiar. His hands cupped her buttocks, pressing her against him, letting her feel the heat of his arousal. "I want you."

She nodded, too breathless to speak.

A long shuddering sigh rippled through him as he swung her into his arms and carried her toward a blanket he had spread beneath a tree.

"It's been so long," he said, lowering her gently to the blanket.

"Too long," Beth replied. Impatient, she slid her hands under his shirt, wanting to touch him.

His hands trembled as he reached behind her to unfasten her dress. He gasped with surprise when his hands encountered bare flesh instead of the layers of underwear she usually wore.

"I was in a hurry," Beth said. She removed his shirt, then reached for the fastening of his trousers. "I'm glad you don't wear anything underneath."

He groaned as her fingertips grazed him. "Beth."

"I know." She reached for him, drawing him down on top of her. "I know. Me, too. Kiss me,

Chase, kiss me and never stop."

He gazed into her eyes for a long moment, and then crushed her close, his breathing becoming ragged and uneven as she guided him home.

Chapter Twenty

It wasn't until much later, when they were lying wrapped in each other's arms, that Beth told Chase about Lester Harbaugh.

"What are we going to do?" she asked, snuggling closer.

"You will not marry him," Chase said, his tone sharper than he intended. "You are my woman. My wife."

Beth sighed. "I know, but I'm afraid my father will never let us be together."

"Then we will leave here."

"I told you we should never have come back."

"I had hoped we could live here," Chase said quietly. He stroked her hair, thinking how soft it was. "I had hoped to get to know my mother better. And my brother. And the sister I have not yet met . . ."

"That's not possible now, is it?" Beth remarked. She propped herself up on one elbow and ran one finger along his jaw. "It's all my fault. I'm sorry, Chase."

Cupping her face in his hands, Chase gazed into Beth's eyes, his expression solemn. He could live without his mother, without his brother and sister, but he would not want to live without Beth. He could not live without his heart, his soul.

"You mean more to me than anyone, or anything else, Beth," he said fervently. "Never doubt that."

"Are you sure? I don't want you to look back and blame me for ruining your life."

"It will not happen." He brushed his thumbs over her lips, then kissed her tenderly. "I love you, Beth. You will be my mother, and my father, my sister, and my brother. So long as I have you, I will need no one else."

"Oh, Chase . . ." she murmured.

He kissed her again, and yet again, each kiss longer and more intense, until kisses weren't enough. He needed to be a part of her again, his body sheathed deep within her, needed to feel their hearts beating with one song, one rhythm, as their bodies and souls merged into one heart, one mind, one flesh.

Beth ran her hands over his back and shoulders, along his thighs, reveling in the hard muscular strength of him, in the tender way he held her, and loved her. Her heart ached for the loneliness he had known, and she vowed that, as long as she lived, as long as there was breath in her body, he would never be lonely again.

She sobbed his name as the tension within her built to a crescendo, her nails raking his back, her arms holding him tight as wave after wave of ecstacy swept through her.

She felt him shudder convulsively as his life poured into her, warm and sweet and satisfying.

He held her close for a long while, one hand stroking her hair, as their breathing returned to normal and the sweat cooled on their heated flesh.

"When?" she asked later. "When should we leave?"

He wanted to take her away now, this minute, but first he must find a way to earn some money. He could not take Beth into the hills and expect her to live in a cave. He needed money to provide for her until he could find a way to earn a living. Life had been so much easier in the old days, he thought morosely, when they could have lived off the land, when the buffalo would have provided all of life's necessities: meat for food, hides for robes and clothing. The paunch could be used as a cook pot, the hair from the tail for thread, utensils could be made from the horn, glue from the hooves. Hide, hair, meat, and bones, nothing had gone to waste.

But those days were forever gone. And Beth was not an Indian, but a white woman. She had not complained about the time they spent in Rainbow Canyon, nor had she had complained about sleeping on the hard ground, or cooking over an open fire, or washing in the river's cold water. But he could not expect her to be happy living in such a way indefinitely. She was accustomed to living in a town, in a house. And a woman, whether red or white, appreciated the company of other women.

"I will ask Ryder if I can work for him," Chase

said. "At the end of October, we will leave this place and look for another."

She didn't want to wait that long, didn't want to have to sneak out to meet Chase as if what they felt for each other was something shameful.

"I think we should go now," Beth urged. "Tonight."

Chase shook his head. "We will need money to live on until we find a place to stay. I will not come to you as a beggar."

"Oh, all right. Maybe I can find a way to earn some money, too."

Chase took a deep breath. "Tell me," he whispered. "Tell me again that you love me."

"I love you, Chase the Wind," she said ardently. "Never doubt it for a minute."

"You will tell me every day?"

"Every day."

"We should go back," Chase said.

Beth nodded. He was right. She had to get back home before she was missed. But she hated to leave him. "Tomorrow night?" she asked anxiously. "I'll see you tomorrow night?"

"And every night," he promised.

Reluctant to part, they dressed slowly, pausing now and then for a quick kiss, a tender caress.

When he couldn't put it off any longer, Chase lifted Beth onto the back of his horse, vaulted up behind her, and rode to the edge of town.

"Until tomorrow," he murmured. Lifting the heavy fall of her hair, he pressed soft kisses to the nape of her neck.

"Tomorrow," Beth said. Twisting around in the

saddle, she kissed him, then slid to the ground. "I'll miss you until then."

Chase nodded. He watched her until she was out of sight, then reined his horse around and headed for home.

Dusty was sitting on the front porch when Chase rode up. Dismounting, Chase stood at the bottom of the steps, idly slapping the reins against his palm. "You are up late," he remarked.

"So are you. Where've you been?"

It did not occur to him to lie. "With Beth."

"You had no right to take her," Dusty said. Rising, he walked to the porch rail and stared down at his brother. "She was my girl. I asked her to marry me."

Chase shook his head. "She never said yes."

"She never said no." Dusty placed his hands on the railing, his fingers curling over the edge. "If you'd get the hell out of town, she'd be mine again."

"No. She is mine."

"Dammit, why the hell did you have to come here?"

Chase took a deep breath. Dusty's words cut into him like a knife, sharp and painful.

"You had no right to come here, causing trouble. Dammit, I wish you'd just stayed the hell away."

"Dusty, what are you saying?" Jenny stepped onto the porch, her voice taut with anger. "Chase has as much right here as you do."

"The hell he does."

"Dusty, I won't have you talking to your mother like that," Ryder said. Walking up behind Jenny, he wrapped his arms around her waist. "You'll apologize right now."

"I'm sorry," Dusty muttered.

Jenny placed her hand on Dusty's arm. "We're a family," she said. "All of us together."

"How can you stick up for him? You don't even know him."

"But I want to. He's my son, Dusty, as much as you are."

"Dammit, he's ruined my life."

"That's nonsense, and you know it," Jenny said.

"Your mother's right. I don't think Ralph Johnson would let Beth marry you any more than he's going to let her marry Chase."

"You don't know that," Dusty said brusquely. He glanced at his mother and father, his expression hard. "I don't want to talk about it anymore." He took a deep breath, let it out in a heavy sigh. "I'll be moving into town in the morning."

"Dusty, no!"

He shook his head. "I'm not staying here, with him." Shaking off his mother's hand, he went into the house and slammed the door.

"He is right," Chase said. "I never should have come here."

"Don't say that!" Jenny exclaimed. Hurrying down the stairs, she reached out to Chase, wanting to touch him but afraid he would rebuff her. "I'm glad you're here, Chase," she said, lowering her hand to her side. "Please don't think of leaving."

"This is Dusty's home, not mine."

"You're wrong. You have as much right to be here as Dusty does, maybe more. I have a lot to make up to you, Chase. Please let me try."

Marshaling her courage, Jenny took one of his hands in hers. His hand was large and brown and calloused. "Please don't go. I can't bear the thought of losing you again."

"Your mother's right," Ryder added. "Your place is here. Please stay."

They wanted him. The knowledge filled his heart, expanding, making him feel weak inside. He swallowed the lump rising in his throat, blinked back the tears he considered a weakness.

"Please, Chase?" Jenny implored softly. "We have so many years to make up for."

"I will stay." His mother's hand, still holding his, felt warm and oddly familiar.

She smiled up at him, her green eyes luminous in the moonlight, and Chase knew why three men had loved her, had fought for her.

Standing on tiptoe, Jenny kissed his cheek. "Thank you. Son." The last word was a caress wrapped in a whisper.

Chase nodded, then looked up at Ryder. "I would like to work for you."

"You're family. You don't need to earn your keep."

"I need a job," Chase said, "a way to earn money for the future."

Ryder nodded in understanding. "All right. You can start tomorrow, and I'll pay you the same wages as I pay the other hands. Just one thing. I don't want you to even think of paying room and board. This is your home, not a hotel."

"Thank you."

"Glad to do it. I could use a hand with the horses."

"Well, that's settled then," Jenny said. "Are you coming in, Chase? It's late."

"Not yet."

"Well, good night, then."

"Good night, Mother." He glanced up at Ryder. "Good night."

" 'Night, son. And don't worry. Everything will work out."

"Will it?" Jenny asked as she followed Ryder down the hall to their bedroom. "Work out, I mean?"

"I hope so, Jenny girl. Hey, cheer up. Dorinda will be home before you know it."

Jenny nodded. At least there was one good thing to look forward to.

The next morning, Dusty was gone. In spite of all that his mother and Ryder had said the night before, Chase couldn't shake off the guilt that plagued him. He had never meant to cause trouble for his mother. He'd only wanted to learn why she had left him, nothing more. He had planned to confront her, and then leave. But that had been before he met Jenny. Before he met Beth.

Jenny and Ryder had tried to put him at ease during breakfast, assuring him that Dusty would be back.

"His pride's hurt, that's all," Ryder had said. "It's not easy to think the girl you love prefers another man."

"Especially when that man is your brother," Chase had muttered bitterly.

"Finish your coffee, cowboy," Ryder had said, slapping him on the back. "We've got work to do."

Sitting on top of a bucking bronc was exactly what he'd needed, Chase thought later that day. There was no time to think about Dusty or Beth or anything else, not when you were sitting on top of a thousand pounds of bucking horse whose only goal was to dislodge you from its back.

Once or twice, Ryder had stopped by to watch him, always with an encouraging word. At midday, Jenny had called them in for lunch. She hummed softly as she filled their plates, smiled often. If she was upset about Dusty moving out, she didn't say so.

Chase had worked the rough string until dusk, then cleaned up for dinner.

Now, sitting at the table, he found himself looking at the clock again and again, counting the hours and minutes until he could see Beth again.

After dinner, he followed Ryder and Jenny into the parlor. Jenny sat on the sofa, mending one of Ryder's shirts. Ryder sat beside her, muttering under his breath as he went over the ranch accounts.

Too restless to sit, Chase stood up and paced the floor.

"Something wrong?" Jenny asked.

"No," Chase said. "I am not used to being inside so much, I guess."

"I imagine you'll be going out for a ride later on," Ryder remarked.

"Yes."

Ryder met Chase's gaze. "Be careful out there in the dark."

"Of course he'll be careful. For goodness sakes, Ryder, he's a grown man." Jenny's voice trailed off. "You're meeting Beth on the sly, aren't you?" she asked.

Chase nodded.

"Do you think that's wise?" Ryder asked.

Chase arched one brow in wry amusement. "What would you do?"

Ryder grunted softly. "The same thing, I reckon. Just be careful. Ralph Johnson can be a vindictive son of a bitch when he's crossed."

"He wants her to marry someone else. Some man from the east."

"Lester Harbaugh," Jenny said with a nod. "I overheard Theda talking about it in town today."

"It will not happen," Chase said.

"Just what is it you're planning to do?" Ryder asked.

"I am going to take Beth away from here at the end of October. She tells me she will no longer need her father's permission to marry after the fifteenth day of December. On that day, we will be married again, in the white man's way."

"Be careful, son," Ryder admonished. "I wouldn't put anything past Johnson. Beth's his only child, and he's always been protective of her. I wasn't kidding when I said I didn't think he'd let her marry Dusty, either. Johnson's got no use for half-breeds, or anybody else that he considers inferior."

"I will be careful," Chase said, "but I will have Beth, one way or another."

"I've never known a day to pass so slowly," Beth murmured. She snuggled against Chase, wanting to be closer, wanting to be part of him.

"I know." He trailed feathery kisses down her cheek, nibbled at her earlobe.

They had met at the river over an hour ago, their hands eager as they undressed each other. The hours they had spent apart, the knowledge that they were meeting in secret, had only served to fuel their desire.

He had made love to her quickly, unable to restrain his passion, his need, and then he had made love to her again, slowly, sweetly, worshipping her with his hands and his lips, whispering that he loved her, arousing her until she quivered with need, until she had begged him to take her.

And now they lay nestled in each other's arms, their legs entwined, her head resting on his shoulder.

"What did you do today?" Beth asked. She traced lazy circles on his chest, gradually working her way lower, lower.

"Worked some of the horses," Chase said, then gasped as her fingertips brushed against his groin.

"Oh?"

He heard the smile in her voice as she ran her hand along the inside of his thigh.

"Yes," he said, his voice growing ragged as her hand continued to move up and down the length of his thigh. "Ryder has some fine animals."

"Really?" She ran her tongue over the hollow of his shoulder, up the length of his neck.

"Beth." Her name was a groan on his lips.

She propped herself up on one elbow and gazed down at him, batting her eyelashes in mock innocence. "Is something wrong?"

Chase looked up at her, awed by her beauty. He was not accustomed to flirting. There had been little time for it in his life.

"Beth, do you know what it does to me when you look at me like that? When you . . ." He groaned low in his throat as her fingertips skimmed over his belly, teasing and tempting and tormenting him. "When you touch me like that?"

"What does it do?" she whispered. "Tell me."

Taking her hand, he pressed it over his groin. "This."

"Are you complaining?"

"No," he said hoarsely, "so long as you do not complain when I do this." And rolling on top of her, he sheathed himself within the warmth of her body.

Beth smiled up at him, sighing with contentment as he began to move slowly deep within her. Safe in his arms, caught up in the passion that engulfed them with the speed and intensity of a flash fire, she forgot everything but the man who kissed her with such ardor, such tenderness, who loved her so completely.

Hours later, they stood facing each other in the waning light of the moon.

She hated to leave him, hated to have to go home to her cold, lonely bed.

"Couldn't we run away now?" she asked. "I miss you so much."

"Soon," he promised. "It takes money to live in the white man's world. I will not have you live like a beggar."

She wrapped her arms around him and held him tight. "I wouldn't mind."

"I would."

He kissed her one more time, then lifted her onto his horse and swung up behind her.

Beth leaned back against him, thinking how romantic it was, the two of them riding double through the darkness. The night wrapped around them, cocooning them in a world of their own, a world of moonlight and shadow. Crickets and tree frogs serenaded them as they passed by.

All too soon, they reached the edge of town. One more fervent kiss, one more fierce hug, and she was standing alone, watching him ride away.

Only a few more months, she told herself as she tiptoed into the house and up to her room. Only a few more months, and they'd be together forever.

Chapter Twenty-one

Dusty sat in his office, his feet propped on the desk-top, his hands steepled in front of him. Five weeks had passed since he'd moved out of the house. In that time, he'd hardly seen his mother or his father. He knew he'd hurt his mother's feelings when he moved out, but, damn it, she'd hurt his feelings, too.

For what must have been the hundredth time, he wished Chase had never come to Twin Rivers. If it wasn't for Chase, he'd still be living at the ranch, and Beth would still be his girl.

No doubt she'd be at the dance tomorrow night. He wondered if Chase would show up. There was a good chance he wouldn't, a chance Dusty might get to see Beth, might get to speak to her for a few minutes alone.

He swore under his breath. This was his town. If he wanted to go to the dance, he'd go. And if he wanted to talk to Beth, he'd talk to her. And no half-brother born on the wrong side of the blanket would stop him.

Glancing at the clock, he jumped to his feet. Damn! It was almost time to pick up Dorinda. She'd rake him up one side and down the other if he was late.

Grinning at the prospect of seeing her again, he left the office. She'd decided to come home early, and she wanted to surprise their mother, so she'd sent Dusty a wire asking him to pick her up. Of course, it meant driving out to the ranch, but he'd do it, for her. He'd drop Dorinda off, and then leave.

Walking down the boardwalk toward the livery barn, he nodded to those he passed. The friendly nods and smiles he received in return lifted his spirits.

He was almost at the livery when he saw Rebecca coming out of Clausen's Meat Market carrying a large package. He hadn't seen her since that day at the ranch, and it hit him with the suddenness of a Texas twister that he'd missed her, that his life seemed as bleak as the Arizona desert without her.

"Afternoon, Rebecca," he said, tipping his hat. "Can I help you with that?"

"Thank you, Mr. Fallon, but I can manage."

In that instant, something deep inside him shifted and he knew he was in love with Rebecca, knew that he'd have realized it far sooner if he hadn't been so blinded by his pride.

Determined to make up for lost time, he turned on his brightest smile. "Come on, Becky, that package looks heavy."

"I said I can manage."

"Okay, okay." He held up his hands in a gesture of surrender. "I give up."

She started down the boardwalk, and Dusty fell into step beside her. When she reached her buggy, he took the package from her arms and placed it on the seat, then took one of her hands in his. "Listen, Becky, I'm sorry I acted the way I did. I never meant to hurt you."

She looked up at him, but said nothing as she very carefully, and very deliberately, removed her hand from his.

So, she was going to be stubborn. "Hey," he coaxed, "won't you give me just one smile?"

"I have to go."

He caught her hand in his again, determined to have his own way. "Dammit, Becky, I said I was sorry. What else do you want from me?"

"Nothing, Dusty. Nothing at all." She looked down at their hands. "Would you let me go, please?"

He shook his head, his hand tightening on hers. "Go to the dance with me tomorrow night?"

"I don't think so. It's obvious that you care for someone else. Please don't bother me again."

Her words were formal, her tone cool and aloof.

"There's no one else, Becky. Not anymore. I've been a fool, and I'm sorry. Won't you give me one more chance? Please, Rebecca? I've missed you."

"Have you?"

He nodded, pleased to see the indifference fading from her eyes. "Pick you up at seven?"

"Well . . ."

"Do you want me to beg?" he asked with a cocky grin. And before she could answer, he dropped to one knee and kissed her hand. "Please go to the dance with me, Rebecca Lynn Winterburn."

"Dusty, please do get up! People are staring!"

"Say you'll go to the dance with me, Rebecca Lynn, or I'll follow you home on my hands and knees."

The idea pleased her even as it embarrassed her. "All right, all right, I'll go. Only do get up!"

Rising, he took both her hands in his, lifting first one and then the other to his lips. "Wear something pretty," he said, winking at her. "Something red."

"Red!"

Dusty nodded. "Red." Lifting her into the buggy, he kissed her quickly on the cheek, handed her the reins, then walked away, feeling better than he had in weeks.

Dorinda was waiting for him outside the depot when he arrived.

"Well, big brother," Dorinda said, grinning as she hugged him tight, "you look like you just dug a hole and found gold."

"I did, little sister, I did."

"Want to tell me about it?"

"Sure." Dusty tossed her bags into the back of the buggy. He turned to help her up, but she'd never been one to wait for a man to help her. She was already seated, smoothing her skirts around her.

"Well? Out with it, Dusty. You look like you're about to burst."

"I'm in love."

"Well, I knew that. How is Beth?"

"It's not Beth. It's Rebecca."

"Rebecca." Dorinda clapped her hands. "But

that's wonderful!" She settled back in the seat. "Tell me everything."

Dorinda was shaking her head by the time Dusty finished his story. "We have a half-brother who's Apache! I can't believe they never told us."

"You'll meet him when you get home. He's staying at the ranch."

Dorinda laughed. "To think, I went to New York looking for excitement. I guess I should have stayed home."

"I'm glad you're back, Dorrie."

"Are you sure you're all right?" she asked. "No ill effects from the shooting or anything?"

"I'm fine."

"I think you should come back home, Dusty. You can't blame mother for wanting to get to know her other son better. And you can't blame him for wanting to stay."

"I know. I behaved badly, but I couldn't help it. It would have been easier if you'd been here."

"Well, I'm here now, and I don't intend to ever leave again. They can keep New York City. It's noisy and dirty . . . but parts of it are wonderful. Oh, Dusty, you should see the Statue of Liberty. And the museums. And the art galleries. I wish I could paint. Maybe I'll give it a try."

Dusty drew the team to a halt. "Here we are. Home sweet home." After wrapping the reins around the brake, he lifted her bags from the back of the buggy and carried them to the porch stairs. "I'll see you at the dance tomorrow night."

"Of course. I wouldn't miss it. You're coming in, aren't you?"

"No, I've got to get back."

"All right. I'll see you tomorrow night. Save a dance for me."

"I will." He pressed a kiss to her cheek. "I'm glad you're home."

Dorinda waved to her brother as he drove out of the yard; then, taking a deep breath, she picked up her bags and went into the house, eager to meet her new brother.

Chase looked up as the door slammed and a voice called, "Hello, I'm home."

"Dorinda!" Jenny practically flew from her chair as she went to meet her daughter. "We didn't expect you until next week!"

"Hi, Mom. I couldn't wait any longer, and I wanted to surprise you, so I had Dusty pick me up."

Jenny glanced out the front door. "He didn't stay?"

"No, but he said he'd see you tomorrow night at the dance."

Chase watched as Jenny and the younger woman embraced. So, this was his sister. She had hair as long and black as his own. Her eyes were a dark blue, laughing now as she hugged her mother, then her father.

"Welcome home, squirt," Ryder said. He took a step back, then shook his head. "New York seems to have agreed with you."

Dorinda twirled around. "I had a fabulous time, but I missed being home." Her gaze came to rest on the man standing beside the fireplace. "You must be Chase."

He nodded, uncertain of his welcome. And then

Dorinda crossed the room and kissed his cheek. "Hello, brother."

"My sister, I am glad to meet you at last."

With a smile, Dorinda took Chase by the hand and drew him toward the sofa. "Start at the beginning," she said, "and tell me everything."

"I think it went well," Jenny remarked later, when she and Ryder were getting ready for bed.

"I was proud of our girl," Ryder said. "She made him feel at home, welcome. I'm glad."

Jenny nodded. "I wish Dusty had stayed."

"He'll come around. What were you and Dorinda whispering about in the kitchen after supper?"

"It seems Dusty told Dorinda that he's in love with Rebecca."

"I wish that boy would make up his mind. One minute he's in love with Beth and can't live without her, and the next he's wild-eyed for Rebecca. I don't think he knows what he wants."

"It'll all work out for the best," Jenny said, feeling suddenly optimistic. "I just know it."

"Yeah, well, I hope you're right. I'm too old for all this matchmaking."

"Hush that right now, Ryder Fallon!" Jenny admonished. "If you're getting old, that means I'm getting old, and that's something I refuse to do!"

"Yes, ma'am," Ryder said, and sweeping her into his arms, he carried her to bed and proved just how young he really was.

"You might as well come to the dance," Jenny said. "Everyone in town will be there."

"Big doings," Ryder agreed, grimacing as Jenny

straightened his tie. "Dinner and dancing."

"What is the occasion?" Chase asked.

"No occasion," Ryder said. "the women just decided we should have a big dance the last Sunday in September every year, and we foolish men agreed."

Jenny made a face at her husband. "I didn't realize dancing with me was such a dastardly chore."

"Now, Jenny girl, you know I love to dance with you," Ryder said, catching her around the waist and holding her tight. "It's getting dressed up that I hate."

"But you look so handsome," Jenny purred. "Besides, it's nice to see you in something besides scuffed moccasins and dusty Levis."

He looked stunning, she thought. His black jacket and white shirt complemented his dark hair and skin. In deference to her wishes, he was even wearing boots instead of moccasins.

Ryder glanced at himself in the mirror, then grinned. "Not too bad for an old man," he muttered.

"Didn't I tell you last night that you'll never be old?"

"Right, I forgot."

"It's true. You look the same to me now as you did twenty-five years ago."

"You keep looking at me with that gleam in your eye," Ryder warned, nibbling on her earlobe, "and we might never make it to the dance."

Chase turned away. It was obvious they had forgotten he was in the room.

He left the house and walked down to the corral. Propping one foot on the bottom rail, he crossed his arms on the top rail and stared into the distance.

He couldn't help it—he envied Ryder and Jenny the love they shared. They had overcome whatever obstacles they had once faced and had built a good life together.

"Chase," Dorinda called, "are you sure you won't come with us?"

"I'm sure." He watched as Ryder helped his sister and his mother into the carriage.

"I wish you'd reconsider," Jenny said. "I don't like to think of you staying home alone."

Chase shrugged. "Perhaps I will come by later."

Jenny smiled, then turned away as Ryder helped her into the buggy.

Ryder climbed up beside Jenny and took up the reins. "We'll look for you in town, son."

Chase nodded and waved, no longer bothered by the fact that Ryder called him "son." He wished that Beth's parents were not opposed to their being together, wished he could stay here, in this place, with his mother and Ryder, but it wasn't possible.

Leaving the corral, he walked toward the river. The night was cool and quiet, with only the lullaby of a gentle breeze and the low murmur of the river to break the stillness.

He walked for a long time, until there was nothing in sight but the river shining like a black ribbon beneath the full moon, and the prairie that stretched beyond, flat and endless.

At times like these, it was easy to pretend that nothing had changed, that he was still a warrior living in the old way, as the Apache had always lived. In Rainbow Canyon, before the soldiers came the last time, he had known who he was, had known where he belonged. Now he felt like dandelion fluff blown by the wind. He had no roots anywhere, no place of his own to call home. A stranger in a strange land. He had heard those words somewhere, knew exactly what they meant.

He picked up a rock and skimmed it across the river. Soon, he would take Beth away here. It amazed him that she loved him enough to leave this place, that she was willing to leave her parents and all that was familiar, to go with him, to be with him. He had nothing to offer her—no home, no land, no way to earn a living, and yet she didn't seem to care.

Somehow, he would make a home for her. No matter what it took, no matter what sacrifices he had to make, he vowed to make her happy, to give her everything she desired, everything she deserved, so she would never regret her decision to go away with him.

Beth. She was the beat of his heart, the air that he breathed. Beth.

He turned back toward the ranch, the need to see her burning strong and bright within him. His mother had said everyone went to the dance. Perhaps Beth would be there. Even if he couldn't talk to her, at least he could look at her, hear the sound of her voice, see her smile.

The thought of seeing her quickened his pace until he was running. Toward Beth. Toward home.

The dance, which was held in the schoolhouse, was in full swing by the time Chase got there. The room had been cleared of desks; chairs had been pushed against the walls. Several long tables held a variety of pies and cakes, as well as a large punch bowl. Colored streamers and paper lanterns hung from the ceiling.

Standing in the open doorway, Chase scanned the room. He saw his mother waltz by with Ryder, caught sight of Dusty twirling a pretty young woman in a red dress around the floor. Dorinda stood off to the side, surrounded by a group of young men and women who all seemed to be talking at once, and then he saw Beth and everything else faded into the background. She was dancing with a man who held her far too tightly. It was all Chase could do to keep from crossing the floor and putting his fist in the other man's face.

When the music ended, the man took Beth by the hand and led her back to where her parents were sitting. Ralph Johnson looked stern in a dark brown suit and tie. Theda Johnson looked like a pumpkin in an orange dress with a yellow sash. And Beth . . . She was a vision in a floor-length gown of dark pink silk. Her hair, held back from her face by a pair of ivory combs, fell down her back in a mass of golden waves. She had never looked lovelier, or more out of reach.

As if she felt his gaze, Beth slowly turned around. He saw the warmth of recognition in her eyes, the smile that curved her lips. A smile that was for him, and him alone.

The man at her side spoke to her, and she turned away.

"Chase! You came. I'm so glad."

He turned to see his mother and Ryder coming toward him. They were smiling and holding hands. His mother's cheeks were flushed, and her eyes sparkled with delight.

"I'm going to get your mother some punch," Ryder said. "Can I get you some?"

"Thank you."

"There's a nice crowd here tonight," Jenny said, "but then, there usually is." She smiled up at him. "Will you dance the next dance with me?"

Chase shook his head. "I do not know the white man's dances."

"Your father couldn't dance either, until I taught him." Jenny smiled at the memory. Ryder hadn't been keen on dancing, but he had admitted, later, that he was in favor of anything that put her in his arms. It had been fun, teaching him to waltz and to polka. She remembered how they had laughed as they whirled around the old cabin.

Chase shook his head again. He didn't want to make a fool of himself here, in front of a roomful of strangers. In front of Beth.

"Who is that man?" he asked, pointing at the man hovering at Beth's side.

Jenny glanced over her shoulder. "Oh, that's Ernest Tucker. He works at the bank."

"I do not like the way he looks at Beth."

Jenny placed her hand on her son's arm. "Chase, please, don't cause any trouble here. It will only infuriate Ralph, and embarrass Beth."

A muscle worked in Chase's jaw as he watched the man called Ernest Tucker lead Beth out onto the dance floor again. Through narrowed eyes, he studied the man. He was of medium height and build, with slicked-back light brown hair and pale brown eyes. He held Beth with confidence, smiling at her often as he waltzed her around the floor.

Chase wanted to kill him.

Ryder returned a few minutes later, carrying three cups of punch. He handed one to Jenny, and one to Chase. "Cheers," he said.

Chase nodded, his gaze riveted on Beth.

"Dusty and Rebecca look good together, don't they?" Jenny remarked.

Ryder nodded, but his attention was focused on Chase. He could sense the tension radiating from the younger man, feel the jealousy that pulsed with every beat of his heart, the hatred that flowed through his veins.

"Chase." Ryder shook his shoulder. "Chase."

Slowly, Chase met Ryder's gaze.

"It isn't worth it," Ryder said quietly.

"He holds her too closely."

"It's just a dance. It doesn't mean anything."

"Doesn't it? I see the way he looks at her."

"But she's not looking at him," Jenny said. "She's watching you."

When the dance ended, Jenny walked over to say hello to Ivy Patterson, who was sitting near Beth's mother. After a few moments, Jenny turned to say hello to Beth, who was, for the moment, alone.

"How are you, Beth?" Jenny asked.

"Fine, Mrs. Fallon. And you?"

"Quite well, thank you." Leaning closer, Jenny whispered, "Chase sends his love."

Beth's smile was radiant. "Tell him hello for me. And tell him . . . Never mind."

"Tell him what, Beth? You can tell me."

"Tell him I'll meet him later, in the usual place."

"I'll tell him."

"Mrs. Fallon?"

"Yes, dear?"

"Tell him I love him. Tell him I'd rather be dancing with him."

"I think he knows that, dear, but I'll tell him."

Giving Beth a pat on the shoulder, Jenny went back to stand with Ryder and Chase. A few minutes later, Dusty and Rebecca joined them.

"Hello, Mother. Father."

"Good evening, Mr. and Mrs. Fallon."

Ryder nodded at his son. "Dusty. Rebecca. It's nice to see you."

"Looks like Dorinda's the belle of the ball," Dusty remarked as he watched his sister waltz by. "She's danced every dance."

"It's good to have her home again," Jenny said. "That's a lovely dress, Rebecca. Is it new?"

Rebecca looked over at Dusty and smiled. "Yes, it is."

"It's a lovely shade of red."

"Thank you," Rebecca said. "Who's this?"

"Oh, I'm sorry. This is my son, Chase," Jenny said. "Chase, this is Rebecca Winterburn. She's one of our school teachers."

Rebecca offered her hand and Chase took it, aware, all the while, of his brother's shuttered gaze.

"Having a good time, Rebecca?" Jenny asked.

"Yes, thank you. Dusty is a wonderful dancer."

"Takes after his old man," Ryder said, grinning.

Jenny laughed softly. "Come on, Twinkle Toes," she said, grabbing Ryder by the hand, "they're playing our song."

An awkward silence rose between Dusty and Chase. Chase watched his parents dance, wishing there was some way to breach the distance between himself and his brother.

"Come on, Becky," Dusty said, "let's dance."

Chase cleared his throat. "Dusty, can I talk to you?"

Dusty shook his head. He knew what his brother wanted to say, but he wasn't ready to hear it yet.

"Excuse me," Rebecca said. "I think I'll go say hello to Mrs. Patterson."

"I am sorry for the hurt I have caused you," Chase said quietly. "I ask your forgiveness."

Dusty took a deep breath. Maybe it was time to get it over with, time to make amends with his brother, especially now, when the reason for their animosity no longer existed.

He turned his back on Chase, needing a moment to gather his thoughts, and his gaze settled on Beth. She was standing near Rebecca, and he studied the two women—each beautiful in her own way. Beth, blond and fair, with dark brown eyes and honey-hued skin; and Rebecca, with her long dark hair and soft gray eyes. One was a lark and one was a dove, albeit a dove clad in a bright red dress, and he knew in his heart that it was Rebecca he loved, Rebecca he wanted to spend the rest of his life with.

He turned around, intending to tell his brother that he'd been wrong, that he was willing to make amends, but it was too late. Chase was gone.

Dusty glanced around the dance floor. He saw his mother and father standing near the punch bowl, saw Rebecca talking to Melinda Patterson, saw Dorinda laughing at something Daisy Patterson had said.

But there was no sign of Chase.

When he turned back to look for Beth, she was gone, too.

Chapter Twenty-two

They met behind the schoolhouse. Hand in hand, they ran into the shadows until they came to a small clearing within a grove of trees.

"This is dangerous," Chase said, glancing over his shoulder.

"I don't care. I couldn't wait any longer."

Beth rose on her tiptoes and pressed her lips to his. She couldn't be in the same room and not be with him, not talk to him. Not want him. Couldn't stand another minute of listening to Ernest Tucker try to sweet-talk her.

She had been sorely tempted to tell Mr. Ernest Leroy Tucker that he was a hypocrite, refusing to marry her but all too willing to make time with her, but it had seemed easier to let him prattle on.

Let people think she was sweet on Ernest. What did she care? In another month, she'd be gone, and she would never have to see any of the people in Twin Rivers again.

"I wanted to kill him," Chase said, his lips moving in her hair.

"Kill who?"

"That *gusano* who was dancing with you?"

"Ernest?" Beth laughed softly. "He's nothing."

"He can hold you when I cannot. He can dance with you, talk to you. Smile at you."

"But you can hold me now," Beth reminded him with a saucy grin. "And kiss me, if you'd just shut up."

"Vixen," he murmured, and slanting his mouth over hers, he kissed her long and hard, leaving no doubt in her mind that she belonged to him and no one else.

Her legs were trembling when he took his lips from hers.

"Beth, I need you so."

"I know." She unbuttoned his shirt and slipped her hands inside, letting her palms slide over the smooth expanse of skin beneath. "I love to touch you," she whispered. "Touch me."

With a groan, he drew her down on the grass, his hands sliding down her back, skimming across her breasts. She came alive in his hands, arching her back, pressing herself against him, until he was blind with need.

It was madness, being with her here, like this. In the distance, he could hear the faint strains of a fiddle, the high-pitched shriek of feminine laughter.

And then everything else ceased to matter. All other sounds faded into the background, and he heard only the harsh rasp of his own breathing, the seductive whisper of silk sliding over flesh as he slipped her dress over her shoulders.

"You wear too many clothes," he muttered as he divested her of her undergarments.

"You don't," she said, a grin in her voice. He wore only a shirt and trousers and moccasins.

At last they were together, fevered flesh against fevered flesh, two hearts beating as one, two souls merged into a perfect joining of mind and body.

Heaven, Beth thought as the earth righted itself once again. Being in Chase's arms was like being in heaven.

She wrapped her arms tight around him when he would have rolled away. "Not yet."

Bracing himself on his elbows, Chase smiled down at her. "I've too heavy for you."

She shook her head. "No."

With a sigh, he rested his forehead against hers, thinking he would like to stay as they were forever, with her arms around him and his body sheathed within her warmth. She shifted her hips beneath him, and he felt the faint stirrings of desire flutter through him once again.

Chase lifted his head, his lips brushing hers. "We'd better go," he said reluctantly, "before . . ."

"Not yet." She closed her eyes, drifting on a warm sea of contentment.

"You slut!" Her father's voice jerked Beth back to the present.

"Father!" She glanced up at Chase, who was still lying over her, shielding her nakedness from view.

"Get up, Injun."

Chase hesitated a moment, then stood up, his hands clenched at his sides.

Jackknifing to a sitting position, Beth grabbed her dress and held it over her breasts. Fear snaked through her, making her mouth dry. Even so, a distant part of her mind couldn't help but think how magnificent Chase looked standing there, his body bathed in moonlight, his expression defiant.

"Get up, Elizabeth."

There was no room for argument in her father's voice. Or in the two rifle barrels leveled at Chase.

"You." Loathing dripped from Ralph Johnson's voice as he leveled an accusing finger at Chase. "Get away from her."

A muscle worked in Chase's jaw. It was in his mind to refuse, but then he looked at the two riflemen. Both looked capable of killing him where he stood. If there was to be any shooting, he didn't want to take a chance of Beth getting hurt. Jaw clenched, Chase took several steps to the left. Naked and unarmed, he felt as vulnerable as a newborn colt.

"Mel, Lowell, get him out of here while my daughter gets dressed."

The man on the right jerked his rifle toward the deep woods behind them. "You heard what Mr. Johnson said, Injun, git goin'."

"If he doesn't cooperate, shoot him," Johnson said. "No one will object to my defending my daughter's honor."

With a last look at Beth, Chase walked deeper into the forest that grew behind the schoolhouse.

Beth clutched her dress to her breasts. "What are you going to do to him?"

"He's going to get just what he deserves. And you're going to watch. Get your clothes on."

Panic rose up within her. She had never seen her

father look so angry, so . . . uncivilized. "What are you going to do?"

"Get dressed, Elizabeth."

She waited until he turned his back. Ignoring her undergarments, she pulled on her dress, her fingers shaking so badly she could hardly fasten the buttons.

"Father . . ."

He turned around, his eyes filled with contempt. "Let's go."

She didn't resist when he grabbed her by the arm and forced her to follow him into the woods.

A few minutes later, they stepped into a small clearing. Chase stood facing Mel and Lowell, his hands tied behind his back, his expression impassive. Blood oozed from a cut in his lower lip.

"Get on with it," her father said.

Grim-faced, Mel and Lowell handed their rifles to her father. Then, with great deliberation, they each pulled on a pair of leather gloves.

"No." Beth shook her head. "Father, you can't do this."

She watched in horror as the two men closed in on Chase, their fists driving into him with steady precision. Hands bound behind his back, Chase was helpless to defend himself.

Feeling as though she were caught in the jaws of a nightmare, Beth watched Chase stumble back. Blood dripped from his nose and mouth. His breath was ragged and uneven, and she wondered how he could endure such a horrible beating without crying out.

"Father, make them stop!"

"Shut up, Elizabeth."

She pressed her hands over her ears in an effort to block the horrible sound of fists striking flesh, but the sound echoed and re-echoed in her mind. She wanted to close her eyes, to look away, but something compelled her to watch. If he could suffer such a brutal beating in silence, then it would be her punishment to watch it, to listen to the harsh rasp of his breathing, to watch the blood drip from his nose and mouth, to know he was suffering and it was all her fault.

"Please, make them stop," she begged. "Please, please, please. This is all my fault." She tugged on her father's arm, desperate to make him listen. "I made Chase come out here with me. He didn't want to."

She tugged on her father's arm again. "Make them stop. Please make them stop!" She repeated the words in a helpless litany that fell on deaf ears.

She groaned as Chase's legs gave way and he fell to the ground, his body curling in on itself in an effort to avoid the punishing blows that went on and on. And on.

She heard each individual blow, each grunt of pain that passed his lips.

"That's enough."

She sighed with relief as her father put an end to the brutal beating.

Mel and Lowell stepped back, breathing hard.

Elizabeth started forward, but her father grabbed her by the arm. "Stay here," he commanded sharply.

Ralph Johnson walked forward until he was standing over Chase. "You know what they do to unruly stallions, don't you, redskin?"

Chase stared up at the man through a red haze of pain, his gut knotting with dread.

"Give me your knife, Lowell," Ralph said.

"Father, no!"

"Shut up, you slut." Rage burned in Ralph Johnson's eyes as he took Lowell's knife.

Chase glared up at Beth's father through eyes nearly swollen shut. But it was not the man who held his attention now, it was the knife that drew his eye in morbid fascination. Moonlight glinted on the long narrow blade.

"They geld rogue stallions," Ralph Johnson said. "That way, they can't pass on their undesirable blood." Ralph glanced at Mel and Lowell. "Hold him down."

Pain splintered through Chase as he struggled against the two men who held him down. He heard Beth scream, cringed as he felt the touch of hard cold steel against his groin.

"Father! No!" Beth stared at her father in horror as she realized what he meant to do. Revulsion rose up within her. "No." She shook her head, unable to accept the horror of it. Chase would hate her now, and she couldn't blame him.

Chase closed his eyes, his whole body taut, his heart pounding in dreadful anticipation as he waited for the blade to cut away his manhood. He only hoped they would kill him after.

"Drop that knife, Johnson, or you're dead where you stand."

"This isn't your affair, Fallon."

"It is now. Dammit, Johnson, drop that knife."

Slowly, Ralph Johnson stood up, the knife still

clutched in his hand. "This dirty redskin defiled my daughter."

"I don't think so. Mel, Lowell, cut him loose."

The two men looked at each other, then at Johnson.

"He's not in charge here," Ryder said, his voice deadly quiet. "I am. Now cut him loose and get the hell out of here."

Moving quickly, the two men cut Chase's hands free, then hurried toward town.

"Drop the knife, Ralph."

Johnson hesitated another minute, then, with a flick of his wrist, he tossed the knife into the dirt. "Come, Elizabeth."

She shook her head. "No, I'm staying here."

"You will come with me."

"Go with him," Ryder told her curtly. "There's nothing you can do here."

"Please, Mr. Fallon," Beth pleaded softly. "I can't leave him. Not now. He needs me."

"I'll take good care of him. I promise. Now, go on home. There's been enough trouble tonight."

With a last, soulful glance at Chase, Beth let herself be led away.

Muttering an oath, Ryder holstered his gun, then knelt beside Chase, who was shivering uncontrollably. Johnson's men had done a thorough job. There was hardly an inch of flesh on Chase's body that wasn't already turning black and blue. Both eyes were nearly swollen shut; blood dripped from a cut on his lower lip. His nose was bleeding and was probably broken. No doubt he had some broken ribs, as well.

"You'll be all right," Ryder said. Removing his

jacket, he draped it around Chase's shoulders. "Just sit tight while I go get some help."

"No." Wracked with pain, it was an effort for Chase to speak. "No one . . . to . . . see me."

"I understand," Ryder said sympathetically, "but I don't think I can carry you all the way back to the schoolhouse."

"No."

"I know, you don't want anyone to see you." Ryder swore under his breath. "I'll go get the buggy."

"What's going on here?"

Ryder glanced over his shoulder, relieved to see Dusty walking toward him.

"Mother said she can't find Chase, and she wants you . . . damn!" Dusty exclaimed. "What happened to him?"

"Johnson found him out here with Beth. He had a couple of his boys work him over."

Dusty frowned a moment, and then grunted softly. "Yeah, I can see that."

Ryder made a sound of disgust low in his throat. "That's not the worst of it. He was gonna castrate him. I got here just in time to prevent it."

"Lucky."

"Yeah. Go get the carriage, will you? And find your mother. We're going home."

With a weary sigh, Chase closed his eyes against the pain throbbing through him.

"Chase? Hang on, son. We'll get you patched up in no time."

With an effort, Chase opened one eye and looked at Ryder. "Thank . . . you."

Ryder grinned. "Glad I got here when I did."

"Me . . . too." It was an effort to speak. Every

breath sent daggers of pain lancing through his rib cage.

"You'll be all right," Ryder said. "Just rest easy."

Fifteen minutes later, Dusty and Jenny drove up in a flatbed wagon. Jenny was at Chase's side almost before the wagon came to a halt. Anger roiled through her as she saw what Johnson's men had done to her son.

"You should have killed him," she said, glaring at Ryder.

"He didn't give me any cause."

"No cause!" Jenny exclaimed. "No cause! How can you look at what he did and say you had no cause?"

"Calm down, Jenny girl. You can rant all you want later. Right now we need to get Chase to a doctor."

"You're right. We borrowed the Pattersons' wagon because Dusty thought Chase would be more comfortable lying down."

"Dorinda went over to the doc's to tell him we're on our way," Dusty said.

"Good thinking, son. Give me a hand here."

As carefully as possible, they lifted Chase onto the blankets Jenny had spread in the bed of the wagon. She covered Chase with a quilt, then climbed in beside him and took his hand in hers.

"You'll be all right," she crooned softly.

Please God, she prayed. *Let it be true.*

Jenny stood up, her arms folded over her breasts, as the doctor entered the waiting room over an hour later.

"He's gonna be fine," Forbes said quickly, reassuringly. "He's got two black eyes, a broken nose, three busted ribs, and more bruises than I've ever seen on any one man, including Lyle Hewitt after he got stomped on by a loco bronc. But as far as I can tell, there's no internal bleeding, no serious damage."

"Thank you, God," Jenny murmured, blinking back tears of relief. "Can I see him?"

Forbes nodded. He knew Jenny Fallon well enough to know she was going in there whether he said she could or not. "He's pretty heavily sedated, so he won't know you're there, but you can go in, if you like. I want to keep him here a day or two, just to make sure I didn't miss anything, and then you can take him home." He ran a hand through his hair, then smothered a yawn. "I don't want him out of bed for at least two weeks. Light meals for the first few days. I'll give you some laudanum for the pain."

"Thank you, Doctor," Jenny said, then hurried into the other room.

"Yeah, thanks, Doc."

"Is there anything we can do?" Dorinda asked.

"I don't think so," Ryder said.

"We'll wait out here," Dusty said.

Ryder nodded, then went into the other room and closed the door. Jenny was standing at Chase's bedside, tears streaming down her cheeks.

"They could have killed him," she said, choking back a sob. "Damn Ralph Johnson."

"You heard the doc," Ryder said, drawing her into his arms. "Chase is gonna be fine."

"I know, I know, but . . ." She blew out a deep breath, reminding herself that not everyone hated

Indians. They had good friends in Twin Rivers, men and women who liked and respected her in spite of the fact that she was married to an Indian, who accepted and valued Ryder's friendship, who saw him as a man, not a half-breed. Johnson was the exception, not the rule.

"Come on," Ryder urged, "let's go home. There's nothing you can do here."

"No, I can't leave him."

"All right, Jenny girl. I'll send the kids home, and we can stay in town. They can look after things at the ranch for a day or two." He kissed her on the cheek. "I'll be back soon."

With a nod, Jenny pulled a chair up close to the bed. Tenderly, she brushed a lock of hair from Chase's forehead. Thick black hair, like his father's. His face was bruised and discolored. Both eyes were black and swollen shut. His lower lip was twice its normal size. Dark bruises covered his chest and arms; there was a cut on his left cheek. His ribs were tightly bound.

She shuddered as she thought of what Ralph Johnson had intended to do. She lived on a ranch; she'd seen stallions gelded.

Jenny swallowed the bile that rose in her throat and knew that, if Ralph Johnson had been in the room at that moment, she would have killed him without a qualm.

It was a sobering, horrifying thought, but true nonetheless.

And in that instant, when every mothering instinct she possessed was screaming with outrage at what had been done to her son, she understood what had driven Ralph Johnson to pick up that knife.

Chapter Twenty-three

Voices. Familiar voices. They penetrated the thick fog of pain that enveloped him. It hurt to breathe, to move.

"Chase, we're going to prop you up a little more so you can eat."

His mother's voice, thick with tears. She was crying, he thought. Why?

"Chase, can you hear me?"

He nodded slightly. He tried to open his eyes, and couldn't. He lifted one hand toward his face, felt someone take hold of it. "Don't. Your eyes are swollen shut. We're going to lift you up a little now."

He bit back a groan as calloused hands reached under him and lifted him up. Someone placed pillows behind his back.

"I've got some broth here," Jenny said. "Try to eat it."

He shook his head, wanting only to be left alone.

"You've got to eat, Chase. You've got to keep your strength up."

He felt the touch of a spoon at his lips and after a moment, he opened his mouth. Warm beef broth trickled down his throat.

Feeling like a mewling infant, he let his mother feed him. It was humiliating. Unable to see, unable to move, he was completely helpless, completely dependent on her.

He felt her wipe his mouth with a damp cloth; then she offered him a drink of water and more broth, until he couldn't eat any more. The simple act of eating left him exhausted.

"Sleep now," she said.

Rising, Jenny stood staring down at her son for a moment. Every breath was labored, and her heart was aching for the pain he was suffering. She removed one of the pillows from behind him, but left the others, knowing it would be easier for him to breathe if he wasn't lying flat on his back.

Voices sounded around him. Ryder's. The doctor's. Chase knew they were talking about him, but the words eluded him like smoke in the wind. And then sleep claimed him, and he heard nothing at all.

When next he woke, there was no light in the room. Lying there, he wondered if it was night, or early morning. Thirst burned through him; his body felt as though it were on fire.

He flung off the covers, groaned softly as pain splintered through him.

"Lie still." His mother's voice, heavy with sleep. "What do you need?"

"Water . . ."

She placed her hand on his brow. "Good Lord," she exclaimed softly. "You're burning up."

She gave him a glass of water, then went in search of Forbes, who prepared a brown paper poultice.

"Here," he said, handing her several small packages. "Dissolve one of those in a glass of water, and repeat the dose every three or four hours." Forbes grinned at her. "Ever think of being a nurse?"

"No," Jenny said. She tore off a corner of one of the packets and poured the contents into a glass of water.

"Well, you're doing a bang-up job."

"You're sure he'll be all right?"

"I'm sure. You can take him home day after tomorrow. He'll probably rest more comfortably in his own bed." Forbes picked up his black bag. "I've got to go look in on Mrs. McBride," he said, reaching for his hat. "Her baby's due any day, and she's out there all alone until Fred gets back from Tucson. I should be back in an hour or so."

"Thanks, Jonas. I don't know what we'd do without you."

"Oh, I reckon you'd get along," he muttered as he settled his hat on his head.

"Oh, I reckon," Jenny said, grinning at him. "I mean it, Jonas. Thank you."

"Try not to spoil him too much," Forbes said. "See ya later."

Jenny nodded, then turned her attention back to her son. "Here, Chase," she said, lifting his head a little. "Drink this."

He took a swallow, grimacing at the bitter taste.

"All of it," Jenny urged.

Chase shook his head, quietly cursing the helplessness that left him at the mercy of others.

"Please, Chase."

He shook his head again. Bad enough to be laid up without having to drink such a vile concoction.

Jenny frowned, and then, remembering how she had gotten Dusty to take aspirin, she went in search of molasses.

A short time later, she was at his bedside once again. "Open your mouth," she said.

Chase shook his head. He felt awful and wanted nothing so much as to be left alone.

"Come on, you'll like this. I promise." When he still refused, she made a little sound of impatience. "You might as well eat it because I'm not leaving until you do."

Resigned, he accepted the medicine, his mouth filling with a thick syrupy sweetness.

She smoothed the covers over him, brushed the hair back from his brow. He heard the sound of her footsteps move away from the bed.

"Try to get some sleep," she said. "I'll look in on you later."

But sleep eluded him. Shrouded in darkness, his body burning with fever, hurting with every breath, he thought of Beth. Beautiful, sweet Beth. What had her father done to her when he got home? Surely even a man like Ralph Johnson wouldn't beat his own daughter, he thought. And then he recalled the look of outrage in Ralph Johnson's eyes, the disgust in the man's voice when he accused his own daughter of being a slut.

Helpless rage churned through him, and with it

the desire to avenge himself on Beth's father, to make him pay for the cruel beating he himself had received, for the cruel words that had whipped Beth like a lash. His hands closed around the sheet that covered him, clenching tighter, tighter, as he imagined his hands at Johnson's throat, slowly squeezing the life out of him.

"Chase, are you all right?"

Loosening his hold on the sheet, he willed himself to relax. Turning in the direction of his mother's voice, he asked, "Have you seen Beth?"

"No, but I'm sure she's fine."

"Go to her . . . make sure."

"I really don't think I'd be welcome at the Johnson house just now," Jenny said dryly, "but I'll see what I can find out."

And then, in the morning, like a miracle, Beth was there.

"Chase?" Her voice, soft and sweet, was filled with gentle concern.

"Beth?" He turned toward the sound of her voice, wishing he could see her face.

"Chase?" Her hand taking his, clasping it to her breast. "Oh, Chase."

Beth blinked back her tears as she looked at him. His face was a mass of swollen, discolored flesh. There was a cut on his lower lip, another across his left cheek. She could feel the fever raging through him, knew each breath was causing him terrible pain. And it was all her fault.

Chase threaded his fingers through hers. "What are you doing here?"

"Dusty brought me."

"Dusty?"

"Yes. He told my father he needed me to come to the jail and make a statement, that you were filing assault charges against him. Instead, he brought me out here."

"Not . . . true." Dusty and Ryder had both tried to get him to change his mind, to bring charges against Johnson, but he had refused. If he wanted revenge against Johnson, he would extract it himself. He didn't need the white man's law to do it for him.

"Well, you *should* file charges against him!" Beth exclaimed. "You can't just let him get away with this." She lifted his hand to her cheek, turned her head to place a kiss in the center of his palm. "Do you hurt terribly?"

"Not now," Chase replied. "Not when you are here."

Beth brushed his hair from his brow, wishing she could hold him, hug him tight, but she was afraid to touch him. There were cuts and bruises everywhere she looked. Bruises her father had inflicted. "Do you hate me now?"

"Hate you?"

She lifted her hand and let it fall. "For what my father did to you. It's all my fault. Oh, Chase, I'm so sorry. I never dreamed he'd do such a terrible thing. And if Dusty's father hadn't shown up . . ." Her voice trailed off as her mind filled with sickening, full-color images of what might have happened if Ryder Fallon had arrived five minutes later.

"Beth." Ignoring the pain that engulfed him when he moved, Chase reached for her, one hand sliding up her neck, loosening the ribbon that held her hair away from her face. "Come, lie beside me."

"I shouldn't," she said. "I might hurt you."

"Please?"

Unable to refuse him, she sat down on the bed, careful not to jar the mattress as she stretched out beside him, her head pillowed on his shoulder. "Am I hurting you?"

"No." He turned his head, his lips brushing her cheek. "How long can you stay?"

"Not long. Dusty's waiting for me outside. Please get well soon. I miss you. Your mother said they're taking you out to the ranch tomorrow. How will I see you again?"

"I will find a way."

It had to be soon, she thought desperately. Lester Harbaugh would be arriving in less than a week.

There was a knock at the door. "Beth? We'd better go before your old man comes looking for you."

"I'm coming, Dusty."

Chase's arm tightened around her. He had a terrible feeling that if he released her now, he would never see her again.

"I've got to go," Beth said, blinking back her tears. "I love you."

"Beth . . ." He wanted to beg her not to leave him, but he knew it would only distress her, knew that it would only cause more trouble with her father if he learned she had come here.

She kissed him lightly on the mouth, then slid out of bed. "You'll come for me as soon as you can?"

"You know I will."

"I don't want to leave you." She took his hand in hers, her heart breaking as she gazed at his battered flesh. *All my fault,* she thought, *all my fault. How will he ever forgive me?*

"Beth?" Dusty's voice called to her through the door.

"I'm coming." She squeezed Chase's hand, bent to give him one last kiss. "Good-bye."

He listened to the sound of her footsteps as she crossed the floor, heard the door open and then close again, and knew he could never repay his brother for that one act of kindness that had brought Beth to him when he needed her most.

Chapter Twenty-four

The ride out to the ranch was long and uncomfortable. Ryder kept the horses to a slow walk, but every jolt, every breath, sent shards of pain splintering through him. Jenny sat in the back of the wagon with Chase, cradling his head in her lap.

Chase had objected at first. He didn't want anyone pitying him, or seeing him when he felt so vulnerable, so damned helpless. But his mother had refused to leave his side, and after a while, he admitted it was pleasant to lie there with the sun on his face and his head resting in her lap. As if he were a small child, she stroked his hair, murmuring low, soothing words of comfort.

For all that her hands were worn and calloused from years of hard work on the ranch, her touch was light and gentle.

"Tell me," Chase said, his hands clenched beneath the blanket that covered him. "Tell me how you met Ryder."

"He was scouting for the Army," Jenny said, smiling at the memory. "Some major had blackmailed him into it. I don't remember why now. Kayitah attacked the patrol at Rock Springs. Most of the soldiers were killed, but Ryder and a few others were taken captive. Ryder was wounded. He's half-Cheyenne, but the Apache had adopted him into the tribe years earlier when he saved the life of one of their young men.

"Anyway, when they got back to the rancheria, some of the warriors wanted to kill him. They said he was a traitor for scouting for the Army, but one old woman spoke in his behalf, and then the medicine man stepped forward and declared that it wasn't right for one Apache to kill another. Only *Usen* had that right, he said, so it was decided that they would keep Ryder bound to a tree for five days. If he was still alive when the five days were over, then they would know it was *Usen*'s will that he should live."

Jenny shook her head. "He was so brave," she said, her voice catching as she glanced up at Ryder's back. "I knew if he lived, he wouldn't remain a prisoner for very long."

"So you helped him," Chase guessed, wishing he could see her face.

"She blackmailed me, is what she did," Ryder said. Glancing over his shoulder, he grinned at Jenny. "Seems like everybody was blackmailing me for one thing or another back then."

"She blackmailed you?" Chase asked. "How?"

"She refused to give me anything to drink until I promised to take her away with me," Ryder said, chuckling with the memory.

Chase grinned. "Is that right?"

Jenny nodded, then, realizing Chase couldn't see her, she said, "It's true."

"Would you have let him go thirsty?" Chase asked.

"No," Jenny said.

"Now she tells me," Ryder muttered with mock despair. "Why don't you tell him how Alope kept me as her slave? He ought to get a kick out of that."

"Alope did that?" Chase asked, the throbbing pain in his side momentarily forgotten.

"Yes. She made him fetch and carry, and when he didn't obey quick enough, she took him outside and whipped him in front of everyone. One day she pretended he was a horse and made him spend the day on his hands and knees."

Jenny looked at Ryder. He was facing forward, but she could tell by the rigid set of his shoulders that he was reliving the humiliation he had suffered at Alope's hands. She had been the one to wash the blood from Ryder's back when Alope finished whipping him. She had been the one to sneak him food when Alope got angry and refused to feed him. On days when Alope had nothing for Ryder to do, she had left him tethered to a tree from dawn till dark, leaving him at the mercy of the sun and the flies. The day Alope had made Ryder pretend to be a horse had been one of the worst. She had put a rope around his neck and led him into the forest. She had collected a pile of wood, then lashed it onto Ryder's back and made him carry it back to the village on his hands and knees, poking him in the ribs and buttocks the whole way to the amusement of the other women in the village. She would never forget how humiliated Ryder had been, how he had refused to meet her gaze.

"I cannot believe she would do such a thing," Chase said. He had never seen Alope be cruel or unkind to anyone.

"Well, it's true," Jenny said. "She was jealous because I was Kayitah's prisoner. I think she hoped to make *him* jealous when she took Ryder for a slave, but it didn't work."

"And so the two of you ran away?"

Jenny nodded. "It was raining that night. We might have made it if my horse hadn't gone down. I went into labor. Kayitah found us the next morning. He threatened to kill Ryder and me both if Ryder refused to give you up. When I realized I was going to lose you, I begged your father to take me back, but he refused."

It had all been so long ago, Chase mused, yet he could hear the pain in her voice, as fresh as if it had happened yesterday. Not knowing what to say, he took her hand in his and squeezed it.

A few minutes later, they reached the ranch.

Within minutes, Chase was settled in bed, as comfortable as could be expected, all things considered.

Jenny hovered over him, wanting to do something, anything, to make the hurt go away. Just looking at her son, at the horrible bruises on his face and body, made her want to hit something—preferably Ralph Johnson.

"Are you there, *Cima?*"

"Yes, I'm here," Jenny said, her throat constricting as he used the Apache term for mother. "Do you need something?"

"Water. And . . . could you send Ryder to me?"

"Of course. Do you need anything else? Something to eat?"

"No." He hesitated a moment. *"Cima."*

"Yes, *ciye?"* she replied, using the Apache word for son.

"Thank you."

"For what?"

"For taking me in. For understanding my anger, and forgiving me for it."

Tears filled Jenny's eyes, sweet tears that washed away all the heartache of the past. "I'll send Ryder in to you, Chase."

For Chase, the next two days passed slowly. With his eyes still swollen shut, he was trapped in darkness. Most of the time, he slept, but when he was awake, his every thought was for Beth. He wondered if she was all right, if her father had dared to beat her, when he would see her again.

Four days after the beating, most of the swelling was gone from his eyes and he was able to get up for short periods of time.

Now, a week later, he stood at the front window in the parlor, staring out at the rain. The horses in the corral stood with their backs to the wind, their heads lowered. Beyond the grass that grew near the house, the earth was a sea of dark brown mud. Thunder echoed across the skies; jagged bolts of lightning rent the clouds. Flames snapped and crackled in the hearth, turning away the chill.

The storm and his inactivity both made him restless.

He glanced at his mother, who was sitting on the

sofa reading a book. Ryder sat beside her, mending a bridle.

"Chase, can I get you anything?" Jenny asked. "Some coffee, or a glass of milk?"

He shook his head.

"I'd like a cup of coffee," Ryder said, looking up.

"Okay."

"And maybe a slice of that cake you made this morning?"

"All right. Chase, are you sure you don't want something?"

Glancing over his shoulder, he smiled at her. "You know I cannot resist your chocolate cake."

"Good," she said, rewarding him with a smile. "Two slices of cake coming right up."

"I've never seen your mother so happy," Ryder remarked, setting the bridle aside. "I can't tell you what it's meant for her to have you here."

"It has been good for me, too." And it had been, except for the trouble with Beth's parents.

"What are you gonna do about Beth?" Ryder asked.

Chase grinned wryly, wondering if his thoughts were so transparent. "As soon as my ribs heal, I am going after her."

"Do you think that's wise?"

Chase shrugged, wincing as the movement pulled on his injured ribs. "Love is not a matter of wisdom, but of the heart. I cannot be whole without her."

Ryder nodded, understanding what Chase meant all too well. Try as he might, he couldn't think of any way out of this mess that would make everybody happy.

* * *

Beth stood in front of the mirror arranging her hair in a braid atop her head. The day she had dreaded had come. Lester Harbaugh had arrived. Her father had gone to pick him up and bring him to the house for dinner.

Pinning the braid in place, she turned away from the mirror and went to the window. Drawing back the curtain, she stared at the driving rain. It seemed fitting somehow.

The last week had been the worst of her life. She'd only been allowed out of her parents' sight once, when Dusty had come for her. Otherwise, her mother and father had kept her under constant surveillance, refusing to let her out of the house, when she wanted nothing more than to go to Chase, to make sure he was all right.

She couldn't forget how awful he had looked the last time she'd seen him, his whole body seeming to be a solid mass of discolored flesh, his face bruised, his eyes swollen shut.

Twice, she had tried sneaking out of the house. Twice her father had caught her and brought her back. The second time he had locked her in her room for two days, refusing to let her even come down for meals. Beth blew out a sigh. Two days of being locked in her room with nothing to do but think. Two days of eating nothing but bread and milk.

And now Lester Harbaugh was here.

Knowing she couldn't ignore the inevitable any longer, she took a last, uninterested look in the mirror to make sure nothing was showing that shouldn't be, then made her way downstairs.

She heard voices in the front parlor and knew

that Harbaugh had arrived.

Taking a deep, calming breath, she squared her shoulders and lifted her chin defiantly. And then she smiled. Maybe he wouldn't want her. Maybe there was a way to make sure he wouldn't want her.

Pasting a smile on her face, she stepped into the parlor. "Good evening, Mother. Father."

"Elizabeth," her mother said, beaming. "How pretty you look." Theda Johnson held out her hands. "Come and meet Mr. Harbaugh, dear."

"Hello, Elizabeth."

She could only stare at him. *This* was Lester Harbaugh, this tall, blond, remarkably handsome man? Extending her hand, she smiled up at him. "It's a pleasure to meet you, Mr. Harbaugh."

"Indeed, Miss Johnson, the pleasure is all mine." Bowing over her hand, he kissed it gallantly.

From that point on, the evening passed in a blur. She had been prepared to hate the man, had expected him to be old and fat and repulsive, but he was none of those things. He was, in fact, one of the nicest men she had ever met. His manners were impeccable. He had a remarkable sense of humor, an easy smile, and guileless brown eyes. If she hadn't met Chase the Wind, she would have been quite swept off her feet by Lester Harbaugh's considerable charm.

The evening passed pleasantly and before she knew it, she was bidding Lester good night and promising to see him again on the morrow.

Needless to say, her parents were delighted that she seemed to have accepted him so readily.

"Well, Elizabeth," her father said, obviously

pleased with himself, "what do you have to say now?"

"I like him very much," she admitted honestly.

"I knew you would," her mother said. "Ralph, we're going to give Elizabeth the biggest wedding this town has ever seen."

Ralph nodded. "Spare no expense, my dear," he said, smiling expansively.

"Let's see," Theda said. "We'll have to send to New York for a wedding dress, order champagne, invitations . . ."

"You might wait until the man proposes," Beth remarked dryly.

"Oh, he will," Ralph said confidently. "He will."

Lester courted Beth for the next two weeks, bringing her candy, taking her to a dance at the church, listening to her play the piano. He told her about his daughters and about his house, telling her, obliquely, that once they were married, she could rearrange the house to suit herself, or buy a new one.

Beth entertained him graciously, partly because she genuinely liked him, and partly in hopes of lulling her parents into believing that she was smitten with the man.

Lester had been there a little over three weeks when he asked her father for her hand in marriage. Ralph gave them his blessing, and they all drank a toast to the occasion. Later that night, Lester took Beth out on the porch and proposed. And because she really had no choice, because it was the only way to appease her father until she could talk to Lester about her plan, she said yes.

* * *

The next afternoon, Beth asked Lester to take her for a buggy ride out in the country. Lester was only too happy to oblige.

It wasn't until they were away from town that Beth relaxed.

"Lester," she said, "we have to talk."

"Of course," he said affably. "About what?"

"I can't marry you."

Startled, he reined the team to a halt, then turned on the seat to stare at her. "What do you mean?"

"I'm in love with someone else."

"Why didn't you tell me this before?"

"I couldn't. My parents don't approve of him."

"Why not?"

"He's part Indian."

"Indian! Surely you can't mean to marry such a man." Lester shook his head in disbelief. "An Indian, Beth. What will people say?"

"I don't care what they say. I love him, and he loves me."

"So, what do you want me to do?" he asked, looking understandably disgruntled.

"I want you to tell my parents that we don't suit."

"I think we suit very well," Lester said. "I don't mean to sound immodest, but I know you're fond of me."

"I am, I won't deny it. But I don't love you, and I never will."

"Far be it from me to stand in the way of true love, but calling off our marriage won't solve anything. Your parents will just find another suitor." He smiled. "Maybe someone you don't like at all."

Beth sighed. What he said was all too true, but

she wouldn't, couldn't, marry Lester Harbaugh. In her heart, she was already married to Chase. "Will you help me?"

"Help you do what?"

"Would you pretend to be my fiancé, and postpone the date of the wedding until I don't need my father's permission or approval to marry?"

He shook his head. "I don't think so. I don't want you to take this wrong, but if we're not to marry, then I need to go home. I have a law practice to think of, not to mention my children. I don't want to be away from them any longer than necessary. Surely you can understand that?"

Beth nodded. She'd tried and failed. Now what? "Well," she said, sighing heavily, "you're right, of course. There's no reason why you should help me. It was wrong of me to ask."

Lester shifted his weight on the seat. Beth was a sweet girl, and she needed his help. And he'd never turned down a woman in need.

"Say, for the sake of argument, that I can convince your father to postpone the wedding a few weeks. Then what?"

"Why, then I'll marry Chase, of course."

Lester chuckled softly, amused by her gall. "Let me see if I've got this straight. You want me to carry on a mock engagement so you can dump me?"

Beth nodded, suddenly hopeful. "Will you do it?"

"I don't know. Give me a few days to think about it."

"All right." She placed her hand on his arm when he picked up the reins. "Would you do me another favor?"

"Is it as flattering as the last one?"

"Would you take me out to see Chase?"

"Bless me, girl, you've got all the nerve in the world, don't you?" he muttered, but he couldn't deny he was curious to see the man who had captured Elizabeth Johnson's heart.

"My father beat Chase when he found us together," Beth explained. "I need to know he's all right."

"Why not," Lester said. "If I can't be Miles Standish, I might as well be John Alden."

Chapter Twenty-five

"Go on," Lester said, reining the team to a halt in front of a rambling yellow house with white trim. "I'll wait for you out here."

"I won't be long."

"Don't hurry on my account," he muttered, chuckling softly.

Feeling as though her feet had wings, Beth flew out of the carriage and up the porch steps. She knocked on the front door, her heart fluttering wildly at the prospect of seeing Chase again.

But it was Dusty who answered the door.

"Beth!" he exclaimed softly. "What are you doing here?"

"Hello, Dusty. I . . . I came to see Chase."

"Of course." He stepped back. "Come in."

"Thank you."

Feeling awkward in his presence, she stepped into the parlor.

"How have you been?" Dusty asked.

"Fine, thank you." She stared up at him, her hands clenching the material in her skirt. "I . . . Dusty . . . I . . ." She shrugged helplessly. "I don't know what to say."

"There's nothing to say," he replied, his tone bitter. "You love Chase, and he loves you. I'd just like to know one thing; How could you run off with a stranger, a man you hardly knew?"

"What do you mean?"

"Just what I said. Chase told me you'd only seen each other twice, once in town, and once at the river. Yet you drugged me and broke him out of jail and ran off with him. How could you do it?" He shook his head. "Why?"

Heat washed into Beth's cheeks. "You make it sound so . . . so sordid," she replied quietly. "It wasn't like that. I can't explain it, Dusty. I wish I could."

Dusty shoved his hands in his pockets. Women! If he lived to be a hundred, he would never understand them. "He's in the back bedroom on the left."

"Dusty, I never meant to hurt you."

"You didn't." It was a lie, but she didn't have to know that.

"Well, I . . ." Not knowing what else to say, she hurried down the hallway.

The door was open and she peeked around the frame. "Chase?"

"Beth!"

His smile of welcome erased everything else from her mind. Crossing the floor, she sat down on the edge of the bed, sighing as his arms closed around her. His mouth captured hers, and he kissed her as if it had been years since he'd seen her last instead of only a few weeks.

"Beth." He whispered her name as he rained kisses on her nose and cheeks, then drank from her lips again, as if he were dying of thirst and she was his only hope for salvation.

Her hands slid restlessly up and down his arms, across his naked chest. It had been so long since they'd made love, she thought, so very, very long.

"Beth, what are you doing here?" he asked between soulful kisses. "How long can you stay?"

"I've so much to tell you," she said.

"Tell me, then," he said. His heart was pounding in his ears, his body, bruised and aching though it was, was thrumming with need.

She drew back a little, her gaze roaming over him. The swelling in his face had gone down. The bruises were no longer black and blue but a hideous shade of greenish-yellow.

"Lester Harbaugh is in town," she said, her finger tracing the colorful bruises across his chest.

"Who?"

"The man my parents expect me to marry."

"You are already married," he said. "To me."

"I know, but he's been courting me for three weeks."

That got his full attention. "What do you mean, courting you?"

"Just what I said. He's a very nice man, tall and handsome, quite charming. Nothing at all like what I expected."

His hands fell away from her waist and he drew back, his dark eyes shuttered and cold.

"Don't look at me like that," Beth snapped.

"How should I look?"

"Just listen. I told Lester that I couldn't marry him, that I loved you. He's the one who brought me out here."

"He does not want you?"

"Well, I guess he does, but I don't want him."

"Are you sure?" Chase asked caustically. "You just said he was tall and handsome."

"But you're taller, and even more handsome," Beth said, grinning because he was jealous. "And I love you."

"Where is this man?"

"Waiting outside in the buggy." Tilting her head to one side, she regarded Chase for several moments. "You look awful. How do you feel?"

"You just told me I was handsome," he muttered.

"Oh, you are." She shook her head in wonder. "I've just never seen so many colorful bruises before." Hesitantly, she touched the yellow bruise on his left cheek. "Does it still hurt?"

"Only a little."

Her hands slid over his chest, then settled on the bandage wrapped tightly around his ribs. "I wish . . ." With a sigh, she looked up at him.

"What?" he asked, though he knew exactly what she was wishing.

"I wish we could make love."

"Soon."

"Not soon enough." Scooting down on the bed, she rested her head on his shoulder, content to lie there while he stroked her hair. For the first time in weeks, she felt relaxed and happy. Somehow, everything would work out for the best. She had to believe that, or she'd go crazy.

"Oh, excuse me!"

Beth jumped off the bed as if shot out of a cannon, embarrassment flooding her cheeks as Chase's mother entered the room. "Mrs. Fallon, I . . ."

"It's all right, Beth," Jenny said, grinning. "I remember what it was like to be young and in love."

"Please, Mrs. Fallon, I . . ." Mortified, she pressed her hands to her burning cheeks.

Jenny looked at Chase, who met her gaze with a rueful grin.

"Next time, we will close the door," he said.

"Good idea. I just came in to see if you were ready for lunch. Would you care to join us, Beth?"

"I'd love to, but I can't." She stood up, suddenly remembering Lester Harbaugh. "I've got to go. The man who brought me is . . ."

"Is in the parlor discussing Shakespeare with Dorinda," Jenny said.

"He's here, in the house?" Beth asked.

"Yes, so you might as well stay for lunch. I'll bring yours in here, so you and Chase can eat together."

Smiling at her son and Beth, Jenny left the room, quietly closing the door behind her.

"Your mother's very nice," Beth said, resuming her seat on the edge of the bed.

"Yes," Chase said. "She is. I wish I had not waited so long to find her."

"Why didn't you live with her when you were younger?"

"It's a long story."

"Well," Beth said, settling her skirts around her, "it looks like I'm going to be here for a while."

* * *

Lester nodded, hardly aware of what the girl sitting beside him was saying. Dorinda Fallon was the most incredibly beautiful woman he had ever seen. Her eyes were dark blue, fringed by thick black lashes. Her hair was long and straight and as black as a raven's wing. Her skin was the color of dark honey, smooth and clear, with a hint of roses in her cheeks. And her mouth . . . ah, that mouth tempted him as nothing else ever had. She wore a blue-and-white print dress that did wonderful things for her figure—and made his breeches seem suddenly tight.

He slid a glance at Dorinda's father, who was sitting in an easy chair across the way, thumbing through a mail order catalog.

". . . so sad," she said. "Don't you agree?"

"What? I . . . oh, yes, it is," Lester agreed, though he had no idea what she'd just said.

"You weren't listening, were you?"

Lester shook his head. For a moment, he considered a polite prevarication, and then he grinned. "Not really."

"Penny for your thoughts?"

"I was thinking how beautiful you are."

"Well, I guess I can't get mad at you for that." Dorinda grinned back at him, charmed by his easy flirtation. Lester Harbaugh was an attractive man. She had always had a weakness for men with blond hair, perhaps because she'd never really cared for the color of her own. His eyes smiled at her, dark brown eyes, as guileless as those of a child. She had liked him immediately. She'd heard other women talk about the way they felt when they met the men they fell in love with, how their hearts had beat fast and butterflies had danced in their stomachs, but she'd never experienced such feelings. Until now.

"I'm glad you're not really going to marry Beth," she remarked.

"Yes, me, too." And just like that, he knew that he'd stay in Twin Rivers as long as Beth needed, and maybe longer than that. He hadn't taken a vacation in years; his junior partner was perfectly capable of looking after things until he got back. His children were being well cared for. And if everything went as he hoped, they'd be a real family again soon.

"I'm going to make some tea," Dorinda said, her gaze never leaving his. "Would anyone else care for some?"

"I didn't think you knew anybody else was in the room," Ryder muttered under his breath.

"I'll help you," Lester offered, anxious for a chance to have a few minutes alone with her.

"Thank you," Dorinda replied.

She smiled over her shoulder as she went into the kitchen, Lester close on her heels.

"Well," Ryder muttered laconically, "that was quick."

Jenny frowned at him as she entered the room. "What are you talking about?"

"Lester and Dorinda. I'd say it was a case of love at first sight."

"You're kidding?"

Ryder shook his head. "The stew's getting thicker every day, darlin'. If we're not careful, we're going to be up to our armpits in newlyweds."

That day set the pattern for the ones that followed. Every day or so, Lester drove Beth out to the

Fallon place so she could see Chase and he could visit with Dorinda.

Sometimes Lester and Dorinda sat in the parlor and played chess, sometimes they walked along the river, or just sat on the front porch. He told her about his law practice, of cases he'd won, and those he'd lost; about his partner, who always wore black suits because Lincoln had been a lawyer and often wore black; of how hard it was to be mother and father to his children.

He listened with interest as Dorinda told of growing up on the ranch, of learning to rope and ride, of the time she'd fallen out of a tree and broken her arm. She told him about going to New York, and how her parents had wanted her to take a companion. She'd refused, arguing that they would have let Dusty go alone without a fuss.

"I never liked being a girl," she said. "It seemed as if Dusty could do whatever he wanted, and no one worried about him, but I always had to be careful."

"Well, I, for one, am glad you're a girl," Lester said, kissing the end of her nose.

"Me, too. Now."

Lester had been driving Beth out to the Fallon ranch for about two weeks the afternoon he found himself alone in the parlor with Chase. Though they'd been passing friendly up to this time, Lester felt vaguely awkward being alone with the man. He had a feeling that Chase didn't like him, didn't trust him, and didn't think he was good enough for his sister.

Lester cleared his throat, uncomfortable to be the focus of the Indian's unblinking stare. It took no imagination at all to imagine those eyes glaring at him over the barrel of a rifle, or holding a knife at his throat. It hadn't been all that many years ago since the very word Apache was enough to strike terror in the hearts of white settlers. Lester's grandfather had served in the southwest when Geronimo was a young warrior. Grandpa Harbaugh had been fond of telling his grandchildren chilling tales about raids and massacres when their parents weren't around to stop him.

Lester cleared his throat. "So, ah, how are you feeling?"

"Better," Chase replied tersely.

"Good, good. Have you and Beth decided when you'll get married?"

"No." Chase settled back in his chair. "Why do you bring her here?"

"Why? Because she wants to see you, of course."

Chase shook his head. "She told me you had come here from the east to marry her."

"That's right, but, ah, things have changed." Lester tugged at his shirt collar. "She doesn't want me; she wants you. You know that. I must admit, I've become quite fond of Beth these past few weeks. I want her to be happy."

"You have a good heart," Chase mused. "In your place, I would not be so obliging."

"Well, to tell you the truth," Lester said with a grin, "it's your mother's cooking that keeps me here. She makes the best pot roast I've ever had. And her apple pie is second to none." He patted his stomach. "I think I've gained ten pounds in the last couple of weeks. You know, a woman's looks fade in time, but her cooking skills last forever."

"You are a poor liar," Chase said affably.

"Excuse me?"

"You are in love with my sister."

Lester ran a finger inside a collar suddenly too tight. "Shows that much, does it?"

Chase grinned at Harbaugh, liking the man more in that moment than he would have thought possible.

"What are you two talking about?" Beth paused in the doorway, wiping her hands on a dishcloth.

"Cooking," Lester replied.

"Cooking! I don't believe you."

"It is true," Chase said. "Are you a good cook?"

"No, I hate to cook."

Lester and Chase exchanged glances. "Maybe you'd better think it over," Lester remarked with mock gravity. "Remember what I said."

"Think what over?" Beth asked suspiciously.

"I was telling Chase that beautiful women don't always make the best wives."

"Is that so?"

Chase nodded solemnly. "He told me that your beauty will fade, but that good cooking lasts a lifetime."

"Well, silly me," Beth said huffily. "Here I thought you were marrying me because you loved me."

She was turning away when Chase caught her in his arms. "Never doubt that I love you, Beth," he said quietly.

"Looks like the game's over, and you two want to be alone," Lester muttered. "Guess I'll just go outside and have myself a smoke."

Beth gazed into Chase's eyes, hardly aware that Lester had left the room. "I love you, too. I wish we could be married now, today."

"It is my wish, also."

"Mama ordered me a wedding gown from New York last week," Beth said. "It's beautiful."

"You are beautiful."

"So are you." She slipped her arms around his waist and rested her head against his chest. It felt so good to be in his arms, to hold him and be held by him. She couldn't wait for the day when she would be his wife, when nothing and no one could keep them apart.

"Beth . . ."

Just her name, but she heard the underlying note of desire, knew that he ached for her as she ached for him. "I know. I wish we could go somewhere and be alone for a while."

"It is my wish also." He drew her closer, letting her feel the very visible evidence of his need.

"Beth, I . . . Oh, I'm sorry."

Beth felt her cheeks grow hot as Jenny entered the room. She tried to disengage herself from Chase's embrace, but he refused to let her go.

"Did you need me for something, Mrs. Fallon?" she asked, mortified at being caught in Chase's arms.

"No, dear, not as badly as Chase needs you," Jenny replied, stifling the urge to laugh. "You two go on with what you're doing."

Chase met his mother's amused gaze over the top of Beth's head. He would have released Beth, but he didn't want his mother to see how aroused he was. Judging from the laughter glinting in her eyes, he had the feeling that she knew exactly why he was keeping such a tight hold on Beth.

"You've got about forty minutes until dinner's ready," Jenny said. "In case you two want to take a nap—or something."

"Thank you, *Cima,*" Chase replied.

With a nod, Jenny went back into the kitchen and closed the door.

"Come," Chase said, taking Beth by the hand.

"Where are we going?" Beth asked suspiciously.

"To take a nap."

Beth pulled her hand from his, her cheeks burning with embarrassment. "I couldn't! I'll never be able to look your mother in the face again."

"Why not? She knows how we feel about each other."

"I know, but . . ." As much as she longed to be in his arms, she wasn't sure she could make love to Chase here, in his mother's house, while his mother was in the kitchen, cooking. "I can't."

"You do not wish to?"

Beth shook her head, certain her parents never talked so openly of such things. No doubt her own mother would have fainted dead away even to think of her daughter wanting to be in a man's arms in the middle of the day. She couldn't even imagine her parents in bed together, let alone caressing each other the way she had caressed Chase. The way he had caressed her.

But then she looked into Chase's eyes, saw her own longing mirrored in his ebony gaze. There was more than just desire reflected in the depths of his eyes—there was love and tenderness and need.

With a shy smile, she took Chase's hand in hers and led the way down the hall to his bedroom, and boldly closed the door.

Chapter Twenty-six

Dusty leaned back in his chair and blew out a sigh. "That was mighty fine pie, Becky. Every bit as good as my mother's."

"It should be," Rebecca replied, her cheeks pinkening. "Your mother told me apple pie's your favorite. It's her recipe."

Dusty grinned, inordinately pleased that she'd gone to so much trouble on his behalf. "I'm glad Dorinda's back home."

"Me, too. I like your sister. When she was away, I really didn't have anyone to share secrets with."

"You can tell me your secrets."

"I don't think so," Rebecca said.

"Why not? I can keep a secret."

A faint blush crept into Rebecca's cheeks. "Well, most of the secrets I had were about you."

"Me? What kind of secrets?"

"Just that I was in love with you, but you were too blind to see, or care."

"I care now." Reaching across the table, he took her hand in his. "I love you, Becky."

"Do you?"

"Don't you believe me?"

"What about Beth?"

"That's all over." He squeezed her hand, willing her to believe him. "Will you marry me?"

"Marry you! Oh, Dusty, do you mean it?"

"With all my heart. Say yes, Rebecca Lynn."

"Yes. Yes, yes, yes!"

Jumping to his feet, he rounded the table and pulled her into his arms. "You won't be sorry, I promise," he whispered, and then he kissed her, gently, tenderly, and all thought of Beth vanished from his mind as Rebecca sealed her heart to his.

Breathless, they drew apart a little, though Dusty continued to hold her in his arms. "I hope you don't want a long engagement," he muttered with a wry grin.

Rebecca shook her head. "Name the day."

"Tomorrow?"

"Well, I would like just a little more time," Rebecca said. "At least a month so I can shop for a wedding dress and a trousseau."

"How about December twentieth, so we can spend Christmas together as man and wife?" Dusty suggested. "That'll give me time to swear in an extra deputy and show him the ropes."

"December twentieth," she agreed, feeling as though her heart would burst with happiness.

"Where would like to go for our honeymoon?"

"Anywhere you want."

"We can decide later," Dusty said. "Right now, let's go out to the ranch and tell my folks."

"Do you think they'll approve?"

"I know they will. Come on, let's go."

Jenny looked up from the stove as Dusty and Rebecca stepped into the kitchen. "Hi, you two," she said. "You're just in time for supper."

"We've eaten," Dusty said. He took Rebecca's hand in his and gave it a squeeze. "Where's Dad?"

"Out in the barn. One of the horses went lame, and he wanted to check it one more time. He should be up any time now." Jenny wiped her hands on her apron. "What's up? You look like the proverbial cat that swallowed the canary."

Dusty grinned at Rebecca. "Should I tell her?"

Feeling as though she would burst, Rebecca nodded. She had always loved Dusty's family, could hardly believe that she was actually going to be a part of it at last.

"I asked Becky to marry me, and she said yes."

"That's wonderful," Jenny exclaimed. "I'm so glad." She hugged Rebecca. "Welcome to the family."

"Thank you, Mrs. Fallon."

"Here now, no more of that 'Mrs.' stuff. You might as well call me Mother, or Jenny, if that would be more comfortable. Oh, I'm just so pleased."

"Pleased about what?" Ryder asked. Taking off his hat, he hung it on the peg beside the kitchen door.

"Tell him, Dusty."

"We're getting married."

"No kidding? That's great. Congratulations, son. You're a lucky man." Ryder took Rebecca's hands in his, then bent and kissed her cheek. "I wish you all the happiness in the world," he said sincerely. "And if he gives you any trouble, you just come and see me. I can still whip his behind if I have to."

Dusty shook his head. "Don't tell her things like that. She might believe it."

"Hey, you know it's true," Ryder said. He clasped Dusty's hand in his. "I'm happy for you, son. Well, this calls for a celebration. I've got some brandy in the den. I say we toast the bride and groom."

They were all in the parlor when Chase and Beth entered the room a few minutes later.

"Come on in," Ryder said, lifting his glass. "We're celebrating."

Chase draped his arm over Beth's shoulder. "What is the occasion?" he asked.

"Dusty asked Rebecca to marry him."

There was a momentary hush. Dusty glanced at Beth and bid her a silent farewell, then he looked at his brother and smiled.

"Congratulations, Dusty," Beth said, meaning it. "And to you, too, Rebecca, I know you'll be happy together."

"Thank you," Dusty said.

"Yes, thank you," Rebecca replied.

The door opened and Dorinda preceded Lester into the room. "Hey, did we miss something?" Dorinda asked.

"Come on in and join the party," Ryder said, handing Lester a glass of brandy. "Dusty and Rebecca just got engaged, and we're celebrating."

"Oh, well, congratulations to both of you," Lester said, and lifting his glass in a salute, he took a drink.

"Well, I just couldn't be happier," Jenny said. "When's the wedding?"

"December twentieth," Rebecca said.

"That's wonderful." Jenny smiled at Ryder. "This is going to be our best Christmas ever."

Lester looked over at Beth, wondering if she was thinking the same thing he was, that their wedding was supposed to be on the third. Yep, he mused, taking another drink, it was going to be some Christmas all right.

Beth stood in front of the mirror, staring at her reflection. It couldn't be true. It just couldn't. She had tried to rationalize her fears away, telling herself she hadn't missed her monthly curse, that she was just late because she'd been under so much pressure.

But she couldn't lie to herself any longer. She'd been sick to her stomach the last three mornings, her breasts were tender, and now that she thought about it, she hadn't missed one cycle, but two.

She was pregnant.

How could she tell her parents? How could she tell Chase? Would he be glad? They had never discussed children. She had always wanted a large family, but not now . . .

She whirled around as her mother knocked at the door. "Lester is here, Elizabeth. Are you ready?"

"Yes, I'll be right down."

Grabbing a heavy navy blue wool coat, she slipped it on, then hurried downstairs.

Lester was waiting for her at the foot of the staircase. He smiled as he took her hand and kissed it. "Good afternoon, Elizabeth," he said warmly. "Are you ready to go for our drive?"

She nodded, unable to speak.

"It looks like rain," Theda remarked. "Are you sure you wouldn't like to stay in this afternoon?"

"No, Mother," Beth said quickly.

"Try to be home in time for supper, won't you?"

"We'll be here, Mrs. Johnson," Lester said, and turned on his most charming smile. "Let's go, Elizabeth." He practically dragged her out of the door in his haste to get to the Fallon ranch.

Lost in the anticipation of seeing Dorinda again, it took Lester several miles to realize Beth hadn't said a word.

"Beth, is something wrong?"

"No."

Les frowned. Turning to study her face, he noticed she seemed unusually pale. There were dark smudges under her eyes, as if she hadn't slept well, and she was fidgeting with the folds of her skirt.

"Beth, I can see that something is bothering you. Why don't you tell me what it is? Maybe I can help."

"You can't. No one can."

"Is it Chase? You haven't had a disagreement, have you?"

"No."

"Is there a problem with the wedding? Don't tell me your dress arrived and it doesn't fit," he said, chuckling.

"Oh, Les," she wailed, and burst into tears.

Startled, he reined the team to a halt. "Beth, it can't be that bad."

"It is," she sobbed. "It's worse."

She was sobbing now, tears welling in her eyes, running, unchecked, down her cheeks.

With a sigh, he drew her into his arms. "Tell me."

"I'm . . . I'm . . ." She couldn't say the word.

"You're what?"

"I'm going to have a baby."

The words hung in the air like a thick fog.

"A baby." Lester looked at her as if she had just sprouted horns and a tail. "You're pregnant?"

"Yes." The admission brought a fresh wave of tears.

"Well, that shouldn't be a problem," he remarked, hoping to console her. "I mean, he loves you, and you love him, and you're planning to be married anyway . . ."

"What if he doesn't want a baby?"

"Well, I think it's too late to worry about that," he muttered wryly.

"How can you joke at a time like this?" Beth exclaimed. "You know how people are, how they talk! Oh, what am I going to do?"

"Just let me think a minute," Lester said, patting her on the back. "It took a while to get into this mess. It might take me a bit of time to think of a solution."

"There is no solution. By the time we're supposed to get married, I'll be almost four months pregnant. Everyone will know! Oh, Lester, my father's going to kill me."

"No, he won't. Here, now, crying's not going to help." Reaching into his pocket, he withdrew his handkerchief. "Dry your eyes and blow your nose. I'm sure Mrs. Fallon will be able to think of something."

"Mrs. Fallon! I can't tell her! What will she think of me?"

"Beth, she knows you and Chase are . . ." Lester cleared his throat. "Well, you know what she knows. She's not going to think any the less of you."

"I can't face them," she said, dabbing ineffectually at her eyes. "Take me home."

"You've got to tell them sometime," Lester said, taking up the reins, "and it might as well be today."

Chapter Twenty-seven

They were all at the ranch—Ryder and Jenny, Dorinda, Dusty, and Rebecca. And Chase.

Jenny opened the door at Beth's knock, a smile of welcome lighting her face.

"Beth, how pretty you look! Hi, Les. Come in, come in. We were just relaxing over cake and coffee."

Forcing a smile, Beth followed Jenny into the parlor, grateful for Lester's comforting hand at her waist.

"Good afternoon, everyone," Beth said.

She hardly heard the words of welcome from the others as Chase rose from the sofa and walked toward her. She felt a catch in her heart as she looked at him. He was so tall, so incredibly handsome. He wore a white shirt that complemented his dark skin and hair, and a pair of black whipcord britches that emphasized his long muscular legs and thighs. He moved with unconscious grace, his moccasins making no sound as he crossed the hardwood floor and took her in his arms.

Smiling down at Beth, he kissed her lightly on the cheek. "I've missed you," he said.

"I've missed you, too. Can we go somewhere and talk?"

Chase nodded, his gaze reflecting his concern as he caught the tremor in her voice. For the first time, he noticed the shadows under her eyes.

He brushed his knuckles over her cheek. "Are you all right?"

"Please, Chase, I need to talk to you. Alone."

"Beth and I are going for a walk," he said to no one in particular. Grabbing a sheepskin jacket from the rack by the door, he took Beth by the hand and they left the house.

It was cold and gray outside. Chase glanced up at the dark clouds gathered overhead and knew it would rain before nightfall. The wind stirred the leaves on the trees and blew a tumbleweed across their path.

They walked in silence until they reached a picnic table situated beneath a cottonwood tree.

"What is it?" Chase asked, drawing her down on the bench beside him. "What's wrong?"

Beth looked up at him, eager to tell him everything in hopes that sharing the burden would make it lighter, and yet afraid to say the words. Once said, there was no going back. Once said, the child would no longer be an abstract problem to be dealt with, but a reality, a tiny human being who would be the living, breathing proof of her love for Chase.

What would he think when she told him?

Her mother had told her time and again that a

woman must zealously guard her chastity and protect her good name. Men, Theda Johnson had explained in a voice thick with contempt, never thought of the consequences of intimacy before marriage, nor did they have to bear the disgrace. It was all right for a man to "sow his wild oats," but a woman's reputation must be above reproach.

The disgrace. She was pregnant and unmarried, at least in the eyes of the church. How could she tell her mother what she'd done? How could she face her father, her friends, Chase's family?

She tried to feel guilty, tried to feel as though she had made a terrible mistake, waited for the mortification her mother had spoken of to engulf her, but she felt neither shame nor guilt. Right or wrong, in her heart she was married to Chase, and she wanted this baby.

But what if Chase didn't?

"Beth." He drew his knuckles across her cheek, then kissed her tenderly. She wore a dark blue dress that seemed to emphasize her wan complexion. "Whatever it is, you can tell me."

"I . . ." She took a deep breath, her gaze sliding away from his as she placed a hand over her stomach. *Please,* she prayed, *please let him want this child as much as I do.*

"Beth?" Her silence frightened him, making him fear the worst. He took a deep breath. "Tell me. Whatever it is, just say it."

"I'm going to have a baby."

Chase stared at her. Of all the things he had expected her to say, all the things he had feared, he had never considered this.

"A baby!" he exclaimed softly. "We are going to have a baby? When?"

"I'm not sure. In June, I think."

"A baby," he repeated. "A baby. In June."

A sudden chill made her shiver. He didn't want it. He didn't want her.

She turned away from him so he couldn't see her tears, couldn't see the pain that must surely be visible in her eyes. She wouldn't beg him to marry her. She'd run away. She'd . . .

"Beth, look at me."

"I can't. I'm too ashamed." She hadn't been ashamed before, when she thought he loved her, but now, knowing she'd have to face the town alone, pregnant and unmarried, she understood what her mother had been talking about. She would be ridiculed, or shunned.

"Ashamed?" Chase drew back, feeling suddenly numb. She was ashamed. Of him, of bearing his child.

Silence stretched between them.

Chase stared into the distance. The sky had turned from gray to black. He smelled rain in the air, heard the distant rumble of thunder. She was ashamed. He had been kidding himself all the time, thinking she loved him.

Beth saw his hands clench into tight fists. Try as she might, she couldn't think of anything to say. If only he'd take her in his arms and tell her it didn't matter, that everything would be all right, that he wanted this child as much as she did, that he still loved her.

"What do you want me to do?" he asked, afraid she would tell him it had all been a mistake, that she didn't love him, had never loved him.

Beth looked up at him then. "What do you want to do?" she asked, afraid he would tell her he was through with her, that the baby was her problem, not his.

"I will not let you keep the child from me."

She looked surprised. "Why would I?"

"Because you are ashamed of me."

"Ashamed of you! I'm not ashamed of you. Why would you think that?" Tears welled in her eyes. "I'm the one who should be ashamed. The one people will point at and talk about. They'll say it was all my fault, that I . . . that I'm a . . . a . . ." She couldn't say the word.

"You have no need to feel shame," Chase said quietly. "We have done nothing wrong, you and I. In my heart, you are my woman, my wife. If necessary, I will protect you and our child with my last breath."

"Oh, Chase," she murmured, "I was so afraid you'd think badly of me."

"It is a proud thing, to bear a child," he said. "Only a white woman would think it shameful."

Beth placed her hand over his. Her skin was the color of honey, his the color of dark bronze. "I *am* a white woman," she reminded him.

He covered her hand with his. "No, you are my woman, a part of me. There can be no shame in what we have done unless you, yourself, are ashamed to be carrying my child."

"I'm not, I swear it. I'm just so afraid of facing your mother and Ryder, of telling my parents."

"Do not be afraid, *shi-aad*." He drew her into his arms and held her close. "No one will harm you."

All her fears, all her doubts, disintegrated like morning mist. He loved her, and she loved him, and between them, there was nothing they couldn't handle.

It took them a moment to realize it was sprinkling. Hand in hand, they ran for the house.

A little of her confidence waned when they reached the porch. She removed her coat, shook the raindrops from her hair, and took a deep breath.

Everyone looked up when they entered the room. A fire burned cozily in the hearth; the glow from several lamps brightened the room.

Lester was sitting on the sofa beside Dorinda. He gave Beth a smile of encouragement, then winked at her.

Chase put his arm around Beth and drew her close against him. "I have good news," he said. "Beth is going to have my child."

"A baby! That's wonderful!" Jenny sprang to her feet, the mending in her lap falling, unnoticed, to the floor as she hurried toward them.

She gave Beth a quick hug. "How do you feel, dear? Here, sit down and put your feet up. Ryder, find me a blanket. There's a chill in here."

"I'm fine, really," Beth said. She looked up at Chase, feeling helpless, as Ryder spread a quilt over her lap.

"When's the baby due?" Dorinda asked. She slid a footstool under Beth's feet, straightened the quilt, placed a pillow behind her back.

Chase grinned down at her, then shook his head. He knew little of childbearing, but he knew enough to stay out of the way.

"A toast," Ryder said, taking a bottle from the liquor cabinet. "We need a toast!"

"A baby," Rebecca said, smiling first at Beth and then at Chase. "How exciting."

Ryder poured drinks for everyone, except Beth. "Not good for expectant mothers," he said, and handed her a glass of buttermilk instead.

Dorinda lifted her glass. "To my brother and his bride," she said. "A long and happy life."

"Here, here," Jenny said.

Beth looked up at Chase and knew she that if she lived to be a hundred, she would always remember this moment, the adoration shining in the depths of his dark eyes, the warmth of his family's love and acceptance.

"I hate to be the one to pour cold water on this happy occasion," Dusty said, his voice as wry as his expression, "but isn't Beth supposed to be marrying Lester next month?"

"That she is," Lester replied. He grinned as he clapped Dusty on the shoulder. "But not to worry, young man. I have a plan."

"Delay the wedding?" Ralph Johnson fixed Beth with a piercing look. "Why?"

"I'm afraid it's my fault," Lester said. Sitting back on the sofa, he stretched his legs. "I'm sure you can understand my desire to have my daughters at the wedding."

"Of course," Ralph said.

"I know we originally set the date for the third, but it seems my daughters can't be here until the eleventh." He lifted his hand in a gesture of appeasement. "I thought we could have the wedding the following Saturday."

"But . . ." Ralph glanced sharply at his daughter. She would be of age on the fifteenth. Should she refuse to marry Lester, there would be little he could do, especially in front of a chapel filled with guests.

"You needn't worry, Papa," Beth said. "I've promised to meet Lester at the church on time."

"Indeed?"

Beth nodded. "And now I give you my word that Lester and I will be married on the seventeenth."

"You swear it to me, on your word of honor?"

"Yes, Papa, on my word of honor, I swear to be married that day."

Ralph considered that for a moment. "Very well. The seventeenth, then."

"Tell me, dear," Theda said, "where do you and Lester go every day?"

Beth blinked at her mother several times as she searched for an answer.

"We've been looking for property," Lester injected smoothly. "I'm thinking of moving here, to Twin Rivers, and we've been looking at land."

"Moving here?" Ralph asked. Leaning back in his chair, he folded his hands over his ample girth and regarded Les with interest.

Lester nodded. "I find I quite like this country. Lots of room for growth. The people are friendly. I think my girls and I would be happy here."

Theda beamed at Lester. "I think that's a simply marvelous idea," she said.

"Do you intend to open a law practice here?" Ralph asked.

"I do indeed," Lester said. "I've noticed that's the one thing this town lacks."

Theda smiled at Beth. "I knew this would all work out for the best. Didn't I tell you it would?"

"Yes, Mother."

"Well," Lester said, rising to his feet, "I think I should be going."

"I'll walk you to the door," Beth said.

Lester shook Ralph Johnson's hand. "Good night, sir."

"Good night, Harbaugh," Ralph replied. "There's a vacant building near the bank. If you want, I'll ask around and see if it's for sale."

"Thank you, sir." Lester took Theda Johnson's hand in his. "Good night, ma'am. Thank you for a lovely evening."

"Good night, Lester. I'm sure we'll see you tomorrow."

Lester smiled. "Indeed, you will." He turned to Beth. "Walk me to the door?"

Beth nodded. Hand in hand, they left the parlor.

"Thank you," Beth whispered. "You saved my life in there."

"No problem."

"Are you really thinking of moving out here?"

Lester nodded.

"I'll bet I know why."

"Yes, I'll bet you do." Bending down, he brushed his lips across her cheek. "Good night, Beth. I'll see you tomorrow."

Jenny and Ryder sat side by side on the sofa, enjoying the warmth of the fire, listening to the sound of the rain.

"Well," Jenny said, snuggling against him. "It's been quite a day."

Ryder chuckled softly. "Quite."

"What do you think Les is planning?"

"I don't know. I got him alone for a few minutes before they left for home, but he wouldn't say. I think I have an idea of what he may be up to, though."

"I just don't see how it can work out."

Ryder shrugged.

"Do you? I mean, the wedding is only a couple of weeks away. It doesn't make sense to keep planning for something that isn't going to happen."

"Maybe that's his plan," Ryder said with a wry grin. "Maybe he's going to surprise us all my marrying her."

"I can only hope you're joking," Jenny exclaimed, punching him on the arm. "What would that solve?"

"Not a darn thing." Gathering Jenny into his arms, he began to nuzzle her neck. "I'm tired of worrying about Chase's problem. He's a big boy. He can work it out."

"I guess so. I saw Martha Crenshaw in town yesterday."

"Oh?"

"She looks awful, Ryder. Old. I stopped to talk to her for a minute, and she said the bank's talking about foreclosing on their ranch."

Ryder grunted softly. "Can't say as I'm surprised."

"She's got no family, nowhere to go."

"Yeah, well, her husband should have thought of that before he took to horse stealing and shot Ned Greenway."

"She's not to blame for what Rance did. And what about her boys? Where will they go if she loses the ranch?"

Ryder shook his head. Jenny had the softest heart in the whole world. He'd once claimed that she'd feel sorry for a snake, and she had replied, *Maybe, if he was sick and hungry and all alone in the world.* She'd been referring to her first husband at the time, but he knew it applied to anyone who was down and out.

"We have so much, Ryder. It breaks my heart to think she might lose her home."

"Jenny, what do you want me to do?"

"Talk to Ralph Johnson. Ask him to give her an extension."

"You know how I feel about Ralph."

"I know."

"All right, all right. I'll talk to him next time I go to town."

"Thank you, Ryder. I knew I could count on you."

"Don't you think I deserve a little reward for being so agreeable?"

"What kind of reward?"

"I'll show you," he said, and leaning forward, he kissed her. With a sigh, she wrapped her arms around his neck and kissed him back.

"We're home alone," he murmured. "And I hate to see that fire go to waste."

Holding her in his arms, he slid down to the bearskin rug that covered the floor in front of the hearth.

"Ryder, not here," she protested softly. "What if someone comes home."

"Let them find their own rug."

"You always were incorrigible," Jenny murmured.

"And you always loved it."

"And you." She slid her hands under his shirt and

raked her nails over his back. "Were you ever sorry, Ryder?"

"Sorry about what?"

"About settling down."

He lowered her to the floor, then gazed into her eyes. "A little late to be asking such a question, don't you think?"

"I know, but I've always wondered. You were such a wanderer when we first met. I know how you hated the thought of settling down. I remember one night, I asked you if you missed the freedom of your old life."

"And do you remember what I said?"

"You said there was a lot of pretty country out there. You talked about canyons and mountains and the beauty of wild places where no one else had ever been." She blinked up at him. It had been so many years ago. A lifetime ago. At the time, she didn't think she could love him more, but she'd been wrong. What she'd felt then paled in comparison to the love she felt for him now.

"And do you remember what I told you?"

Jenny laughed softly. "I remember."

"So do I. I told you that you had hills and valleys that put the *Paha Sapa* to shame."

"I'm afraid my hills are sagging," Jenny muttered ruefully, "and my valleys have filled with flab."

Laughter rumbled deep in his throat.

"Are you laughing at me?"

"I wouldn't dare. After all, I don't claim to be the same mighty warrior I was back then, either. But I love you, Jenny girl. More than my own life."

"And I love you," Jenny replied tremulously. "So much. So much."

"If Beth and Chase are half as happy as we've been, they'll do fine."

"And Dusty and Rebecca," Jenny said.

"And Les and Dorinda."

"Les and Dorinda! Do you think so?"

"I told you when they first met, Jenny girl. They can't keep their eyes, or their hands, off of each other."

"I guess I was so caught up in worrying about Chase and Beth, I didn't pay any attention, but now that you mention it, I think you're right." Jenny smiled at him. "Quite a crop we've harvested, Mr. Fallon."

"Well, they come from good stock," Ryder replied. "What can you expect?"

"I expect you to shut up," Jenny said, slipping her arms around his neck and drawing him close, "and kiss me."

"Always willing to oblige a lady," Ryder said, his voice suddenly husky. "All you had to do was ask."

Thanksgiving dawned cool and cloudy. By afternoon, it was raining. Beth fretted over having to stay home and eat dinner with her parents. It was a holiday, and she wanted to spend it with Chase.

Lester came over late that afternoon, bringing a box of candy for her mother, a box of cigars for her father, and a frilly pink bonnet for her.

Sitting in the parlor, Beth kept staring out the window, wondering what Chase was doing, wishing she could go out to the Fallon ranch. She was certain the Fallon family was having much more fun than she was. Her mother was crocheting an afghan; her father and Lester were playing chess.

Was there ever such a boring game?

With a sigh of exasperation, she picked up the book in her lap and tried to read, but she couldn't concentrate on the words, couldn't think of anything but the minutes slowly ticking by.

Once, Lester looked up and caught her gaze. Giving her a half-smile, he shrugged, as if to say, "I'm sorry, but there's nothing I can do."

Might as well grin and bear it, she thought ruefully, and staring down at the book in her hands, she read the page again.

Chase regarded his family as they sat around the dining room table after eating a huge meal. He hadn't seen so much food at one time since he'd been a boy back in Rainbow Valley. Dorinda sat beside him, looking forlorn because Lester was spending the day at the Johnson house. Dusty and Rebecca sat across from Dorinda and Chase, smiling foolishly at each other every few minutes. Ryder sat at the head of the table, Jenny at the foot.

"I'll bet the Indians on the reservation aren't celebrating today," Ryder remarked as he sat back in his chair.

"Now, Ryder, don't start," Jenny admonished. She tossed her napkin on the table, then began stacking plates.

"Well, it's true. Hell, if the Indians had been able to see into the future, they would have killed the Pilgrims and burned the Mayflower."

"Here, here," Dusty said. "And we'd all be living wild and free and feasting on buffalo hump and tongue instead of turkey."

Chase grinned. Even though he'd just eaten his

fill of turkey and ham, his mouth watered for the taste of fresh buffalo meat.

Jenny glanced at Dusty, and then at Ryder. "I hate to bring this up, but neither one of you would be here if the Indians had burned the Mayflower," she remarked dryly. "Or have you both forgotten that you're only part Indian?"

"I haven't forgotten," Ryder muttered.

"And," Jenny said, her eyes twinkling as she poked Ryder on the shoulder, "you wouldn't have me."

"Okay, okay, I give up," Ryder said, grinning at his wife. "Maybe burning the Mayflower wouldn't have been such a good idea."

"I hope you all saved some room for pie," Jenny remarked as she carried an armload of dishes into the kitchen. "Cause we've got apple and pumpkin."

Chase watched his sister get up and begin helping their mother clear the table. Dorinda had hardly said anything during dinner, and he knew she was thinking of Harbaugh, wishing he could be there. In the short time since Chase had met his sister, he'd grown to love her. She had a quick smile and a wry sense of humor. He thought it odd, considering that they hadn't been raised together, that they shared the same ideals, that they held the same views on a good many subjects.

Chase looked out the window, the conversation at the table fading into the distance as he wondered what Beth was doing. He should be able to get along without seeing her for one day, he thought ruefully. But it seemed as though it took hours for the minutes to pass and he resented each second, each minute, that kept them apart.

The depth of his feelings for her amazed him. He had never thought to fall in love, especially with a white woman, yet Beth filled his every thought, his every dream for the future. If she wanted to spend her life here, he would do it. If she decided she wanted to move to the east, he would take her there, though it would kill him to leave this land.

Beth. Her love had filled his heart, obliterated years of loneliness. Only a few more weeks, and she would be his for all time.

Chapter Twenty-eight

With Thanksgiving over, plans for the wedding became uppermost in everyone's mind.

The dress Beth had ordered arrived from New York on December first. It was the most exquisite thing she had ever seen. Made of soft white satin, it had a square neck and long fitted sleeves. Hundreds of tiny seed pearls adorned the bodice.

It was beautiful, if a trifle snug. Thank goodness the wedding was only a few weeks away. In another two months, the dress wouldn't fit at all.

She was standing in front of the mirror when her mother entered the room.

"Elizabeth, how lovely you look," Theda exclaimed. And then she frowned. "Did they send the right size? It looks a little small."

Beth swallowed hard as her mother tugged at the material. "We'll have to have the seams let out a little. I'll have Mattie Kennedy see to it tomorrow.

Hurry and change now. Lester is waiting downstairs."

Theda walked to the door, paused with her hand on the knob. "You'll be a beautiful bride, dear," she murmured, and left the room.

Beth stared after her mother. Compliments from her parents had been few and far between.

After removing her wedding gown, she put on a blue wool dress, brushed her hair, then hurried downstairs to meet Lester.

It struck her again that he was a very handsome man. The time they'd spent driving back and forth to the Fallon ranch had tanned his skin, making his blond hair seem even lighter. Dressed in a dark brown suit and tie, he looked positively dashing as he sat in the parlor, conversing with her father.

He stood up when she entered the room. Crossing the floor, he took her hands in his and pressed a kiss to her cheek. He was enjoying this, she thought. No doubt he found it quite amusing to play the part of her fiancé when she was in love with Chase, and he was in love with Dorinda.

Imagining what her parents would think if they knew the truth made her smile.

"Good afternoon, Lester," she said. "Are you ready to go?"

He nodded. "Best take a coat, Elizabeth. It's cold out."

"All right. See you later, Father."

"Have a good time, Elizabeth. By the way, Harbaugh, I checked into that vacant building next to the bank. It's available. I think you can get it for a good price, if you're looking to buy."

"That's good news," Lester said. "I'll stop by the bank tomorrow morning and we can discuss it."

Ralph Johnson nodded, pleased at the prospect of having a successful lawyer in the family.

"Well," Les remarked as they drove out to the Fallon ranch. "Who'd have ever thought things would turn out like this?"

"Who, indeed?" Beth said. She chuckled softly. "If I hadn't met Chase first, I think I would have fallen in love with you."

"Really?"

"Yes. You're quite charming, Mr. Harbaugh," she remarked candidly, "and easy to talk to."

"And handsome," Lester added, throwing her a self-mocking grin. "Don't forget handsome."

"And handsome," Beth agreed, grinning back at him.

"Why, thank you kindly, Miss Johnson."

"You're welcome, Mr. Harbaugh." She watched the scenery pass by for a few moments, then placed her hand on his arm. "I really mean it, Les. Dorinda is a lucky girl."

Lester shrugged one shoulder. "I think I'm the lucky one."

Beth smiled. "I want you to know how much I appreciate your help in all this."

"It was nothing. Sort of exciting, all this sneaking around. Do you think you and Chase will stay here in Twin Rivers after you're married?"

"I don't know. I'd like to. I think he would, too. I guess it all depends on my parents."

"Your parents? How so?"

"If they won't accept Chase, our living here could

be—I don't know—awkward, I guess. You know what I mean?"

"I think so."

"What about you? Are you really going to settle here, or did you just say that to throw my father off?"

"No, I meant it. See that?" He pointed at a stretch of land to their left. "Twenty-five acres. I bought it day before yesterday."

"You did?"

Lester grinned at her. "I've got an architect drawing up plans for a house."

"Have you told Dorinda?"

"Not yet."

"What will your children think about moving west?"

"My oldest isn't very happy about it. She doesn't want to leave her school or her friends, but she's still young. She'll adjust. At least I hope she will. The younger ones are excited about being able to have all the animals they want in the backyard."

Beth laughed softly. "When my father first told me about you, I pictured you as short and fat and as old as my father."

"No wonder you didn't want to marry me."

"I hope you'll be happy here."

Lester reined the horses to a halt, then turned to face Beth. Leaning forward, he kissed her on the cheek. "If you and Chase ever need anything, you let me know."

"I will. Thank you."

He smiled at her, then took up the reins and clucked to the horses.

A short time later, they drew up in front of the Fallon house.

Chase drew Beth closer, thinking that, if they lived together for a hundred years, it would not be long enough. He placed his hand over her belly, trying to imagine his child growing within her womb. Was it a boy or a girl? He told himself he didn't care, so long as the child was healthy, but deep inside, he hoped for a son.

"What are you thinking about?" Beth asked.

"The baby."

"What about it?"

"I was wondering if it is a boy."

"Oh. I guess every man wants a son."

Chase nodded.

"Will you be terribly disappointed if it's a girl?"

"Not if she looks like you."

With a sigh, Beth settled back in his arms. They were sitting on Chase's bed, a blanket spread across their legs. It was raining again, a soft gentle rain. Earlier, they had locked the door and made love.

She still felt shy about making love in Chase's room, knowing his relatives were in the house, but not making love was unthinkable. She couldn't be near him and not touch him. His kisses drove her wild, his caresses made her pulse pound and her heart race like a runaway locomotive. She loved to touch him, to run her hands over his hard-muscled flesh, and know that he was hers. He had a beautiful body, taut and strong.

Turning her head, she ran her tongue over his chest, heard him groan low in his throat.

"Beth . . ."

"Hmmm?" She looked up at him innocently. "Is something wrong?"

"Not a thing," he replied, his voice hoarse. Lifting his hand, he cupped her breast, heard her gasp of pleasure as she arched against him.

"Kiss me," she whispered, turning her face up to his. "Kiss me, kiss me, kiss me."

Lowering his head, he claimed her lips, his tongue delving into the sweetness of her mouth. His hands roamed up and down her back; in minutes, they were locked in each other's arms again, all else forgotten as they renewed the love they felt for one another.

Lester and Dorinda sat on the sofa, trying to pretend they were alone. Dusty and Rebecca were playing checkers across the room; Ryder and Jenny had gone into the kitchen to brew a pot of coffee.

"Tell me about your children," Dorinda said. "Do you think they'll like me?"

"They'll love you, don't worry. Alice is six. She's the youngest. She's a sweet thing. Big smile. Big dimples. Curly hair. Kathy is the middle child. She tends to be very quiet, very introspective for one not yet ten. She's quite bright, and very talented at the piano." Lester sighed. "Polly's twelve going on thirty. She doesn't want me to marry again. She doesn't want to move out here." Lester sighed again, heavily this time. "Actually, I expect her to give us a lot of trouble."

"Don't worry about it. I'm sure we'll all be friends, eventually." Dorinda smiled up at Les. "I'm so glad you came out here to meet Beth. And so glad she fell in love with my brother and not you."

"Me, too." He slid a quick glance at Dusty and Rebecca. Seeing that they were both intent upon the checkerboard, he pulled Dorinda into his arms and kissed her. "I'll be glad when we get to spend some time alone."

"Me, too."

"When do you think that might be?"

"Well," Dorinda said, grinning at him, "if all goes as planned, Chase and Dusty will both be married by the twentieth."

"Yeah, except my girls will be here by then."

Dorinda sighed in mock despair. "Maybe we'll never be alone."

"Oh, yes, we will! I don't know how, but we will." He groaned softly, his hands sliding up and down her arms. "Do you know how much I want you?"

"I can guess."

"Maybe when the rain clears up, I can drop Beth off here, then you and I could go for a ride, a long ride. Maybe check out the land I just bought."

"I'd like that."

"Good. It's a date then."

"A date," Dorinda agreed. "If it ever stops raining." She grinned up at him, so happy she thought her heart might burst with it. "At least we're all paired up two by two if there's another flood!"

Dusty reached across the checkerboard and took Rebecca's hand in his. "I love you," he whispered.

"I know. I love you, too," she whispered back.

"Do you think we'll ever get to be alone?"

Rebecca glanced over at Dorinda and Lester, who were huddled close together, doing some whispering of their own. "I don't know."

"It isn't fair," Dusty muttered. "Chase and Beth get to spend hours in his room, just the two of them."

"Well, they *are* married, sort of."

"Yeah, sort of."

"We'll be married soon," Rebecca reminded him. "And that reminds me—I should be getting home. I have a lot to do between now and the wedding."

"Okay. Come on, I'll take you home." He helped her with her coat and scarf, handed her her gloves, then leaned forward to nuzzle her ear. "Any chance your mother might have gone visiting an old friend tonight?"

Ryder sat back in his chair, one hand fisted around a cup of coffee as he watched Jenny slice apples for a pie.

"Do you think we'll ever have the house to ourselves again?" he asked.

"Someday, I reckon." She tossed the apple peelings into the scrap bowl to feed the hogs later. Wiping her hands on a towel, she stood behind Ryder's chair and began to massage his shoulders. "It's nice to see them all so happy together."

"I'd like to see *us* together," Ryder muttered.

"We will be. They'll all be married and have homes of their own soon enough."

"You don't sound too happy about that."

"Oh, I am." Her hands moved to his neck, gently kneading his nape. "It's just that the house won't seem the same when they're all gone."

"I can live with it."

"Ryder, has Les said anything to you?"

"About what?"

"About what! About the wedding, that's what. He's supposed to be marrying Beth on the seventeenth."

"Yeah?"

"You don't think they're going to let everyone show up for the wedding, and then just call it off, do you? I mean, aside from the expense, think about how embarrassing it would be for Beth's parents."

Ryder let his head roll forward, giving her better access to his back. "I don't know what they're gonna do. I asked him about it a couple of days ago, and he told me not to worry. He said he and Beth and Chase have everything under control."

"So you're not going to worry?"

"That's right."

Turning his chair away from the table, he drew Jenny onto his lap. "The first night that we're alone, I'm gonna build a big fire in the fireplace, lock all the doors, shut all the windows, and make love to you all night long."

"Sounds wonderful," Jenny murmured.

"It sure does."

Jenny sighed as he pressed his mouth to her breast and blew softly, the warmth of his breath heating her skin.

"What do you say we just throw them all out tonight?"

"Ryder, it's pouring outside."

"So what?" He looked up, and she saw the heat smoldering in the depths of his eyes. "They won't melt."

"Ryder, did you ever talk to Ralph about extending Martha's loan?"

"Yeah, I talked to him. I even offered to bring her loan up to date. He said it was too late for that, that the bank had already sold the property to someone else. She has to be out of there by the first of the year."

"They sold it? To whom?"

"He wouldn't say."

Jenny sighed with regret. "Thanks for trying." Cupping his face in her hands, she kissed him deeply, thoroughly. "Have I told you lately how much I love you?"

"Probably, but it wouldn't hurt to tell me again."

"I love you, Ryder Fallon."

"And I love you, Jenny girl," he whispered, his voice suddenly husky. He ran his hands over her back, slid his thumbs along the supple curve of her breast. Aching with need, he kissed her, wishing, for one fleeting moment, that they'd never had kids in the first place.

They were still kissing when the kitchen door swung open.

"Oh, sorry."

Ryder glared at his son over Jenny's shoulder. "What is it?" he growled. "Can't you see I'm busy?"

"I'm gonna take Rebecca home," Dusty said, a grin in his voice, "and as long as I'm gonna be in town, I think I'll just spend the night at the jail so I don't have to ride back in the rain."

"Fine. See you tomorrow."

Dusty nodded, stifling the urge to laugh. "Night, Dad. Mom."

"Good night, Dusty," Jenny said sweetly.

Ryder looked up at Jenny and grinned lecherously. "Two down, two to go."

Chapter Twenty-nine

Dusty's face was grim as he sat back in his chair, his feet propped on his desk. Life was full of surprises, he mused. He'd no sooner figured that the road ahead would be clear sailing than he'd gotten a wire informing him that Rance Crenshaw and Joby Berland had escaped from prison on December fifth. Both men were armed and thought to be headed back toward Twin Rivers.

Damn, what a mess. No doubt Martha had written to tell Rance that the bank had foreclosed on the ranch. No wonder Crenshaw had busted out of prison. Dusty knew he'd do the same thing under the circumstances. A man couldn't sit by and let his wife and kids be tossed out into the cold. Still, Crenshaw would be stupid to come back to Twin Rivers. Surely he knew that was the first place they'd look for him.

But then, Crenshaw had never won any medals for being bright. After pondering his options, Dusty had deputized Pete Hampton and Lenny Wible and then he'd ridden out to the ranch and asked for his father's help, as well.

His mother hadn't been thrilled with the idea of her husband pinning on a badge again, but she understood Dusty's need to have someone beside him whom he could depend on, someone he could trust with his life, if need be.

Propping his elbows on the arms of his chair, Dusty rested his chin on his clasped hands. Damn. Today was the tenth. He was supposed to be getting married in ten days; Beth was supposed to be marrying Harbaugh in seven. He didn't know whether to hope Crenshaw and Berland stayed out of sight until after his wedding, or if he hoped they'd make their play beforehand and get it over with. He had a feeling that Crenshaw wouldn't be taken without a fight.

Damn. It just wasn't fair. He didn't want to have to worry about Berland and Crenshaw right now, didn't want to think about anything but marrying Rebecca—without wondering if he was going to marry her, and then make her a widow.

Rebecca . . . . It was getting increasingly difficult to let her go at night, to hold her and kiss her without giving in to the desire to possess her. The fact that she wanted him almost as badly didn't make things any easier. And as tempting as the thought of making love to her might be, he was determined to keep his desire in check until she was truly his.

Still, the thought of marrying her only to leave her a widow preyed on his mind.

He glanced up at the clock. Almost noon. Swinging his legs to the floor, he grabbed his hat and left the office, bound for the schoolhouse. Crenshaw and Berland could wait. He had a date for lunch with the prettiest school teacher in town.

Rance and Joby pulled up on the outskirts of the Crenshaw farm shortly after sundown.

"You sure this is smart?" Joby asked. He glanced around, his movements quick and nervous. "I mean, anybody lookin' fer us is sure to come here first."

"You damn fool, don't you think I know that? But I've got to talk to Martha and my boys. We need to figure on a place to meet up later."

Joby nodded. He hated himself for being such a coward, but he didn't have the guts to cross Rance twice. In prison, Rance had beaten the crap out of him for snitching on him. Joby hadn't complained, and he hadn't turned stoolie. He'd deserved that beating. Still, he considered himself lucky to be alive. Rance Crenshaw was a soft-spoken man most times, but he had a vile temper when he was riled, and Joby didn't intend to rile him again, at least not in this lifetime. For better or worse, he'd cast his lot with Crenshaw. Anything was better than rotting in prison.

"You wait here," Rance said, thrusting the reins of his horse into Berland's hand. "I won't be long."

Joby nodded. He'd tried to talk Rance out of stealing the Harveys' stud horse, too, but Crenshaw hadn't listened. He'd needed to get his hands on some money to meet a mortgage payment, and Rance had insisted that stealing and selling the Harveys' stallion would be a piece of cake. Not only that, but he'd said there would be enough money left over to fix up Joby's place if Joby wanted.

Nothing had gone as planned. They'd lost the horse, Rance had goten shot, and they'd wound up in jail.

Joby grunted softly. Sometimes he thought he had more brains than Rance. All he needed was a chance to prove it.

He glanced up at the moon, hanging low and full in the sky, and wondered what was taking Rance so long.

By the time an hour had passed, his palms were sweating. Something was wrong. He knew it.

Maybe he wasn't as smart as he thought, Joby mused as he tethered the horses to a low-hanging branch. If he was smart, he'd climb into the saddle and ride for Texas just as fast as he could.

With a sigh, he sneaked up to the side of the house and peered in one of the windows.

A vile oath escaped his lips as he heard the prison doors clanging shut behind him one more time. Forever this time.

Muttering under his breath, Joby walked around the house, took a deep breath, and stepped inside. "Rance, you damn fool, what the hell are you doing?"

"Shut up," Crenshaw hissed. "And close that door."

Feeling the hand of doom clamping down on his shoulder, Joby closed the door, his gaze moving from Jenny Fallon's face to her daughter's face to that of Elizabeth Johnson, and back again. The three women were seated on wooden chairs, their hands and feet tied. They were all gagged. Martha Crenshaw sat on the edge of the sofa, worrying the hem of her skirt.

"Martha, get me some coffee," Rance said, "then fix us something to eat."

With a nod, she went to do as bidden.

Joby waited until Martha left the room, and then his temper exploded. "Dammit, Rance, Ryder Fallon's gonna come down on us harder than a duck on a June bug when he finds out what you've done."

"I told you to shut up."

"Not this time. Turn them women loose, and let's get the hell out of here."

"Don't be any more of a fool than you already are," Rance growled. "Don't you see what I've got here?"

"All I see is trouble, and lots of it."

Crenshaw shook his head in disgust. "This is the answer to all my problems," he said, grinning.

Joby wiped hands gone suddenly sweaty on the sides of his pants. "Fallon will kill you for this."

Crenshaw snorted softly. "I ain't gonna hurt 'em none. All I want is enough cash money to get Martha and the kids settled somewhere's else. I figure Fallon and Johnson ought to be good for at least a couple grand between them."

Joby held up his hands, palms out. "I don't want no part of it. Ryder Fallon's a hard man. He ain't gonna take kindly to you holding his wife for no ransom."

"You wouldn't be thinkin' of walkin' out on me, would you, Joby?"

Berland shook his head. "Of course not, Rance. We're in this together, you know that."

"Yeah, that's what I thought." Crenshaw smiled at his wife as she handed him a cup of coffee, then offered one to Joby. "Stop worrying, Martha. Everything's gonna work out fine."

"I'm not worried," Martha replied, but Joby knew she was lying. Her voice was shaking almost as badly as her hands.

"Good. How's that food coming?"

"It's almost ready." Martha laid a hand on her husband's arm. "Are you sure this is the best way, Rance? Ryder and Jenny tried to help me."

"Sure they did. That damned 'breed' helped me go to jail."

"Listen to what I'm saying, Rance. Ryder went to the bank and offered to pay off the mortgage, but Mr. Johnson said it was too late." She looked up at her husband, frightened by the harried, desperate look in his eyes. "Don't you think we should let her go?"

"Is that what you think?"

"Yes. Please, Rance, do it for me."

"Maybe tomorrow," Crenshaw said. He dragged a hand over his eyes and down his jaw. "I can't think straight right now."

"All right, dear," Martha said. "You just relax. I'll get you something to eat, and some more coffee."

Rance smiled at her. He'd let the Fallon woman go tomorrow. He'd give her a note to deliver to Johnson, and another to Fallon. He'd tell Johnson he wanted five thousand dollars cash or he'd never see his daughter alive again. The note to Fallon would be pretty much the same, except that, in addition to the money, he'd demand safe passage out of town for himself and Berland in exchange for his daughter's life.

It would work. It had to work.

* * *

Ryder paced the floor of the sheriff's office, his hands clenching and unclenching as he glanced at the clock. It was after six. Dammit, where were they?

"Staring at the clock ain't gonna make the time pass any faster," Dusty muttered. Sitting back, he propped his feet on the desk.

Ryder grunted and continued pacing.

He whirled around, his hand streaking for his gun, as Chase and Harbaugh entered the jailhouse.

Chase came to an abrupt halt. Harbaugh's face went white.

"Sorry," Ryder said, his expression sheepish. "Old instincts tend to take over when I'm upset."

Lester swallowed hard.

"Any sign of them?" Dusty asked. He sat forward, the chair's front legs slamming against the floor.

Harbaugh shook his head. "No."

"Dammit," Ryder said, holstering his gun. "Whose fool idea was it for them to go out to Crenshaw's anyway?"

Lester cleared his throat. "It was Mrs. Fallon's idea. She wanted to take Mrs. Crenshaw some foodstuffs, and Beth and Dorinda said they'd go along to keep her company."

Ryder drummed his fingers on the desktop. "And you let them go?"

"I didn't see any harm in it," Lester retorted, his voice rising.

"Well, if I'd been home, you can be damn sure they wouldn't have gone."

"Well, a fat lot of good that does us now," Lester snapped. "I went over to the Johnson place to see if maybe they'd dropped Beth off at home, but

Johnson said he hasn't seen her since she left with me this morning."

Ryder swore under his breath. Every instinct he had told him that Jenny and the girls were in trouble, and that Rance Crenshaw was behind it.

"Don't you think you're worrying too much?" Lester asked. "Maybe they just decided to stay for dinner. Maybe they're still talking. You know how women are. You put four of them together in the same room, and they can gab all day."

Ryder shook his head. "Something's wrong, I know it."

Chase nodded in agreement. "Beth is in danger."

Lester glanced from one man to the other. He could feel the tension rising within them. A muscle worked in Fallon's jaw; Chase stared out the window, his shoulders taut, his hands clenched. And suddenly Les was tense, too. If Beth was in danger, so was Dorinda.

Abruptly, Ryder crossed the floor and took a rifle from the gun rack. He tossed it to Chase, then took another for himself.

Ryder checked to make sure the Winchester was loaded. "Harbaugh, you go on out to the ranch and wait for us there."

Lester ran a hand through his hair. He felt like he should offer to go along, but he knew his inexperience in such matters would be more of a hindrance than a help. "All right."

"Dusty, you stay here in case they show up."

"If you're not back by midnight, I'm coming after you."

"You do that. Ready, Chase?"

Chase nodded. "Let us go."

Dusty stared after them, then grinned ruefully. If Crenshaw was mixed up in this, he'd sure as hell hate to be in the man's shoes when Ryder got hold of him.

It was full dark when Ryder and Chase reached the Crenshaw place. A single light burned inside the house.

Ryder counted six horses in the corral. The matched grays wore the Fallon brand. Jenny's carriage was parked alongside the house.

Ryder swore under his breath. At least he knew she was here. He brushed his hand against the knife sheathed on his belt. Crenshaw would die a long slow death if any harm had come to Jenny or Dorinda.

He slid a glance at Chase. "You go around the back. I'll take the front."

Chase nodded.

One minute he was there, the next he was gone. Ryder shook his head in awe. Chase moved through the darkness like a wisp of smoke, making no sound, leaving no tracks.

He held his ground, giving Chase enough time to get to the back door, then, keeping to the shadows, he made his way to the front of the house. Peering through the window, he saw Jenny. She was sitting in a chair, her hands tied behind her back, her feet lashed to the chair's legs. A gag covered her mouth. She seemed to be sleeping. How she could sleep trussed up like that was beyond him, he mused, and then grinned ruefully as he recalled the nights he'd spent tied to a log in the Apache camp years ago. When the body was tired enough, it slept.

Shifting slightly, he saw Dorinda and Elizabeth, both similarly bound.

There was no sign of Crenshaw, or his wife and kids.

Ryder frowned. Drawing away from the window, he tried the latch on the front door. Locked.

He peered in the window again, swore softly as he saw Crenshaw enter the room. Where was Berland? In the kitchen? Asleep in one of the back rooms?

He swore as a shrill cry broke the stillness of the night. There was a crash from the rear of the house, a harsh cry, the sound of a gunshot.

Ryder cocked his own pistol as the front door flew open and Joby Berland came barreling out, his gun at the ready.

"Hold it!" Ryder ordered.

Berland came to an abrupt halt and immediately raised his arms over his head. "Don't shoot!"

"Drop your gun."

Joby quickly did as bidden. Ryder kicked the Colt out of reach, then handcuffed Berland's hands. "Where's Crenshaw?"

"I'm in here, Fallon. Turn Joby loose, then give him your gun."

"And if I refuse?"

"I'll kill the women."

"Don't be a fool."

"The Injun's dead." Crenshaw laughed bitterly. "I got nothing to lose."

In the stillness that followed, he heard the muffled sounds of weeping, and Ryder knew Jenny was crying for Chase.

Damn.

He took a deep breath. "Turn the women loose."

"Not until I see you in here with your hands up."

"I want your word, Crenshaw."

"You've got it."

Muttering an oath, Ryder unlocked the cuffs from Berland's wrists, then handed Joby his Colt.

Berland aimed the gun at Ryder, using both hands to keep the weapon steady.

"Where're Martha and the boys?" Ryder asked.

"In the back bedroom. I think she's afraid to come out."

"You'll never get away with this," Ryder said, his voice pitched low so only Berland could hear. "You know that, don't you?"

"I got no choice. Dammit, don't you understand? He'll kill me if I cross him again."

Ryder nodded; then, hands raised over his head, he walked into the house.

Crenshaw stood behind Jenny, the gun in his hand leveled at the back of her head. Tears tracked the faces of all three women. Chase lay on the floor near the kitchen doorway. Blood welled from a wound in his left temple, pooled beneath his head to make a bright red stain on the hardwood floor.

"I'm here," Ryder said. "Turn the women loose."

"Do it, Rance," Berland urged. "We gotta get out of here now."

"No. Not until I get the money from Johnson."

"Is that what this is all about?" Ryder asked. "Money?"

"I got nothing left, Fallon," Crenshaw exclaimed. "The bank's takin' my land. My wife, my kids, they got no place to go."

"I've got money," Ryder said. He kept his voice

calm, refused to acknowledge the anger raging through him. "How much do you need?"

Crenshaw snorted. "You must be crazy if you think I'd trust you."

"What other choice do you have?"

"He's right," Joby said. "Let him get the money. He won't try nothing while we got his womenfolk."

Crenshaw shook his head, his eyes wild and unfocused. He needed sleep. He needed time to think. The scent of the Injun's blood filled his nostrils, reminding him of another night, the night he'd killed Greenway. He hadn't meant to shoot Ned. They were friends. But he'd been afraid of getting caught. He shook his head. Sleep. He needed sleep . . .

The gun in his hand felt heavy, so heavy.

"Rance, what are we gonna do?"

"I'm thinkin'! Dammit, Joby, I've got to think. Handcuff the breed. I'm gonna get some coffee."

"Put your hands behind your back, Fallon," Joby ordered, though his voice lacked authority. "Don't try nothing."

"Listen to me, Berland," Ryder said, keeping his voice low. "I need your help."

"No." Joby wiped the sweat from his brow with the back of his hand. "No, I can't."

"I'll testify for you in court. I'll tell them you helped me. They'll go easy on you, I swear it."

Joby shook his head. "I can't. Don't ask me . . ."

"What's he askin', Jobe?" Crenshaw stepped into the parlor, his gun in one hand, a coffee cup in the other.

"Nothing, nothing."

"Do I have to cuff him myself?"

"No, I'll do it."

From the corner of his eye, Ryder saw a movement behind Crenshaw. It was now or never.

Whirling around, he lunged at Berland, driving him backward. They crashed to the floor. Berland lost his hold on the gun and it skittered across the floor.

One well-placed punch rendered Joby unconscious. Breathing hard, Ryder scrambled to his feet in time to see Crenshaw pitch forward, a knife buried to the hilt in his back.

"Chase! Dammit!" Running forward, Ryder caught the younger man around the shoulders before he collapsed. Gently, he eased him to the floor. Taking the gag from Jenny's mouth, he pressed it over the gash in Chase's head to staunch the blood.

"Is he all right? Ryder! He isn't . . ."

"He's not dead, Jenny girl." Taking the gag from Dorinda's mouth, he used it to hold the other piece of cloth in place.

Moving quickly, he untied Jenny and the two girls. Leaving them to look after Chase, Ryder checked on Crenshaw. The man was stone cold dead. Berland was still unconscious. After handcuffing Joby's hands behind his back, Ryder went to stand by Jenny, who was kneeling beside Chase. Beth knelt on the other side of Chase, his head cradled in her lap. Her face was wet with tears.

"How's he doing?" Ryder asked.

"I think he'll live," Jenny said.

Taking Jenny by the arm, Ryder lifted her to her feet. "Let Beth look after him."

"But . . ."

Ryder shook his head. "I've got to go tell Martha about Rance. She'll need a woman with her."

Jenny nodded. "You're right, of course." She looked at Chase, as if to reassure herself, and then she followed Ryder down the narrow hallway.

Martha Crenshaw was sitting on the edge of the bed, her arms wrapped around her sons. From the look on her face, Ryder knew there was no need for him to say anything.

"I'm so sorry," Jenny said. "Is there anything we can do?"

"Haven't you done enough?" Martha asked. She stared at Ryder, her eyes red-rimmed and filled with hatred. "Get out of my house."

Jenny took a step forward. "Martha, it's not Ryder's fault."

"Why couldn't he just leave us alone?"

"Martha, please, listen to me."

"Let it go, Jenny," Ryder said quietly.

"But . . ."

"I'm gonna take Chase home. Harbaugh's there, waiting."

"All right, I'm coming." She waited until Ryder left the room. "Martha, I know how upset you must be, but you can't blame Ryder for what happened. Rance would still be alive if he'd just let us go."

The anger drained out of Martha Crenshaw's eyes. With a sob, she drew her children closer and began to cry. Seeing their mother's tears, the boys began to cry, too.

"Martha, do you want me to stay the night?"

Martha shook her head. "No, I just want to be alone with my boys."

Jenny didn't argue. When she got home, she'd send someone after Doc Forbes. Maybe he could give Martha something to calm her down and help her sleep.

Ryder was waiting for her in the parlor. "I put the body in the back of Crenshaw's buckboard. I'll drop Joby off at the jail, take Chase to the doc's, then leave Crenshaw's body at Rickman's. You take the girls and go home. Les is waiting there. Tell him to tell the Johnsons that his horse went lame and they had to walk home, and that's why Beth's so late."

Jenny nodded. "After Doc sees to Chase, send him out to Martha."

"Yeah, I will. You ready to go?"

"Yes."

"Did he hurt you, Jenny girl?"

"No." Jenny sighed as Ryder put his arm around her shoulders and led her outside. "Poor Martha. I feel so bad for her."

"I'll make sure she's got enough money to get a fresh start somewhere else."

Jenny nodded, suddenly too weary to think.

Ryder helped Jenny into the carriage, then tied Chase's horse and his own to the back of the buckboard.

"You gonna be all right, Jenny girl?"

"I'll be fine. You just hurry home."

"I will. Come on, Beth, get in the carriage."

"I'm going with Chase."

"There's no room in the buckboard."

"Make Mr. Berland ride in the back with . . . with the body."

"Let her go with him, Ryder," Jenny said.

"All right. Listen, Jenny, tell Harbaugh I'll see that Beth gets home. Joby, climb on into the back."

"What?"

"You heard me. Get in the back."

Muttering under his breath, Joby climbed into the back of the buckboard, sitting as far away from Crenshaw's blanket-wrapped body as he could get.

Ryder lifted Beth onto the seat, then walked around the wagon and climbed up on the seat. Taking up the reins, he glanced at Chase, who was leaning against Beth, his eyes closed.

Ryder clucked to the horse. Hell of a night, he mused as he followed Jenny down the road. Hell of night.

Chapter Thirty

It took eight stitches to close up the wound in Chase's head.

Beth sat on the operating table beside him, his hand clutched in hers, flinching every time the thin silver needle pierced his flesh. Ryder had tried to make her wait in the other room. The doc had tried. Chase had tried. But she wasn't leaving. By the time the doctor tied off the last stitch, her face was as white as the sheet that covered the table.

"He ought to stay here overnight," Forbes said. He wrapped several layers of gauze around Chase's head, snipped off the end.

Chase looked at Ryder. "No."

"You heard him, Doc."

"Suit yourself. See if you can't make him stay in bed, at least until day after tomorrow. Head wounds always bleed profusely, and he's lost a lot of blood." Doc shook his head as he taped the gauze in place. "I seem to spend a lot of time patching up your family, Ryder."

"Somebody's got to keep you in business. And speaking of business, Jenny wants you to go out to the Crenshaw place and look after Martha. She's in a bad way."

"I'll take care of her. In the meantime, try to stay out of trouble, you two."

"Right, Doc," Ryder said, reaching for his hat. "Thanks."

"You'll get my bill."

"Glad I'm still around to pay it," Ryder retorted with a grin.

Chase stood up, wincing a little as the movement sent a flash of pain through his skull. He took one look at Beth, and slipped his arm around her shoulders, thinking she looked worse than he felt.

Ryder lifted Beth into the buckboard, helped Chase up beside her, then drove to the Johnson house. She gave Chase a quick kiss on the cheek, then ran up the path to the front porch. She turned and waved, then went inside. They had all agreed not to mention what had happened at the Crenshaw house. Instead, Beth was going to tell her parents that the carriage horse went lame and she and Lester had had to walk back to town, and that was why she was so late getting home.

"That was a close call," Ryder remarked as he turned the buckboard toward home.

Chase grunted softly. "Too close." He slanted Ryder a wry grin. "I did not receive this many wounds when I fought against the bluecoats."

Ryder chuckled softly. "Civilization is a dangerous thing." He frowned thoughtfully. "This wedding could prove dangerous, too, if Lester's plan backfires."

Chase nodded ruefully. He did not like trickery or deceit. Had it been up to him, he would have taken Beth away from Twin Rivers, but she had urged him to give Lester's plan a try. If all went well, they wouldn't have to leave. He could stay in town and get to know his family better; she would not be estranged from her parents.

"Well," Ryder mused, "it should be interesting."

"Yes," Chase agreed. "Interesting."

Lester's daughters arrived the following afternoon. Beth accompanied him to the depot to pick them up, stood back while three pretty little girls with their father's blond hair and brown eyes flew into his arms, smothering him with hugs and kisses, all talking at once, until he began the introductions.

Kathy and Alice smiled shyly at Beth. Polly's expression was sullen and defiant.

Lester kept up a steady stream of conversation on the way back to the house, telling the girls of the land he'd bought, promising the two youngest girls ponies of their own. Beth pointed out the schoolhouse as they passed by, assuring them that they'd love their new teachers. She pointed out the church, and the ice cream parlor, and said she'd introduce them to some girls their age so they'd feel more at home. And all the while, Polly sat with her arms folded across her chest, her expression belligerent, her gaze focused straight ahead.

By the time they reached the house, Alice and Kathy were laughing and talking with Beth as if they'd been friends forever. Polly remained sulky and silent, refusing to be drawn into their conversation.

Lester glanced at Beth and shrugged. She smiled at him in return, secretly glad that it would be up to Dorinda to win Polly's affection.

For Beth, it was a long day. Her father wanted them to spend the rest of the day at home. Theda insisted on serving an enormous lunch. After that, she showed the girls their rooms, then took them on a tour of the house. Later, Lester and Beth took the girls outside so they could look at the horses and take a walk through the gardens.

Alice and Kathy were thrilled with the horses, the dogs, the cats. Polly sat on a bench and refused to budge.

"I'm sorry my parents insisted we stay in today," Beth said as they followed the girls back to the house. "I know you wanted to go out to the ranch and see Dorinda."

"It's all right," Les said with a shrug.

"No, it's not. I want to see Chase, too, you know."

Les patted her hand. "I know, but there's always tomorrow."

"This plan of yours had better work," Beth said with a rueful grin. "I'm too young to be the mother of three children."

"It'll work," Lester said. "It has to work."

"Your daughters are lovely," Beth remarked, watching Alice try to catch one of the barn cats.

Lester nodded, his expression melancholy. "In spite of the fact that they've got my coloring, they all look like their mother."

"You loved her very much, didn't you?"

"Yes. Shirley was a wonderful woman. A wonderful wife and mother."

"What happened to her?"

"She died of pneumonia when Alice was three. It happened so fast." He shook his head. "It was hardest on Polly. She doesn't want to move out here. She says it's because she doesn't want to leave her friends behind, but I think it's because of the house. She feels close to her mother there."

"I hope you'll all be happy here."

"We will be," Lester said, and there was no room for doubt in his voice.

Beth stood on a stool, her arms outstretched, while Mrs. Kennedy made the final alterations to her wedding dress. Thank goodness, the wedding was only a day away.

"I think you've gained some weight since the last fitting," Mrs. Kennedy said. "Most brides lose weight due to nervousness."

"Not me," Beth said, forcing a smile. "When I'm nervous, I eat."

It was a bold-faced lie. She'd hardly eaten a thing in the last week, and what little she did eat just came up again. Fortunately, her mother attributed her queasy stomach and poor appetite to a bad case of prewedding jitters and didn't give it a second thought.

Beth fretted as Mrs. Kennedy turned the hem. It had been five days since she'd seen Chase. Five long, lonely, agonizing days. She needed to see him, needed to know he was all right, needed to feel his arms around her. But every day her mother found some reason why she and Lester had to stay home—she was having some of the town ladies over to meet Lester's daughters, they needed to discuss last minute details for the wedding, they needed to discuss the menu for the reception.

Yesterday had been her birthday. She had put on a smile and tried to pretend she was having a good time, but all she could think of was Chase, and how much she wanted to be with him.

Her father had taken her aside to wish her a happy birthday and had reminded her of her promise.

"I haven't forgotten, Father," she said. "I promised you that Lester and I would be married on the seventeenth, and we will be."

Tomorrow was the seventeenth. She could only hope she had told her father the truth.

That night, lying in bed, she tossed and turned and tossed some more as she thought of all the things that could go wrong. She had visions of her father standing behind her with a shotgun, insisting she marry Lester or he'd shoot Chase. She imagined herself chained to the altar, watching helplessly as Lester and Chase and Ernest Tucker ran out the door, while Lester's daughters laughed at her because no one wanted to marry her.

She was about to go downstairs for a cup of warm milk when she heard something strike her window.

Throwing back the covers, she jumped out of bed and ran to the window. And smiled. And waved.

Grabbing her robe, she ran down the stairs and out the back door and straight into Chase's arms.

His kiss was long and hard and she gloried in it until, breathless, they drew apart. "Are you all right?" she asked. She lifted a hand to touch the bandage on his forehead.

"Fine, now," he whispered. "I've missed you."

"Oh, and I've missed you."

His gaze moved over her face, his eyes dark and searching. "You have not changed your mind about marrying me?"

"Of course not! It's just that my mother won't let us out of the house."

"I love you, Beth." He caressed her cheek with the backs of his knuckles, then bent to kiss her once more. Five days without her, and every one longer and lonelier than the last. Five days of doubts, of being afraid she had changed her mind, that she had decided she would rather marry a man of her own race. Five days.

He groaned softly as he crushed her close. "Tell me you love me."

"I love you. I'll always love you." She kissed his cheek, her arms hugging him close. "Only you."

He held her close for a long while, wishing he could make love to her. His need for her burned like a dull ache, relentless, like a fire that could not be quenched.

Beth went suddenly still. "Someone's coming."

"It is Harbaugh."

"Lester? What's he doing out at this time of night?"

"No doubt he has been doing what I am doing."

Beth frowned, and then grinned. "You mean he sneaked out to see *his* girl, too?"

Chase nodded.

"Hey, you two," Lester called with a cheery wave. "Tomorrow's the day, Chase. Don't be late."

"I should go," Chase said. He looked deep into her eyes. "If things do not go as planned tomorrow, will you leave here with me?"

"You know I will."

"Rest well, beloved."

"You, too."

He kissed her once more. "Until tomorrow."

"Tomorrow."

She smiled as she watched him disappear into the darkness. Tomorrow. Hugging herself, she ran back into the house. Tomorrow.

Ryder rolled over in bed and drew Jenny into his arms. "Well, today's the big day. How are you holding up?"

"I'm fine. How about you?"

"Lookin' forward to it, actually. Should be quite a show if Lester does what I suspect."

Jenny punched him on the arm, giggling as he rolled over on top of her. "Not now," she admonished. "There's no time."

"You didn't used to say that."

"I've never been to a wedding like this before, either." She glanced at the clock on the bedside table. "Ryder, look at the time!" She pushed against his chest. "Get off me, you big lump. We'll be late."

Chase and Dusty were already in the kitchen, drinking coffee, when Ryder and Jenny entered thirty minutes later.

"Anybody hungry?" Jenny asked, then grinned when all three men shook their heads. "Me, either.

A moment later, Dorinda entered the kitchen. "Just coffee for me, Mom," she said, then frowned as everybody else laughed. "What's so funny?"

"I think we've all got a bad case of nerves," Jenny said, patting Dorinda on the arm. "Well, if no one's hungry, we might as well get ready to go."

Forty minutes later, they were ready. Jenny looked at Chase, her eyes damp with tears. "You look so handsome," she murmured. "Just like your father."

"Thank you, *Cima,*" Chase said, and loved her more in that moment that he would have thought possible.

"Well, let's go," Ryder said. "They aren't gonna wait on us."

Beth paced the floor of the small room outside the chapel. She peeked out the door, wishing she could see Chase, but he was nowhere in sight.

"Calm down, Beth," Dorinda said.

"I am calm."

Rebecca grinned at Dorinda. "Right. Is my hat on straight?"

"You both look beautiful," Beth said. As her maid of honor, Dorinda wore a floor-length gown of jade green satin and lace. Rebecca wore a similar dress in a lighter shade.

Too soon, she heard the music that was her cue. Dorinda took a last look at Lester's girls, then opened the door and Polly, Alice and Kathy began walking down the aisle. The girls looked like rose-buds in varying shades of pink. Even though she'd been against the wedding, Polly hadn't been able to hide her excitement at being asked to be a flower girl at her father's wedding.

"Here we go," Dorinda said. She smiled at Beth and crossed her fingers. "Good luck."

Beth nodded, her heart pounding as she watched Dorinda and Rebecca walk down the aisle.

Her hand was shaking as she placed it on her father's arm.

"Ready, Elizabeth?" he asked.

"Ready."

"Don't be nervous," he said. "You're getting a fine man."

"Yes, indeed," she said. "He is that."

And then they were walking down the aisle. She was hardly aware of the people rising to their feet as she passed by, hardly aware of the tears in her mother's eyes, or the half-smile on Lester's face as he awaited her in front of the altar. Dusty stood beside him. Both men looked elegant in black broadcloth suits and crisp white shirts.

As from a great distance, she heard the minister ask, "Who giveth this woman to be married to this man?" heard her father's clear reply, "Her mother and I do."

With a smile that could only be called smug, her father placed her hand in Lester's.

She stared at Lester. Her whole future depended on what happened in the next few minutes.

And then the fateful words: "If there is anyone here who knows just cause why this marriage should not proceed, let him speak now or forever hold his peace."

There was a moment of silence, and then, in a voice that easily carried to the back of the church, Lester said, "I find that I must object."

The minister blinked at him. "Excuse me? What did you say?"

"I'm afraid I can't marry this woman," Lester

said, releasing Beth's hand. "I don't love her, and she doesn't love me."

Murmurs and gasps spread through the congregation.

"I say, this is quite irregular," the minister said, glancing from Beth to Lester and back again. "I . . . uh . . ."

At that moment, Chase emerged from the side door and took Beth's hand in his.

"I wish to marry this woman," he said. And knew, deep in his heart, that he would never forget this moment, or the way Beth looked at him, her face radiant, her eyes shining with love.

"And I wish to marry this man," Beth said, squeezing Chase's hand.

"And I wish to marry this man."

Dorinda's voice, soft yet clear, broke the stillness as she took her place at Lester's side.

Beth smiled up at Chase. She could hear her father sputtering behind her, hear her mother trying to calm him.

"Well, then," the minister stuttered, "I . . . uh, that is, will you please join hands. Oh, you're already doing that . . ."

"Wait!" Dusty stepped forward and offered his hand to Rebecca. "How about it, Rebecca Lynn? Will you marry me today?"

With a grin, she placed her hand in his. "I'd love to marry you, Dustin. Today, or any day."

"Dustin!" Chase grinned at his brother. "Dustin."

Holding hands, Dusty and Rebecca turned to face the minister.

Beth choked back her laughter. Truly this would be a wedding they would never forget. She could hear her father muttering dire warnings under his breath, heard her mother's voice rise as she tried to calm him. Murmurs of surprise and shock continued to ripple through the church.

Glancing over her shoulder, Beth saw Ryder stand up and offer his hand to his wife. "Would you marry me again, Jenny girl?" he asked.

Chase's mother looked young and carefree as she smiled up at her husband, her eyes bright with unshed tears.

"And again, and again, and again," Jenny replied.

Beth couldn't hold it back any longer. Laughter bubbled up inside her like champagne as she held out her free hand to her parents. "You might as well join the party," she said.

Face red, Ralph Johnson took his wife by the hand and led her to the altar. "You told me you'd marry Lester today," he said to Beth under his breath.

"No, Father, I said Lester and I would be married today. I never said we'd marry each other."

The minister cleared his throat. "Are we ready now?" His gaze moved over the congregation. "Perhaps every married couple here present would like to renew their wedding vows at this time," he said. "If you would like to join in, please come forward."

Beth looked up at Chase and smiled as the married couples took their places near the altar.

Truly, this was a day they would never forget.

Chapter Thirty-one

There was a resounding chorus of "I dos" as the minister spoke the final words of the wedding ceremony.

A round of applause followed from the few people remaining in the audience, the sound of laughter as children ran down the aisle to join their parents.

Jenny kissed Ryder, then Chase and Beth, Dusty and Rebecca, and Dorinda and Lester.

"Well," she exclaimed, "this has been quite a day."

"I'll say," Ryder agreed. He put his arm around his wife and drew her up against his side.

Ryder glanced down at Jenny. "Shall we tell them now, or later?"

"Now," she said, her smile betraying her eagerness.

"Tell us what?" Dusty asked, glancing from his father to his mother and back again.

"We've got three hundred acres of prime land

across the river, a hundred acres for each of you. The land is yours, free and clear, unless you decide to sell, and then I want first chance to buy it."

"A hundred acres," Dorinda murmured. She looked up at Lester and grinned. "Now we've got two pieces of land."

Lester grinned back at her. "Maybe we'll build two houses; one for us and one for the girls." Lester shook Ryder's hand, gave Jenny a hug. "Thanks."

"Yes, thank you," Dorinda said, hugging her folks.

"We'll definitely build on ours, right Rebecca?" Dusty remarked.

Rebecca nodded. At last, a real home of her own. "Thank you so much," she murmured.

"Thank your mother-in-law. She was afraid you'd all leave town if we didn't figure out a way to keep you here."

"Well, it worked," Dusty said, giving Rebecca a squeeze. "Thanks to you both."

Beth looked up at Chase and smiled. "We'll stay, won't we?"

Chase shrugged. He had never owned land before, never considered the possibility. But then he looked into Beth's eyes and knew he would stay if that was what she wanted. He was about to say so when he saw her parents bearing down on them.

Beth's smile grew ragged around the edges as her mother and father approached, both looking grim-faced on what was supposed to be a happy occasion.

Hoping for the best, expecting the worst, she took a deep breath, grateful for Chase's arm around her waist. His nearness gave her the courage to face her father. There was nothing he could do now. She was of age, and, under the law, old enough to marry whomever she wished.

"Well, Elizabeth, what have you got to say for yourself?" Ralph Johnson asked.

"Congratulations, Mother, Father. You make a lovely couple." And indeed they did. Her father looked quite handsome in a dark brown suit and tie; her mother, dressed in a pale yellow dress, looked younger somehow, less severe. Perhaps it was the bonnet she wore, a yellow and white confection made of lace and silk flowers.

A dull flush spread across Ralph Johnson's face; Theda smiled at her daughter, then glanced at her husband.

"I trusted you," Ralph said, his gaze fixed on his daughter's face.

"I'm sorry you're disappointed in me, Father, but I love Chase, and he loves me. I couldn't marry anyone else."

"I could disown you for this."

"You must do what you think is best," Beth replied, her voice and posture stiff with hurt.

"Ralph, don't."

"Be still, woman."

"Listen to me, Ralph Johnson. I won't let you drive Beth away. She's our only child. For once in your life, think before you speak."

Ralph looked at his wife, a stunned expression on his face. It was obvious that Theda rarely disagreed with her husband.

"My father didn't want me to marry you, either, remember?" Theda said. "He said you'd never amount to anything. He was wrong, wasn't he?"

"Yes, but . . ."

"No buts, Ralph. I want you to welcome Chase to our family. If you drive him away, drive Beth away, I'll never forgive you. Never."

The flush staining Ralph's cheeks grew darker as he offered his hand to Chase. "Welcome to our family, young man," he said, his tone bordering on belligerence.

Chase hesitated a moment, then took his father-in-law's hand. "Thank you. Sir."

Ralph Johnson nodded, then, with a sigh, he hugged his daughter. "Be happy, Elizabeth," he murmured. "I shall expect you—and your husband—to visit often."

"Thank you, Father," Beth replied. "Please be happy for me."

"I'll try," Ralph said.

"Well," Jenny said brightly. "Shall we cut the cake and toast the newlyweds?"

Beth grinned up at Chase, happier than she'd ever been in her life. How handsome he was, this husband of hers. He wore a black suit and white shirt that emphasized his dark good looks. His long dark hair framed his face, a face she loved. She caressed his cheek as she imagined the years stretching ahead of them, good years. He would be there to kiss her good night before she fell asleep, to smile at her when she woke.

"I love you, Beth," Chase whispered, placing one hand over the slight swell of her belly. "Both of you. And we will make our home here, if that is your wish."

"It is," she replied fervently. "Oh, it is."

Chase nodded at his parents. "Our thanks for the

land, and for . . . for . . ." He took a deep breath. "For making me feel welcome in your home, and in your life."

"To the newlyweds!" Jenny said. Tears of joy sparkled in her eyes as she lifted her glass in a toast. "May you all live happily ever after."

"Here, here," Ryder said, touching his glass to hers.

"To love and laughter," Lester said, smiling at Dorinda.

"To long life and happiness," Dusty added, brushing his lips across Rebecca's lips.

Jenny grinned up at Ryder. "To grandchildren!" they said in unison.

Chase glanced at his mother, at Ryder, at Dusty and Dorinda, and then his gaze settled on Beth.

"To coming home," he said softly, his voice choked with emotion.

And as Beth squeezed his hand, Chase knew he had found everything he had been searching for, and more.

Epilogue

Christmas Day
Six years later

Jenny sat at the foot of the table, her gaze moving from one beloved face to the next. How quickly her little family had grown!

Dusty and Rebecca had a five-year-old daughter, Allison. Three years ago, Rebecca had given birth to twin sons. The boys, Jeff and Benjamin, were the spitting image of their father, who acted as if no one else had ever produced twins. Much to Rebecca's dismay, Dusty was bragging that he'd done it again, that she wasn't carrying one child, but two. They were outgrowing their little house in town and planned to build on their property come spring.

Dusty was still sheriff, and now had two full-time deputies. In addition to keeping law and order, he ran a couple hundred head of cattle on their land.

Dorinda and Lester had five children now: in addition to Lester's three girls from his first marriage, they now had a four-year-old-boy, Lester, Junior, and an eighteen-month-old daughter, Melinda. They had sold the property close to town and built an enormous two-story house across the river. It was the biggest house in the valley.

Chase and Beth had also built on their land, though their house wasn't as elegant as the Harbaughs'. Built of stone and oak, it blended into the landscape. Chase had refused to abandon his old way of life completely; he had built an Apache wickiup and a large sweat lodge behind the house so that his children would not forget their heritage.

In the summer, Jenny and Ryder sometimes spent the night in the wickiup with the older grandchildren. On occasion, Chase and the men used the sweat lodge. One hot summer day, the women had gathered inside to see what all the fuss was about. They had used it several times since then.

Chase had gone into partnership with Ryder, and between them, they raised the finest horses west of the Mississippi. And he and Beth raised the prettiest children. Their oldest son, William Kayitah, looked just like his daddy; their daughter, Jennifer, had her father's black hair and her mother's expressive brown eyes. Beth was expecting another baby in the spring.

Jenny knew it was wrong to favor one child over another, but she had a soft spot in her heart for Chase's son. Of all her grandchildren, he was her favorite. Perhaps it was because he so reminded her of Chase when he'd been a baby; perhaps it was because, on rare occasions, she saw a resemblance to Kayitah. Once, she had thought she hated the Apache chief, but she knew now that was impossible. How could she hate the man who had fathered Chase, who had spared Ryder's life?

Beth's parents had finally come around. They sat side by side at the far end of the table, looking a little overwhelmed by all the commotion. One thing was sure, whenever the Fallon clan got together, it was never quiet! And she wouldn't have it any other way.

Jenny bowed her head as Ryder said grace, giving thanks to *Usen* for the bounty before them, a bounty measured not only in the banquet spread on the table, but a bountiful harvest of friends and family gathered close to share their love at the most wonderful time of the year.

As Ryder said, "Amen," Jenny murmured her own thanks that her family was here, beside her, that they loved and respected each other.

She felt that love swell around her as steaming platters were handed back and forth and the merry laughter of her grandchildren filled the air.

She met Ryder's gaze across the table, and knew she would ask nothing more of life than what she had now—a husband who loved her, happy healthy grandchildren, and the promise of more on the way.

Truly, life was good.

Dear Reader:
Sequels are always interesting to write (and I hope to read!) because it gives me a chance to go back and find out what happened to old friends.

I hope you're as happy with the way things turned out for Jenny and Ryder and their family as I am.

I had a lot of fun writing the wedding scene at the end. Originally, the only two getting married were going to be Chase and Beth, and then I thought how much more fun it would be to have a double wedding, and have Lester and Dorinda decide to get married at the same time. That spurred the thought of . . . what if Dusty and Rebecca also decided to tie the knot? Well, I couldn't leave Jenny and Ryder out of the excitement, and the next thing I knew, practically the whole town was involved. I could picture it so clearly, it just had to be written.

Here's wishing you all love and laughter and happy endings!

Madeline

Reckless
Love
Madeline Baker